ANOTHER CUP OF COFFEE

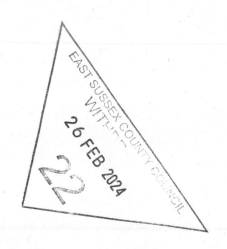

ANOTHER CUP OF COFFEE

Jenny Kane

Acknowledgements

This novel is dedicated to Steve – with love.

Special thanks must go to KD Grace, Lucy Felthouse, Hazel Cushion, and all my friends in the world of erotic writing, who have been as supportive as ever while I've been dipping my toe into the contemporary romance genre.

To Greg Rees for his wonderful editorial support, to Lisa and Anneke for their proofreading skills and encouragement, and to Debs for her frequently proffered cups of coffee.

A big hug must also go to Alan, Dave, Bec, Bren and Pete – just for being who they are.

Finally, thanks to Sue and Dave, the regulars at the Madhatter Tearoom, and to Jules and the staff of my local Costa. Without you, your coffee, and your happy banter, there would be no words.

Jenny Kane, 2013

JULY

In which Amy Crane finally finds out why ...

One

July 2006

Shrugging off her khaki jacket, Amy bent to pick up the pile of post that lay waiting on her doormat. As her hand reached to retrieve the small brown package half-buried beneath some junk mail, Amy froze. She knew that handwriting. She also had a funny feeling that she knew what was going to be inside.

But why return it now, after all these years?

The poorly wrapped parcel broke open as her fingers fumbled at the sticky tape, and a music cassette fell into her hands. The cover was unmarked, just as it had been when he'd taken it from her. Amy stared in disbelief, the blood draining from her already pale face. She remembered recording at least two tracks onto it herself. Maybe there were more now.

Amy's brother had given her the blank tape as she'd been climbing into their parents' car, about to be driven away to start her new life as a student. She hadn't seen Mike since he'd moved to Australia not long afterwards, but she could still picture his face clearly as he'd passed over the unusual gift. 'To record your musical memories along the way,' he'd said with a grin. Back then Amy had had every intention to fill her gift with each musical memory associated with her student life, but the reality of actually living through those experiences had left her with little time to record more than a couple of tracks.

Flustered, Amy shook the torn packaging in her hunt for a note of explanation. A small white envelope fell to the floor. Jack's familiar spidery scrawl stretched across its front.

Dearest Amy. Please listen to the tape BEFORE you open this. The letter will explain afterwards. J x

With a feeling that she was outside of what was happening,

detached, as if she was a spectre floating above herself, Amy walked into her tiny living room and put the tape down on her coffee table, as gingerly as if it was an unexploded bomb.

What was on it now? She knew she couldn't avoid this unexpected intrusion for long – but, on the other hand, a brief delay in order to clear her head suddenly felt essential.

Taking refuge in the kitchen, Amy placed her palms firmly onto the cool, tiled work surface, and took a couple of deep yet shaky breaths. Forcing her brain to slip back into action, she retrieved a bottle of white wine from the fridge, poured a large glassful and, squaring her shoulders, carried it through to the living room.

Perching on the edge of her sofa, her throat dry, Amy stared suspiciously at the tape for a second, before daring to pick it up and click open its stiff plastic box. Two minutes later, her hands still shaking, she closed it again with a sharp bang, and drank some wine. It took a further five minutes to gather the courage to re-open the case and place the tape into the dusty cassette compartment of her ancient stereo system. It must have been years since she'd seen a cassette, she thought, let alone listened to one. She wasn't even sure the stereo still worked …

Swallowing another great gulp of alcohol, Amy closed her eyes and pressed *Play*, not at all sure she wanted to take this trip back in time …

The hectic bustle of the place had hit Amy instantly. Being brought up by parents with a serious café habit, the energy buzzing around the student coffee shop had felt both newly exhilarating and yet comfortably familiar. She'd instantly enjoyed walking anonymously through the crowds with her plastic mug and a soggy salad roll.

Sitting in the coffee shop one day, during the second week of her first term as a student archaeologist, Amy noticed two lads, whom she'd seen in her Prehistory lecture only ten minutes before, struggling to find seats. Surprising herself by inviting them to share her wobbly plastic table, Amy recalled how she'd been even more surprised when they'd accepted her offer.

With that one uncharacteristically impulsive gesture, Amy had met Paul and Rob. Those cups of strong black coffee in the overcrowded student café were only the first of many coffee stops they shared over the next three years ...

The first track, which Amy remembered recording herself, was only halfway through, but her wine glass was already empty. With closed eyes Amy thought of them now. Rob was married with three small children. Paul was travelling the world, his archaeological trowel still in hand. Both were miles away. Their friendships remained, but were rather neglected on her side, she thought sadly. The sigh which escaped Amy's lips was a resigned one, as the sound of Bryan Adams' 'Summer of '69' continued to fill the room.

Amy sighed again, but couldn't help the hint of a smile as she remembered how the student coffee shop had only appeared to own one CD, which it had played on a continuous loop. It had quickly become traditional for Amy, Paul, and Rob to time their departure to the sound of Adams belting out the last lines of his song.

As track one of her tape died away, and the second began, Amy realised she'd been holding her breath. Expelling air slowly as the first notes hit her ears, Amy's racing pulse was calmed by the recollection of a happy memory that had led her to record the song fifteen years ago ...

The rain was thudding down so violently that it seemed to be angling for status as a monsoon. The trainee archaeologists were still hard at it, though, stoically ignoring their soaking backs as drips ran down their necks, crept inside their T-shirts, and even permeated their underwear. Nobody knew that it was Amy's nineteenth birthday as she stood, waist-deep in mud, in a Roman drain in South Wales during one of the wettest summers ever, soaked to the skin with her blonde ponytail plastered to the back of her neck. In the few months they'd known each other, Amy, Rob, and Paul had discussed everything from their

5

favourite curries to their preferred sexual positions, but somehow dates of birth had never come up.

Despite the appalling conditions, it had been a considerable surprise to everyone when the site supervisor had called a halt to their labours and announced they could all have the afternoon off. Heaved bodily out of the hole by two of her fellow diggers, Amy had struggled her way through the thick, squelching mud to a sad-looking group of tents huddled together at the edge of the field. Almost pointlessly, she'd replaced the day's soaking clothes with yesterday's damp ones, before joining her waiting colleagues and climbing into the site minibus.

As soon the bus had reached the town centre, Paul and Rob had tugged a confused Amy out, and waved goodbye to the other passengers. Bewildered, Amy had been led by the boys into a blissfully warm tearoom. Paul had spoken to the owner, explaining and apologising for their bedraggled appearance, while Rob had manoeuvred Amy to a table, complete with a green tablecloth and dainty, but rather clashing, Spode china.

When the pot of beautifully strong jet-black coffee had arrived, Amy had felt a huge surge of love for her friends – but when the plate of cupcakes arrived, each with a small pink candle glowing on top, she'd been forced to bite back tears.

As they hungrily bit into the birthday treats, Paul had told Amy that the site supervisor had discovered it was her birthday when he'd been tackling the overdue student insurance forms. He'd told the lads, and they'd hit upon the perfect birthday treat, and an excuse to escape the rain.

The music in the teashop had been gently lilting classical, but it wasn't the calming strains of Vivaldi's *Summer* which Amy had recorded onto her tape once she had returned to dry living. Having taken pity on her soggy customers for having to live without running water or proper toilets for two weeks, the kindly café proprietor had given Amy the best present she'd ever had: a hot shower and freshly tumble-dried clothes.

The neat, white-tiled bathroom in the compact flat above the café was filled with the sound of the owner's radio. Standing in a spotless cubicle, washing the mud off and getting the tension out of her aching muscles, Amy had sung along as 'Here Comes the Rain Again' by the Eurythmics blared out with well-timed irony …

Amy pressed *Stop*. The remaining wine wouldn't last the length of the cassette if she carried on like this. She was hungry too, after a day of dishing out tedious advice to various dull clients from various boring businesses. Without changing from her work suit into her beloved jeans and a chunky jumper, Amy put her coat back on.

Grabbing her long-abandoned Walkman from a kitchen drawer, and thankful that the batteries miraculously worked, she slid the tape in and stuffed the unopened envelope into her pocket. Rejecting her hated court shoes, she slid on her cosy brown Hush Puppies, barely registering the sartorial clash with her smart navy trousers, and hit the road in search of supper.

With the cool evening air of Aberdeen blowing against her face, Amy walked from the granite-grey terrace that she called home towards the even greyer Union Street and its array of restaurants. Choosing an Italian that was just busy enough for her to hide in and think while not sticking out as a single woman dining alone, Amy opted for a calzone and a fresh orange juice to counteract the wine sloshing around her empty insides. Her order was taken by a young olive-skinned guy, who stared at her as if she might be genuinely insane when she started fiddling with her museum-piece technology.

Knowing neither her curiosity nor her nerves could wait any longer to find out what else lurked forgotten on the cassette, Amy settled back onto her red padded seat, positioned her unfashionably large headphones on her head, and started the Walkman.

Her heart thudded. She hadn't recorded anything else herself.

But Jack had.

The shiver that shot down her spine as the first bar of the next tune kicked into life was enough to make Amy slam the *Stop* button down with unusual violence. The pretty-boy waiter came back with her drink, looking concerned: perhaps he'd seen her shocked expression. *Or perhaps he desperately wants to tell me about MP3 players or iPods*, Amy thought, forcing herself to aim a fake smile of reassurance in his direction.

Amy slowly counted to three. How bad could it be, anyway? She pressed *Play*. This time she wouldn't be taken by surprise.

She couldn't believe Jack had recorded it. But then of course he had: that's why he'd taken the tape in the first place. He'd owned a copy of the track in question, and had promised to record it for her. It had seemed funny at the time.

Amy had forbidden herself to think about Jack for so long that, now he was pushing himself back in, she feared she wouldn't be able to cope with the reason why.

She'd had a handful of boyfriends at university. Although they had all been rewarding experiences, each liaison being flirty and fun, they had also all been ultimately brief. But the moment she'd seen Jack walking down the library steps with Rob, one Monday morning fourteen years ago, Amy had known he was different. His dark hair and soulful hazel eyes had made an instant impact. Yet, both of them being reticent to make the first move, they had managed to ignore their obvious mutual attraction for three months, driving their friends mad with their inaction. Rob, frustrated by what was fast becoming an awkward situation, had finally set them up on a friendly 'getting-to-know-each-other' date out of sheer desperation.

The butterflies had been stirring in Amy's stomach before she'd even got to the pub chosen for the occasion. She'd just about convinced herself that Jack wouldn't show up anyway, and was going to call the whole thing off, when Rob had phoned to assure Amy that no thumbscrews had been used to force Jack to come along. In fact, no persuasion had been required at all.

The pub had been poky to say the least, and the lack of sawdust on the floor was an opportunity severely missed by the management. The smoke from the customers' cigarettes had been at smog levels, and there was standing room only. Even as she'd walked through the door Amy had experienced an overwhelming temptation to run, to escape before the inevitable hurt happened, but there'd been a tiny voice of hope screaming somewhere in the back of her head. So she'd stayed. And then Jack had arrived.

Amy couldn't remember how they'd got talking, but in a remarkably short time they had covered their early childhoods, school days, past relationship disasters, and their hopes and fears for the future. They'd also discovered a mutual love of real, good-quality coffee – preferably served to them by someone else. By the time the barman was declaring last orders it had seemed perfectly natural for Jack to walk her home.

When they'd reached her rented terraced house, Amy hadn't hesitated before inviting Jack in. The kettle was boiled and drinks made before she'd even thought about the social connotations of inviting a man 'in for coffee'.

Their drinks had never been drunk. The two chipped mugs sat on the magazine-strewn table in front of the tiny sofa upon which they'd cuddled while they chatted. Jack had been the one who suggested putting on some music, and not knowing where to hunt for a suitable tape, had simply turned on Amy's radio. They'd laughed out loud when Joy Division's 'Love Will Tear Us Apart' burst into the room; agreeing that, even if it wasn't too pathetic to have a song that was 'their song,' that that particular track would never be it.

Despite the fact that the restaurant was filling up around her, Amy didn't try to hide the tears which had begun to slip down her face in time to the music. It seemed absurd to remember how happy she'd been.

Forcing herself into further reminiscences, Amy remembered how Jack had left at about two o'clock in the morning, after arranging to take her to see *The Bodyguard* at the cinema the following evening. Before leaving, he'd given Amy the most delicious, gentle, and loving kiss she'd ever experienced. A kiss full of future promise. It had been a moment locked in time.

She told him all about her brother's tape, and promising to

return it soon, the cassette had been secured in Jack's vast coat pocket, so that he could record their non-song. Amy hadn't been able to stop grinning, and by the time she met up with Paul and Rob the next morning, her jaw had ached with the strain of being so elated.

Making an emergency dash to the ladies' cloakroom, Amy gazed at her 34-year-old reflection in the mirror. Her fair hair was tied back into its practical work-day ponytail. Dark shadows circled her intensely blue eyes. Suddenly feeling very tired, Amy splashed her face with cold water. Then, telling the woman in the mirror to get a grip, she returned to her rapidly cooling meal.

The discarded Walkman lay accusingly on the table. No one had pinched it as she'd half-hoped. No one had made her life easier by stealing the past away. Amy couldn't begin to guess what the remainder of the tape contained. She had loved Jack so much; no one else had stood a chance.

Her year with Jack had lurched from starting to stopping, re-starting to re-stopping, until whatever they had finally collapsed into an unrecognisable heap right in the middle of her finals. The confused feeling which had swamped her then had remained ever since, like a hostile shadow, blighting any chance of further meaningful relationships. Overwhelmed by a rejection she hadn't understood, Amy had finished her exams, packed up her belongings for her parents to collect later, stuffed a suitcase with clothes and books, and run.

That was almost exactly thirteen years ago. Amy inwardly groaned. Here she was in her mid-thirties, in a dull job, with no real local friends, no partner, and no children. Eking out her spare time sitting in unspectacular cafés, inhaling coffee fumes and reading novels. She had to do something about her life. And fast.

Slipping her mobile out of her pocket, Amy punched in the number before she had a chance to change her mind.

Rob answered the phone with blessed speed. Just hearing his delighted voice when he realised that the prodigal daughter was on the line made Amy feel so much better that she silently cursed herself for not calling him more often. She found herself accepting the frequently made, but usually refused, invitation to visit, and was amazed by how happy he sounded, and by how quickly Rob made plans to invite Paul over from his current dig so that they could all make some coffee stops like they had in the old days.

Amy briefly explained what had happened. Did Rob still work with Jack? He did.

By the time she'd put the phone down on Rob, Amy's indecisive metabolism had decided she was starving and she ate her meal without registering what it tasted like. Once she'd finished, Amy slid her hand into her pocket and fingered the envelope nervously. Placing the headphones back over her ears and pressing *Play*, she flinched as Jack's soft voice spoke to her.

'I'm sorry Amy. I'm sorry I hurt you. I hope you don't mind, but I've put two more tracks on your tape. I tried to imagine what you'd have put on it, if I'd returned it. I hope I got it right. I did love you. Still do, really, but, well, open the letter as you listen, it'll explain. Oh, and as far as the last track goes, remember we had very wide musical tastes back then – don't tell anyone who knows me I own a copy!'

The wounded lyrics of the first new track, Massive Attack's 'Unfinished Sympathy', crowded her head, and Amy found she was shaking. Fresh tears threatened as she opened Jack's letter with clumsy fingers …

So that was it.

Amy felt odd; relieved, bereft, used, but strangely free. It hadn't been her fault. Her head thudded and an incredible anger welled up inside her. She'd wasted so much time over something beyond her control.

When the last track came on Amy couldn't help but laugh. No wonder Jack didn't want anyone to know they'd liked it. She could feel the weight of the last thirteen years lifting from her. He was gay. As simple as that. He must have felt as confused as she'd felt worthless. It was time to find him. Time to ask all the questions she should have demanded answers to years ago, not to mention the new ones that crashed through her head.

What had he seen in her? Amy wasn't naïve enough to believe she'd turned him gay, but why the hell had he gone out with her in the first place? Whatever had been the point? And why hadn't Rob ever told her? He must have known for a while if he worked with Jack every day.

Her brain did an abrupt U-turn and, with her thoughts spiralling out of control in another direction, Amy was seized with panic. Why had he told her now? What had happened to make him get in touch after so many years? Was Jack in trouble? Had someone hurt him?

As Whitney Houston's version of 'I Will Always Love You' completed her tape, Amy fished the letter back out of her pocket. There was no address, but there was a mobile number.

Coming to a vastly overdue decision, Amy pulled her mobile back out of her pocket and pressed re-dial.

'Rob. I'm not coming to visit. I've made a decision. I've been hiding long enough. I'm moving south. Please don't say *anything* about *anything* to Jack yet. OK?'

OCTOBER

In which Amy heads south, we meet an erotica writer, and discover the perfect coffee house – and Jack has some explaining to do ...

Two

October 2nd 2006

Jack sat on the edge of the stool. It was hard and unyielding against his buttocks. He suspected it had been specifically designed not to encourage lingering at the bar.

Wiping his hands down his faded jeans, Jack remembered how carefully he'd wrapped the package before posting it north. In July it had seemed so much the right thing to do ... He'd visualised Amy opening it, and had contemplated her reaction for a while. Then, in typical Jack style, he'd moved on, and placed the whole event into that part of his brain where the best-forgotten actions of his life dwelt.

Propped against the bar counter behind him, Jack stared at his mobile phone. He hadn't expected this. He read the text again.

Got tape. Got letter. Moving to London. Will c u maybe. Hope u ok. Amy

Jack gulped down a giant mouthful of Worthington's before allowing his eyes to rove around the pulsating dance floor. He needed a distraction. Something – someone – to stop him thinking. Jack's eyes fell on a tall slim man, about thirty, nice hair, dark eyes. He'd do.

Jack put his pint down and joined the fray.

Cramming the foot cream and moisturiser back amongst the more familiar clutter of books, tissues, and scraps of paper that adorned her bedside table, it struck Kit that not long ago she'd scorned such additions to her life. Nightly applications of unguents to stave off the evidence of aging were a paranoia reserved exclusively for other people.

Somehow that had changed recently. It was as if on her last birthday a trigger had gone off in Kit's head, and the fear of looking old, rather than being old, had consumed her. Phil had laughed when Kit had bought a pot of Nivea. Not in an unkind way, but in a 'so you *are* growing up at last' sort of way. She knew it had annoyed her far more than it should have done, as she'd sulked in their bedroom, embarrassed at the ownership of something that the rest of the female race had taken for granted since adolescence.

As if having to admit she wasn't twenty anymore wasn't bad enough, other aspects of her life seemed to be losing their certainty as well. The twins were growing up way too fast. Although only nine years old (an age which in Kit's opinion was definitely the new thirteen), they seemed to need her less and less beyond the functions of taxi driver, housekeeper, and meal-provider. To top it all, writing her erotica, which had once given her so much pleasure, somehow didn't feel quite so satisfying these days.

'I'm not even forty!' Kit flicked a stray strand of red hair out of her eyes and, slamming the offending lotion away with her socks, pulled open her knickers drawer for consolation. It always made her feel better to see her pile of delicate silk, satin, and lace undies. They felt soft between her fingers as she trailed a hand through the fabric. These were also a relatively new innovation for her, though not one that her husband joked about.

Confidence, that was what it was about, and since she had, after five years of moaning and a further two gruelling years of actually trying, lost the weight she'd gained during pregnancy, Kit had rewarded herself by throwing her hated cheap and boring knickers into the dustbin, and built up a pile of lingerie to be proud of. She had to be careful though. For the first time in her life Kit saw how buying clothes could become addictive. This was a new sensation to someone who didn't give a damn about fashion, and regarded shopping as something inconvenient to be slotted in between coffee breaks.

Kit smiled and closed the drawer, ignoring the glint of a

shiny silver vibrator Phil had given her as a present after the publication of her first smutty story. He'd be up in a minute, and the real thing was always preferable. Or perhaps she should try and get some sleep. After all, she was seeing Jack tomorrow afternoon, and judging by the tone of his voice when he'd called, it sounded as if their inevitable caffeine overload might be accompanied by some pretty heavy conversation.

October 3rd 2006

Fishing around in her kitchen cupboards, Kit produced two school lunchboxes, and began buttering slices of bread before facing the fact that she didn't have much to put between them.

As she worked, Kit's brain was abruptly dragged out of its sandwich-preparing stupor by the radio. 'Let's Dance' was oozing out of the speakers. David Bowie's gravelly voice made her skin chill and her heart leap at the same time. It had been so long since she'd heard it. Her mind slipped back to those precious months back in 1994. She was in his old bedroom with him then, dancing in time to the words, and …

'Mum.'

Helena was staring at Kit with a mixture of scorn and disbelief. 'Mum, what are you doing? You've put milk in your coffee. You *hate* milk.'

Coming reluctantly back to the present, Kit bit back an expletive, and put on her "Mum is in control" face. 'Hello love. What do you want for breakfast?'

'Shreddies please, Mum, I *always* have Shreddies.' Helena gave a 'grown-ups are so stupid' shrug and sat imperiously at the kitchen table, expecting full waitress service. 'And blackcurrant juice!'

Moving around the room, completing her everyday routine, Kit's brain totally disengaged, but her subconscious carried on dancing.

Three

October 3rd 2006

Kit had begun working from home three years ago. Except she hadn't, because she couldn't.

Phil had designated their home's box-sized spare bedroom as Kit's office, had bought her a new desk, a laptop, and evicted the twins' baby toys and all their other clutter to the loft, but it was no good. Try as she might, Kit could not take on the persona of her pseudonym, Katrina Island, and think up intricate plot lines and erotic acrobatics in a house she knew needed dusting. So each morning Kit stuffed a notebook into her bag and, after walking the twins to school, headed to her favourite café.

Kit loved Pickwicks. Cluttered with dubious antiques and mismatched furniture, it had shuttered windows and a solid wooden floor that echoed as you walked across it. Classical music played gently in the background. It was the perfect venue in which to avoid real life, and become immersed in her brand of literary progress.

As a regular customer, Kit frequently found that her arrival had been anticipated, and a piping hot cup of black coffee would already be waiting on her usual table before she'd got through the door. Today however, Kit didn't find her essential caffeine injection awaiting her, but a plotline dying to be exploited.

Her friend Peggy, resident waitress, manager, and dogsbody combined, was leaning so far across the glass cake counter that her head was dangling down over the other side, her feet only just touching the floor. Her shiny black hair had escaped from of its grips and cascaded downwards, obscuring the view of all the mouth-wateringly fattening cakes on offer.

'What the hell are you doing?' Kit threw her bag down and crossed the room to rescue the sprawled waitress.

'I was trying to clean the glass and I slipped.' Peggy, her round face apple-red from the blood that had rushed to it, smiled broadly, adjusting her ample white blouse and black trousers.

'Oh really?' Disbelief dripped from Kit's lips, 'Why didn't you go around the front then?'

'Gets boring doing the same old thing every day,' said Peggy with a mischievous grin, 'I fancied a change.'

'And I don't suppose that husband of yours is just out of sight, wishing that a customer wasn't so inconsiderate as to want serving, and thus causing him to quit playing waitress and chef?'

'I don't know what you mean!' Peggy brandished the cake-tongs in Kit's direction. 'Danish?'

'Only after you've disinfected the counter, you hussy.'

'Like you can talk.' Peggy grabbed her cloth and began to wipe it down.

Childishly sticking out her tongue, Kit sat down at her table. Feeling inexplicably happy, her early morning visit into nostalgia forgotten, she opened her bag, grabbed a pen and began to write; hoping that the strong image in her head wouldn't disappear before she'd committed it to paper.

... as her mass of black hair swept past the cake display, he pushed her body further across the counter...

Friends who knew which literary genre Kit wrote for a living could never understand where she got her ideas from. She'd tried to explain that simply by picturing a location she could stimulate the background of a story. Then all she had to do was invent ways to get rid of everyone's clothes – or not.

When Kit told people what she did for a living, they generally looked at her with a mixture of incomprehension, admiration and, more frequently, amazement. Kit simply didn't fit their stereotype of the writer of erotica. Happily married with two children, she wore no make-up or scent, never wore skirts (let alone mini ones), had a strong aversion to body piercings, and her shoulder-length bobbed hair remained its natural red.

When people she sensed wouldn't be able to cope with the knowledge of how she made a living, asked her what she did, Kit always told them that she worked for an online company. Hardly anyone ever asked 'doing what?' They usually assumed she was doing something dull and low-paid to fit in with school hours. As it happened, Kit *did* work for an online company, and it was anything but dull. She'd been writing for *Pearls* for some time now, but it wasn't the sort of website she wanted to discuss in the playground.

Checking the clock on the wall, Kit saw she'd been writing steadily for three hours. Satisfied with her initial story draft, she gathered up her belongings, waved goodbye to Peggy and headed off to find Jack.

The moment she arrived Kit spotted Jack at their usual table. His brown leather jacket was thrown across the back of the wooden chair on which he was perched. He didn't look right somehow. Normally he'd be virtually reclining, a flirty smirk playing across his face as he watched her walk towards him. Today Jack seemed pale and almost twitchy. Kit's stomach turned over; what if he was ill? It was a possibility, especially in his world. She instantly told herself off for such a stereotypical thought, but a voice still nagged. Something was wrong.

It was a relief to come to her turn in the queue. Paying for a large Americano and two Chelsea buns (it looked as though they might need extra sugar); Kit took up her tray and headed towards Jack.

'Do you think it's possible to love someone, love them very much, and still know in your heart that it will never work between you?' The sentence exploded from Jack's mouth like bullets from a gun; not even waiting for Kit to take her coat off before blurting out what was on his mind.

'Bloody hell, Jack! That's a heavy question for a Monday lunchtime.'

'Sorry …' Instantly abashed, Jack seemed almost ashamed.

Too late, Kit realised that in her relief that Jack hadn't announced he was sick; she had made a huge error in making light of his question. Such soul searching was so out of character that she'd been taken by surprise. He'd probably been building up to asking that all night.

Amazed, Kit watched as Jack stood up, ignoring his drink and cake, grabbed his jacket, and walked out. He'd always had a taste for the dramatic gesture, but this was different. Kit sat where she was, fighting her natural instinct to run after him. Sipping her coffee, she ran his words through her head. Who did he love hopelessly? Maybe he wasn't referring to himself at all? Kit snorted into her coffee; of course it was about him. It was always about him. Perhaps he'd fallen for a married man who wouldn't give up the more traditional part of his life? *Or maybe ... no, don't be ridiculous!* Kit quashed a treacherous thought. Picking up her phone, she fired off a text.

Come drink ur coffee. I'm sorry, u took me by surprise. K x

Jack's drink was stone cold by the time Kit had given up on him sending a reply.

22

Four

October 4th 2006

It was only once she'd checked in at Aberdeen airport, her luggage safely stowed, that Amy finally stopped moving. Slumped on a bench, looking around at the people rushing by, she realised that this was the first time she'd been inactive for weeks.

Once her impulsive decision to go home to England had been made, she'd barely stopped for a break in the haste to work her notice period, sort out the ending of the lease on her rented flat, and arrange somewhere to stay in London. Now that stillness was about to be forced upon her, Amy had to face the reality of what she'd done by throwing in a good job and a nice flat for no job and a rented room in a shared house in London that she'd never even seen.

'I need coffee,' she muttered to herself. Hoisting her tatty fabric handbag higher onto her shoulder in a bracing gesture, she headed for the café located next to the departure checkpoint.

Having successfully managed to convey her order to the Chinese-speaking assistant via a mixture of words and what could almost pass for semaphore, Amy sat down on one of the fiendishly uncomfortable steel seats. Ignoring the unsightly build-up of used cups, half-eaten meals and spilt fizzy pop, she briefly allowed herself to contemplate her situation. Almost instantly her nerves regrouped in her gut, and Amy decided to put off any serious thoughts about the future until she was on the plane. That way, any possible temptations to chicken out and stay in Scotland after all would no longer be an option. Major life planning could wait. For now she would just indulge in her drink and watch the world go by. Then she'd have a wander around the meagre collection of shops, and perhaps buy a book or magazine for the flight, putting reality off for a bit longer.

Unable to put off the moment, Amy picked up her backpack and headed over to the departure gate. As she passed the newsagents' her eyes landed on a copy of one magazine in particular – it had the appropriate headline *New Job, New Home, New Life*.

Amy muttered the words over and over in her head like a mantra as she purchased the magazine fate seemed to have left there for her, before joining the queue of people who were also turning their back on the Granite City, for to business commitments, holidays or, as in her case, for ever.

During the seventy-minute flight, Amy had managed to concoct enough excuses to delay any plan of action as to what to do next for a little longer. She'd examined the flight safety card thoroughly, had uncharacteristically engaged her fellow passengers in mindless conversation, and flicked through her magazine. Amy had read the occasional relevant passage, but had been disappointed not to find an article entitled *You've Ditched Your Life – So Now What*?

Now, trudging down the gloomy concourse at Heathrow to retrieve her luggage and trying to ignore the patina of perspiration on her palms, Amy was suddenly aware that someone was talking to her.

'You OK?'

The man striding next to her spoke with a soft Irish lilt. 'You've been chatting to yourself ever since we landed.'

'Oh, God, have I?' Amy's face flushed. 'I'm sorry, I'm always talking to myself. You must think I'm nuts.'

'No!' His eyes twinkled at her as he spoke. 'Well, maybe just a bit.'

Amy wondered how old he was. Roughly her age perhaps; she always found it difficult to tell with men in suits. Amy didn't want to think about it, or she'd get onto thinking about how much time had passed since she'd last smiled at a man of her own age, let alone spoken to one, and that way lay madness.

'You're probably right. I've just chucked in my life, so perhaps I'm insane.'

'A lot on your mind, then.' He nodded his bespectacled head.

Amy carried on rambling. 'No job, a new home I've only seen on a computer screen … I'm getting a serious case of cold feet.'

They reached the dimly lit baggage collection area as the carousel sparked into life. The whole room spoke of transitory lives, and the dank atmosphere made Amy shiver inside.

The man had obviously noticed her growing unease. 'Look, I know I'm a total stranger, and it's none of my business; but if it helps, I think it sounds fantastic. Exciting and brave.'

Spotting her luggage heading towards her, Amy grimaced. 'I don't feel very brave.' She grabbed her heavy bag before it lumbered out of reach.

'You have a blank page. A new canvas to start on. I'd swap what I've got for that, and so would most of this lot.' He gestured to the anonymous crowds that surged around them. 'Go with the flow, have fun, be yourself, and smile. You have a nice smile.' Then he scooped up his navy executive wheeled suitcase, extended the handle, and rapidly disappeared, his grey suit merging with hundreds of others in the crush.

Amy stood there, oblivious to the fact that she was in everybody's way. *A blank page*. For the first time in days excitement overtook the fear, as she hurried off to hail a taxi to transport her into the unchartered wilds of Richmond.

Five

October 4th 2006

Phil's extra-long limbs were beginning to feel quite numb as he stamped his six-foot-four frame up and down the street. To be fair, his client had warned him that her flight may be delayed, and that her time of arrival would depend on both that and her ability to quickly find a taxi, but her non-appearance was tedious nonetheless.

He knew it wasn't really the cold that was bothering him; he was bored. In fact, his whole day stretched ahead in a rather onerous fashion, and once again Phil considered the practicalities of packing it all in. The business was doing well, and now that Kit had a regular buyer for her stories he really didn't need to work such ridiculously long hours, but he was the bloke, right? Isn't that what he was supposed to do? Support his family. Earn the money. He didn't consider himself old-fashioned, but giving up a good regular income just because his job was driving him mad with its utter dullness seemed terribly selfish.

As the founder and director of Home Hunters, Phil didn't usually do the initial visits with clients any more. He had underlings who he sent out, via Tube, taxi and bus, to usher people into their new flats and new lives. Today, though, Phil's discontent with his work had reached boiling point, and he knew he simply had to get out of the office. Glad of a genuine excuse to get away from the perpetual hum of the air conditioning, and to breathe in some of what passed for fresh air in London, Phil had decided to deal with the Richmond let himself. Plus it was close to home anyway: after he'd sorted this Amy Crane out, he'd knock off early for once.

The drizzle which had threatened to start all morning had finally broken through the clouds when a black cab pulled up outside 8 Princes Road. Amy had been sent a photo of the small end-of-terrace, but she hadn't expected it to look so cramped against its fellow homes. It appeared as if an overly optimistic builder had shoe-horned it into place. As Amy fumbled through her purse for money to pay the driver, she tried to swallow down a feeling of rising panic. £800 a month for a room in that tiny, squat-looking place? Bloody hell, what had she done? Was this really the 'new home' part of her 'new life'?

Phil, recognising the glaze of uncertainty that was typical of clients new to London, came over and took her bag. 'Miss Crane?'

'Yes, I'm Amy.' She stared about her. Perhaps it was the rain, but right now Richmond seemed every bit as grey and gloomy as Aberdeen had done.

The tall man from the agency seemed to be psychic. 'Come on. It'll feel better when you're dry and have a cup of something warming in your hand.'

Steering Amy up the short gravel path, Phil produced a Yale key from a large bunch. He opened the front door. *Her front door. In Richmond.*

Amy clutched her rucksack like a security blanket, reluctant to put it down as she lingered in the dark, narrow hallway. Phil was talking to her, but only his name and the fact he was going to put the kettle on had registered.

Once she reached the kitchen, though, Amy could barely disguise her relief. It was compact, neat and spotless. Rows of gleaming white and stainless steel cupboards lined the poster-free walls, and the work surfaces held only biscuit tins and cooking appliances. There wasn't a leftover meal, an unwashed dish, or even burnt toast crumbs, in sight.

'You didn't think I'd let you live in squalor, did you?' Phil smiled, then picked up a mug and waved it at her. 'Tea or coffee?'

'Coffee, please, if the other tenants won't mind me scrounging some.'

'No problem, I always come equipped.' He produced a handful of sachets from his inside pocket. 'The only thing we have to steal is milk.'

'I don't take it; but thanks, I need a caffeine fix fast.'

'You sound like my wife.' Phil starting chatting away about his wife's café obsession, but Amy wasn't listening. She was surveying the clean crisp white walls, the tastefully chosen pictures, the floor-to-ceiling bookshelf crammed with novels and DVD boxes. Why had she assumed this would be a return to student-land? That she was taking a step back, not forward?

The kitchen opened onto a small dining area with a table big enough for four. Then, passing through an archway she was drawn into a compact living area. Two mini navy sofas lined two sides of the room, a gas fire occupied a third, and the TV and a large bay window took up the fourth. In the centre of the room sat an oversized coffee table.

Phil was looking at her as if he expected an answer to a question.

'Sorry, I'd phased out, I missed what you said.' Amy admitted shyly.

'Not to worry. Do you like it so far?'

'Yes, I do. I didn't expect to.' Amy gave a nervous laugh. 'I hope the people here like me.'

'They're very nice.' Phil passed Amy her coffee. 'To be honest,' he called over his shoulder, 'you probably won't see that much of them, I think they work all hours.'

'I guess you'd have to so you can afford the rent.'

'I'm afraid so,' Phil shrugged apologetically, trying not to think of his company's cut. 'Have you got work sorted down here?'

'No,' Amy lowered her eyes, inwardly cursing her honesty, and hurriedly continued. 'Not yet, anyway. But I do have all the money from the deposit on the flat I was renting in Scotland. I can pay the rent.'

Phil changed the subject. 'I'll show you upstairs.'

Pointing out a perfectly adequate but unspectacular bathroom, Phil indicated her fellow housemates' bedroom

29

doors, and then opened the final door. 'This is you then.'

As she stepped into the spacious room, any fears Amy had about damp dark lodgings were blown away for good.

'You wouldn't think there was space for all this when you look from the outside, would you?'

Smiling, Phil said, 'I'll give you a minute,' and headed downstairs, experience telling him his client wouldn't need him for a while.

Dark maroon curtains hung thickly over the bay window. Pulling them back, Amy let daylight fill the room, but ignoring the view for a moment, she concentrated instead on the furnishings. The double bed, complete with a pine headboard, had been made up for her. A note lay on the pillow: *We didn't think you'd want to go shopping for linen straight away, so you can borrow these sheets and things until you're sorted.* It was signed *James and Sarah.* Amy felt reassured to think that her housemates were already proving so thoughtful, and mentally thanked them. In her rush to leave Scotland she'd totally forgotten to bring bed linen with her. The removal van holding the few bits of furniture that actually belonged to her, rather than having been rented with her flat, wasn't due to arrive until tomorrow.

A large pine chair sat by the window, and a built-in wardrobe occupied the wall by the door.

'I'll need to get a bedside table,' Amy told the curtains as she ran her fingers over them, appreciating their weight and thickness, which would help keep her room warm in the winter and protect her from the sun's early morning glare in the summer.

'Miss Crane?'

Amy actually ran downstairs. 'Hi, sorry, I got carried away. I love it, thank you.' Barely blinking at the amount, she signed the already-prepared contract and the first three months' rent cheque before waving her new landlord goodbye.

The second Phil left, Amy retreated into the living room and burst into tears. She was here. She had no idea if she was crying from relief, happiness, excitement, or just in reaction to being herself at last. For the first time in years she didn't feel as if she was the wounded girl who had fled to Aberdeen and hidden for the past thirteen years.

She knew she'd been a fool to run in the first place, but she had, and there was nothing that could change the past, but perhaps she could return to being the sociable, chatty person who'd existed before? Before Jack had abandoned her with no explanation other than a few heartbreakingly devastating words.

'I'm sorry Amy, this is going too well. It's over.'

Six

October 4th 2006

The power shower thundered, sending a searing-hot cascade of water down onto Jack's head. Squeezing far too much shampoo into his hands, he began to viciously scrub his short hair. What the hell had he been thinking? Well, actually, he hadn't been thinking, had he? He never looked beyond himself. The moment. The day. He was so stupid. So angry with himself.

Why the fuck had he posted that tape? And, more immediately, where was he? And how soon was he going to able to get away from whoever it was he'd spent the night with? Jack could feel the familiar sensation of suffocation closing in on him as he abandoned his hair and began to furiously soap his torso.

He was a shit.

But then you have to be good at something.

And now Amy was coming here. It hadn't crossed his mind that she'd even visit, let alone move her entire life back south. And not just south, but bloody *London*. Being back in touch, and hopefully forgiven, was one thing when she was safely tucked away in Scotland. But here. Face to face. Jack hadn't banked on that at all.

He really didn't want to see Rob today. It was his fault this had happened. Rob had come into work one day, back in the summer, going on about how worried he and Paul were for Amy. How she seemed to have hidden herself away, completely off the emotional scale. The combination of bright sunshine, happy reminiscences, and the weight of a conversation he and Amy had never had, had brought his buried guilt racing to the surface.

Then, a few days later, Paul had visited Jack and Rob's bookshop, passing through on one of his rare visits between archaeological digs. He'd been sorting out some of his university mementos, and had come across a load of photographs.

They were all there, at university, more years ago than was acceptable if Jack was still going to pass himself off as thirty at the clubs he frequented. Amy, Rob and Paul huddled together in a muddy ditch, laughing. Rob, Paul, and him, pints of Tiger lager in hand, outside their favourite pub. Paul, Amy and him, all cuddled together on Rob's battered and suspiciously stained brown sofa. Amy and him. Amy and him together. Smiling. Together.

That had been the killer. That was the photo that had made him think. Her eyes had shone at the camera. If Jack was honest, so had his. So, in a state of happy but unrealistic nostalgia, he'd gone home, dragged a box of assorted junk out from under his bed, and pulled out the tape.

He had weighed the clear plastic box in his hand. It was time to explain. If Amy was half the girl he used to know then she'd forgive him. And suddenly, from nowhere, Jack had found that he really, really needed to be forgiven.

That was why he'd put 'Unfinished Sympathy' on Amy's tape. He wanted her to understand that he knew he'd hurt her. That he, himself, had been hurt by having to leave her. But for reasons he hadn't totally understood at the time, he'd felt he had no choice. A fact which had led him to the record the unbearably twee, but wholly accurate, 'I Will Always Love You'. It seemed to say how sorry he was. It said everything he'd wanted to say then, but couldn't. He was sorry, really he was. But for Amy to turn up here! *Bloody hell.*

Stepping out of the shower, Jack began to dry himself with a suitably punishing rough brown towel. Now he was going to have to tell Rob he'd returned the tape, *and* have another go at talking to Kit.

He hadn't deliberately failed to tell Kit about Amy. Specific conversations about individual exes had never come up. Jack was pretty sure that Rob hadn't mentioned Amy to Kit either. Amy had been part of their old life, and Kit was part of their current one. Simple.

Jack knew he had to see Kit soon, before someone else filled her in. He wasn't sure why he'd walked out on her now he came to think about it. At least she'd understand. Kit always understood. After all, they'd remained friends. Great friends. They had moved on smoothly.

'Talk about my past catching me up,' he muttered to his sleep-deprived reflection as he dragged a borrowed razor over his chin. 'It's pretty much tripped me up, into a pile of shit, and it's entirely my fault. Bloody sentimental tape. *Fuck!*'

Approaching his bookshop, Jack peered up at the sign which swung from its low eaves, and silently thanked his grandfather for leaving him that money in his will.

Even though he'd attained a first-class degree in Ecology, Jack had never had any intention of taking up a career in that arena. The idea of running a bookshop had started as a faint possibility; an option amongst many. It had developed into a dream, and then, when he'd accidentally come across the empty premises in Kew, it had blossomed into an exciting and challenging project.

Now Reading Nature was a source of real pride, and despite his self-inflicted gloom, Jack got a kick of achievement from seeing its single bay-windowed frontage ahead of him. Through the glass Jack could see Rob's cropped ginger-haired head bent over the counter. He was busy sorting the morning's post into piles: to do, to send, the ubiquitous bills to pay, and junk to recycle.

'Morning,' Rob smiled up at his friend as he came in, but adjusted his expression as he saw the cloud hanging across Jack's face. 'What's up? Club no good last night?'

'It was fine, busy, you know.'

'Not really, mate, but then I'm a boring old married fart.'

Jack attempt at a smile failed, 'I've done something stupid. I think.'

Rob pulled a face that clearly implied *no change there then*, but simply said, 'Go on.'

'I've got in touch with Amy.'

'Oh, is that all! God, I assumed you were about to tell me something dreadful.' Rob chucked a whole pile of pointless post into a tub under the counter. 'Anyway, I know.'

'What?' Jack stopped dead.

'I know you wrote to Amy, and sent her tape back. She called me a while ago.'

Jack was stunned, 'Why on earth haven't you mentioned it?'

'She asked me not to.'

Jack slammed his hands flat onto the counter and fought the urge to shout. 'Oh great, and you have to do what *she* says I suppose. Who's your mate here, exactly?'

Rob's hackles rose as he confronted Jack. 'Oh, no. You are *not* doing this to me again. It was bad enough being caught in the crossfire when you and Amy were together, and then not together, and then together again, and then not, all the bloody time! Christ, you were on and off like a tap! I am *not* being put in that position again.'

'But we work together every day, Rob!' Already feeling guilty for taking his anger at himself out on his friend, Jack sighed; he felt as if his customary fight had been snuffed out of him. 'You should have told me you'd heard from Amy. I'd like to have known she was all right.'

Relenting a little, Rob spoke more gently. 'Look, Jack, Amy asked me not to talk about it, and, quite frankly, I didn't want to. I didn't want to end up being piggy-in-the-middle again. You can understand that, can't you?'

'But she's coming to London!'

'I know.'

'But she'll want to see me.' The panic that had been building in Jack's brain began to leak out of his mouth.

'After the way you treated her, I wouldn't bank on it.'

Jack spoke urgently, 'Why, what has she said?'

Realising he wasn't going to be able to escape being the middle-man once again, Rob bit down his annoyance. 'She's said very little. Amy called me in July, told me she was coming down. Apart from a text last week to say she'd found a room to live in, and that she'd call me when she arrives, I know nothing.'

'Yeah, right,' Jack dripped disbelief.

Rob gave up trying to be calm and let go of his temper. His voice was unusually sharp as he snapped his reply. 'Right! Now you listen to me carefully, Jack. Beyond birthday and Christmas cards, Amy has hardly been in touch with either me or Paul for these last ten years. Ten *years*, simply because we are friends with you. Don't you *dare* blame anyone but yourself for that!'

Jack slouched onto the stool behind the counter, and ruffled his fringe through his fingers. 'I'm sorry. I shouldn't be taking this out on you. I didn't think she'd do it, you know. Actually come here.'

Sighing, Rob's voice returned to its normal level. 'Neither did I.'

'Look, mate,' Jack stretched a consolatory hand towards his friend, 'I've not had much kip. I need to sleep. Think. You know.'

'Who was he this time?'

'Ouch!' Jack grinned up at his friend through his long eyelashes.

Rob didn't need Jack's fake flirting right now. He screwed up his eyes as if to gather strength, 'Just go home, Jack. Sleep, go for a walk, anything. Come back when you're in a more receptive mood, OK.'

'Thanks.' Jack got up. He had to find coffee fast, but alone. Today was not the right time for more confessions. 'And I'm sorry, it's just I ...'

'Forget it.' Rob made a dismissive gesture with his hands, 'Just leave me in peace to have a non-productive day on my own.'

Seven

October 4th 2006

Kit clicked *Send* and watched the screen as her latest manuscript headed invisibly, electronically, across the Atlantic to the States. She hadn't been required to write more than a couple of short pieces of flash fiction that week, and had quickly completed her allotted work.

As always, Kit was apprehensive. What if this was the month that her work wasn't up to standard? What if today was the day when her publishers emailed her to say, 'Hey honey. Sorry babe, but we've got a new source, you understand?' It would happen sooner or later, which was why she knew she should crack on with a proper novel. The snags were that she had no ideas, limited time, and no belief in her abilities.

Kit was also feeling guilty. She'd been so engrossed in her latest story, *Waitress Service*, and in caring for the twins, that she hadn't called Jack since he'd walked out on her. Well, now she had some free time before the next requests came in. *If* they did. Kit picked up her mobile and sent Jack a text.

Stories for this fortnight done. Coffee? Cake? Shoulder to cry on. Ears open. Promise. K x

By the time she had been to the loo and dug out her autumn boots, her phone was beeping.

Good on stories. Can't do coffee. Busy. J x

'Damn,' Kit sat down on the edge of the bed. That was not the answer she'd expected. Jack was never too busy for coffee.

Perhaps she'd offended him more than she'd thought. Kit mentally kicked herself. She shouldn't have just left things. Why hadn't she taken him more seriously? It was so out of character for him to ask for any sort of opinion when it came to matters of the heart. Jack usually went out of his way to stay impervious to the emotional tangles that afflicted the rest of the world. Sometimes Kit wondered if she knew him as well as she thought she did.

'Well, if the gay man in the leather jacket won't come to the writer, then the writer must go to the gay man in the leather jacket.' Kit announced as she picked up her coat and headed off to apologise for whatever the hell it was that she'd done; or not done, or whatever.

'Hey, Kit,' Rob looked up from the article he was reading while he sat behind the short maple-wood counter, 'as you can see we are *insanely* busy just now, so perhaps you'd like to join the queue.' He gestured to a non-existent line of customers and beyond to the small deserted bookshop.

'Business booming then?'

'Bloody Internet, it's killing us.' Rob rustled the magazine he was studying at her. 'Reading up on how to get us online. Jack's been on at me for ages to get a website going; reckons it's the way to fill in the lull between the summer and Christmas trade. I know he's probably right, but unless it involves straight typing or emails, I know nothing about this stuff. I'm about as computer-literate as a banana, so I'm swotting up a bit.'

Kit surveyed the customer-free space. 'Being out of season can't help.'

'True. The lack of enthusiastic American tourists with a desperate need for a tree spotter's guide before they hit Kew Gardens is certainly a hindrance to sales.' Rob oozed sarcasm. 'Anyway, how are you?'

'Where's Jack?'

'Home I guess. He was in for a while this morning, but then headed off. It doesn't need two of us here this time of year. And I was asking about you.'

'I'm fine.' Kit brushed a stray hair from her eyes, 'Jack told me he was busy, I assumed he'd be at work.'

'Trust me, Kit, "busy" is not an adjective you can associate with this place.' Rob picked up the book he'd been about to

40

return to the shelves, 'I don't suppose you want to buy a blockbuster on the Great British Hedgerow? Lots of sex and violence!'

'Thanks, but no thanks.'

Rob faked a dramatic groan. 'If Jack's not at home then he'll either be with his latest bedmate, walking around Kew, or lurking in one of the myriad of caffs that litter our part of town.'

This was a bit too dismissive for Kit. 'You two haven't had a row, have you?'

'Not really; but hell, he's a prickly sod sometimes. I know he can be more precious than the crown jewels, but this week he's been so damn jumpy and snappy, he's been about as useful as a broken brolly.'

'Jumpy?'

'Every time a customer comes in, he reacts as if a rocket's been jammed up his backside.'

Kit wrapped her coat tighter around her chest as the early autumn wind blew the door open and sprinkled a handful of rust-coloured leaves across the carpet.

'I was out with him the other day. He was so serious; not his usual fly-by-night self. I didn't know what to say to him. Jack was trying to open up to me, and I was so surprised that I handled it badly.'

Rob was intrigued. 'What did he say?'

'Something about "loving someone not being enough." I wasn't too clear about what he was saying. Do you think he's met a bloke he likes beyond a quick shag?'

'No. No I don't think so. It sounds to me as if this is about someone else,' Rob began to mumble as if talking to himself, Kit temporarily forgotten, 'but honestly, she's never even asked where the shop is. I don't think even she knows what it's called or anything, let alone the hours Jack works.'

Kit moved around to the staff side of the counter, her brow furrowed, 'Rob? Who and what are you talking about?'

'I'm not sure I should say. Anyway, I could be wrong. It might not be that at all.'

'Oh for fuck's sake, Robert, don't go all mysterious and

loyal on me now. I'm worried about Jack.'

Rob got up and slammed the shop door shut. 'OK,' he sounded resigned, 'like I say, I could be wrong, but I think the name Amy might sum the situation up nicely.'

Kit was stunned.

'Who on earth is *Amy*?'

Eight

October 4th 2006

*She shifted slightly, in an attempt to prevent the bookshelves
that were digging into her back from bruising her permanently.
Closing her eyes, Jayne felt his ...*

Despite her lack of success in tracking down Jack, the bookshop
had inspired Kit, and directly after her visit she taken refuge in
the nearest café to scribble down some lines for a potential
story. Now, as she sat in her study, copying her draft on the
computer, a call from downstairs broke through her line of
thought.

'Mum!'

Kit hastily pressed *Save* and switched on her screen saver.
'*Mum!*' Helena was bounding up the stairs two at a time, and
threw open the door.

Kit swivelled around on her chair and faced her irritated
daughter. 'Helena, will you please knock before you come in
here.'

'Tom is being horrible. He won't let me watch my
programme, and you promised I could.'

Kit bit down a choice expletive and turned her monitor off
completely. 'Which programme?'

'*Walking with Dinosaurs*. He knows I love it. Oh, Mum!'

Kit stood up, ushering her daughter through the door and
down the stairs so she could adopt the role as referee. 'What is
it you're watching, Tom?'

'*Walking with Dinosaurs*.' Her son was in his usual spot on
the sofa, his drainpipe-thin legs and sockless feet stretched out
so that they had the optimum chance to trip up unwary passers-

43

by.

'He wouldn't, Mum, he ...' Helena, whose hands seemed permanently to be attached to her hips these days, launched into another protest.

'Be quiet, Helena.' Kit turned back to Tom, 'Your sister's just told me that you wouldn't let her watch it. Well?'

Tom's eyes remained fixed on the television screen. He answered calmly, plainly pleased to have successfully wound up his sister. 'I changed my mind. I like it too.'

'You *pig*, Tom, you said that ...'

'ENOUGH!' Stopping her daughter before she hit full steam, Kit took away the remote control. 'You will both sit quietly and watch this. Then it is going off.'

This made Tom sit up. 'But Mum, I wanted to see ...'

'No, Tom. Then it is going off.'

Kit left the last vestiges of arguing behind her and sought refuge in the kitchen. She flicked the radio on and, submerging herself in the music, started peeling potatoes while playing around with the lyrics for future storylines. She was just speculating on how she could manipulate Depeche Mode's 'Personal Jesus' into a plotline, when the twins' mutual cries of 'Dad!' told her that it was time to put the kettle on, and to cook the pork chops that she'd forgotten to put under the grill.

'So, how's it gone today?' Phil lounged against the kitchen units cradling his mug of tea.

'Good.' Kit started to clear the table for dinner, 'I popped in to say hi to Rob, and got a bit of story done. *Pearls* haven't ordered anything new yet, but I started banking up a few ideas in case of a literary emergency. It's been more of a thinking day really. You?'

'Escaped the office for a bit to show a new client her new home, but apart from that it was the same old same old.'

Kit looked at her husband as he sipped his tea. How could she tell him to give up his life's work? She could see how bored he was, but knew she couldn't be the one who pulled the plug. 'I tried to have coffee with Jack, but Rob tells me he's got his knickers in a twist again about something or other.'

'Sounds normal.' Phil loosened his tie as his wife flitted around the kitchen.

'What was the new client like?'

'Nice. Quiet. New to London.'

'Really?' Kit spoke absent-mindedly as she stirred the gravy.

'Yeah, Amy something. Crane! Amy Crane,' Phil dug out some plates so Kit could serve up, 'I don't think she'll be here long though.'

At the mention of the name Amy, Kit found herself paying more attention than she usually did when Phil ran through his day. 'Why not?'

'No job,' Phil sat down at the table, 'so no money coming in. Apparently she's living off her last deposit and her savings; she's just moved down from Scotland. Still, she probably thinks the streets are paved with silver and gold instead of rotting leaves and dog shit.'

Kit felt unaccountably cold as she sat down to eat. It *had* to be her. It had to be that Amy.

'You not hungry, love?' Phil shovelled a forkful of hot roasted vegetables into his mouth as Kit felt her appetite slip away. For some reason she couldn't fathom, Kit felt as if she was slowly being boxed in; or maybe pushed out.

Nine

October 5th 2006

'Jack, it's me again. I'm sorry if I upset you. You caught me by surprise, that's all. I've spoken to Rob. Please call me. Coffee sometime?'

Kit left a third message on Jack's voicemail as she trudged thoughtfully towards Pickwicks. Since Rob had told her Amy was Jack's ex, and then Phil had mentioned an Amy, Kit hadn't been able to shake the feeling that she'd wandered into the plot of a third-class soap opera. It had to be her. The same name, new in town, and fresh from Scotland. How clear did it need to be for God's sake?

Kit hadn't mentioned to Phil that his client could be one of Jack's other exes; she hadn't even asked him what this Amy was like. Kit felt uncomfortable as she negotiated her way through the busy streets, as if she was keeping secrets from her husband, but she wasn't sure why.

'Coffee's coming,' Peggy called out as Kit pushed open the café door.

Inhaling the comforting aroma of freshly ground beans and cakes baking, Kit headed towards her table as if it was a place of sanctuary, 'Thanks, I need it.'

'What's up? The smut not pouring forth from the pen?' Peggy winked theatrically as she finished checking the till.

'That's it; tell the world what I do for a living why don't you!' Kit spoke rather more sharply than she had intended.

'Hey?'

'Sorry, Peg. Lot on my mind.' She smiled with gratitude as Peggy brought her a cup of coffee so large that it could have doubled as a soup bowl. 'You're so good to me, petal.'

'And am I rewarded? No!' Peggy put her hand to her forehead in mock despair.

'Actually, you are. Here.' Kit passed her a couple of pages with five hundred words of carefully constructed thrills neatly typed onto it.

'What's this?'

'You inspired it, so it seems only right that you own a copy, but for God's sake don't flash it about; my publisher would not appreciate you getting an advanced copy.'

'Wow!' Peggy scanned the first paragraph, 'I'm surprised the paper isn't singed around the edges. You wait till Scott reads this!'

'Yes, well, I'd rather not know.'

'You're amazing. How can you be so prudish and yet write this stuff?'

'I've always been complicated, honey. Now, be a good little waitress and go yonder to serve that poor woman by the window, she's been sat waiting for her pot of tea for ages.'

As she watched Peggy zip toward her new customer, her mobile announced the arrival of a text.

What Rob say?

Kit read Jack's message with a mixture of relief and foreboding. She really didn't want to land Rob in the doghouse. On the other hand …

Told me someone called Amy was in town.

Kit pressed *Send* and sat looking at her phone, willing Jack to respond, yet full of apprehension as to what his reply might contain.

When Peggy arrived back at her table an hour later with a fresh coffee, Kit realised that she'd been staring into space and hadn't written a thing. Depeche Mode's words were still whizzing around her head, but she couldn't decide what to do with them. Some sort of bondage and punishment story seemed obvious, and fitted in nicely with the rather vague story request she'd received from *Pearls* early that morning – but where to set it?

It was time to call in a second opinion and ignore the lack of activity on her phone.

'Peggy, help!'

'You bellowed, your writer-ship.' Peggy put down the cake tongs and moved towards Kit.

'I'm stuck.'

'Oh, great. What is it this time?' Peggy pulled out a chair and sat down, rubbing her hands together as her head trotted through a selection of her own highly charged fantasies with which to assist her friend. 'You stuck on a character's name, or can't you think of what unspeakable things they should do to each other?'

'Sometimes I wonder why it's not you writing and me serving coffee.' Kit lay down her pen. 'I need a location to work from. I can't picture anywhere suitable in my head.'

'Where have you used recently?'

'Here for one. I've got something drafted set in a bookshop, and last week I had a go at the bus station.'

Peggy nodded, running possible situations through her mind, 'What sort of story?'

'Bondage, possibly with some punishment, but nothing too heavy.'

'Cool. I'll have a think.' Returning to the counter to collect some cheese on toast, Peggy delivered it swiftly to another regular, and returned to Kit with a wicked expression across her face. 'How about the snooker club?'

'What the hell has snooker got to do with bondage?'

'Think snooker tables, balls, and rope. Oh, hang on. It's for the US, right? Better make it a pool table.'

Kit's eyebrows rose. 'Bit clichéd?'

Raising her own eyebrows suggestively, Peggy answered, 'Don't knock it till you've tried it.'

Not for the first time, Kit looked at her friend with incredulity. 'Peggy, why do I get the feeling I don't want to know?'

Peggy laughed, and with a curtsey said, 'More cake, madam?'

49

I suppose his first reaction was to be expected. 'But it's such a cliché! I mean! A pool table! There isn't a month goes by without some girlie mag having a babe spread across a pool table.'

'Exactly,' I replied, but Karl didn't ask me about my fantasies again, and I felt like maybe I should've made a bit more effort. Perhaps I should have invented something more glamorous, but as I've always been a bit of a tomboy; getting down and dirty with the lads in a grubby, badly lit pool hall with a few beers has always been more my style. Anyway, there's something about the sound of pool balls clicking against each other ...

Kit had written over two sides of erotic activity by the time Jack's text came through.

Did Rob mention a tape?

Kit re-read the message and muttered, 'What bloody tape?' into her coffee. All Rob had told her was that Amy was a friend from university, that she had done archaeology with him and his friend Paul, and that she was one of Jack's exes. From what Kit knew of Jack's past, that just made Amy one of dozens, be they male or female.

A tape, though? With Jack that *did* make a difference.

Kit felt a new wave of unease flow over her as she sat cradling her phone. Pool, ropes, and interesting cue positions were all forgotten. She was remembering.

Ten

October 5th 2006

Amy awoke with a smile.

The evening before, waiting for her new housemates to come home from work, she'd been a bag of nerves. She'd boiled and re-boiled the kettle countless times before a key had turned in the lock.

Arriving together, James and Sarah had been delighted to walk in and discover freshly brewed tea and coffee (she wasn't sure which to make, so had settled for both), and a box of Scottish shortbread arranged on the dining room table. They were neither as young nor as trendy as Amy had feared, and in no time they'd thrown off their coats and shoes, discarded their briefcases, and were slobbing out on the sofa.

After asking Amy countless questions about herself, they told her as much about the house and the local area as she wanted to know, plus loads about themselves, including the fact that they'd recently become a couple after years of house-sharing.

Dragging on her faded blue jeans, Amy reflected on how, as with the be-suited man at Heathrow, she hadn't minded answering their queries. Strange; she thought, she'd always been so guarded before. She hadn't mentioned Jack though; that would have been a confidence too far.

Drawing back her curtains, Amy looked through her window properly for the first time. Brick-built terraces, cars, motorbikes, deafening aircraft noise, litter clogging the kerbside drain, and people, masses of people. Richmond; right on London's doorstep. A place simmering with possibilities. All she'd have to do was overcome her natural nervousness and

51

grasp every opportunity. It was all out there for her. Even in its dark, damp, autumnal state, everything appeared inviting. She'd have to wait to hit the sights though; today she was going to be sensible. Today Amy was determined to take the first job she could find, and then tomorrow she'd start writing a CV and hunt down a proper career. Well, OK, maybe the day after tomorrow. Then she was going to call Rob. Jack could wait.

Amy felt a small rush of pride just thinking it.

Now she was here, Jack could wait.

The winter boots had been a mistake. Her feet felt uncomfortably prickly and hot. Amy smiled ruefully; this wasn't Aberdeen. London was wet, true, but not half as cold as Scotland. It was incredible how having unpleasantly over-heated feet could make her feel good about her situation.

Amy passed by the grubby and well-worn *Part-Time Help Required* sign that had been stuck to the window of the small newsagent's nearest the house, promising herself that if she hadn't found anything else by the end of the day, then she'd enquire about it on the way home. Crap money was better than no money at all.

By ten o'clock Amy had already explored employment opportunities at Waitrose, Tesco, and WH Smith, and her need for a caffeine hit had reached epidemic proportions. Caffé Nero seemed to be calling to her, siren-like, from across the street, but it was packed and she couldn't face being penned in with so many strangers. Looking around for an alternative, she spotted a faded sign advertising that Pickwicks Coffee House was lurking down a narrow side street. Amy strode off to discover where it was hiding.

She loved it instantly. An eclectic huddle of flower-filled vases and jars vied with each other for space on the crowded windowsill. Cream and blue Victorian tiles were embedded here and there in the plastered walls, and dark beams made the ceiling feel deceptively low. A higgledy-piggledy mixture of dark wooden furniture, a stripped pine floor, mismatched china, and a dominant aroma of coffee and sugar-coated pastries created a cocooned atmosphere of warmth and safety. Caffé Nero could keep its crowded convenience. In here, Amy thought, she could hide from the world.

'Can I get you anything, love?'

The waitress, her incredibly long dark hair drawn back into a thick ponytail that almost reached the waistband of her black trousers, stood beaming at Amy as if she was the most important person she'd seen all day.

'I would love a really huge black coffee please.'

'Well, you're in luck; we deal in really huge cups of coffee.' She pointed across the room to a lady sat in the far corner scribbling away at something, a soup dish-sized mug of hot liquid caffeine in front of her. 'That cup about the right size for you?'

'That would be perfect, thanks! Oh, and a Belgian bun if you have one?'

'Coming right up.' The waitress shimmied away, returning almost instantly with Amy's order.

Amy stared into her drink. It was so fresh that it steamed as if smoke was rising from its opaque surface. The cup's welcoming presence gave out that special kind of comfort that you only get from coffee when it's black. If she could find a job locally she'd be able to come in here for lunch every now and again. Maybe she'd meet Rob here sometimes. They'd always made time for plenty of coffee stops back then, so why not now?

'And if you press this then you'll get a nice steady stream of hot milk frothing on top of the coffee.'

Amy had been in Pickwicks for almost two hours, and her head was so full of new information that she thought it might burst. Anyone who considered being a waitress an easy option was under a serious misconception. Her booted feet had almost reached tropical temperatures, and were beginning to distract her as she struggled to concentrate on everything Peggy said.

'So, do you fancy it?' Peggy was bouncing around behind

the counter like an exuberant puppy – how could she say no? Anyway, she did feel comfortable in here. Perhaps it was fate. Amy nodded, unable to believe her luck in finding employment so fast.

'Thanks, yes! Although I think you'll probably have to show me how to work the cappuccino machine a few more times before I get the hang of it.'

'Not a problem. I'm just so glad to get help.'

'Were you advertising then? I didn't notice a sign in the window.'

'Not really.' Peggy tossed her ponytail from her shoulder, 'I keep an eye out every now and then, and pounce on anyone remotely suitable. The last girl who worked with me was a regular customer. She ended up working here so she could afford to eat here. Nuts!'

'I'm really grateful. Like I said, I've only lived here a day and I need something to tide me over. Something to work at, while I find something to work at. If that makes sense.'

'No one makes much sense here, honey. You'll fit in fine.' Peggy ripped a piece of paper off her order pad and began to write. 'Now, these will be your hours for this week, starting with a sort of training day tomorrow. The hours will vary each week, depending on the season and how lazy I'm feeling, but it will include most weekends until after Christmas. After that we'll see if you want to stay, or if you're off to become a captain of industry, OK?'

'More than OK. It'll give me a bit of free time too. Catch up with friends, develop a career, marry a millionaire, that sort of thing.'

Peggy laughed again, 'Let me know if you find one, I'm still looking.'

'For a millionaire or a career?'

Shrugging her shoulders, her new boss replied, 'Both! I've been here five years and have been far too busy to actually look!'

'Oh?' The number of tables crammed into the room illustrated just how busy Peggy could be, especially if she didn't always have waiting staff to help her.

'And being married to the owner sort of helps the time fly.'

Now it was Amy's turn to laugh, 'I'll see you tomorrow. I'd better pull myself together and go home. My removal van should turn up quite soon.'

'Sure. Take care, honey.' Peggy beamed at Amy's retreating back, feeling very pleased with herself for securing someone to help her without having to go through all the hassle of advertising.

Kit looked up. Peggy was free at last. The girl she'd been showing round must have gone. She waved in her friend's direction. Peggy picked up the percolator jug from behind the counter and crossed the room to refill Kit's cup. 'How's the snooker – sorry, *pool* – tale going? You've hardly raised your head since you put pen to paper this morning.'

Deciding not to tell Peggy that she'd spent more time locked within her own memories than writing, Kit replied, 'Pretty good, thanks for the inspiration.'

'Any time.' Peggy tapped the side of her head. 'Constant supply of material nestled in here, you know.'

Kit laughed 'You're a star, a grubby star, but a star nonetheless!'

Peggy began to sing 'Twinkle, twinkle, little star' as she danced back to the counter to fill out an employment form for one Miss Amy Crane ...

Eleven

October 6th 2006

Jack wasn't slumped in his seat this time. In fact, he was looking pretty good, as he waited for Kit at the back of the department store café. Not as relaxed as usual, granted, but not blatantly uncomfortable either. Jack winked at Kit as she crossed the room, her tray laden with highly calorific treats. He patted the round-backed chair next to him.

Sinking down, Kit found herself embraced in one of Jack's familiar hugs. She inhaled the smell of his leather jacket and felt reassurance and relief flood through her. It was Jack's equivalent of saying sorry for walking out on her, and she accepted it without question.

'How's Phil doing?'

This was not the opening question Kit had been expecting, but if Jack wanted small talk, then fine. 'Still hating work and pretending otherwise.'

'He needs to get out before he burns out.'

Kit emptied the contents of the tray onto their table, 'Tell me about it. Trouble is, he's run Home Hunters for ages. I'm not sure he knows how to let go.'

'He could sell up. Must be worth a bit; going concern and everything?'

'I'm sure it is, but until he's ready, I can't make him change his life.'

Understanding Kit's dilemma, Jack asked, 'Have you talked about it?'

'Not really. There never seems to be a minute, what with work, writing, the twins; time seems to evaporate.'

'Oh, that old excuse.' The corners of Jack's mouth twitched into a wry smile.

'Yes that old excuse.' Kit trailed fingertips through the icing sugar that had fallen from her croissant. She glanced at the inexpertly done wildlife paintings that adorned the walls, and not for the first time thought that they'd be better suited to a second-rate country hotel, rather than this genteel corner of an otherwise smart high-end department store.

Dragging herself back to the reason she'd arranged this meeting; Kit steeled herself to change the subject completely.

'So, what tape?'

Jack was still squeezing Kit's hand long after he'd finished talking. Kit hadn't said a word, but had sat motionless, her body stiff as his words filtered into her brain. She already knew about his time as a student, about how he'd played the field when he'd been at university, while at the same time he hadn't really been sure of his sexuality.

What she hadn't known was that, just as Jack was starting to think about giving up the whole 'women thing', he'd met Amy, and for a while everything had felt OK. That he'd never loved anyone like he loved Amy, and he'd dared to think that maybe he was straight after all, and that the first flickers of suspicion that he might prefer men had been happily extinguished.

Without looking at her, Jack told Kit of how he came to realise though, as the months passed, that something was missing, wrong even. That, although he'd never loved anyone like Amy before, and when he'd slept with her it was fun and inventive, it wasn't, well, *right*. He tried to describe the frustration that coursed through him each time he failed to feel content after sex.

It hadn't only been the sex either; it was as if something was out of kilter all the time. Jack explained that he'd broken up with Amy, and got back with her again, more times than he dared to think about. How The Clash could have written 'Should I Stay Or Should I Go' just for them. That he saw now how badly he'd treated her; that Amy couldn't have known if

58

she was coming or going.

He explained how Amy's tape had been a gift from her brother, and about the music he'd put on it for her. And how, more than anything else, he wished he'd left it all alone. Kept it buried. Never sent it back. For now Amy was here, in Richmond, he'd have to explain. He'd have to face all the guilt he had run away from.

Kit couldn't speak. She extracted her hand from Jack's grip and replayed his words in her head. "I never loved anyone like her." It went through her like ice. He'd said it twice. *Twice.* And the music! Amy and Jack together had taken music as their own. But that's what *she*, Kit, did with Jack. Had done, anyway. They'd frequently had entire conversations in song lyrics; it was rarer in these days of parenthood and responsibility, but they still did it now and again. Bile rose in Kit's throat as she had a vivid recollection of dancing around the kitchen to David Bowie a few days before, her daughter watching with mystified disdain. It seemed ridiculous now. Worthless.

'Kit?' She was vaguely aware that Jack was talking to her, his hazel eyes clouded with confused concern. 'What's the matter?'

Kit studied his face like it was new to her. He really didn't know. He genuinely had no idea that he'd just cut her to the bone. *'I never loved anyone like her.'*

Plus a tape. *They* had been going to make a tape of all the songs that had reminded them of each other, the important events in their lives, the things they'd said and the places they'd been. Jack had never got round to making it though. It had never mattered before, but suddenly Kit felt cheated.

'Kit?' There was an edge of panic to Jack's voice as he watched his friend stand up, her legs wobbling beneath her. Jack grabbed her arm, 'Where are you going? What is it? What's up?'

Pulling herself free from his grip, Kit hoisted up her bag. She wasn't sure how far she'd get, but she knew she had to leave. Turning towards Jack, a complex conflict of emotions etched onto her neat round face, she glared at him as he sat, a mass of incomprehension. 'You like to express yourself with music? Go listen to *our* tape. Oh, of course, you can't, can you, 'cos you never bloody recorded it. *Did you!*'

Jack wasn't sure how long he'd been sat there. He felt exhausted. It had cost him so much, telling Kit all that. Never in his life had he been so open with anyone. Even when he'd come out, he'd never gone into details about his feelings. He shook his head as if trying to remove the image of Kit's ashen face when she'd stalked out. He had truly thought she'd understand. Kit *always* understood.

With a hazy realisation that the café was crowded, and that other customers were looking for a seat while he cradled an empty mug, Jack got up, uncertain what to do. Was this how Kit had felt when he'd walked out on her the other day?

He'd go for a walk. He'd go to work. Anything but think, because he wasn't sure what the hell to think.

Kit?

Twelve

October 7th 2006 – 1.00am.

With his duvet clenched around his shoulders, Jack attempted to get comfortable in bed. Turning over, he untangled the sheet that had somehow become looped around his legs. But even when he finally felt cosy, he was unable to prevent himself from thrashing through his conversation with Kit. Conceding a win to his subconscious, Jack gave in, and allowed himself to remember ...

June 2nd 1995

Jack could hear her laughing even before he opened the pub door. It was an infectious, light laugh that always started in her eyes. He loved her eyes, probably more than the rest of her. Kit knew that though; she knew this was for fun, and that was exactly what he needed.

His recent experience in Nottingham had unnerved Jack more than he cared to admit. He really ought to think about it properly, but if he acknowledged to himself that it had gone well, felt right; then he'd have to face the bigger truth, and he wasn't ready for that yet. Anyway, he was having fun with Kit. She was so different from the other girls he'd dated. She could drink as much as him without passing out, never bothered about her hair, told blue jokes, played Twister in the nude, and did whatever he wanted her to in the bedroom. She was perfect. For now.

Kit was sat squashed up around a small table with Rob, Paul, and a petite blonde student archaeologist Paul had brought with him from his latest excavation. 'What's so funny?'

Extracting Kit from her seat, Jack pulled her up onto his lap. 'Well?'

Kit wriggled until she was comfortable, causing Jack's dick to sway promisingly beneath her pert backside. 'There was this thing going around work today. You have to choose five songs that sum up pivotal moments in your life.'

'We are so stuck. Come on, Jack, you're always spouting lyrics and stuff, we need your help. Rob keeps coming up with total crap.' Paul smirked into his beer.

'Thanks a lot,' Rob smiled, 'but I happen to think that *never* buying a copy of George Michael's "Careless Whisper", despite my girlfriend of the time nagging insistence of its brilliance, *was* a pivotal moment in my life.'

They hadn't talked any more about their musical highlights in the pub. Paul had got another round of drinks in, and the conversation had moved on. But once Jack and Kit were back in the semi-squalid bedsit he rented, he'd asked her what music she would choose.

Sat at Jack's coffee table, her hands cupping a steaming mug of hot chocolate, Kit had immersed herself in thought. Watching her from the comfort of his lone armchair Jack waited quietly for her response. After a while she sighed audibly, 'It's too tricky. There are just too many songs, too many events,' Kit ran a finger around the top of her mug. 'I can think of hundreds, getting them down to five is impossible. What about your top five?'

Jack reached out his hands and she came to him. 'Well, I can think of one straight away.' He stood, putting his arms around Kit, dancing her around the tiny space between the end of the bed and the living area to no music at all. '"Let's Dance", by Bowie.'

'Of course! I love that one. Can I have it too?' They swayed together to the imaginary music.

'Only if you can tell me why it is so important.'

Kit beamed up at him, 'I'm stunned you remember. I didn't have you down as the sentimental type.'

'Cheek! You'll pay for that one.' Jack grabbed hold of Kit's wrists.

Squeaking out a reply, Kit giggled as Jack towed her towards the bed, 'It was playing in the bar when we first met.'

'It was! Congratulations! Your two-point prize for remembering is: one, you can have it on your list as well, and two, you can bend over the edge of the bed, yank your jeans down, and let me smack that gorgeous butt of yours until you beg for mercy.'

October 7th 2006 – 1.30am

Jack closed his eyes and banged his fist against his pillow in a feeble attempt to smother his memories. A crisp frost was gathering outside. He'd forgotten to put the heating on before he went to bed, but it wasn't the temperature of the room that made him shiver. He didn't want to remember how good it had felt. Jack tried to block out the image of smacking Kit until she was screaming to be screwed. It was hopeless. Somehow he'd allowed the box that he kept sealed at the back of his brain marked *Kit Past* to be opened. All he could do now was subject himself to the consequences. It was all Amy's fault, what did she have to come back for?

June 3rd 1995

He'd been awake for hours. Tucked up behind Kit's back, Jack listened to her gentle breathing. He was finding it harder and harder to settle next to her at night these days. The waking hours were fine, but at night, as he watched her sleep, usually content after sex, a growing sense of discontent, suffocation, and guilt would engulf him.

He had almost told Kit that he suspected he was gay twice before. That when he shagged her, his mind was full of images of the various fit men he'd seen walking around the city, but each time he had shied away from a confession at the last minute.

How could he be gay anyway? He'd loved Amy, and he

adored being with Kit. Why throw all that away? Why give up a more accepted life on the off-chance his suspicions were correct? Perhaps he was bi? Yet the vision of the men dancing before him at the club in Nottingham haunted him, and in the dead of night, Jack knew he was kidding himself.

Their discussion last night about music had prompted Jack to remember one track in particular. As Kit's unconscious body turned away from him, he wondered if he should use the opportunity she'd unwittingly presented him with to tell her about it. To help him come clean.

Only minutes after waking the following morning, Kit sat abruptly up in bed. The cool of the room made her exposed nipples stand to regimental attention as she blurted out two more song titles.

'"Come on Eileen", by Dexy's Midnight Runners, and "Gypsy Woman" by Don Williams.'

Jack, who had only just dropped off to sleep, rubbed his eyes as his brain frantically backtracked to what they'd been discussing the night before. He spoke with incomprehension, wishing, not for the first time, that Kit wasn't so lively first thing in the morning. 'What? "Come on Eileen"? You must have been about eight years old! And who on earth is Don Williams?'

'"Eileen" was on almost constantly when I was at college. I loved the oldies nights we had there! And Don Williams is a really famous country-and-western singer. I'm amazed you haven't heard of him! His song "Gypsy Woman" reminds me of my Dad. He loves Don Williams. It reminds me of being a kid.'

Jack propped himself up on one elbow beside her and laughed. 'You're priceless.' Tucking her straggly red hair behind her ears, abruptly serious, Jack's heart was pounding so fiercely he could almost hear it, as she said, 'You'll want to know one of mine now, I suppose?'

'Yep. But I'll allow you to put the kettle on at the same time.'

'So gracious.' Jack put the kettle under the tap, his thoughts in a quandary. Should he tell her about the tune that was whirling around his head? It could ruin everything, yet he had to. Every day he ignored the facts he was misleading her, not to mention himself. Keeping his back to Kit, Jack inhaled deeply, 'I guess one of mine has to be Kylie's "Better the Devil You Know".'

Kit pulled one of Jack's old oversized T-shirts over her head. 'Kylie? You're kidding me. How textbook camp are you?'

Jack spoke levelly, knowing she had given him a second perfect lead into a confession. His brain remained undecided about whether to say anything more, but his mouth carried on regardless. With his eyes cast down he replied, 'Well, my tastes are pretty camp to be honest, although I'm not sure about the textbook bit.'

Kit moved closer to him, refusing to acknowledge the tension which had filled the room. She spoke softly and carefully, already sure of what he was going to admit, 'Tell me.'

'I heard it when I was in that club in Nottingham.'

'The gay one you went to with your mates for a laugh?'

'Yes. Look, Kit, I need to come clean about something.' Jack put down the mugs he'd been fiddling with and sat on the edge of the bed. He wanted to study her, gauge her reaction, but he couldn't bring himself to see the expression on her face. 'The thing is I, well. First I … I do like you, I really, really like being with you, and I don't want to finish this, but it's just …' Jack sprang up and began to pace the room, taking out his confusion and frustration on the poorly carpeted floor boards.

Kit shuffled up behind Jack and grabbed his shoulders, making him stand still as she let him off the hook with a whispered, 'But you can't work out if you're a straight bloke with kinks, bisexual, or as gay as a maypole with a totally understandable need to hang onto one last female relationship, in case there is a slim chance that you've got it all wrong.'

Jack stared at her in disbelief, whispering back, 'How on earth did you know that?'

Kit mumbled something into the floor that Jack didn't catch, before she turned his face towards hers and looked him straight in the eye. 'I've known you a while. Your uncertainty is kind of obvious sometimes.' She grabbed the edge of the duvet, pulled him towards her and covered his lips in tiny kisses. 'While you're deciding which side of the game you want to play on, perhaps you can make do with me.'

He peered into her face, his shock at her calm response to his bombshell, preventing him from moving away from what Kit was about to do. He spluttered out, 'Why aren't you angry? Why aren't you throwing things?'

'What would that change?' Kit tugged him back onto the bed and slid under the duvet.

October 7th 2006 – 3.00 a.m.

Jack gave up trying to sleep and headed for the bathroom. His dick had gone stiff. He could almost feel the blowjob Kit had given him. Angry with himself for not pushing her off then, and for the effect the memory of it had on him now, he wanked fiercely into the toilet. Why had she even done that? Why hadn't he seen it as a bloody weird response to what he'd just told her? And how could a memory, a memory of a *woman* for fuck's sake, get the better of him after all this time?

Jack wiped himself dry, sat back on the edge of his bed, and tried to concentrate, determined to be honest with himself.

After Jack had told Kit everything she wanted to know, their relationship had got better, not worse as he'd expected. She'd let him do what he needed to do. He'd explored more and more of the local gay clubs and, providing he kept Kit fully informed of all his activities, she was always there to come back to whenever he needed her.

Kit hadn't been offended when he brought gay porn magazines into the flat, or if he chose male porn movies instead of the hetero stuff they'd occasionally enjoyed together. It was like leading two separate but happy lives, with one boot on each side of the fence.

Now, for the first time, as he shivered against the early

morning chill, Jack realised he'd been a fool to stay with Kit once he'd admitted his doubts. A greedy fool who'd hung onto her, keeping his options open, just in case. It had suited him. After all, the idea of sex with a woman didn't repulse him, it never had. He was just damn sure he preferred it with a man.

Jack had been so relieved once Kit knew the truth that, not only did he stop pretending to himself; he stopped considering her feelings altogether. He'd felt so free, he'd pleased himself. A habit Jack now realised he hadn't really broken.

Why, oh why, hadn't he recorded that tape like he'd promised? When Amy had passed on her cassette, he hadn't hesitated to add Joy Division's number, even if it had taken him years to return it afterwards. If only he could remember what else Kit had chosen as her top five songs. Jack slid off the bed onto the floor, his head in his hands. How had this happened? Amy was in London, and now he'd upset Kit. He felt bewildered and disorientated.

Jack always avoided thinking about the past. It didn't fit with his happy-go-lucky image, not to mention his club-cruiser role. He'd never felt uncomfortable about his history of female conquests. But he was who he was, surely Kit could accept that? Even as he mulled things over, he knew he'd got that wrong too. Kit *had* accepted it. She'd been amazing. As soon as he'd admitted his confusion she'd been a tower of strength, had pledged undying friendship, and had helped him sort his life out. Kit was incredible. He needed her in his life. He'd call her.

Sounding bleary and disorientated, Phil's voice radiated anger, 'Jack, it's nearly four o'clock in the bloody morning. What do you want?'

'Sorry Phil, I just … is Kit awake?'

'No she isn't, and neither was I. Whatever the problem is, you sort it on your own for once.'

Phil slammed the phone down. 'Bloody man.'

Jack made tea and turned on the gas fire in his lounge, his mind see-sawing between the past and present, until it rested on that life-changing evening in Nottingham all those years ago.

Even now he was surprised by how comfortable he'd felt there. Although he'd been the one who'd organised the trip to a gay club with his friends, to see how the other half partied, Jack's palms had been sweaty, and it had taken more bottle than he'd care to admit to cross the threshold.

Before going in, he'd had visions of pink furnishings, twee gypsy styles, and muscly blokes in sailor-suits or minimal black leather outfits. Jack had been fractionally disappointed when it almost lived up to the cliché. Purple and stainless steel ruled, rather than pink, and although it favoured modern, rather spartan décor, it had hung onto the essential floor-to-ceiling mirrors.

There were indeed 'sailors', S&M fans, and the most incredibly short shorts he'd ever seen, but they were definitely in the minority, giving way to the ubiquitous young men's uniform of T-shirts and jeans.

And women. Not that many of them admittedly, but women. He had been so worried about betraying himself to his mates that he'd forgotten about the lesbian contingent. He cursed himself for being so stupid, hoping his mates wouldn't leer too much. They all had serious fantasy issues in that direction.

The music, which was so loud it bounced off the walls, was a fantastic mix of the undeniably camp and general dance stuff. The regulars were used to students coming in to check the place out, and teased them enough to let them know they were tolerated, so long as they were only passing through and didn't take the piss.

Jack had suspected he was giving off mixed signals, as he got rather more attention than his mates, much to their amusement and weeks of subsequent banter. This was confirmed for him when, plucking up enough courage to go to the gents', a laid-back young man with shoulder-length ginger hair and a soft Irish brogue had approached him.

'When you've made your decision, come back and see me. I'm usually here on a Friday night.'

He'd left Jack then, moving out of the cloakroom and into

the seething mass of bodies. Jack tried to locate him later, but couldn't spot him in the crowds, so he'd contented himself with watching the talent immediately before him, drinking way too much Diamond White while listening to Kylie blasting out of the speakers, and gradually feeling at ease in a nightclub for the first time in his life.

Thirteen

October 7th 2006

Jack woke with a start. He felt disorientated. Damn. He'd fallen asleep at his kitchen table, and at some point he'd knocked over his half-drunk mug of coffee. Pulling some paper towel from the roll, he began to mop up the sticky brown puddle that had started to form over the wooden table. Jack glanced at the clock. 8.30. Shit. He'd told Rob he would open the shop at nine, and now he was going to be late.

Staggering through to the bathroom, Jack splashed his face with cold water, sprayed too much deodorant under his arms, and stuffed his electric razor into his jeans pocket to use later. Throwing on a clean white shirt, Jack grabbed his keys and wallet and, ignoring his pneumatic drill of a headache, ran out of the door.

As Jack stood in the anonymous crowd of commuters, awaiting the next train from Mortlake to Kew, he caught sight of an advert pasted on the opposite side of the station. *Cinema Tickets – 3 for the price of 2.*

'Three for two.' Jack played the phrase around his mouth, like a tongue irritating a sore tooth. As he took the tatty railcard out of his wallet, Jack winced, the now familiar tide of rage rising within him. An anger that was aimed solely at himself as he recalled that not only had he let Kit give him a blowjob that morning, but that he'd had sex with her the next day as well. For God's sake! What the hell had he been thinking? And what about Kit? Had the woman got no pride at all?

Standing cheek by jowl with his fellow passengers, Jack suddenly remembered the song Kit had decided would be suitable for him the day after their 'top five' discussion.

71

It had come to her as she'd showered, and was a piece of music that, Kit declared, should be dedicated to him; one that summed up how she felt about him, about their relationship. Jack cringed inwardly as he remembered how he, caught up in Kit's childlike enthusiasm, had thoughtlessly announced that he'd decided on a tune for her too. He hadn't even had to think, it had come to him instantly as he stood with her. He wished it hadn't.

Kit had chosen 'I'll Stand By You' by The Pretenders for him. With particular reference, she'd said, to the bit about confessions not changing anything. Jack had been blown away. It had fitted their last twenty-four hours together so well. It said so much. It still did. It might even have been amusing, if Kit had got in first. But she hadn't.

If only he'd hesitated. If only he hadn't blurted out that he'd always associate Meatloaf's 'Two Out Of Three Ain't Bad' with her *before* Kit had mentioned her choice for him. The hurt had clouded her face for only a millisecond before she'd replaced it with her 'I don't mind' mask; but Jack had seen her momentary lapse. The hurt had shown, however briefly, before Kit laughed, claiming the lyrics were 'most fitting'.

'Barely a crack in her mask,' Jack mumbled to himself, thinking of the younger Kit as the crowded train moved off, 'until now.' Suddenly it seemed so obvious that she'd been in love with him. *Too up yourself to notice, as usual.* Jack felt sick as he closed his eyes to London as it whizzed past the train window.

For a change, Jack was glad the shop was so quiet. Time to stop making excuses, and start putting together the endlessly discussed website. Rob would never actually do it, and anyway he needed to work, keep his brain active before it unearthed anything else from the dusty catacombs of his memory.

After an hour of failing to get the initial stages of the site started, Jack slammed his fist against the computer mouse, cracking its top and sending it skidding across the desk. It was a relatively simple task, but his psyche kept veering off into the diverse cock-ups of his past.

'Sod this.' He got up and filled the kettle.

The door swung open, and Rob walked in, 'Jack?'

'Making coffee, you want some?'

'Thanks.' Rob came through to the back, catching sight of the cracked mouse as he circumnavigated the desk, on his way to the tiny kitchen-come-stock room. 'You OK?'

'Sure.' Jack stirred an extra spoonful of sugar into his drink.

'You don't look OK, you look rough.'

'So would you if you'd been trying to get that fucking computer to do what you want. Christ, this place is depressing! What the hell are we doing here anyway?'

'Well, I'm hanging up my coat, getting ready to earn a meagre living, and you're earning pocket money to supplement the family fortune.'

Rob exhaled deeply. He'd been in a relatively good mood only a moment before and, once again, Jack had brought him to only a decibel away from shouting. 'What are you talking about? This is what we do. Given the odd customer we do all right. It's a bad time of year for us, you know that. Once the tourists return at Easter, we'll be fine again.'

'Oh I don't mean … Oh shit. I have no idea what I mean.'

Rob was quieter now, sensing that this wasn't just Jack being Jack. This was something else. His friend appeared somehow defeated. 'Do you want me to have a crack at the web site instead?'

Jack sat back down at the computer, 'No, it's fine. I'll do it. I can't focus today that's all.'

'You want to talk about it over this repulsive brew?' Rob pulled a face at the instant coffee. Decaf, for God's sake! If ever there was a morning that required full-strength, good-quality coffee, then this appeared to be it.

Jack laughed despite himself, 'No thanks, mate. Sorry. I never function well without any sleep.'

'Shouldn't pick them up on a school night then, should you?' Rob said teasingly.

'Whatever.' Jack's handsome face darkened again. 'Just

unpack the orders that came in with the post, will you?'

Rob was extremely grateful when Jack asked if he'd fetch the sandwiches for lunch. He felt as if he'd been caged in with an irritated tiger all morning.

Normally Rob just grabbed the nearest vaguely appetising sarnies, but today he surveyed the refrigerator shelves at length. He needed time away from the black cloud that hung over Jack and everything he touched. Rob couldn't remember a time when they'd sniped at each other so much ... well, not since Jack had broken up with Amy, of course.

If Jack hadn't wanted Amy to get in touch, then why on earth had he returned her tape? Jack wasn't stupid. He was foolish sometimes, but far from being an idiot. There must be something else wrong. Rob considered his friend's behaviour as he counted out his change; exactly the right amount for a tuna and sweetcorn with salad on rye, and a coronation chicken on white, hold the butter. Exchanging polite smiles with the shop assistant, Rob waited as she slid his chosen purchases into the compulsory brown paper bag, before he escaped back into the cool London air.

Maybe Jack was bored. The shop was always a bit dead this time of year, but why would that worry him? Jack didn't need the money, the death of a fabulously wealthy relative had seen to that, yet Rob had always thought the shop meant more to Jack than a hobby. Rob held a percentage, but the shop was Jack's, no question about that.

Rob felt his body chill. What if Jack wanted to sell up? Move away? *After all our hard work*! Rob began walking faster, his imagination heading off full-steam in the direction of personal employment disaster. Rob decided to tackle Jack as soon as he got back. This was too big to ignore. It would gnaw away at his brain. It had started to already.

'What *are* you talking about?' Jack looked confused as Rob weighed in, talking at ninety miles an hour, with his selling-the-shop theory. 'Why on earth am I fighting this computer if I wanted out?'

Catching his breath after his outburst, Rob took a bite of his sandwich. 'So what is it then? If you don't want out? This mouse-battering and daily bickering can't be all about Amy, can it?'

'Amy?' Jack put his own sandwich on the counter.

'Yes, you know, the girl you've been dreading walking through that door. Ever since you found out she was heading this way you've been as edgy as a … well, as something edgy.'

Putting up his hand to calm Rob, Jack continued to chew his mouthful before he replied. 'I've cocked up, mate. Really cocked up.'

'What do you mean? You haven't got someone pregnant, have you?'

'Ha fucking ha.'

'All right, spit it out.'

Jack spoke with genuine sorrow now. 'I've upset Kit.'

Rob suddenly remembered he'd seen her. 'Hey, Kit was here searching for you the other day; she was concerned about you. Told me you'd walked out on her.'

'I did,' Jack wiped his sleeve across his mouth. 'We had coffee, and Kit said you mentioned Amy. I wish you hadn't.'

'Then you should have told me not to. I'm not a bloody clairvoyant.' Rob concentrated on not getting cross again, 'I assumed she knew. And let's face it, Amy's ancient history relationship-wise, and so is Kit for that matter.'

'That's what I thought when I filled Kit in about Amy.'

Rob's brow furrowed as he listened. He was having trouble keeping track of this conversation, 'How did that upset Kit? She's got a hide like a bull elephant.'

Jack sighed, realising he seemed to be doing that a lot lately as well. 'Kit didn't know about Amy. I didn't think there was any need to tell her details about my past when we were together, and then, well, I moved on, and so did she.'

Resisting the urge to make a joke out of Jack's use of the phrase 'cock-up', Rob scrunched up his sandwich packet. 'At the risk of labouring the point, what happened?'

'She went quiet. *Angry* quiet. You know, the way women do.'

'Ever the diplomat. Go on.'

'It was the tape that did it I think. The music.'

'Really?' Rob tried to sound as if he understood.

'I don't know.' Jack began waving his hands about in his struggle to describe Kit's reaction. 'It was like she was jealous of the lousy tape, for fuck's sake!'

'I think you'd better take me through this from the beginning, I'm lost.'

'You and me both, mate. It was like I'd got the reaction I'd expected from her when I came out all those years ago. Well …'

'*Crept* out, you mean.'

'Whatever.'

Fourteen

October 12th 2006

Amy waited wordlessly with the other Starbucks customers. It felt so sterile, so alien. One of the few things she'd loved about the corner of Scotland she'd lived in was the coffee places. They were clean, quiet, and had the best scones on offer anywhere in the world. Her favourite café, The Acorn, tucked away in a luxury food and countryside supplies store in the remote village of Midmar, had pretty tablecloths, welcoming waitresses, and friendly customers. In London, with the occasional exception, things were very different. For a start, she was one of the older customers, even though she was only in her thirties. In Aberdeenshire she was used to being the youngest coffee-swiller by at least twenty years.

There was none of the innocent banter with strangers about the weather, the traffic, or the appalling state of British television. You simply queued quietly, paid, and stayed within the confines of your own little world, drinking as quickly as possible so that the next customer could occupy your seat in a never-ending stream of changing clientele. Amy sent up a silent word of thanks for having found Pickwicks as soon as she had.

Amy sat at the most secluded table possible, which wasn't that private, but would have to do. She removed a newspaper that had been left on the table, not wanting to be distracted or depressed by things she could do nothing about. Running a moistened finger across the plate which held her almond croissant, she mopped the crumbs which had fallen off in transit and licked them up, before producing a copy of *Jane Eyre* from her bag, to re-read for the umpteenth time.

Five minutes later Rob sat down, making Amy jump.

Engrossed in Jane's trials and tribulations, she hadn't noticed him come in. He put down his tray of cakes and coffee, and placed his Timberland jacket neatly on the back of the chair.

'Is it me?' Rob asked with a grin, 'or is this a tiny bit surreal?'

'Very surreal! Good, though.' Rob grasped Amy's hands tightly before hoisting her into his arms. A forgotten, and yet familiar feeling of rightness engulfed Amy along with Rob's hug.

His slim frame looked the same, but his ginger hair was fading with the first streaks of grey, and his green eyes seemed puffy and tired. His grin, though, was as impish as it had always been. 'Christ, I've missed you, girl. Sorry it's taken me a while to get the time off work to meet up.' Rob pinched a bit off her pastry as he sat down. 'Even if things go pear-shaped down here, promise you'll stay in touch this time. Proper touch.'

Amy hung her head, 'I'm sorry.' Then, looking her friend in the eye she said, 'I promise. And I'm sorry. I shouldn't have let all that past come between us. I missed so much by hiding.'

'It's OK.' Rob reached his hand out to hers.

'No, really, you'll never understand how sorry I am. I've been pathetic. I daren't let myself think how much I've missed, how many opportunities I've let pass me by through fear of rejection, of not matching up.' Amy spoke into her cup, focusing on what she was saying, and on not welling-up while she said it.

'Well, you're here now, and I'm glad.' Rob began to munch on his bacon and Marmite bagel. 'Debbie wondered if you'd like to come over for dinner on Sunday.'

Suppressing a twinge of nerves at the prospect Amy said, 'I'd like that; she looks so nice from the photos you've sent. I'm sorry I missed the wedding,' Amy let the fact she'd chickened out of attending because Jack would've been there remain unsaid, 'Trouble is, I'm working on Sunday. When do you normally eat?'

'Not until about eight o'clock. It's the one evening when we don't try and instil civilised table manners into our tribe. We eat after they've passed out in bed.'

'In that case, thanks.' Amy smiled, and began asking about the three daughters, Rose, Flora, and Lily, that Rob referred to as his "bunch of flowers", exclaiming at how old they were already, before they settled back into happy shared reminiscences.

Half an hour later, as he stirred his second latte, Rob broke the spell of nostalgia. 'I didn't think you'd do it, you know.'

Amy glanced at him sideways, 'No?'

'Debbie said you would, but I thought you'd visit, panic, and run away again.'

'But Debbie doesn't know me.' Amy started to twiddle a packet of brown sugar between her fingers.

'I've told her a lot about you.' Rob tilted his head towards her, 'I suppose I'm trying to say I'm proud of you. That's not too patronising, is it?'

'You're proud of me?' The packet split open and a stream of golden sugar crystals spread through Amy's fingers across the table. 'Why?'

'Big decision, chucking in your life like that.'

Amy grimaced, 'Not so big. I missed my friends, hated my job, and never felt as if I fitted in up there anyway.'

'But you always talked Scotland up so much. When you did get in touch, of course.'

'OK, enough with the teasing, I've said sorry, I'll keep in touch now.' Amy kept talking, feeling the need to explain, 'Aberdeenshire is a lovely place. The people are really friendly. I just didn't fit. It wasn't even that stupid English versus Scottish thing. I was on the outside peeping in. Aberdeen was somewhere to go, far enough away to be gone, but not truly gone, and not so far away that I had to learn another language.' Amy's mouth twitched into a smile as she remembered the occasional bizarre conversation with the older members of the local farming population, where neither understood a word the other said. 'Although it did feel a bit like a foreign language sometimes.'

'Do you fit now?' Rob collected up the spilt sugar with a

folded napkin. He wasn't a father of three for nothing.

Amy paused to consider her answer, 'Waitressing for Peggy is good for now, and the house is great. But ... well, ask me when I've done what I came to do.' She sat up straighter as she reeled off her mantra, 'New job, new home, new life. Well, that's the plan, anyway.'

Rob nodded approvingly, 'Amy?'

'Yes?'

'Don't leave it too long before you see Jack. He's like a cat on hot bricks.'

'Good.' Amy felt strangely satisfied that she'd managed to unsettle Jack.

'He wasn't expecting you to move to London.'

'I bet he wasn't.' Amy looked about her. By the door, an impossibly young mother was struggling to force a toddler into a bag-laden pushchair. Mature students were laughing over their bacon baguettes, and crosswords were being completed at top speed by business folk on a break. At every alternate table a mobile phone was tucked under a chin, a mixture of conversations with invisible drinking partners filled the room. 'I didn't expect to come either. I didn't let myself think. I just sold up and came. You were here. It seemed the right place to start afresh. I doubt if I'll stay forever.'

Rob's forehead crunched, his freckles creasing as he scrutinized his friend's face. 'You might stay though. If you get a grown-up job?'

'I might.' Amy went quiet for a moment, rubbing a fingertip around the top of her cup. 'Is he OK?'

'Not really. He needs a good friend.'

'He has you.'

'Yes, but right now he needs you.'

Amy gathered up her things. She didn't feel ready for an in-depth "Jack" conversation yet. 'Right Rob, I've got to go to work.'

Accepting her dismissal of both the subject and their meeting, Rob asked, 'See you on Sunday then?'

Amy kissed his cheek. 'See you then.'

Fifteen

October 16th 2006

'Would you like milk with that, or is Primo OK?' The waiter placed an extra-large black coffee in front of Jack. 'Sir?'

Jack snapped his head up, vaguely aware that someone was speaking to him. 'Sorry?'

'Hot or cold milk, sir? With your Americano?'

'Sorry, no, just Primo thanks.'

The waiter placed the tray containing Jack's coffee, complete with complimentary oatmeal biscuit, onto the octagonal table next to his armchair. 'Are you all right, sir?'

'Yes, thanks. Heavy night.' Jack grimaced weakly and picked up his cup.

'I see.' The waiter seemed to pack a heap of innuendo into those two words, and with a brief flash of his white teeth, retreated towards his other customers.

Cute bum. Jack watched the slimly built man move away. Then, as he burnt his top lip on the scalding drink, he hissed sternly under his breath, 'I've got to stop this.'

It was eight o'clock on a Monday morning and he felt awful. Zipping his coat right up under his chin in an attempt to block out the cold which seemed to shroud him these days, Jack sent a text to Rob, apologising for the fact that, once again, he was going to be late for work.

Jack had left the CXR nightclub bar at three in the morning, and his successful cruising activities had already been consigned to the 'best forgotten' part of his brain. The brief thrill his submissive conquest had given him was already a distant memory. Stumbling onto an unfamiliar street about an

81

hour away from home, Jack had sought sanctuary in Ashford's, the first early opening coffee shop he considered safely out of range from the particular apartment block which he'd departed at an undignified pace.

His awkwardly shaped triangular cup was too hot to hold, so he sank bank into the over-plump purple seat to examine his surroundings. The other customers, all wedged into similarly curved armchairs, also seemed to be immersed in their own worlds, either cradling solitary cups of hot liquid or tucking into breakfasts at breakneck speed, lest their plates be whisked away before they'd finished.

As he surveyed the fixtures and fittings Jack accidentally caught the waiter's eye, and hastily turned away. *Nice eyes too.* He allowed himself a second to consider making a move. Blue eyes and blonde hair. Like Amy's ...

Gazing blankly towards the window, Jack tried to picture the guy he'd spent the early hours of the morning with. Fairly short, dark hair, stocky, a northern accent, and a good thick dick, which had utilised one of the condoms he optimistically kept in his jacket pocket. *Christ*, he thought to himself, *I'm not even sure of his name. Mark? Matt?* How on earth had he allowed his life to get like this? It wasn't even as if he could use alcohol or drugs as an excuse. He hadn't drunk more than two pints of beer all evening, and it'd been years since he'd experimented with the various methods of getting high. The kick he got from casual sex was enough of a drug anyway. Kit said he was too high on the power of conquest to need artificial stimulants. *Used to say.*

It was nearly two weeks since he'd heard from Kit. Two weeks without snatched coffee, daily texts, advice, moans, gripes and grumbles. Jack had relived their conversation over and over again. He just didn't get it.

Eleven years ago she should have acted like this. Eleven years ago she should have been hurt and insulted. He'd used her, pretty openly too in the end, but she'd simply shrugged it off. 'The situation,' she had frequently declared, 'suits us both,' and he'd believed her.

Rob, always the king of clichés, had told him at the time that it would 'all end in tears.' Jack cowered over his half-empty cup as he remembered how he'd openly laughed back at Rob when, on finally ending the thing he'd had with Kit, their association had remained amicable. Six months later Kit had met Phil and been happily settled with him within weeks, enjoying a far more regular relationship with a bright future.

As soon as Kit had begun to see Phil seriously, Jack had gone mad. It was as if, once she was being taken care of by someone else, the last hurdle of his uncertainty had been taken down. He'd met like-minded folk via the various gay sites that littered the Internet, even in those days, and with them Jack had visited club after club, bar after bar. Some of these new acquaintances had turned into his earliest, often terrifying, short-term conquests, but most were simply friends, who he continued to meet and go clubbing with, as his confidence began to grow within the world he'd entered.

Jack's life, from that time on, became split in half. Not a secret life and a public life, but a gay social life with new friends, and a working and social life filled with old friends. Sometimes the two groups crossed, but largely they sat alongside each other, running side by side on comfortable parallel lines.

About three months into Kit's relationship with Phil, Jack had met Ryan. He was built like a bear, but was as gentle as a lamb. He had fallen hopelessly for Jack, who'd liked him back, but not enough. For when he had introduced Ryan to Kit and she hadn't been particularly impressed, Jack had unceremoniously dumped him. There was no way he could seriously date someone Kit didn't like.

Since watching Ryan crumple before him, Jack hadn't let anyone get emotionally close to him again.

He'd broken Amy's heart and badly hurt Ryan. Jack was determined not to do that to anyone else ever again, and he didn't ever want to feel that way himself. *Anyway*, he told himself, *I don't need anyone special*. He had his friends, and he was attractive and, Jack privately admitted, arrogant enough to get regular sex, so why worry?

Over the last two weeks Rob had started to twitter on about 'chickens coming home to roost.' Jack had listened to his friend's well-meaning advice, and then completely ignored it, preferring to throw himself into the fledgling bookshop web site by day, and into gay bar and club life by night. Only six of the past fourteen nights had he spent alone. He never took anyone home to his house though. He'd never been one for drama on his own doorstep.

The waiter reappeared at Jack's side, 'Can I get you anything else, sir?'

He's got a nice smile too. 'Another coffee would be great, thanks. Maybe a Danish pastry if you have any?'

'Almond, custard, cinnamon, fruit? I could go on.'

Jack laughed. A real, genuine laugh. He felt like he hadn't laughed for weeks, and it took him by surprise. 'Almond would be great, thanks.'

'No problem.' The waiter, whose name badge announced him to be called Toby, headed off on his new task.

Jack's eyes followed him. His brain sternly reminded his body that he'd screwed some other guy only a few hours ago, and that to make any sort of move now would be low, even by his current standards.

Jack began to fiddle with his mobile. He'd tried to call Kit several times over the past fortnight, but the voice-mail seemed to be permanently on, or else the call was stalled by Phil, who claimed Kit was either out or busy.

It was no secret that Phil didn't really like Jack. He'd never been able to understand the strength of his wife's relationship with an ex. Wallowing in self-pity, Jack imagined that Phil was secretly pleased that they'd fallen out.

'I've put extra sugar in your drink already.' Cutting into Jack's thoughts, Toby produced a tray holding a cup of black coffee and an almond croissant. 'Don't argue. You look like you need it.'

Then he turned away before Jack, open-mouthed, could say thank you, protest, or do anything other than meekly drink it.

Sixteen

October 16th 2006

Honey, what's going on?

You've never been late with a story before. You're usually the one who keeps us to schedule! Sorry if there's a crisis or something, but we need those Christmas stories by yesterday. Can you email them ASAP?

Thanks, Pearl

Kit re-read the email and then glanced down at her doodle-covered notebook. So far she'd decided on a naughty fairy theme, possibly with a secret Santa's grotto. Beyond that she'd produced nothing. Not a single word of erotica in nearly two weeks. Normally she would have produced two stories in that time.

There was a soft knock on her office door. Phil pushed it open, 'You OK, love?'

'Not really.' Kit swivelled the laptop around so he could read the email.

'How much have you done?'

'Nothing.'

'I see.'

Phil knelt beside Kit as she sat on her black leather chair. 'Look love, I'll help all I can, but I can't sort this thing with Jack out for you. Especially as you say you can't explain it to me.' He stroked her sleek red hair.

'I know. It's silly and irrational. Thanks though, but it's no good pretending you like Jack now.' Kit turned to face Phil, her shoulders drooped, 'I'm not keeping secrets, love, I just can't explain.'

'It's OK. He's OK.'

Kit spoke in a quiet, matter-of-fact way. 'Come on Phil, you've never liked him. This must be a relief for you.'

From the first moment Jack had met Phil, he'd tried to include him, to make Kit's new partner part of his friendship with Kit, but every attempt had proved awkward and stilted, and in the end both sides had graciously, and without rancour, given up trying.

'No.' Phil shuffled into a more comfortable position, 'I've never got on with him that well, it's true, Jack's too into himself for my liking, far too me-me-me,' Phil raised his hand, seeing Kit was about to argue, and continued, 'but he's important to you. Call him. What's the worst that can happen?'

'I have no idea. I'm not sure why I feel like this anyway.'

Phil's brow crinkled, 'Feel like what exactly? I'm having trouble understanding this one, Kit.'

'You and me both.' Kit reached up and put her arms around her husband's neck, 'I really appreciate you being here. I love you, Philip Lambert.' She kissed him on the nose. 'Now get lost and make sure those lovely children of ours are ready for school. I have to write some flannel to appease our American cousins.'

For days Kit had replayed every conversation she'd ever had with Jack in her mind. She knew she wasn't, and never had been, angry about his coming out. If you're gay, you're gay. If you're gay with the need for an occasional female fuck to reassure yourself that you've got your preferences right, then so be it. Kit didn't care which of these categories Jack fell into, and she suspected that if she could have asked him he wouldn't have known.

The morning after Jack had come out to her, Kit recalled that they had slept together again, just as they always did when they weren't working. It was as if nothing had been said, right up until they reached the local tea room they had hit the town in the search of a late breakfast ...

June 3rd 1995

Jack passed Kit the sugar and stirred his own mug of coffee.

'I think I'll give up having sugar,' she had pushed the bowl back to its original place on the easy-clean lemon yellow tablecloth, 'Time to start watching the weight if I'm going to be on the pull again.'

Jack flinched at her directness.

'Come on honey, you've just told me that we aren't exactly going to be together forever.' Ignoring the screaming voice at the back of her head that told her she loved this man, Kit marched down the boringly practical route, accepting things; giving the world a face which said she was blasé about everything. Burying how she felt.

'So, when did you first start to suspect that you wanted to share more than football chat over a pint of beer with the male half of the population?' Kit asked, as she began to make headway into the mountain of toast and marmalade before her.

Jack looked carefully at Kit, searching to see if she generally wanted to have this conversation. 'You don't mind me talking about it?'

'Of course not. Anyway, what are friends for?' Kit wiped some of the tangy orange spread from her lips, 'I'm all ears.'

Appreciating the opportunity to share his early suspicions, Jack eagerly confided in her, 'You know we were talking about how music can remind you of salient time in your life? Well, whenever I hear "Unbelievable" by EMF, then I'm taken back to where I began to suspect I was a bit different. The Ziplight.'

'The what?' Kit accidentally spluttered toast crumbs across the table.

Jack put his head in his hands, 'It was a disco at uni every Friday night. Oh God, how old am I, a bloody disco!'

Kit mopped up the mess she'd made, 'Calm down, Grandad, I remember discos being called discos too! So, the Ziplight? That really is a crap name.'

'I know, but that at least is not something I'm responsible for.'

Kit put her hand out to stop Jack's violent stirring before he splashed his drink across the table, 'What about "Unbelievable" then?'

'It's so clear in my memory. It's as if I close my eyes, I could almost be there.'

'So, sit back, shut your eyes, and describe what you see to me.'

'Well, OK. I'll try.' Jack sat back and attempted to recapture the scene for Kit.

'It was a Friday night. A crowd of two hundred or more students would all be cavorting together in your approximation of something which might possibly be called dancing. Mostly first-year undergraduates like I was, all cramped into the dark, sweat-smelling hall, whose floor was virtually an ice rink of spilt alcohol by about eleven at night. The girls all wore interchangeable, brightly coloured oversized cardigans and black Lycra miniskirts, and flirted shamelessly with the lads, in their eternal black jeans and slogan covered T-shirts. Everyone thought they were dressed so distinctively, and yet we were all more or less interchangeable with the next.

The DJ was always positioned in the middle of one side of the room, away from the bar queue, which was usually at least six layers of thirsty students deep, all waiting impatiently for their plastic pint glasses of Tiger or McEwen's lager. Now and then the odd would-be sophisticate would order a bottle of Beck's, or a Diamond White if it was a particularly heavy night.

There, for the first time, I saw I didn't quite fit, although I hadn't yet worked out why. My whole teenage life I felt I was watching an alien world through the wrong end of a pair of binoculars.

My mates and I usually danced together most of the night. Outlandish movements to "Sit Down" and, of course, "Dancing Queen"!' Jack grinned wider as he recalled how he, Rob, Paul, and his other friends had regularly managed to clear the floor as the attended masses watched, goggle-eyed, at their wild response to such numbers.

Returning to the point of the conversation, Jack shifted

uncomfortably. 'I had no trouble in attracting the attention of the girls. In fact, it always irritated me how keen some of them were when they didn't even know me. I watched the boys, the men, and felt safer. I assumed at the time that it was because they didn't demand anything of me. But I had also liked some of the girls well enough, so I shrugged off the out-of-place feeling and kissed them, screwed them, used them, and left them, anyway. After all, I was a teenage boy, that was what I was supposed to do wasn't it?'

October 16th 2006

Kit yawned into her coffee, and snapped back to the present as Peggy approached.

'Keeping you up, are we?' Peggy placed a warm croissant and accompanying pot of butter before her bleary-eyed friend.

'I was up at six o'clock staring at a computer screen, willing myself to write for America.'

'What? All of it?' Peggy's eyes twinkled.

Putting a hand over her mouth as she replied, so Peggy wouldn't see her semi-chewed breakfast, Kit replied, 'Oh, ha, ha. No, I've got a bit behind.'

'But you're never behind. You're more punctual than a full stop.' Peggy dragged out the chair opposite her friend and sat down concerned. 'So if you haven't been scribbling away furiously for our American cousins, what have you been doing in here? I've barely heard a peep out of you lately, except the faint scribble of pen on paper.'

'Sorry, Peg, nothing personal.'

'I swear I saw steam rising from your pen yesterday. What are you working on?' Peggy emptied the contents of her percolator jug into Kit's mug.

'Not sure to be honest. Just thoughts.'

'You OK?' This wasn't like Kit, Peggy shrewdly observed; her friend normally took salacious pleasure in sharing her plotlines.

'Not really, but I can't explain it. Wish I could.'

Peggy sighed for her friend, 'You haven't called Jack yet, have you?'

'No.' Kit changed the subject. 'How's the new girl shaping up?'

'I'm surprised you've even noticed I have a new girl! You've barely raised your head from the table recently. Scott was dead worried about you on Friday. He said you'd left some coffee to go cold.'

'OK! I've said sorry.'

Peggy put her hands on the table and pushed herself up, 'Oh, honey, I have no idea what's going on, but it sounds like teenage angst to me. Jack's your mate, not your bloody lover. Be an adult and call him, for fuck's sake.'

'Thank you, Mary Poppins.'

'No problem. Now drink up and write some pornography. And not another word, young lady! Or I shall have to call in a number of chimney-sweeps with fake Cockney accents to make you work. I'll get them to dance across the tables, soot and all, if you're not careful!'

'Yes Mum.' Kit giggled as Peggy did a Dick Van Dyke-style jig across to her counter.

Looking down, Kit contemplated her notebook. A novel. She was almost sure she was writing a novel. She just hadn't told anyone yet, not even herself.

Seventeen

16ᵗʰ October 2006

Nothing, Amy thought as she scuffed her feet, is quite as satisfying as scrunching through freshly fallen leaves.

Last autumn Amy had kicked her ankle wellies through the satisfying crackle of pine needles and cones at the impressively Scottish Crathes Castle. Kew Gardens was quite a different proposition. Even though she'd never been before, Amy had optimistically handed over the rather steep yearly membership fee and wandered through the main gates.

Pickwicks was work now, so it could no longer function as her place to hide. She needed a different bolthole, somewhere to disappear into whenever she felt like it. 'Like a security blanket, but for adults.' Amy had tried to explain her need to Peggy, who'd simply shrugged, openly declaring Amy insane for spending a precious day off in the freezing cold, and paying for the privilege.

As her blue boots flashed through the contrasting russets and orange of the autumn fall, Amy reflected on the weekend just past. Sunday dinner had been good. Rob obviously fitted the role of family man perfectly. His three girls were delightful, with shy smiles and shocks of curly ginger hair; they had mumblingly introduced themselves to her earlier. Having read them a collective bedtime story, and promising Flora that she would come round to play Lego sometime soon, Amy had left Rob to tuck them into their beds, and escaped into the kitchen.

Despite being nervous, Amy had forced herself into conversation with Debbie. Shorter than Amy, with shoulder-length brown hair which curled like her daughters', she was every bit as nice as Amy had hoped. In fact, after several hours of regaling her with tales of Rob's less auspicious university escapades, Debbie had been in hysterics, and Rob had had the air of a hunted man, torn between being fed up at being the butt of the jokes, and pleased that his wife and his long-lost friend were getting on so well.

The grounds of Kew Gardens were very quiet. While most of London coped with the horror of another Monday morning, Amy revelled in the peaceful solitude of freedom. Clutching her foam-topped mug of cinnamon- and marshmallow-sprinkled hot chocolate, she watched two squirrels dance around the trunk of a nearby oak tree, as she took stock of her short time in England.

Over the past few years, Amy had become adept at phasing out the image of Jack. In the beginning, once the initial sobbing self-pitying stage had passed, anything that reminded her of Jack was treated to serious diversion therapy. She would concentrate on anything else; the weather, the people nearby, the view. Any distraction would do. Amy had become so good at it that her brain had learned to short-circuit the whole process for her. Sometimes she found herself thinking about one thing, and suddenly her mind would flick elsewhere, a well-honed self-defence system, before she'd even registered that a Jack thought was imminent.

Now that she was in London, only a short distance from the cause of her self-imposed exile, her defences had slipped. Even though they'd never lived in London together, there seemed to be reminders everywhere. Bitter coffee, couples taking lengthy walks in the cold, music (any music), pubs, laughter, and the smell of leather jackets in the rain. He was everywhere.

Rob had asked her again last night. When was she going to get in contact with Jack? She'd hesitated, knowing that she was suffering, not just from cold feet, but also from the need to sit back a while and adjust to the increased influx of memories, before she faced the reality. Everything had changed so fast. She simply wasn't ready to meet him yet. To appease Rob, Amy had agreed to take the address of the bookshop in Kew.

Fishing out a sunken pink marshmallow from the bottom of her mug with a finger, Amy supposed that she couldn't be far from Reading Nature right now. Maybe she should turn up there today? The mere idea of finding the shop, let alone seeing Jack, brought on a fit of butterflies.

'I'm a coward, that's the trouble,' she told the squirrels as they continued to chase each other around the trees. 'Don't knock cowardice,' the squirrels seemed to reply.

Shouting a thank you to the waiting staff, Amy continued her walk, temporarily burying the decisions she needed to make beneath the opportunity to investigate the huge tropical greenhouse that stood before her.

Two hours of slow meandering later, Amy sat down on an old grey metal bench beside the Waterlily House. Just for now she could live like this. A poorly paid waitress in a small Richmond café, an explorer in a city she hardly knew. A visitor on the edge of other people's lives. 'For another day or two,' she told a passing blue tit, 'just a couple more days, that's all, and then I'll text Jack, start applying for permanent jobs, and re-enter the real world, however scary it is.'

Eighteen

October 16th 2006

Jack put the cup back into its saucer with a crash, grabbed his jacket and, before he could change his mind, crossed to the till and waited to pay. He barely acknowledged Toby as he thrust a ten-pound note at him and, without waiting for change or looking back, Jack sprinted from the café. He'd got about three strides down the pavement, when he ran back.

Toby was still by the till. Jack marched straight up to him. 'Sorry. It's a bad time, there's stuff I have to ... Anyway, I might come back here some time.'

Toby held his gaze, but said nothing.

Jack continued, more uncertain. 'If that's OK? Some time?'

Toby inclined his head a fraction.

'Good. That's, um, good.' Jack felt strangely satisfied, but rather awkward, as he dashed towards the Underground, determined to carry out his newly formulated plan of action.

Jack had promised Kit that he'd never meet her at Pickwicks. That was her space, especially since she'd started writing there. His presence, they had long ago agreed, would cause too many distractions. But this was an emergency, and anyway, Jack had already broken so many rules that he wasn't going to worry about one more. It was only ten o'clock. If he hurried he could get back to Richmond by eleven and catch Kit before she packed up, and headed home to type up her morning's labours.

He stared impatiently down the track at the strangely quiet Leicester Square station, willing the train to arrive. Now he was doing something positive Jack felt better; enlivened. What he was about to do might not help, but he had to at least try to sort things out.

As the Piccadilly Line tube arrived, Jack leapt into the grey and red carriage and did his best to relax. He could picture Kit hunched over her table, pen and notebook in front of her. He had given up trying to persuade her to carry a laptop around with her ages ago. One of the few things Jack had in common with Phil was the inability to understand Kit's preference for a pen and paper; that she gained genuine satisfaction from leafing through a book filled with her own hand-written work.

A thought of Toby flitted through his head. Toby was certainly something to look forward to. Blonde and blue-eyed, that he'd registered at once, but now Jack had allowed himself time to think, he saw that Toby was also elegant, with light freckles and slender hands. Jack reflected, as he watched subterranean London rocket past the windows, that he and Toby were probably of about equal height, although the waiter was certainly slimmer. Toby was feminine, there was no doubt about that. But not camp, for which Jack found he was grateful. Beyond the requirements of a drag act, Jack had never been a fan of camp, or of any sort of unnecessary affectations for that matter.

Crossing to the District Line at Hammersmith, Jack stopped his thoughts in their tracks. Just because Toby had piqued his curiosity, it didn't mean that the feeling was reciprocated. It was ridiculous to even consider it. Toby wouldn't be interested in someone like him. He was a slut, a tart, a slapper, and he knew it. Reaching Richmond, Jack switched his contemplation away from his own sexual shortcomings towards Kit, and the conversation that awaited him. His palms began to sweat.

Walking past Pickwicks' window to check that she was there, Jack saw it was very busy. Full of elderly women with shopping trolleys, ladies who lunched, and Kit. She was in the corner just as he'd imagined, head down, her right hand speedily moving back and forth across the table as she scribbled down her words. Jack was about to open the door when he saw Peggy approach her. He hung back, watching their exchange as

Kit's cup was refilled. Jack couldn't help but smile. He wondered how much coffee she'd unconsciously drunk that morning, and not for the first time, marvelled how Kit's body coped with such high levels of caffeine on a daily basis.

As he stood there, Jack realised that it had been a long time since he'd looked at Kit properly. Without him even noticing she'd turned from a girl into a woman, a mother, and a wife. Her hair was still red; no grey was peeping through. It was shorter than he remembered, though. Maybe she'd had a trim recently, or more likely it had been like that for ages and he just hadn't noticed. Despite the coffee-and-cake lifestyle, she was still relatively slim, but childbirth had changed her shape, and the chest he used to admire was bigger than it had been. There she sat, quiet, motionless, and slightly scruffy. The last woman. Jack knew how much he owed her. It was high time he told her so.

Peggy had gone to tend her other customers, so the coast was clear. Jack wiped his tacky palms on his jeans, suddenly conscious of being in last night's clothes. They smelt of stale smoke and beer. Jack ran a hand around his face; the stubble had crept beyond its usual fashionable shadow. Still, he hadn't crossed London to back out because he was a touch less than hygienic. Pushing the door open, Jack approached her table. 'Kit?'

She looked up. Her oval-shaped face went white as she saw who was standing before her.

'May I sit down?'

She didn't say anything, but nodded, gripping her pen tighter as he sat down on the spindle backed chair opposite her.

Peggy, who'd noticed Jack's hesitant approach to the corner table, immediately recognised the urgent need for another cup of extra strong coffee. Quickly filling a mug, the waitress scooted forward, and placed it wordlessly in front of Jack before retreating to her counter, keeping her ears wide open, ready to witness the potential showdown.

Words tumbled out of Jack's mouth as he plunged straight in, 'I want to apologise. I didn't *not* tell you about Amy. It just

97

never came up. *She* never came up. Time moved on and stuff.'

Kit twiddled a biro between her fingers, looked Jack directly in the eye, and spoke with a calm voice that belied the turmoil within. 'You have absolutely no idea why I'm so upset, have you?'

He hung his head, 'No. Not really. Sorry.'

'You didn't make our tape, did you?'

Jack felt uneasy. 'No, I've remembered some of what would have been on it though. I've remembered quite a lot actually. It's been quite a fortnight.'

'Hasn't it.' Kit picked up her drink, trying to resist her natural tendency to forgive instantly, determined not to tell him it was OK; that she was being silly, and that he should forget it. Because it wasn't OK, not this time. Trouble was, she still didn't really know why – but she was damned if she'd tell him that.

'Peggy,' Kit hailed her friend, 'we need sugar over here. Fast.'

Without a word, Peggy headed for the cake display, placed two large slabs of carrot cake onto a plate, and returned to the frosty silence which hung over her corner table.

'Thanks,' they spoke in unison, both Kit and Jack thankful to have something to focus on as they sat opposite each other and, for the first time in their lives, didn't know what on earth to say.

98

Nineteen

October 16th 2006

Hearing the shop bell, Rob abandoned checking his email, and turned the radio to a more customer friendly volume. 'Hi, Phil, haven't seen you for ages. How's tricks?'

'No need to turn it down on my account,' Phil gestured towards the shop's sound system. 'I'm fine, but work's been mad recently, you?'

'Yeah great, although work isn't so much mad, as on a life support machine. You killing time before a viewing?'

Phil's usually gentle voice rapidly lost its friendly tone, 'No, I'm hunting down Jack.'

'Jack?' Rob instantly felt wary. This had to be about Kit.

Phil peered around the small empty space, 'Is he here?'

Rob shook his head, 'I doubt I'll see him this side of tomorrow. He's currently taking the phrase "burning the candle at both ends" as his code of honour.'

'I see.' Phil sounded blunt as Rob continued.

'When Jack is here he's either so damn tired and miserable that he merely grunts into the computer, or he's so angry that he snaps at everything and everyone.'

'A regular delight to be around then.'

'Absolutely.'

Picking up a Christmas promotional leaflet from a pile next to the till, Phil began flicking through it, noticing the well-constructed mix of gardening books, children's natural history sticker books, and easy-to-follow nature spotters guides, 'You've got some nice stuff here.'

Rob smiled. He'd worked hard on getting the balance of that

pamphlet right. 'Thanks. Hopefully other people will think so, like the odd paying customer.'

Phil looked about him, 'Have you ever considered expanding the range a bit further, you know, cuddly toy robins and coal tits next to the British Birds section, model hedgehogs by the Natural History shelves?'

'We've considered doing that sort of thing in the past, but it's a question of finding the room.' Rob gestured around the shop-floor, 'Space is a bit of a premium here.'

'True. The joys of being your own boss I guess.' Phil considered saying something else about the shop, but drew himself back to the matter in hand. 'Kit's in a bad way. I don't think she's writing.'

'Ah,' Rob nodded, 'I wondered how she was. I was going to call her, but I took the cowardly option and decided to keep out of it as much as I could.'

'Very wise,' Phil inclined his head towards his friend, 'Jack hasn't said anything then?'

'Beyond that he'd, and I quote, "cocked up with Kit," he hasn't said a thing. I've just heard the occasional self-pitying murmurs. All I know for sure is that ever since he sent that tape back to his ex-girlfriend, all hell's broken loose.'

'Jack has another female ex!' Phil was stunned.

'He has a fair collection of them actually.' Rob sighed, realising he was going to have to tell the whole story all over again. 'I think we should have coffee.'

'Tea, if that's all right. Had I better sit down for this?' Phil pulled one of the counter's stalls out far enough to accommodate his long legs.

'Quite possibly,' Rob left Phil studying a selection of books waiting to be parcelled up and posted; the first successes from Jack's website.

Leaning against the patchy magnolia wall, Rob shook his head as he waited for the kettle to boil. How could one man, one *gay* man for God's sake, have this much disruptive influence over two otherwise perfectly sensible women?

Returning to the shop floor, Rob presented Phil with his tea.

100

'Are you sitting comfortably? Then I'll begin.'

'So, if I follow you correctly, Kit is upset because she didn't know about this particular ex?' Half an hour later Phil was still struggling to work it out.

Less than convinced, Rob replied, 'I think so.'

'Why? We all have exes.'

'True, but I think it was a shock, you know, that he loved one particular woman, rather than just bonking them in general.'

'As opposed to a man you mean?'

'I think that's it.' Rob shrugged. 'Hell, I don't know, there was something about music too.'

Phil ran a hand through his short black hair, ruffling it out of its usual neat office style into tuffs and spikes. 'Music? The tape you mentioned?'

'Yes.'

Phil finished his tea, and put the mug on the counter. 'Well, this has all the common sense of a Whitehall farce. Kit's a married woman now, for Christ's sake. Married to me! *I'll* make her a damn tape if that's all this is about.'

Rob began to feel guilty for saying anything, 'Sorry Phil, I really didn't mean to make trouble. I ...'

'It's OK Rob, I'm not cross with you, or Kit really, but it's so petty. So, so, so damn *Jack*!'

Rob spoke more softly, hoping to calm Phil down a bit, 'I think they know that too. They just don't know what to do about it.'

Twenty

October 16th 2006

'Amy doesn't know about you either.' Jack had tried small talk, but it hadn't worked, so he dived back into the fray between mouthfuls of cake.

Kit sounded exhausted, 'What does she know?'

'Very little.' Jack tried to take her hand, but she moved it out of reach, 'Kit,' he sounded almost pleading now, 'you did know I had girlfriends at university.'

'I did, but until our last discussion, I was under the impression they were of the snog 'em, shag 'em, leave 'em variety. That for you, loving a woman was totally out of the question. Period.'

'That's mostly true.' Now it was Jack's turn to sound tired.

'But not her.'

'No, not Amy, but so what?' Jack was getting fed up with this now. He wasn't used to having to justify his actions. 'You must have been in love with someone other than Phil surely, otherwise how did you know that you loved him?'

Kit swallowed. The cake she'd eaten suddenly transmogrified to lead in her stomach. In ten years she'd never given herself away. The truth was now dangerously near exposure; it could change everything. She'd probably freak Jack out so much she'd never see him again, and as the past two weeks had shown her, that as a permanent prospect, was something she didn't like at all. She daren't even contemplate how Phil would react if he found out she'd felt. So she simply said, 'I'd have said.'

Jack watched Kit, his growing temper dying as quickly as it

had risen as realisation dawned. He knew he'd been stupid, now it seemed he'd been blind as well. Yet she hadn't said it. Why not? Choosing his words carefully he said, 'I don't want a life without you in it.'

Kit acknowledged his words with an inclination of her head, but ignored the obvious response, saying instead, 'Have you seen Amy yet, since she's come south I mean?'

Jack took the change of tack gratefully, 'No. I don't know where she's living.'

'I do.'

'What?' Jack abruptly lent forward again, 'How on earth do you know that? Rob hasn't told you, has he?'

'Rob knows?' Kit frowned as she spoke.

'Yes, but he's not saying. Apparently she'll find me when she's ready. Very bloody mysterious.'

Good for her, Kit experienced an unexpected second of respect for her unknown protagonist. 'Phil knows too. Although he has no idea he knows of course.'

'Phil? How on earth …?'

'She's renting a room through Home Hunters.'

'Small world.' Jack let out a sigh as he ran a hand through his hair.

'Isn't it.'

Letting silence fill the gap between them for a moment, Jack rubbed the tension from his forehead before saying, 'You and Amy have quite a lot in common.'

'Really?' The tone of Kit's voice clearly indicated she didn't want to hear it. A nuance completely lost on Jack.

'Sure,' Jack attempted to move closer to her, but Kit lent back. 'You both fidget when you're nervous or uncertain about something. You're both kind and generous. And you're both far too good for me. You both let me get away with murder.'

Kit grunted a begrudging response, 'That bit sounds right anyway.'

Jack was warming to his theme; the more he thought about it, the more similarities there were. 'You like the same types of music, neither of you care much about clothes beyond comfort, and despite your angelic faces, you're both dirty beggars in the bedroom.'

Kit stared at him in disbelief, 'A thought too far, Jack. *Much* too far.' Kit scowled. 'At least now I know why you were attracted to me; I was just like her.'

Jack's mouth dropped open. He'd walked straight into that one. 'Don't be ridiculous, I liked you for you, but you're right, I went too far with the comparisons. I was trying to help. Sorry.' Jack began to shred the napkin he'd absentmindedly been playing with into haphazard strips.

Kit watched him carefully, unable to prevent a tiny smile hitting the corner of her lips, 'Amy and I aren't the only ones who fidget when we're uncertain then.'

'Well, I have a fair bit to be uncertain about right now.'

Peggy finished serving the group of pensioners, who had come into Pickwicks for their regular pots of tea and toasted teacakes, as fast as possible, and scooted back to within earshot of Kit and Jack. This was better than a soap opera! To think she'd thought that Kit, despite all literary evidence to the contrary, was a goody-two-shoes in the men department. She'd known Kit and Jack were good friends, and that Jack was gay. Peggy had always joked that they were like the characters from the nineties sitcom, *Will and Grace*, without realising how close to the truth she was.

Making a play of wiping the counter, Peggy felt troubled as she listened. *Amy?* It had to be the same girl that waited here. Kit had been so self-involved recently that she'd barely noticed the new waitress, and why would she? Peggy always served Kit and the other regulars herself, leaving the passing-trade clients to Amy.

Thanking whichever God was on patrol that morning that it was Amy's day off, Peggy picked up some freshly brewed coffee, headed into the currently hushed war zone, and topped up their mugs.

Taking a sip of her fresh drink, Kit savoured the hot bitter liquid as it slid down her throat. 'So, why did you let us go on for so long?'

'Why did you stay with me once you knew the truth?' Jack countered.

'I asked first.'

'Don't be childish.'

Kit slammed her cup into its saucer, 'Just answer the sodding question, Jack.'

'Poison.'

'I'm sorry?' Kit's eyes rolled menacingly in their sockets, in a blatant warning to Jack that he should explain himself very, very carefully.

'The song, Alice Cooper, you know, "Poison",' Jack explained. 'Everything about you had me caught up, like ... well, like "Poison"'

'Am I to be flattered or supremely insulted? Anyway, that makes no sense in this context.'

'Look. I'm trying to tell you, I was addicted if you like.' Jack leaned forward desperately trying to work out how to make her understand.

'Addicted! Oh great, first I'm poison, now I'm fucking heroin.' He'd never seen Kit so cross or offended.

'Kit, will you shut up and listen for a second, I'm trying to explain.'

Forcing herself not to use some of the words she never spoke out loud, but frequently wrote down, Kit hissed, 'Then tell me, preferably *without* the aid of lyrical references.'

'OK, OK.' He sat up straight and prepared to explain himself as best he could.

Jack spoke without drawing breath for at least ten minutes. He was afraid to stop just in case Kit jumped in with a comment, and right now he had to get out what he wanted to say without interruption. He knew he was repeating himself, and that he'd already apologised at least three times for being selfish, and mentioned how comfortable he had felt with Kit, five times after that. He stressed how he hadn't wanted to let go of a good thing. That that was what he meant about being addicted. He'd told Kit more than she ever wanted or needed to know about the past fortnight, and how he'd used the men he picked up to block out the mess he'd made of his life; was continuing to make of it.

'So,' Jack concluded, 'here I am, thirty-five years old, with no special partner and no prospect of kids. I'm sat here opposite my closest friend and I feel sick to the pit of my stomach that I've upset her. I'm sorry Kit. Sorry for my behaviour then, sorry for my behaviour now, sorry for not understanding how you felt or how you feel. Sorry for always putting myself first. Sorry.'

Jack collapsed back into his chair, aware he'd probably raised his voice rather too loud for a private conversation, and waited for Kit to react. She was cradling her massive cup, her pen and notebook lay open before her, the meagre amount of words she'd managed that morning had been scribbled out viciously in red pen.

Eventually Kit spoke, 'Did you mean it?'

'Which bit?'

'You said you didn't want a life without me in it.'

'I meant it. I also meant all the other stuff as well. I need you, Kit.'

She nodded, a resigned expression across her hurt face, 'And you even wanted me once upon a time, but more than that? I guess it's back to that old Meat Loaf number, isn't it, Jack. "Two Out Of Three Ain't Bad", huh?

'Ouch.'

'That's exactly what I thought at the time.'

'But you didn't react then,' Jack could feel his hackles rising, his hands whirling in frustration, 'you just carried on.'

'Phil always says I have one major character flaw. He says I'm too nice.'

'Don't flatter yourself! You're not too nice; you've just taken selflessness to a bloody ridiculous level. You were allowed to argue with me, to tell me off. You were such a fucking martyr. You still are.' Jack was one decibel short of shouting now, earning him a black look from Peggy.

Kit murmured at him, her words barely audible as she put

107

her mug down with a clatter, 'I'm not saying I wasn't at fault too. I know I should have stood up for myself more, had some pride in myself. Argued with you or something. Oh, what's the point!'

Suddenly Kit felt overwhelmingly tired. 'Look, Jack, it's all done, OK. This is an argument eleven or twelve years too late. I was upset. You've said sorry, so that's it.'

'That's it?' Jack briefly dared to hope she meant it. 'You can't get all angry and then suddenly stop being cross – can you?'

'Actually, I can. This is so utterly pathetic and pointless. We can't rework the past, can we? It is what it is. Which I'm glad about, because for a while I was happy with you. And as a consequence of you and me splitting up, I met Phil. I love him to bits, and we're happy together with the twins. So it's OK.'

'And us. Are we OK?'

Kit sighed again, 'I need some time Jack. It's as if … I don't know how to explain it. As if I have accidentally discovered I was a failed experiment. You know the sort of thing? "Let's see if Kit will take it up the arse, let's see if that is enough, see if treating her like a man will make up for the fact that she'll never feel or think or touch like a man, and then maybe I won't need one."'

Jack paled, 'Kit, I never …'

'And lucky you! Kit did like it that way, didn't she? Lucky sod. I bet they had plenty of laughs about that at whichever gay bar you told that story at.'

'I … it never occurred to me … Kit?' The last drops of blood drained from Jack's face as he realised that what she said was, in some way the truth, although a totally unconscious truth on his part.

'As I said,' Kit paused to collect her quiet, faltering voice, 'I'm sure we'll be fine, I don't want a life without you either, but I do need some time.'

'OK.' Jack felt choked, digesting a feeling of unaccustomed hopelessness as he acknowledged her request.

Kit glanced at the clock that hung above the counter. 'Oh

God, it's getting late. I have to go.'

'Right.' Jack watched, still slumped, as Kit stuffed all her writing paraphernalia into her faded handbag. She put her coat on and, as she hoisted her bag over shoulder, said more kindly, 'This is nothing to do with you being gay, Jack. Really. I know what I said might make it seem that way, but it isn't. It's about being taken for granted. You do get that, don't you?'

Jack said nothing so she continued, 'Perhaps it is me. Perhaps I'm the problem not you. Everything around me is changing. You producing another version of your past, Phil hating his job and carrying on like no one's noticed, the twins growing into teenagers way too early before my eyes, me needing to use medicinal cream on my feet and moisturiser on my hands, and I can see forty approaching me from the other side of the hill. So it probably is me.' She started to walk away.

'"Everybody's Changing."'

Kit turned back sharply. 'I'm sorry?'

'Keane. "Everybody's Changing". The lyrics sum everything up perfectly.' Jack instantly regretted disclosing his musical reflection.

Kit felt more sad than angry. 'Of course. Good old Jack, a song for every occasion.'

Twenty-one

October 16th 2006

Phil pushed the remainder of his late pub lunch aside. He dug his mobile from his jacket pocket and phoned Chris at the office. Crossing his fingers as he spoke, he said, 'I'm sorry mate, Kit's not well, can you cope without me this afternoon?'

'Sure. Nothing urgent has come up. Hope she feels better soon. See you tomorrow?'

'Hope so. Thanks mate.' Striding fast, slipping his mobile back into his coat, Phil felt cross. And scared. Jack. Bloody Jack. Why the hell did he feel threatened by him?

Phil loved Kit and she loved him; but when was the last time he'd told her? What if that idiot Jack had changed his mind about the whole gay thing and wanted her back? *Oh God*. Phil stopped dead, almost causing an old lady to walk into his back. No, that wasn't it; think logically, man. Get a grip. Perhaps this was all simply an overdue, inevitable spat. Maybe his wife had stood up for herself for once. He damned well hoped so.

Flowers; he'd get some flowers and go home early. He'd almost reached the florist when he realised what he was doing. Kit hated cut flowers, what the hell was he thinking? He tried to stop the panic rising in his chest. He wasn't going to lose her. Even though he knew in his gut that this wasn't about Kit leaving him, in fact, it wasn't about him and Kit at all, Phil couldn't shake the feeling that he had to do something before it was too late.

Then it seemed obvious. A tape. All this was sparked, or so it appeared, over some stupid tape. God knew why, but maybe he could use the idea. He'd make a CD, and burn onto it all the

111

tunes that told Kit how much he loved her. He turned and almost ran back to the bookshop. Rob had a computer with Internet access, and was bound to have a spare CD he could borrow. Jack clearly wasn't going to make an appearance today. Phil had the feeling he needed to work fast.

Her confused anger evaporated as Kit stamped out of the café towards home. With each step she felt an easing of pressure at the realisation that, for almost the first time in her life she'd stood up for herself. Yet she felt ashamed. She should never have said all that about the sex life she'd shared with Jack. If she hadn't been up for it, then he'd never have made her do any of that stuff.

She didn't know why she felt so upset about the existence of Amy. Perhaps it was because of the tape? The fact he'd cared enough about Amy to finish her tape off, but had never bothered to even start hers. But then, Kit reasoned, that was unfair too. It hadn't been Amy's idea to make a tape really; it had been her brother's. Kit felt that it was still worth taking a stand over though, even if her logic was confused. Despite her underlying guilt, Kit felt her argument with Jack had done her good. Maybe it would do him good too?

Reaching her front door, and turning the key in the lock, Kit smiled as she remembered that she'd managed to have the last word. *Blimey, what's happening to me? That never happens!*

Dumping her bag and discarding her shoes, Kit grabbed an apple instead of a late lunch, and went straight up to her office. It was high time she caught up on those Christmas stories for *Pearls,* and suddenly she was in the mood to steam a story onto the screen …

'Hi, love!'

Kit hit *Save* on her sexy Santa's Grotto story as she heard the front door slam behind Phil, clicked on her screen-saver, and set off towards the kitchen, 'You're early, everything OK?'

'Yeah, fine. I've had an out-and-about sort of a day, and I was closer to home than the office, so I called it a day.'

'Great,' Kit reached out and kissed her husband, 'Is an easy dinner OK? Omelette or something? The twins are at a friend's house for tea, and I've taken advantage and tried to catch up on some stories. Lost track of time. Sorry.'

'Sounds great, especially the having-the-house-to-ourselves bit,' Phil came up to his wife as she poked a tea bag around his mug and put his arms around her. 'You feeling better?'

'I am, actually. I'm sorry I've been low.' Kit looped her arms around her husband's waist.

Phil cocked his head to one side in enquiry, 'You and Jack talked?'

'Sort of. He apologised and I listened.'

'Jack apologised! Boy, that's a first.' Phil hugged Kit closer to his side. 'So is that it? Normal service resumed?'

'No, but I think I'm in control for once, and although I'm probably being mean, it does feel good to have *him* dangling on the hook for a change.'

'That's my girl. I'm proud of you.' Phil gathered Kit up and whispered into her ear, 'When do you have to collect the twins?'

'*You* have to collect them at 6.30.'

'That's a whole hour and a half away.'

'True.' Kit smiled up at her husband, and telepathically agreed with his unspoken idea that they could make better use of the time than just eating omelette.

Jack watched his friends among the mass of male bodies jumping about in an approximation of dancing. His pint, discarded and forgotten, sat on the table beside him, and his brain seethed with confusion. The usual vibrancy of the place felt stale. The background beat pounded through his head like a constant irritation, rather than an exciting rhythm of expectation. When on earth was Amy going to call?

He dug his mobile from his pocket and re-read the text Kit had sent only moments after his arrival at the club.

Don't shag for revenge. Take care. K x

'Shit,' Jack said to no one in particular. He wasn't even sure what he was doing at the club again anyway. Kit had assumed he'd pitch up here tonight. And as usual, she was right.

An image of Kit sat writing at her corner table in Pickwicks floated into Jack's head. It quickly merged into one of Toby serving coffee, before becoming Peggy's stern glance as he'd struggled to keep his temper under control, until finally it fixed on a picture of a youthful Amy, walking hand in hand with him through the university grounds.

This was ridiculous.

He knocked back his beer and went home.

Twenty two

October 17th 2006

'And then he got a CD out of his briefcase.' Kit couldn't stop smiling.

'Hang on,' Peggy put down the spray detergent and cloth she'd been using to clean off a neighbouring table. 'Let me get the story straight so far. You had great sex, fetched the kids, put them to bed, had supper, and then Phil produced a CD?'

'You got it.' Kit's grin was contagious; Peggy couldn't help but began back at her.

'Go on. What next?'

'He took the stereo upstairs, tucked me up in bed, and then brought up two glasses of wine. Honestly! Phil has never done anything remotely romantic before. I have no idea what got into him.'

'Who cares?' Peggy was thrilled to see her friend so happy again.

'True.' Kit smirked the smirk of a woman who'd recently been thoroughly made love to. 'Anyway, we snuggled down together, and he turned on the stereo.'

Peggy flicked her fingers through the serviettes. 'What was on it?'

Kit blew across the surface of her coffee, cooling it before she spoke. 'It was perfect, Peggy, he chose such great stuff, but best of all, the last track was the first song played at our wedding, "The Power of Love" by Frankie Goes to Hollywood. We both love that.'

'That's so cute! I like that one too. Ooh, and all that stuff in the lyrics about protection – does that mean Phil's going to guard you from Jack's stroppy moods?' Peggy began to sing the relevant lines in her happy off-key way.

'I never thought of that!' Kit laughed at the idea, 'Anyway, it's a great piece of music and it was a fabulous evening. God knows where Phil got the idea from ...'

Kit stopped short, the happiness wiped from her face.

'What? What is it?'

'The tape. He knows about the tape. Well, the lack of tape.' Kit could feel horror rising in her gullet.

Peggy raised her hand in a do-not-move gesture, rushed over to the cluttered but clean counter, and fetched the coffee peculator jug and a straw. 'Here you go. Forget the mug; you might as well take it straight from source.'

Kit laughed through her sudden gloom, before saying, 'Oh hell, but what if ...?'

Her friend interrupted as she sat back down, 'I heard enough of what was going on yesterday with Jack to fill in the gaps between what I already knew. You've been holding out on me big time!'

Groaning, Kit rested her head in her hands, 'It was another life ago, Peggy. Not my finest hour.'

'That doesn't matter. Nor does it matter if Phil knows more than you thought he did.' Peggy put her hand on Kit's shoulder, 'What *does* matter is that he cares enough to find out about what was making you sad. He obviously doesn't blame you for whatever it was, and has done something amazing to show you how much he loves you.'

'You think so?'

'I do.' Peggy's tone was definite.

Kit lifted her head back up. 'Thanks, Peggy.'

'Don't thank me, honey. You have a great man there. Do *not* screw up a good life over a mistake you made however many years ago.'

'You are a wise old thing, aren't you?'

'Student of life, me,' Peggy reached forward, and spoke in a hushed tone, 'You loved Jack, didn't you?'

Kit lowered her eyes again. 'I never told anyone. Not even him.'

'But he knows, doesn't he?'

'I think he might.' A fog of uncertainty clouded at the edges of Kit's eyes.

'It doesn't matter if he does,' Peggy was uncharacteristically serious, 'the question is: do you love Phil?'

Kit snapped her head back up and looked directly at her friend. 'More than anyone. Ever.'

'Then you having loved Jack once upon a time doesn't matter. You haven't done anything wrong. You haven't cheated on anyone; you've just been made to feel cheated. I think. Now,' Peggy stood up straight and smoothed her apron in a businesslike manner, 'would you like a cup for that coffee or is the straw enough?'

Kit grinned. 'If it comes complete with a scone, then I'll have a cup, ta.'

'Coming up,' Peggy fetched Kit's order, 'Oh,' she called across the room, 'you haven't forgotten to tell me anything else apart from the fact your gay best friend was once your lover, have you?'

'What the hell could top that?' Kit felt her earlier smile begin to return.

'That you secretly write erotica for a living?' Peggy put her hand to her mouth in mock outrage, 'Oh, but you do that anyway, don't you?'

'To be honest, Peggy, I'm not sure I do anymore. Not exclusively anyway.'

'What?' Peggy rushed back to the table. This was serious; her free supply of smut was in jeopardy, 'What do you mean? You're so good at it!'

Kit accepted the compliment gracefully, 'Well, thanks, but although I am very proud of what I've written, I'm running out of ways to grind people's bits together in new and original ways. I feel it's time to move the writing on a bit. Try something straight before returning to the kink.'

'You should be proud! I am bloody proud of you. I love telling people that one of my best friends writes erotica. The whole stun factor, you know?'

'Yes, I know.' Kit smiled modestly. 'And thanks, I'm touched that you're proud of me, but there's no need to be.'

Peggy stared at her friend with incomprehension. 'Ye gods, woman, you've got the lowest self-worth on the planet!'

'Sorry?'

'And don't apologise.'

Kit almost said 'sorry' again, but swallowed the word down. 'What are you talking about?'

Peggy tugged her ponytail in frustration, 'It's damned annoying sometimes, listening to you running yourself down.'

Kit started to mumble again, 'That's more or less what Jack said'

'As much as I hate to agree with him, he was right,' Peggy poked a finger through the depleted bowl of sugar sachets, making a mental note to top them up later. 'So, a novel then?'

Kit brightened up, 'I've always wanted to write one, but the time has never been right. Either we haven't had enough money for me to be able to give up work, or I simply haven't had the time to get down to writing anything lengthier than a couple of thousand words.'

'But now you have got the time and the money?'

'The time, yes, but I need to talk to Phil about it properly. The money side, I mean.'

Peggy was curious. 'So, what's this magnum opus going to be about?'

'That would be telling.' Even as she spoke, Kit's vague literary ideas began forming more solid patterns in her mind. By the time Peggy had crossed the room Kit was writing furiously; scared to slow down in case her ideas leaked out of her brain and were lost to her forever.

Twenty-three

October 19th 2006

Amy typed the words into her phone, before pressing delete for the second time. Maybe she'd text Jack when she got home instead – or perhaps tomorrow morning would be better?

She had been happy to immerse herself in another day of filling sandwiches, pouring coffee, and gentle banter, before facing the next step in her new life. Now, gathering up her bag, Amy buttoned her coat over her black trousers and white blouse, and set off from the café. Head down and umbrella up, she walked into the rain, oblivious to everyone and everything, until she reached the door of the local newsagent, and reluctantly purchased the local job paper.

The night before, her new housemate James had told Amy that she could use his computer any time, and he'd also recommended several useful websites for job-hunting. Early that morning she'd done just that, reluctantly acknowledging that she couldn't survive on a waitress' pay long-term. The only snag was that she had no idea what she wanted to do. All Amy could be absolutely certain of was that she never wanted to give failing companies marketing advice *ever* again.

Kicking off her sensible black shoes with a groan of relief, Amy switched on the kettle. With a cup of sadly inferior instant coffee to hand, she collapsed onto the sofa and reluctantly thumbed her way through the jobs section of her rain-dampened newspaper.

Ten minutes later, Amy forced herself to recognise the fact that she was almost totally unemployable for anything other than the dreaded 'business market advisory' sort of job she'd so recently escaped from. A realisation made even more depressing by the fact that there weren't even any jobs like that available in the vicinity anyway.

'New job, new home, new life.' Amy recited her mantra firmly, and started tapping out a text before she could back out. As she did so, she told the phone, quite abruptly, that as the new home was sorted, and the new job was going to take eons to track down, she'd better make a start on the new life section of her ambitions. Amy knew she couldn't do that until she'd laid a ghost to rest. That ghost's name, of course, was Jack …

Hello Jack. It's Amy. U ok?

Jack stared at the message, a combination of relief and horror creeping over him. He had to reply, but what should he say? Amy hadn't said anything much. Testing the water, he supposed. He fumbled over a selection of possible responses. Should he seem cool and off-hand, restrained and vague, or eager and keen? This whole meeting up thing seemed to have had a bigger build-up than the World Cup, and he was no longer sure how he felt about it. He decided on a simple response.

All well with me. U?

Amy leapt off the sofa when the mobile beeped. She'd been expecting the sound, or at least hoping for it, but it still made her jump as it echoed around the quiet room. Her heart thumped louder in her chest as she read Jack's reply. With hasty but clumsy fingers, Amy typed her reply.

Better than ever thanks. Want to meet?

Jack's uncertainty vanished. He had to see her. The depth of his need surprised him; perhaps it's because of how things stand with Kit, he thought. A moment's doubt flitted through his mind – but Amy was 'better than ever thanks', which was a definite improvement on the "angry and out for revenge thanks," that he'd been expecting. Of course, he pondered, *she could be bluffing?*

No. Not Amy. If she was angry, her text would have revealed the fact. She couldn't keep her emotions hidden, which was how he'd known that she loved him. She'd never had the confidence to say she did, but Jack had known. *And Amy isn't Kit. No. Don't think about that now.* He sent his reply.

Shall we have a coffee stop then?

Amy fired one back almost immediately.

No. Can we walk while we talk? U a member of Kew Gardens?

Amy thought hard. *Should I put a kiss at the end of the message?* No. Better not. It's too soon for that.

Jack swore as his predictive text went weird for a second, before shooting back.

I am. See u at main gate. Ten a.m. tomorrow?

Amy's hands shook as she responded. Should I add a kiss at the end? Oh, why not, what harm could it possibly do now?

Sure. Tomorrow then. x

Amy couldn't sleep. Tomorrow seemed both aeons away and frighteningly close. She couldn't decide if she was excited or terrified at the prospect of their scheduled walk.

Jack couldn't sleep. He couldn't shake the feeling that he was about to get himself into another mess.

Twenty-four

October 20th 2006

Amy's stomach lurched as she saw the distant figure approaching on the opposite side of the road. She knew it was Jack. His walk, his dark hair, even his faded brown leather jacket: they all looked the same. She wondered if he'd spotted her yet. She thought that he probably had by the way he was staring at the pavement, rather than at her or at the gateway to the gardens. In spite of her nerves Amy felt an excited smile settle on her face.

Jack's brain was in overdrive as he plodded forward. *Do I really want to face this now?* Kit was still 'thinking', and the idea of coping with another disgruntled female was not an appealing one. Especially *this* disgruntled female. Still, Amy was only a few yards ahead of him now. Jack had spotted her the minute he turned the corner from the bookshop. *Always early then, always early now.* Jack couldn't suppress a grin. Perhaps it would be all right ...

'Hello.'

They spoke in unison; not quite ready to make eye contact yet, they flashed their membership cards at the man on the gate and walked straight into the gardens, bypassing the handful of tourists queuing to pay for a day ticket.

So much had happened. There was so much to say. The air between them seemed textured with awkwardness, stilted, as if its very essence had filled itself with all the things they had left unsaid. Never one to be able to cope with an uncomfortable silence for long, Amy took a bold step and decided to ignore the mindless chatter option.

'So, when did you come out then?'

As she had intended, Jack was taken aback by her directness. That wasn't the Amy he'd known, always so reticent, so reluctant to take the lead; but then recent events had made him question everything he'd believed he knew about the women in his life.

'Eleven years ago.'

'Eleven *years*!' Amy turned, facing him head on.

'Don't shout, Amy,' Jack put his hand up to calm her down.

'Eleven years, though, Jack! I'd assumed it was a recent thing, you know, seeing as you only just returned the tape. Christ, you could have said something!'

'Didn't Rob ever say anything about me, then?'

Don't try and drag Rob into it!' Amy snapped at him. 'And no, no he didn't! He probably thought it was your place to tell me.' She began to fiddle with her signet ring.

Jack's eyes twinkled as he watched her, belying the solemn expression on his face. 'Still practising displacement then?'

Amy couldn't help but laugh. 'So it would seem.'

Jack examined his ex more closely as they strolled past the first large greenhouse. Still very much the same. Curvy in all the right places, and almost as tall as he was. Jeans with small holes in each knee, more from over-wear than the requirements of fashion; a chunky maroon jumper that was at least one size too big, and clumpy unflattering boots. She'd made no effort for him whatsoever. Vintage Amy.

'You look great.'

'Thanks. You too. You haven't changed; you still have the same gorgeous jacket.' Even as she spoke, Amy could vividly picture herself snuggled up against him, inhaling its battered leather aroma.

The hush that fell between them lasted long enough to get uncomfortable, before Amy jumped in with a new line of conversation. This time she headed for safer ground. 'So, your parents OK?'

'Dad's fine. He's actually Grandad now!'

'No way! So is Susan married with all the ticks in the right boxes?'

'Yep, my sister has done things properly. Married a steady bloke with a steady career, and had two children. A boy and a girl, naturally.'

'Naturally. Always the one for getting things exactly right, your Susan.'

'Oh, yes.' Jack's eyes lowered for a split second, but it was enough of a pause for Amy to be able to read his thoughts.

'Christ, Jack! They don't know, do they?' Jack said nothing, scuffing his feet through the leaves. 'Do you think they have any idea? Or have they spent the last decade sat at home waiting for their only son to turn up with a brand-new wife and heir? I mean, bloody hell Jack, where do they think you are every night? Sat in front of the television tatting?'

'Will you calm down? Why are you taking my not telling them so personally? And what the fuck is tatting?'

Amy wasn't listening, her arms waved around as she walked faster and faster. 'I bet your mum knows. I bet she does.'

'Amy!' Jack shouted through her rant, 'Will you please slow down! Just stand still a minute and stop talking.'

'But Jack …'

'Listen a minute,' Jack cut in, 'come on.' He grabbed Amy's hand to pull her into the Pavilion café, but dropped it the instant he felt her skin beneath his. They looked at each other in shock for a split second, and then simultaneously thrust their hands deep into their pockets. Neither of them had expected the old electricity to be there. And as tactfully as possible, neither of them mentioned it.

Quietly sitting on a seat, under the shelter of a large and totally un-seasonal parasol, Jack tried to focus on what he was going to say. 'Mum died, Amy. Mum died five years ago.'

'No!' Amy blanched, 'Oh Jack, I'm so sorry. I just blundered on. Oh hell, I'm so sorry, she was lovely. Your mum, I can't believe it.'

'Cancer. It was very quick, mercifully. No one had any idea that anything was wrong until the doctor announced she only had weeks left. She'd only gone to see him about a mild pain in her chest.'

'Jack, I … I don't know what to say.' Amy brought her chair closer and, given their apparent electricity, risked being singed by putting her hand on his shoulder. 'Your mum was great.'

'I'm sorry I didn't tell you before. Mum was very fond of you. Back then, well … she had hopes, I suppose.'

'Well, I liked her too,' Amy paused while a waitress deposited two hot chocolates on their table, 'Is that why your dad doesn't know about you? Too much, now he's on his own?'

'Actually, he's not on his own anymore, but yes, that was it really. At least it was at first.'

Jack began to explain.

'In fact, I had got all geared up to tell them one particular weekend. I rehearsed what I was going to say over and over and over again. I can't begin to tell you how terrified I was. But as soon as I arrived at the house it was clear that something wasn't right. Mum and Dad sat me down and Mum told me about her visit to the doctor. I instantly ditched the idea of my confession. How could I possibly add to their burden then? And I've pretty much clung onto that excuse ever since.'

Amy was quiet for a moment, before asking, 'Do you like your dad's new girlfriend? It *is* a girlfriend, I take it?'

Jack laughed. 'Yes, there's only the one poof in the family!'

Amy winced, 'Please Jack, don't call yourself that. I hate that word.'

'Surely I should be the one who hates it?'

'I just hate it, OK. Christ, it makes you sound like a squashy footstool!'

Jack shrugged, and ploughed on. 'Anyway, things picked up for Dad a bit when Grandad died.'

'I take it that's not as dreadful as it sounds.' Amy sipped at her drink, feeling its thick warmth glide creamily down her throat.

'Oh no, Grandad was very old, and went peacefully and everything. He sold off his business about two years before he died, and left a fortune. Some to Dad, some to me, and the remainder to Susan.'

Amy looked worried. 'She's not a gold digger, is she?'

'Susan?'

'No, your dad's partner, silly!'

'Jane?' Jack laughed. 'No way! It just meant that the inheritance has allowed him to retire early. They travel a lot. If I did pluck up the courage to tell Dad, I'd have to track him down first.'

Amy toasted her hands around her mug, 'What about you? Your fortune?'

'My house, some money to keep me comfortable and safe from the unforeseen, and the bookshop.'

'Of course. That was pretty obvious. Sorry.' Amy felt silly. It had been such a stupid question.

'Don't apologise.'

'Sorry.'

'Amy!'

The corners of Amy's mouth twitched with amusement, 'Just seeing if I could still annoy the hell out of you.'

'Cow!'

'Moo.'

'And tatting is?'

'A form of lace crocheting.'

'You're insane!'

'True.'

Twenty-five

October 20th 2006

Without really seeing them, they had circumnavigated the entire gardens, talking non-stop. Amy had told Jack about her new home, her housemates, how pleased her parents were that she'd moved back to England, and her quest to find a new career. The fact she was surviving on her fast-disappearing savings and a stop-gap job, and about her Sunday lunch with Rob and Debbie. Jack chattered about how he'd come to London to do a year-long business course after university, that he'd not really known what to do with it until he found his bookshop; of the thrill he'd felt at finding and buying his terraced house in Mortlake, and how he'd designed his back garden.

'If I hadn't opened the shop, I would probably have gone back to college to train as a landscape gardener.'

'Why didn't you then? I would have thought a life outside would be more attractive to you than a life in a shop. More flexibility and all that?'

'My hours are pretty flexible. Rob's my nine-to-five man. Anyway, I didn't want to leave London.' For the first time since they'd left the café, traces of unease returned to Jack's voice. If he answered the question "Why?" that Amy was bound to ask next, then they would have to abandon their happy chat in favour of the underlying reason for their meeting. Could she possibly understand his need to be close to the gay scene he was now so much a part of?

Amy asked the question. 'Why not? There is life outside the big city, you know.'

'I wouldn't know where to start.' Jack stopped walking, and

129

turned to study Amy intently for the first time in years, before echoing what he'd written in the note he'd sent to her in the summer. 'I am sorry, Amy. So sorry I hurt you.'

Amy felt her insides contract. Things had been so relaxed ten seconds ago; she'd almost forgotten they were supposed to having a serious discussion. There was no doubt he was sincere, but for a minute she couldn't respond. She feared that all the years of pent up waiting and wondering about what she did wrong would explode out of her mouth in a fit of either tears or incomprehensible babble. It was way too late for any of that to be worthwhile now, but Amy needed Jack to understand her point of view so she could finally let the scar heal.

'It's just ...' Amy faltered, unsure how to continue. 'It was all so confusing, Jack. There are so many questions, you know? And I'm not sure I know how to ask you any of them.'

'Try?'

Amy looked at Jack for reassurance as they started to stroll again. His expression was attentive and serious as she launched into what needed to be said. 'It's like, when we were together, we'd be fine, then maybe we'd have a particularly good day and the next minute you'd disappear. I wouldn't see you for days. Nothing would be said. You wouldn't take calls. Your housemates made excuses for you as you struggled to cope with each fresh wave of Amy-induced panic. Then, when we did meet up, everything would be fine again. Until the next time a day went particularly well, and the whole damn cycle would start again.'

Amy shook her head as she spoke, in disbelief at her stupidity at putting up with his behaviour as much as at Jack's treatment of her. She risked a glance in his direction. He was looking away from her, but she knew he was listening.

'Other times, of course, you ended it properly. But never for long. Never for a real reason. So when it did end because, as you told me, "it was going too well," I didn't really believe you. I assumed it would be all right again.'

Amy steered them towards the Victoria Terrace Café and sat Jack down, leaving him to ponder what she'd said while she ordered sandwiches for them both, giving herself the chance to gather some courage for the next bit of their conversation. Returning, Amy continued as if she hadn't paused, 'Then I saw you with that Tina.'

Jack's head snapped up. 'You saw that?'

Amy was almost whispering now, the facts still hurting after all this time. 'Oh yes. Unintentionally, but I saw.' She took a tiny bite of her sandwich and watched Jack's stricken face. She had always thought he'd done it on purpose to convince her they were over. Apparently this hadn't been the case.

Chewing her bread, Amy pressed on with her side of the story. 'So, I went home. I cried, wrote an essay and did some more crying. Revised, cried, did another essay, and cried. Passed my exams, cried, booked a ticket to Scotland on the sleeper, and cried. I spent a couple of nights in a youth hostel, cried, found cheap lodgings in Aberdeen's student quarter and cried. I got a part-time admin post, which grew into a full-time marketing position and, about two months after that, I found I'd been so busy I'd stopped crying.'

Jack's voice was small. 'I didn't know you were there, in that pub, to see the Tina thing ... you know ... I mean, she just happened to be there, and she'd made it very clear she liked me. It was so easy. It was nothing. And I'm sorry. I truly didn't intend it to hurt you.'

'Does that make it better or worse, Jack?' Amy managed a weak smile. She hadn't found him again to start hating him. She'd tried to do that years ago, but hating him just didn't seem like a possible option. 'Jack, we were students. Kids, really. It hurt like hell, and I never *ever* want to feel like that again, but what did we know of life then? Nothing. The point is this: it's selfish of me, perhaps, but I need you to understand how awful it is to live with the fact that the person you loved left because everything was going *too well*! Where is there to go relationship-wise after that?'

Jack shook his head sadly, 'Did I really say that?'

'You did.'

'But you're saying this like ... um ... like it's so matter of

131

fact. Aren't you *angry* with me?' Jack felt bewildered as he tried to understand the facts from Amy's perspective.

'I was, but I was angry with me more.'

'What the hell did *you* do?'

'I let you walk all over me. I was so damn blind when it came to you.'

Amy reached out a hand to reassure Jack, who was staring into his rapidly cooling coffee. 'Are you OK?'

'I didn't deserve you.' His face was drawn as he looked back up at Amy.

'Don't talk rubbish.'

'I assumed you'd rip into me today. I thought you'd accuse me of using you as an experiment or something.' Kit's bitter words rang out, echoing in Jack's ears.

'Jack, I have a million questions about the gay thing, and I may well ask you some of them one day. And I confess that my first reaction on receiving your note was to feel a bit lab-rat like, but not for very long.' Amy stretched her hand out to Jack as she spoke. 'Like I said, we were young. If you suspected you were homosexual back then, I doubt if you knew for sure, and you probably didn't want to know anyway.'

'It wasn't really obvious to me at the time. I just knew something wasn't quite right. I mean, I'd had heaps of girls, and I was in love with a woman. I loved *you*, so how could I be gay?' He almost pleaded with Amy as he sat opposite her, hating himself more than ever for how he'd hurt her all those years ago, but knowing he'd had no control over it.

'Did you?'

'Of course I did! It's like that Edwyn Collins song, "A Girl Like You", and sometimes I wish …'

Holding up her hand, Amy interrupted. 'Well, in that case your current sexuality status doesn't matter, does it?' She didn't think it would help if they started on the 'what ifs'.

Amy almost moved to hug him, but held back as she said, 'I loved you too, and I wouldn't have missed my time with you, not for a second. Now, come on, drink your coffee before it gets cold.'

Jack paused, not sure if he should continue, but they'd come this far, 'It wasn't just the gay thing. As you said, I wasn't sure anyway.'

'It wasn't?'

'I didn't finish it because I thought I might be gay. How could I have? I didn't know for certain then, did I.'

Amy's mouth opened and closed, but no words came out. His uncertain sexuality had seemed to have answered all her questions so neatly. She could even have forgiven him the salt he'd rubbed into her wounds in the form of Tina. But now?

'No, I didn't admit that to myself for another few years. I went to this club in Nottingham and ...'

Amy wasn't listening. A blanket of new confusion was smothering her. Noticing that Amy wasn't really with him, Jack stopped talking. He moved directly in front of her, and took both her hands. 'You scared me.'

Dragged out of her illogical musings, Amy felt her blood chill a little. 'Scared you?'

'You loved me so much. I know you never said it, but I knew. It was sort of overwhelming.'

'Well, as I said,' Amy hid her face, staring at nothing in particular out of the window, 'everything was potentially scary back then.' She wiped her wounded expression away in a manner that reminded Jack scarily of Kit. 'Come on you, we've got more walking to do, I want to see the Palm House.'

Returning home several hours later, Jack felt light-headed. He had been prepared for shouting, crying, disbelief, fear, and resentment – in fact, pretty much *anything* from Amy. But not acceptance.

None of his friends had given him a rough time when he came out, and for that he knew he was very lucky, but Amy had simply dismissed it, like being gay was normal. Which it was, but that still wasn't a common reaction, even in these enlightened times. Relieved wasn't even close to how he felt. He was happy. The spectre of Kit vied for his attention, but now he began to dare to hope all would be well there too. Now he had Amy. He had a female friend to help him understand.

They'd left the gardens once the cool afternoon air had begun to stretch its damp grasp beneath their coats, turning walking into a chore and not a pleasure. As Jack sat in his own small garden, breathing in the sharp evening air, he reflected on the day now past. They must have circumnavigated Kew so many times they could have been going for the world record, before they had passed through the exit and, arm in arm, ambled towards his shop.

Amy had told him that she'd been past the door of Reading Nature a couple of times already, and had admired and praised the shop exactly as he'd hoped she would. They had chatted to Rob who, thrilled to see them so comfortable together, was most effusive about how nice it was to see Jack smiling after being such a misery for weeks. Jack had interrupted Rob, not wanting him to raise the subject of Kit. That conversation could happen next time he met Amy; now that he was confident that there would be a next time. More walks, more coffee stops, more chats. He could hardly wait.

The best bit of the day had happened as they'd said goodbye. Amy had turned to him, 'Jack?'

'Yes?'

'The tape. The music you added at the end.'

Jack cautiously asked, 'Was it OK?'

'It was perfect. Thank you.'

He had hugged her then, and the tension of the past weeks began to unravel and drain away.

Crawling into bed, without the idea of clubbing even crossing his mind, Jack smiled to himself. Amy. He still loved her. She still loved him. But it was a different kind of love now. Better even.

As sleep claimed him, Jack's brain began to flick through his vast mental catalogue of music. *There must be a song that sums this situation up perfectly ...*

Twenty-six

October 23rd 2006

Kit looked down at the notebook. It was not the black book with interesting white swirls spattered across one corner that she usually used. That notebook was at home on top of her study bookshelf, out of the sight of children and inquisitive husbands. This was a new notebook. It was bright orange with silver stars splashed across it. Even the cover seemed optimistic. It was for her novel, and it was filling up fast.

Between her numerous coffees and rapid swaying of opinions over the last few days, Kit had concluded that, if she planned her time more efficiently, took less breaks to see Jack (no longer a problem anyway), and ignored the housework even more than usual, she could continue to honour her contract with *Pearls,* and satisfy her need to crack on with her new project. The problem with the novel, now Kit had hit upon a plot that was going somewhere, was that it seemed to consume her. She was already resenting the hours she sacrificed to cooking and cleaning.

She'd have to make more of an effort to talk to Phil; he'd always been so supportive of her writing. Kit had attempted to chat to him about it several times, but something always seemed to get in the way. Maybe she'd have better luck tonight?

Sitting at his desk at the end of another hectic Monday, Phil surveyed the small square office before him. It was an airy, open-plan, and friendly place in which to work. The computers at each of the four other work stations had been off for almost an hour now. He was the only one left.

It was a good team, he thought. From just him, a laptop, and a desk in a rented room above a hairdresser's twelve years ago, Phil had expanded his continually growing business. The end result was these nice premises in a shared office block near Clapham Junction, a handful of employees, and numerous satisfied landlords and tenants. Naturally there had been problems, a fair few in the early days, and the occasional crisis to sort out – but these days they were few and far between. Home Hunters had built up a reputation, and it was a very good one.

As well as the residential private lets, oil companies across Scotland and America used them regularly to provide short-term lets for business clients. They in turn usually recommended them to other businesses that needed accommodation for their own visiting employees in London. Yes, Phil was a success, and he had never been so well-off financially.

'So why am I so fed up?' he demanded of the empty space in front of him.

He had intended to talk to Kit about his dissatisfaction with work last night, but Tom had been stuck on his maths homework, and Kit had been grumpily ironing. By the time he'd read to Helena and helped Kit threaten both twins to stay in bed and not keep popping downstairs for extra juice and biscuits, he'd been too tired for an in-depth discussion about *anything*, let alone their future. The problem was that this sort of thing happened every evening.

Perhaps it would be OK tonight. He'd try anyway.

Kit was singing. Phil could hear her as he walked up the short block-paved driveway to their Victorian red-brick semi. She'd have her MP3 player plugged into her ears. Kit had many talents, but singing was definitely not one of them. Phil winced as he opened the front door in time to hear her failing to hit the high notes with Robbie Williams.

As she spotted her husband, Kit turned off her device of musical torture and gave him a squeeze. 'Hi love, good day?'

Kit bustled about around the kitchen, making them both a hot drink and checking that the casserole she'd put in the oven two hours ago was cooking nicely.

'Yeah, fine. You?'

'Not bad at all. I'd like to talk to you later. The thing is …'

'Mum!' Helena's shrill voice severed the air as she marched into the room.

'What is it this time?' Kit snapped. She suspected she was being unfair, but every time Helena opened her mouth these days, it seemed to be to whine.

'I've spilt my juice.'

'Oh, great!' Kit grabbed a cloth and towel and ran into the living room, in time to see a lake of blackcurrant squash soaking into her beige sofa cushions.

'Can't you be more careful?' she snapped.

'I didn't mean to drop it, Mum.'

Kit didn't trust herself to reply, as she shooed the children away, and took the sticky cushions off the sofa into the kitchen.

Phil grimaced. 'Looks like I arrived in time for a healthy dose of real life.'

'Ha bloody ha.' Kit struggled to free the cushions from their loose covers and stuff them into the washing machine.

'What did you want to talk about?' Phil asked as he watched Kit set the machine's washing cycle.

'What? Oh, that'll have to wait now; as you say, this is real life.'

Phil bit back a flippant remark when he saw Kit's face, and decided he'd better stop standing there with his cup of tea and do something useful. As he put knives and forks on the dinner table, he suppressed a sigh. Unless things improved pretty quickly, it didn't look as if he'd be talking to Kit about their future tonight either.

Twenty-seven

October 24th 2006

'Peggy? Peg? What's up?'

Something wasn't quite right. Peggy wasn't humming to the radio that should be leaking out of the kitchen. But then the radio wasn't on. She wasn't swearing at the cappuccino machine as she tried to clean its various parts. She wasn't dusting, or cleaning tables, or doling out sachets of sugar to the bowls on each table. It was ten-past nine in the morning, but Peggy was just sitting there, staring into space.

'Peg?' Kit felt fear ooze up her spine, 'Peggy?'

Peggy turned to Kit, silent tears cascading down her blotchy face, 'Oh, Kit.' She spoke with such despair that Kit felt her heart constrict.

'Tell me.' Kit grasped Peggy's clenched fist, which wrung her apron between shaking fingers. 'Tell me, please.'

'Scott. It's my Scott.'

'Oh, my God.' Kit's concern turned to panic. 'What about Scott?'

'There … there's been an accident.' Peggy couldn't say anymore, the words stuck in her throat as, exhausted, she dissolved into a sobbing heap on Kit's shoulder.

Eventually Kit freed herself from Peggy's shaking body, got up, made sure the closed sign was up, bolted the door from the inside, and rushed back to her friend.

Crisis after crisis ricocheted around Kit's head, what sort of accident? Car, tube, train? Anyone else hurt? She hadn't heard the news that morning; had there been another bomb? Phil? The kids? She shook herself. No. An accident, Peggy had said. She clutched at her friend's hunched-over form. 'Peggy, please talk to me. Was it a car accident? Where is Scott now?'

'Royal Free Hospital, I …'

Peggy collapsed again as Kit, holding her close, fished her mobile from her pocket and tapped in Phil's number, silently chanting '*please answer, please answer*' as the phone rang and rang. 'Come on!'

Just as the answer service was about to come on Phil mercifully picked up. 'Hey, Kit, you got writer's block?'

'What?' Kit felt confused. What was he on about?

'Well, you never call me in the day unless you can't write.'

'Please, Phil! Thank goodness you're there.'

Picking up on his wife's distressed tone, Phil was all attention. 'Is it the kids? What's going on?'

'No, not the kids, thank God, but I'm at the café. Peggy's incoherent, there's been an accident. Something's happened to Scott. Can you get here? Please, love. Can you come?'

Thanking a God he had no belief in that the trains seemed to be waiting for him one by one, Phil sprinted from the station towards Richmond's main street, before heading down the lane to Pickwicks. Kit was sitting in the middle of the room, her arms around Peggy. He banged on the window, startling both of them.

'I am so glad to see you.' Kit enveloped herself in Phil's welcome embrace, whispering, 'I can't get a word out of her. She should be with Scott, or with a doctor. I think she's in shock.'

Phil knelt down next to Peggy. He gently held her cold hands, 'Hey, Peg. Can you tell me where Scott is, I need to see him?'

Peggy's eyes tried to focus, 'Phil?'

Phil spoke as if coaxing a frightened child. 'That's right, Peg. Where's Scott? I really need him, love.'

'Not here.'

'OK, so he's where?'

'Hospital. They said I should come home. Said I should

sleep. How can I sleep? Stupid.' Peggy's grief turned to sudden fury and confusion, and then died away again to mumbled terror. 'So I came here. I'm not sure why now. Except I always come here, so I came here.'

'Of course, quite right.' Phil smiled at Peggy, smoothed her un-brushed hair with his palm and pulled back to talk to Kit. 'I think you're right, she's in shock. What the hell were they thinking of letting her come home alone? Which hospital do you think he'd be in?'

'She muttered something about the Royal Free earlier.'

'I'm going to call them.'

'But they won't tell you anything.'

'They will if I say I'm his brother or something. Where's the phone?'

'But that only works on the telly, not in real life!' Kit took off her fleece-lined coat and wrapped it around Peggy's shivering shoulders. She could faintly hear Phil talking on the phone in the kitchen. He seemed to have been on the phone for ages. Every now and then he raised his voice, but she was grateful that he'd not started shouting; they'd only have hung up on him.

A fresh knock sounded on the door as Phil came back through to the café. It was the new waitress. Kit had forgotten all about her. Customers had just come, shrugged when they saw the closed sign, and wandered off to pastures new. The new girl would require an explanation.

'Hey, that's Amy! The girl from the house share.' Phil, his face grave from the information he'd convinced the hospital sister to give him, waved at the waitress as he opened the door, 'Hello again, what are you doing here?'

'I work here.' Amy looked around her, 'What's going on, Mr Lambert?'

Kit stood up and stared. 'You're Amy?'

'Yes. You're the writing lady.' Amy turned to Peggy, 'What's going on? Peggy?'

Kit opened her mouth to explain, but no words came out. All her determination to be in control of her conversational standoff

141

with Jack began to crumble as she stood, staring. There was something badly wrong with Scott. Peg was crying, Phil appeared desperately serious, and now, in the middle of all that, she'd just discovered that Peggy's new waitress was called Amy. Jack's Amy. She had to be.

She probably hadn't been gazing into space for long, but Kit realised she must have gone white because Phil had started fussing around her, and Amy rushed to the kitchen, returning with a glass of water for both her and Peggy. Kit shook herself in disgust. *So what if that's Amy? So what if she was pretty, and helpful, and was now kindly cradling Peggy, easing some water gently between her dry lips? Concentrate. None of that mattered now. None of it. Scott. What about Scott?*

'Phil?' Kit felt as if her voice was coming from far away, 'Phil, what did the hospital say?'

Twenty-eight

October 24th 2006

By ten o'clock a taxi had been ordered. Peggy had been eased into her coat, and Amy had pinned a notice up on the door saying that, due to unforeseen circumstances, Pickwicks would only be serving drinks and pastries for the time being. None of them had been sure if that was the right thing to do, but as Phil had said, Peggy couldn't afford to lose too much custom, especially now. Amy had agreed, convinced Kit that she could manage, and had ushered them out of the café, just as the cab parked up outside.

Kit and Peggy sat together in the back, holding onto each other, for strength as well as for warmth. Phil scrambled into the passenger seat and explained to the obliging driver where they were going, and that a gentle ride would be appreciated.

No one spoke as they wove through the mid-morning traffic, each individual privately wrestling with the fear of what might need to be faced.

It had been a car crash. Scott had been admitted to hospital early yesterday evening. Phil had found the hospital sister surprisingly helpful. They'd sent Mrs McIntyre home, she'd explained, as she was clearly exhausted. Peggy had assured them she had someone to go home to. They would never have let her go otherwise if they'd realised that wasn't the case. Naturally she was welcome any time.

Mr Scott McIntyre's car, Phil learned, had been involved in a head-on collision with a van, which had left Scott in a serious condition and the van driver with a multitude of broken bones. Mercifully, neither vehicle had been going fast, or there might

143

have been fatalities.

Scott was in a coma, although the Sister was pleased to say that his hands were already responding slightly to pain applied to the nail beds. This, she assured him, was a hopeful sign, although they were unsure of the ultimate prognosis. The Sister had refused to be drawn about the chances of brain damage, but admitted that they were openly worried about Scott's spine.

Paralysed. That had to be one of the most frightening words in the human language. Kit swallowed waves of nausea as they swam from her belly up into her throat. Phil had told her to be prepared for the worst, and to be thankful that Scott's brain hadn't been starved of oxygen. Otherwise things would have been even worse.

'How could it be worse?' Kit asked disbelieving.

'If he'd been oxygen starved, then right now the doctors would be asking Peggy if she wanted them to turn life-support off.'

'Oh my God.' Kit unconsciously flung her hand to her mouth in horror.

'Exactly.'

Amy sat down on the nearest chair and tried not to let panic engulf her. This fear was ludicrous. Peggy was the one with the crisis not her. Running a café alone was nothing by comparison.

As she still hadn't sorted the float for the till, and the most popular tea break period for Richmond's shoppers crept up on her, Amy new, if this was to be done right, then positive action was called for. Speaking to herself firmly, she said, 'It's time to use that common sense of yours girl. Time to call in reinforcements and get the beverage machines brewing.'

Making a snap decision, she picked up her mobile and punched in Jack's number. 'Jack, it's Amy.'

'Hey, you fancy another walk?'

'Listen, Jack, this is an emergency. Do you know Pickwicks in Richmond?'

'Sure, that's Peggy's place.'

'You know Peggy?' Amy was momentarily confused, but

brushed the feeling aside.

'Sure. How do you know her?'

'There's no time for this conversation now. There's been an accident and her husband is in hospital. I'm in the café trying to keep things ticking over, but I haven't got a clue what I'm doing beyond the actual serving. Help! Will you come? Can Rob spare you for a few hours?'

'I'm already on my way.'

Grabbing his jacket, telling Rob what had happened as he moved, Jack ran from the shop with Rob yelling after him, 'I'll come too if it gets rough.'

Jogging along the busy pavement towards the station, Jack's brain yammered with questions. Pickwicks? Amy was at Pickwicks? *Did that mean that she knows Kit?* What's more, did that mean that Kit knew Amy? Christ!

Scott, though. Poor sod. Scott was a decent guy. He was fairly quiet, and Jack hadn't chatted to him as much as he'd have liked to since he'd finally decided to cross the threshold of Pickwicks. They'd always got on when they had talked, though, especially since they shared a love of music, and Jack knew that Peggy absolutely worshipped Scott.

He began to run faster.

The second he arrived Amy told him all she knew about the accident, and about how she'd offered to keep the café ticking over. Taking stock of the task ahead of them, Jack started by opening up the till with the keys Amy handed him. Arranging the remaining change, and making a note of the float, Jack got the financial side of things sorted with practised speed. There was no doubt they were going to do their best by Peggy. Now was not the time to be asking questions about Kit.

'You ready?' Jack asked ten minutes later. Amy nodded, looking far more confident than she felt, 'Then unbolt that door. Let's earn Peg and Scott some cash.'

The room was full of horrifying beeping equipment. Kit felt as if she'd strayed onto the set of *Casualty* or *ER*. The nurse had said she and Phil could only have five minutes with Scott, although obviously Peggy could stay as long as she liked.

Scott didn't look like Scott. His shock of tightly curling black hair was plastered back beneath a stark white bandage, which contrasted alarmingly with his dark skin. Somehow he seemed shorter than before; even though Kit knew for a fact he was over six feet tall. There were wires everywhere. A potassium-sodium mix drip pumped into his right arm to keep him hydrated, and his heartbeat shot lines across a monitor. His neck was in a brace, his body was stiff, and terrifyingly, he was tethered to a board.

'We don't want Mr McIntyre moving violently when he comes round,' the nurse explained gently. 'It looks awful, I know, but it's for the best.'

Peggy perched on the rigid plastic chair Phil had placed for her next to Scott's head. Laying a hand on his arm, she looked lost and frightened. Kit realised that she had probably sat in that exact position for most of the night, not knowing what to do, feeling totally helpless. No one knew what to say.

'Peggy,' Kit asked, 'do you want tea or anything?' Peggy shook her head, leaving Kit wondering why she'd asked if she wanted tea? Peggy always drank coffee. *How very English,* she thought ruefully, *always a cup of tea in a crisis.*

Kit and Phil had been sat in the waiting area for hours, surviving on lukewarm coffee from polystyrene cups, and damp, cling film-clad ham sandwiches. Peggy had been told that the consultant would be around to see Scott as soon as possible, but he still wasn't there. It was nearly half-past two, which meant that one of them would have to fetch the twins from school in an hour.

'I'll go if you like,' Phil said, 'if you'll be OK here. I don't think we should leave Peggy alone until Scott's parents arrive.'

'Nor me. Do you mind going?'

'Of course not. I hate the circumstances, but it'll be nice to see the kids a bit more.'

Kit squeezed Phil's hand, 'Thanks love. I'll call you if there's any news.'

146

Phil stood looking at his wife for a second, as if undecided about something. 'Kit?'

'Yes?'

'Do you want me to call Rob to sit with you, or Jack maybe?'

'No thanks love. I'll go in with Peggy. I'm sure that'll be OK if I don't get in the way.'

'OK, take care sweetheart.' Phil bent down, and kissed his wife.

'Sure. You too.'

Even though she'd told Phil she'd be fine alone, Kit had to admit to herself, as tears of fear for Scott and Peggy slipped down her cheeks, that she would have loved Jack to be there. One of his massive bear hugs would have been more than welcome right now. But this wasn't the place for a reunion. *Anyway,* Kit sighed out loud as she watched the nurses and porters scuttle around the corridors in a permanent hurry, *he was probably busy.* Again, she started to question if Peggy had known that her new waitress was Jack's Amy. *But then, why would she?*

Twenty-nine

October 24th 2006

As the last customers left, asking for their best wishes to be passed on to both Peggy and Scott, Amy felt high on achievement but utterly exhausted. Turning the open sign to closed, she lent her back against the locked door, gazing at the tables waiting to be cleared, and beyond to where Jack was cashing up.

'We did it.' Amy's speech was strangled with emotion.

All day she'd kept going, pushing herself, ignoring the reason why she was there without Peggy. As they'd worked, Jack had moved quietly amongst the tables, apologising to new customers for the diminished service, and assuring them it was merely a temporary state. He'd approached the regulars, as Amy pointed them out to him, tactfully explaining why Peggy was missing. Amy had heard them all talking in hushed tones. That was what it would be like until they came back. She wasn't ready to think about the possibility that they might not both return. That it could be just her keeping the place ticking over for not days, but weeks or months.

'You OK?' Jack raised his eyes from the till.

Amy nodded, but any words she might have uttered stuck in her throat.

'Come here.'

Amy almost ran across the room, and felt herself fit against Jack's shoulder as if she'd never been away. Tears of worry and fatigue streaked down her face, and her body heaved.

'When did you last eat?' Jack asked.

Amy didn't even have the energy to shrug. 'I'm not sure. I

think I grabbed a biscuit at lunch.'

'It's not surprising you're shaking. Sit down; I'll heat up some soup. There must be a bog-standard tin of Heinz around here somewhere.' Jack sat Amy on the nearest seat and headed into the kitchen.

Served up complete with hot toasted fingers, Amy had never tasted better tomato soup in her life. 'Thanks Jack. Not just for the soup, but for today, I'm not sure what I'd have done without you.'

'You'd have coped.'

Amy shook her head sadly, 'Not me, Jack. I hide. I don't cope, never have.'

'Well, you do now. You should be proud of yourself.' Jack leaned forward and kissed the top of her head. 'I'll help again tomorrow. We'll keep this place going.'

'Are you sure?' Amy looked up at him. 'What about your place, though? Won't Rob mind?'

'Of course he won't. Haven't you ever listened to "A Little Help From My Friends?"'

Amy laughed as Jack sang wildly off-key, and hugged him, 'That has got to be your corniest song link yet!'

Their cuddle was interrupted by a knock on the door.

Kit was there, staring through the glass, watching Jack holding the new waitress, stroking her perfect blonde hair. Amy. The last vestiges of doubt fell away.

Jack let go of his ex and unlocked the door, not sure of what to say. He stood open mouthed, just as Kit did in silent response.

Amy broke the spell. 'Hi, what news?'

'Oh, hello, Amy.' Without pausing Kit pressed forward, adopting the no-nonsense tone she used on her children, and marched towards the kitchen, 'Can I grab a coffee? I'm parched. I'll tell you everything while I help load the dishwasher.'

'Help would be great, thanks, I'll get them.' Amy would have smiled, but the grave expression on Kit's face, and her hostile mannerisms stopped her, 'This is my friend Jack. He's been great today. Really helped me keep the place going, I'd have been lost without him.'

Kit glared at Jack, 'Hello.'

He looked back at her, trying to keep his face neutral. 'Hello, Kit. I've missed you.'

'Yeah well, me too.' Kit gave him a non-committal glance and walked towards the sinks.

'Do you two know each other then?' Amy turned from Kit to Jack, the tension between them blatantly clear.

'Yes. *Very* well indeed.' Kit heaved a tray of plates towards the dishwasher's open door and started loading it up. Instantly regretting being childish in stressing the 'very', Kit sighed, 'I'll tell you about Scott.'

They formed a tray-and-stack crocodile from the kitchen to the café, working quickly and quietly as Kit made her report.

'Well, the good news is that he's out of the coma, and the doctors are as confident as it's possible for them to be, that he isn't going to die from his injuries.'

'Oh, thank God.' Amy spoke to herself as she poured some leftover lemonade down the sink.

'There is more uncertain news though.' Kit frowned at the dishwasher controls, trying to work out how to turn it on, 'I stayed with Peggy until Scott's parents arrived, which was at about the same time as the consultant, luckily. Peggy wanted me to stay to hear his prognosis.'

Amy and Jack put down what they were doing, their faces solemn as they concentrated on every word Kit said.

'In order to establish how far up the spinal cord Scott has sustained damage, and there *is* some damage, they need to do a CT scan, an MRI scan, and some spinal X-rays,'

'When?' Jack asked.

'About now, I think. As I understand it, the higher up the spine the damage, the more severe the problem; the scans will show how bad things are. Although the consultant did rule out quadriplegia, thank goodness.'

Jack muttered, 'Bloody hell.'

'Exactly, but nothing else can be ruled out. He's strapped to a spinal board. It's horrible.' For the first time since her arrival at the café, Kit's voice wobbled, showing the strain of the last few hours.

'Will he definitely be paralysed then?' Amy asked quietly.

'They won't say. If it's muscle damage alone, then no. If it isn't, we'll have to see.'

'How's Peg coping?' Jack studied Kit closely.

'She isn't. Scott's parents aren't too good either, as you'd expect, but at least they have each other. I promised Peggy I'd come and make sure this place was still standing.' Kit looked around her, trying to keep the unexpected acid of resentment at how well things had been taken care of out of her throat. 'Obviously it's in good hands.'

An uncomfortable hour later, Pickwicks was as clean and tidy as possible, and the dishwasher was humming through its last cycle. After some hunting around for the relevant phone numbers, the pastries and refills of juice for the following day were ordered, and a quiet calm descended over the customer free space.

'It seems strange, doesn't it, without Peggy.' Amy wasn't sure she should be the one to say so. Kit was evidently the 'official' friend of Peggy's present, but someone had to say something; the lack of conversation was getting to her.

'It does,' Kit managed a smile, 'it's so empty without her. I had no idea how much her mere presence filled this place.'

Jack turned to Kit, 'Do we open tomorrow?'

'We?'

'Yes. *We*. Rob doesn't need me at the shop. The Christmas trade is picking up, but it isn't a two handed job yet. So, I'll help.'

'Are you sure?' Kit wasn't. She'd planned to run Pickwicks on her own for a while.

'*Yes*,' Jack was emphatic, 'we could all do it? Perhaps get sandwiches back on the menu for lunch time?'

'That would be good,' Amy added, 'I could make them while you guys are serving. Loads of people asked for them today.'

Kit considered this briefly, before saying, 'No. You're the only one who can operate that bizarre coffee machine, I'll do the sandwiches, and you do the waitress bit.' She passed Amy a set of keys, before dismissing her with, 'Here at nine to do preparations, open at ten. Yes?'

'Definitely.'

'Good.' Kit suddenly registered how hard Amy must have worked to keep the place open all day, and added a belated, 'Thanks.'

'Oh, don't worry, this is for Peggy.' Amy said as she put on her coat, mentally adding *certainly not for you*.

As she walked out of the door, waving back at Jack, it struck Amy that Kit was probably the first person she'd ever spoken to who she couldn't get on with pretty much instantly. She wasn't even sure she liked her at all. Strange, because Peggy had said she was really nice. Amy began to walk faster, her yearning for a hot bubble bath and a takeaway spurring her towards home.

'She's very pretty.'

'Yes.'

'And kind.'

'Yes.'

'When did she get back in touch?'

'Last week.' Jack's feet fidgeted against the floor.

'She forgave you?'

'Obviously.'

'Go home, Jack. I'm too tired.'

'Goodnight, Kit. I'll see you tomorrow.'

Kit watched as, without looking back, Jack disappeared towards Richmond Station.

'I'm an ungrateful, bitter cow,' she said to the world in general, privately acknowledging that the nasty taste in her mouth was only partly to do with her fears for Scott.

153

Thirty

October 24th 2006

Amy jumped as she heard the knock on her front door. James and Sarah were both out at an early Hallowe'en party, and, anyway, no one ever knocked on their front door. Especially not after eight o'clock at night.

Fresh from her bath, wrapped in her baby blue towel, Amy called from the safety of the hall towards the unopened door. 'Who is it?'

'It's me, Jack. Can I come in?'

Amy instantly panicked as she fumbled with the door's catch. As she threw it open she was already asking, 'What's happened? Is it Scott?'

'No, I've not heard anything new. I need a word, if it's OK. I mean ... um ...' Jack looked over Amy's head into the vacant hallway, 'I'm not interrupting something am I?'

'What?' Amy was momentarily nonplussed, 'Oh, the towel. No, I've just had a bath that's all. I was in the middle of deciding if it is too early to flop out in pyjamas, or if I should be less sluttish and put my clothes back on.'

Jack winked as he entered the hall, 'Well, I think I prefer the towel, it's very you.'

Privately pleased with his remark, Amy shouted back at him as she ran upstairs, 'Idiot! I'll go and put my PJs on. Stick the kettle on, will you, it's through the archway there.'

'No problem.' Jack ambled through to the kitchen, listening to the sounds of Amy rushing about upstairs. She wouldn't be long. There'd be no frantic brushing of her hair or hurried application of lipstick or mascara. Jack smiled; she really hadn't changed much at all.

'You all right down there?' Amy called down only a minute after she'd disappeared into her room.

'I'm hunting down the coffee.' Jack was randomly opening and closing cupboard doors.

'Left corner cupboard, bottom shelf.'

Jack had found his quarry and was putting a teaspoon into the jar when it dawned on him that, but for a small nagging doubt and a heavy dose of commitment phobia all those years ago, this could be his daily life. Amy flapping about, not caring what she wore, throwing together weird mixtures of food for dinner, and failing to clean the stains out of their cups. Jack exhaled noisily, he knew he'd made the right decision, the flirting idea of Toby that entered his head with increasing regularity confirmed that, but even so, it would have been nice. It would have been…? He abruptly shook himself; there was no point in continuing with that line of thought. No point at all.

Jack poured the boiling water into their mugs as Amy's elephant-like footsteps hammered down the stairs. 'Cool pyjamas!'

Amy bounced into the kitchen in a red top and black fleece trousers, her heart pounding more than it would have been if Rob had come to visit, but not beyond hope. She wasn't stupid, but despite his preferences Amy accepted that it was bizarrely important to her that he noticed her a little bit.

She beamed at Jack, 'Hey, I had a thought in the bath. A song that sums things up for us now?'

'Really?'

'Yep. "Days", the Kirsty McColl version of course.'

'Of course!' Jack looked at her curiously. 'Which bit?'

'Oh, you know, the bits about remembering things forever. *Nice* things.'

'Thanks, Amy, that's very flattering.' Jack grinned at her as he ran the rest of the song through his head, and thought it was probably the bit about knowing that your lover was always going to abandon you that she really associated with him, not that she'd ever say so.

'Like I say, it came to me as I hid under the bubbles.' Amy

stared out of the window as she spoke, momentarily unsure if she should've shared her musical whim. 'So, to what do I owe the pleasure of your company?' Steering Jack through to the living room, Amy curled into the corner of one of the sofas as her ex sat on the other.

'I wanted to apologise for Kit's behaviour this afternoon.'

'That's not your job. Anyway, she's under a lot of pressure with Peggy and everything.'

'I thought perhaps I should explain.' Jack balanced his mug on a pile of magazines and crossed over to join Amy on her sofa. 'It wasn't just because of Scott. I've known Kit ages. I knew her after I knew you.'

'Ah.'

'Yes. Ah.'

'I wasn't the last girl then?' Amy realised she was disappointed, but then she reasoned, she should never have assumed she had been.

'No. You were the only one I loved though, if that helps?'

'It shouldn't,' Amy said as she snuggled into his side, 'but it does. Thank you.'

He put his arm around her, marvelling at how comfortable he felt. 'We were together for about six months, Kit and I. It was very much a convenience thing for me to tell the truth. I assumed it was for her. She said it was. I have recently had cause to find out that that wasn't in fact the case.'

'She was in love with you.'

'I had no idea. Until about three weeks ago.'

'What happened three weeks ago?'

'You came.'

Amy cradled her mug, 'What's my arrival got to do with anything?'

'I never told her about you.'

'Oh.' Amy looked puzzled. Her 'why not?' lay unspoken.

'You were then. You were special. I didn't discuss you with anyone, not even Rob.'

A happy glow fluttered inside Amy's chest. She had been special to him after all. 'I didn't talk about you either.'

Jack wasn't sure if he liked that. His inherent vanity had always been easily bruised. 'You've never told other boyfriends about me then?'

'What other boyfriends?' Amy moved away, her coffee in hand, and stood before him. 'There were no other men, Jack, there are no others.'

'Not one? In all that time?' Jack was openly shocked.

'Not one.'

'Why?'

Amy looked at Jack's crumpled brow and decided against answering that question in favour of asking one of her own, 'Why is Kit angry at me? It isn't my fault you loved me when you couldn't love her. If she'd met you first, and then me, it could easily have been the other way around, but it wasn't, and that's not my responsibility.'

'She isn't angry with you. She's angry with me and herself, so she says. Although I don't really get that bit.'

Amy laughed. 'Stick to men, Jack, you'll never get the hang of us girlies.'

He grinned as Amy sat back down next to, but no longer touching, him. 'I think that's the best advice I've had all day.'

'That's why you're here then, is it? To tell me that Kit hates me, but doesn't really hate me, because of something you and I had over a hundred years ago?'

'Yep.'

'Well, I guess it makes as much sense as anything else you've ever said to me.' Amy grabbed a handful of take away menus from off the table, 'So, I've been told. Your duty is done. Biscuit with your coffee, or shall we dial a pizza and watch a crap DVD?'

Glad of Amy's unquestioning acceptance, Jack relaxed into his seat, 'Pizza and a film.'

'Extra anchovies as usual?'

'Bloody hell, don't you forget anything.'

'Nothing. Not ever. Oh, and by the way,' Amy pointed towards the dining area as she reached for the phone, 'there's a copy of *The Bodyguard* on the bookshelf through there.'

Thirty-one

October 24th 2006

Phil came off the telephone and sank down next to his wife, making the sofa creak under his weight as he turned the television's sound down with the remote.

Kit cuddled up to his side as Phil slipped his arm behind her head. 'So?'

'Peggy sounds shattered. Her in-laws are taking her back to their place tonight for some mutual T.L.C.'

'Good. Best thing. And Scott?'

'No change. The results of the scan will be in tomorrow.'

Anxious, Kit said, 'I guess no change is good at this stage. No other news.'

'He's mumbling a bit, but not much. Peggy says he doesn't seem to remember anything about the accident, and he's so drugged his words are slurred. Mostly he sleeps.'

'I'm glad he can't remember.' Kit shuffled closer to Phil, her conscience pricking after her appalling behaviour in Pickwicks, 'Can I talk to you a minute?'

'You are.' Phil's eyes flickered towards the television.

'No. I mean about something else.'

'Sure, what's up?'

Kit wasn't absolutely sure if she should discuss this, but something drove her on. 'The waitress, Amy?'

'Yes?'

'Is she the girl you took to the house in Richmond?'

Phil frowned, 'You know she is.'

'She's really pretty isn't she, and kind.'

'Yeah, I suppose she is. Well, she seems friendly, Peggy's

lucky to have her just now.'

Kit closed her eyes as she spoke, 'She's Jack's ex.'

'Oh.' Phil felt a haze of gloom blanket the room.

'Yes.' Kit pulled out a cushion from behind her back and began to fiddle with its corners.

Not sure he was going to like where this conversation was heading, Phil growled, 'And?'

Kit felt more and more awkward, 'I will be working with her at Pickwicks. It feels odd.'

'Why odd?'

'Well, it's difficult to explain.' Kit swivelled out of her comfortable position to look at Phil properly, 'When I got back to the café today I was exhausted, and well, it's difficult to admit, but I expected to see the place in chaos. I hoped to if I'm honest. I didn't want her to be able to cope.'

'Because …?'

Kit got up and paced as she attempted to explain, exasperation at herself seeping into her voice, 'because I'm horrible, and well, I'm sort of, well … I'm jealous. It's nuts, I don't even know her.'

'Jealous. Oh, thank you very much!' Phil's face went dark.

Kit hurried on, holding her hands out beseechingly, 'No! Not like that. I wouldn't have Jack back for anything, you *know* that. Even if he woke up one morning straighter than a beanpole. We've been through that more times than I care to mention. I love you. It's just …'

Only the knowledge of his sleeping children upstairs made Phil hiss his response instead of shouting it. 'What? What is it? Tell me! For Christ's sake, Kit, you're a writer. *Find* the words, will you?'

Kit sat back down, scrunching her eyes shut again. She really hadn't banked on a fight, but the guilt that riddled at her made her desperate to confess. But confess to what exactly? She attempted to grapple her fractured concentration and tried again, 'Jack was there, at Pickwicks with Amy, running the café. They did a fantastic job. They did Peggy and Scott proud.'

Phil's voice sounded dangerously close to the edge. 'So,

that's good. The man obviously has a decent streak in him somewhere.'

'He's going to help tomorrow too.'

'Good. Peggy needs all the help she can get right now.'

'But I'm not ready to forgive him yet.' Kit pleaded, willing Phil to understand.

'Forgive him for what, exactly? For loving her more than you? Is that it? For Amy moving on when you can't?' Exasperation gripped Phil; this was bloody ridiculous, he thought they'd long gotten past all this Jack stuff.

'Both, I guess,' Kit lowered her eyes, she felt helpless and defeated. She really hadn't intended to upset Phil, and right now she hated herself more than anyone in the world.

'I can't help you with that.' Phil spoke remarkably coolly as he got up, 'Why can't you ever be happy with what you have. With what *we* have?' He headed for the door without looking back, leaving Kit sitting alone on the sofa, listening to the sickeningly empty echo that came after he slammed the front door.

Thirty-two

October 25th 2006

Walking slowly through the damp early morning air towards Pickwicks, Kit tried to focus on the day ahead. Not on the silent bed she had failed to sleep in last night. Not on the fact that Phil had left for work before anyone else had got up. Not on the reason why she was about to spend the day working with Jack and Amy.

It was already a quarter to nine when Kit reached Pickwicks. Pleased to find that she'd arrived first, Kit turned the key in the door, dealt with the burglar alarm as per Peggy's instructions, and headed for the kitchen.

She wasn't sure how any of this had happened. For years she hadn't let Jack know how she'd felt. No one had known, and that had been fine. And now it was out, and her life felt like it had been tilted on its axis. All because of ... what? Amy? The tape? Or was it all bound to have exploded at some point anyway?

Picking up her mobile, Kit typed in Phil's number, and then hung up. What was the point; she had no idea what to say? She'd explained herself so badly last night. All she'd wanted to do was share her confusion with him; include him in her thinking. To admit her faults. To tell Phil how rocked her confidence felt.

She hadn't imagined Phil would take it personally. None of this was a reflection on him. The gut-wrenching terror that had consumed her all night began to rise again. How on earth could she sort this? What if he'd had enough of her illogical neurosis and left her? What about the twins? Kit's galloping thoughts were interrupted by opening of the café door. Amy had arrived.

As she walked to work Amy had resolved to try extra hard to get on with Kit. She was under pressure, worried about Scott, and was evidently having her own personal crisis Jack-wise. If she was involved in creating that, then Amy was sorry, but it wasn't her fault. Amy was determined to prove to Kit that she was a nice person.

As she approached the café door Amy noticed that the kitchen light was already on. Kit must be here. 'Here we go,' Amy mumbled into her scarf as she crossed the café's threshold.

Stepping off the train, Jack reflected on the evening he'd shared with Amy. They'd overindulged on spicy chicken pizza with anchovies, drunk too much wine and watched *The Bodyguard,* laughing and groaning at its sheer corniness in turn. It had been so comfortable; he'd been reminded of the apt, but wholly unflattering, 'pair of old slippers' metaphor. Now it was morning. Time to work with Kit and Amy in the same space. He desperately hoped that it would be frantically busy, so that they wouldn't have time to talk to each other. The last thing Jack wanted was for Kit to find out about their cosy night in. There was nothing wrong with it, but he didn't think Kit knowing about it would help right now.

Although the initial greetings between herself, Amy, and Jack had been rather stilted, Kit had to admit that the day was going well. Morning coffee had come and gone without a hitch, and now the last lunchtime customers were tucking into her sandwiches. Amy was wiping over the tables as each one emptied, and Jack was charming the customers at the till. Kit had barely had time to think, which she considered, was probably a good thing.

Jack encroached on her thoughts. 'Is this a good time to call the hospital?'

'Could be, I'll give them a try.' A new wave of guilt washed over Kit. She'd been so consumed with feeling bad about upsetting Phil, that she'd almost forgotten why she had been making sandwiches in the first place.

The phone rang for ages before it was answered. The nurse sounded even sleepier than Kit as she reported that there is no change in Mr McIntyre's condition. Kit bit back her frustration. She wanted proper news.

'Would you tell Mrs McIntyre that Mrs Lambert will be in to see them both later?'

'Of course, I'm heading that way soon anyway.'

'Thank you nurse.' Kit hung up, and went back into the now much quieter café.

'What news?' Amy paused in her labours.

'Nothing really. He's the same.'

Amy felt awkward, not sure what to say. It all sounded like platitudes, but the gap in conversation made her speak anyway. 'Well, that's good, isn't it? Better than being worse.'

'I'm going to head to the hospital later. I'm sure Peggy could do with some company.' Kit spoke quietly, her eyes cast to the floor.

Jack came over and took hold of Kit's hands as they hung limply at her sides. 'What else is up? Apart from Scott.'

'Else?' Kit rubbed her forehead, 'Well, I've got a splitting headache for a start.'

'I'm not surprised. You've probably got severe caffeine withdrawal. Comes from serving it, and not drinking it,' Jack poured her a mug brimming with coffee, 'but I didn't mean that. You've hardly said a word all day.'

Jack gestured to Amy to see if she would deal with two customers that had were steering laden shopping bags towards a table, and lead Kit back into the privacy of the kitchen. 'This is silly, Kit. Let's call a truce. You and I have a great friendship. Why are you so determined to ruin it?'

'Me? You're the one. Why didn't you tell me about her?' Kit pointed an accusing finger towards the main café.

'Oh for God's sake! Change the bloody record. I told you,' Jack's expression reminded Kit of Phil when he was trying to keep his temper, 'Amy was the past. My business. My guilt.

165

Something that I have to deal with. And I *will* deal with it. On my own.'

After a brief pause Kit spoke, so quietly that Jack had to strain to hear her. 'I tried to explain how I felt to Phil last night, about all this.'

'And?'

Kit stared at the floor, shame filling her, 'I didn't put things very well and he stormed out.'

'What!' Jack couldn't believe it. Phil was such a level-headed guy.

'He came back about midnight and slept on the sofa. When I got up this morning, he'd already gone out.'

'What on earth did you say to him?'

'I'm not that sure anymore. I think I told him I was jealous of Amy.'

'Well, I think we've established that. Why did that upset Phil?'

'He got it into his head that I'm in love with you.' Kit mumbled the words, unable to meet Jack's gaze.

Jack spoke cautiously. 'But you're not. Are you?'

'No. Not anymore. But I was, years ago, and lately, well, all this forever-suppressed stuff is coming out, and it seems to be preventing me from thinking straight.'

'Bloody hell, Kit, you're such an idiot.'

'I know.' Kit thumped down on the stool next to the sink. 'Jack?'

'Yes, honey?'

'I do love Phil. I love you too though, but not like I did.'

'I know that.' Jack held her quivering body as Kit dissolved into the tears she'd held back all day.

Through her sobs, Kit said, 'And I feel so guilty about being so self-centred when Scott is lying in that hospital bed.'

Amy came into the kitchen to ask for two toasted teacakes, but Jack put his finger to his lips. Instantly understanding, Amy quietly retreated, politely telling the customers in question that there was a small problem with the toaster. Perhaps they would like some fruit cake instead?

166

'Kit,' Jack eventually prised her away from his shoulder, 'we're here for Peg.'

'I know. I shouldn't be doing this. I should be thinking about Scott.'

Jack passed her a tissue. 'Why don't you head off to the hospital now? Peggy will be pleased to see you, and it'll put your own problems into perspective.'

'Can you guys cope here?'

'Of course we can. Go on. Go and tell them that Pickwicks is still standing.' Without waiting for Kit to reply, Jack left her alone, while he told Amy that they would be two handed for the remainder of the afternoon.

'Give them our love, won't you.' Amy called out a few moments later, as Kit pulled off her borrowed apron and grabbed her coat.

'Of course,' Kit headed to the door, turning as she got there, 'and thank you. Both of you. See you tomorrow?'

'Definitely,' Amy smiled. Perhaps Kit wasn't so bad. Tomorrow she'd try and find five minutes to talk to her properly. Maybe she'd ask her about her writing? Peggy said she wrote really good stuff.

Thirty-three

October 25th 2006

Jack carried the last tray of dirty cups and saucers into the kitchen, and passed them to Amy, who stacked them in the dishwasher.

'Have you got the number for Home Hunters on you?'

'Sure. What do you want it for?' Amy stood up and punched the washing up machine into life.

'Kit's husband, Phil. I want to talk to him.'

Amy dried her hands across her apron and fetched her bag. 'It's in here somewhere.' Rifling through the entire contents of her bag, she eventually found the business card she was looking for squashed next to a half-eaten packet of mints, crumpled and inexplicably damp. 'Here you go.'

'Thanks.' Jack flicked the card between his fingers, 'I may be about to help Kit out.'

'Or?'

'I may be about to drop her even further into the shit.'

'Ah.' Amy regarded him, a smile playing at the corners of her mouth.

He beamed back at her, 'You aren't going to tell me to keep my nose out are you?'

'Nope. But if you need someone to bandage your soon-to-be-broken nose, then come round later.'

Jack laughed as he hung up the last tea towel of the day and checked he'd secured the takings correctly. 'I may well do that.'

Phil hadn't sounded too thrilled with the prospect of meeting up after work, but then why would he be? Jack tapped the coaster his coffee should have been stood on against the edge of the

169

table; he knew his charm wasn't going to work this time, but he had to say something. He owed it to Kit. She'd bailed him out enough times over the years.

When Phil eventually appeared, twenty minutes late, Jack was reading an ancient Sunday supplement that someone had left on the table.

'Sorry; last-minute call I couldn't ignore.' Phil sat down, keeping his coat on in a clear, "I'm not hanging around" gesture.

Noting the unspoken statement, Jack asked, 'Drink?'

'No. What do you want, Jack?'

Jack put his own mug down with a thump, 'What I don't want is my best friend and the man she loves, i.e. *you*, to be arguing because once upon a time I screwed up.'

'You really are an arrogant bastard. What gives you the right to …?'

'Nothing gives me the right. Not a thing,' Jack raised his voice over Phil's cracking temper, 'except that I know that Kit loves you and the twins more than anything.'

'More than you?' Phil accused sharply.

'Christ, yes!' Jack snorted, 'Don't get infected by her insanity, Phil. This is all a confidence thing, or lack of it. None of it is about how she feels about you. I don't really think it's about me either.'

'Then what the hell is it about?'

'Her. Everything around Kit seems changed to her. She thought she understood and accepted her past, Amy turns up and she begins to question it all. Not us, but herself. *Her* role in her own life.'

'That's all bollocks, Jack.'

'No it isn't. You know it isn't.' Jack got up from his seat, 'I'm going to get you some tea, now sit down for a minute and think about it.'

When Jack returned with his pot of tea, Phil inclined his head in thanks, but stayed silent. What Jack had said made no sense, but he had a nagging feeling that it was at least partially true.

Eventually, as he poured out his tea, Phil spoke, 'One of the things I first loved about Kit was that she was the most illogical woman I'd ever met.'

'Sounds about right.' Jack couldn't help but smile as Phil continued.

'When we first got together, she said I'd saved her from a road to nowhere.'

Jack knew that that had been a long ago reference to his relationship with Kit, but simply said, 'Talking Heads'

'Sorry?'

'Kit loved that song, "Road to Nowhere", it was by Talking Heads.'

'Ah, yes. You and your lyrics.' Phil sipped his tea, 'I made Kit a CD, you know. Thought it might help. I expect she told you.'

'No. She hasn't told me much lately. I bet she loved it.'

'She did.' Phil's eyes twinkled as he recalled their wonderful evening together.

Sensing that he was beginning to win the argument, Jack pushed further, 'You don't want to give up on all that do you?'

'Of course I don't.' Phil heaved a sigh as he put his cup down.

'Phil?'

'Yes?'

'As I'm here, putting my life on the line by speaking out of turn, tell me, when are you going to give up the business?'

'What?' Phil was surprised by the sudden change of subject.

'You're bored.'

'How the hell do you know that?'

'That was something Kit did tell me.'

Phil studied the table, concentrating on the tan liquid shimmering in his mug, 'I didn't think she'd noticed.'

Jack sat up decisively, 'It's time you two had a proper talk to each other. Is Kit going back to the hospital tonight?'

'I don't know.'

'How about I babysit and you go out for dinner? Actually spend some time together as Kit and Phil, and not Mum and

Dad.'

'You?' Phil was unable to keep the shock out of his voice.

'Yes, me.' Jack was affronted, 'I have a niece and nephew about the same age as your two, I do know the drill. Anyway, I'm their godfather. I should spend more time with them.'

'I'm not sure, Jack …'

'Look, Phil,' Jack put down his empty mug, 'call my mobile if you want. It's a genuine offer. If not tonight, one night very soon.'

'OK. Thanks. It'll depend on Kit, and on Peggy of course.'

Jack pulled his jacket back on as he asked, 'Heard anything new about Scott today?'

'Not a thing. Each time I dialled the hospital the line was engaged. I'll ask Kit when I get home.'

'You are going home then?'

'Of course I am.'

'Good.

Phil added, only semi-grudgingly, 'Thanks, Jack.'

'Any time.'

Phil pushed his chair back to go. 'I still think you're a shifty bastard though.'

Feeling as if they'd called a truce after years of uncertainty, Jack laughed as Phil downed the remains of his tea, 'Oh I am, Phil. I am.'

Thirty-four

October 25th 2006

Kit looked guiltily at the takeaway boxes slowly heating in the oven. Since she'd been so mixed-up over Jack, as well as working all day at Pickwicks, she hadn't cooked much at home beyond the twins' beloved fish fingers and potato waffles for quite some time.

Glancing at her watch, Kit stood at the kitchen window watching for Phil. It was nearly eight o'clock already. Where was he? Surely he'd come home tonight? The twins had already had their bedtime stories and were tucked up for the night. Kit had told them that Daddy had a late meeting and that he'd see them in the morning. She hoped that was true.

The fresh notebook, with her novel in progress safely scribbled inside, sat by the kettle. Picking it up, Kit thumbed through the pages. Re-reading snatches of her work she felt a rush of satisfaction. Kit knew what she'd written was good, and she badly wanted to get back to it. Sitting at the kitchen table, Kit took up a pen and began to write.

... the influence he seemed to have over her was almost frightening. There was no real reason why she hung around. Yet something tangible, but beyond her grasp, made her need to be near him, despite everything he'd put her through ...

Unobserved, Phil watched his wife for a minute; her head bent to her notebook, her hand moving swiftly across the page, studied concentration on her face.

'Hello, love. I bought Chinese.'

Kit jumped, and stood up quickly, uncertain. She pointed to the pizza in the oven.

Phil laughed. 'Well, that's a taste combination worth trying. Come on, woman, get some wine out of the fridge!'

'Phil?' Kit felt confused. She hadn't heard from him all day. She'd expected him to shout, or worse, continue his frosty silence.

'It's OK.' He crossed the room and took her in his arms, 'I've been talking, walking, and thinking. I'm sorry I got so cross. Hurt pride, I'm afraid.'

'You had every right to be cross. I messed up my explanations so badly. I'm sorry, Phil. I love you.'

'I know you do, and I love you too.' Phil took off his raincoat. 'Now, let's stop being soppy. I'm starving. Tell me how Scott and Peggy are today while I serve up this lot.'

By the time they'd discussed the lack of change in Scott, Kit had apologised several more times, and Phil had told her it was all over and to forget about it, they'd demolished the pizza and a good two-thirds of the chicken chow mein. Phil pushed back his plate. 'I'm stuffed.'

'Me too.' Kit agreed as she scooped up a further forkful of food.

'I saw Jack today.'

Kit hadn't expected that, and almost choked on her mouthful of noodles. 'You did? When? He was at the café all day.'

'He called me after work. We went to Costa.'

'But you hate Jack!' Her mouth had dropped open, displaying her semi-masticated food, and Kit closed it hastily.

'No, I don't; I'm wary of Jack, but he knows that.'

Kit felt the relaxed dinner they'd just shared revolve in her stomach as her insides went into a spin cycle. *What on earth had Jack said that had calmed Phil right down?* 'So?'

'He offered to babysit the kids so that you and I could talk.'

'*Jack* did?'

'That was more or less my reaction.' Phil put his hand over Kit's, and cupped it gently, 'I think it's a good idea.'

'You do?'

174

'Yes. We have things to talk about. Like, how come you can suddenly write at home, without a mug of coffee by your side?'

'Blimey, so I did. I didn't think about it. I just wrote,' Kit smiled, 'I guess Pickwicks feels more like a working stop than a coffee stop at the moment.'

Phil sounded decisive, 'I'm going to ask Jack if he'll look after the kids on Saturday night. OK?'

'OK.'

'As he said himself, it's about time he proved to me he is worthy of the role of godfather.' Phil began to collect up the empty food cartons. 'Anyway, I've got something I want to talk to you about, properly, without child-induced distractions.'

'Me too.'

'Anything I should worry about?'

'Absolutely not. Me?'

Phil shook his head, 'Not a thing. I'm going to give Peggy one last call before bed.'

'Then, can we listen to our new CD again?' Kit fluttered her eyelids coquettishly at her husband, and the tension she'd felt at the mention of Jack slipped away.

As Amy was about to settle down in front of television for an evening of mindless nothing, the front door bell rang. She smiled; she'd been half expecting him.

'Oh, rats, you're dressed.' Jack was leaning against the door frame, a burger box in one hand, and a bag full of beer cans in the other.'

'Sorry, Jack, I thought you might pop round, and I didn't want to inflict my PJs on you again.'

'Idiot. You look great in your night-time gear. Do you remember those blue stripy ones you had?' He gestured with his full bag of cans. 'Beer?'

Amy decided against commenting about her student pyjamas, and took a tin as they headed to the living room.

'Where are your room-mates tonight then?' Jack flopped down onto the sofa and tucked into his dinner. 'I'm beginning to think that they don't exist.' He waved his takeaway at her,

'You don't mind, do you? I've not been home yet, and I'm starving.'

'They're out clubbing or something, not my thing anymore I'm afraid.' Amy waved towards the mayonnaise-dripping burger. 'I'll get you a plate for that, after all, it isn't my sofa.'

'Fair enough, thanks.'

'So,' Amy called through from the kitchen where she grabbed a glass for herself, a plate, and handful of mopping up kitchen roll for Jack, 'I see your nose is intact, Phil didn't punch you then?'

'Nope. It went well, even if I do say so myself. At least, I think it did. It's up to him and Kit now.'

'Why did you feel you had to talk to him anyway?'

'I owe Kit. She has stood by me through countless relationship, or, more specifically, *non-relationship* nightmares. I thought it high time I tried to help her.' Jack brushed some crumbs off his lap, changing the subject. 'How's the job-hunting?'

'What job-hunting? I can't possibly leave Peggy in the lurch. I'll start the search again once she can come back to work.'

'That's lovely of you, sweetheart, but how will you support yourself? Peggy probably won't be able to pay you for more than your usual hours, you know.'

Amy felt a bit deflated. She'd been so busy getting on with things that she hadn't considered the financial implications of what had happened. 'Well, I guess I'll have to spend a bit more of my savings than I planned.'

'You don't have to. I can help Kit, and you can get a new career.'

'But you two aren't being paid at all.'

'I don't need it, and Kit is making money from stories she's already written. Anyway, I know they don't flaunt it, but Phil earns a packet.' Jack wiped his mouth on a piece of paper towel, and put his arm around Amy. 'What do you want to do then, when you grow up?'

Amy rested comfortably against him. 'No idea. But I'll tell you this, Jack Brown, I've spent the past decade or so trying to

176

prevent companies going under, there is no way on earth I am letting Pickwicks sink. It's too special.'

He suddenly engulfed her in a bear hug. 'I'm glad you came south, Amy. And that is something I didn't think I'd say. It's a special girl that can stop me clubbing with my mates.'

Amy felt a glow spread through her. Not only had Jack remembered her pyjamas, he was here, with her, when he could have gone out on the town. Totally ignoring the distant alarm bell that began to ring at the back of her head she said, 'I'm glad too. Now, what crap shall we watch on the TV?'

'Anything you want.' Jack rearranged a cushion behind his back and settled himself into his seat, 'Shall we go out tomorrow, a film perhaps?'

Amy's grin spread across her face until it lit her eyes. 'Why not?'

Thirty-five

October 26th 2006

'Amy!' Jack called over to the front door where Amy was locking up after another busy day at Pickwicks.

'You bellowed?' Amy took her cloth from her apron pocket and headed to the nearest table.

Busy cashing up the till, Jack didn't look up as he spoke, 'I'm sorry, but I've just had a call from a mate. He's not well. Nothing like as bad as Scott, probably flu or something, but, well ... can we postpone our cinema trip tonight? I feel I ought to go and see him. Do you mind?'

'No, of course not. We'll do it another time.'

Jack smiled, 'Thanks Amy, you're a star.'

Kit came through from the kitchen and collapsed onto her normal chair in the corner of the room. She was exhausted. It was not just lack of caffeine and unaccustomed hard physical work that made her shake, but a reaction to the phone call she'd just received from Peggy.

Amy, immediately understanding that Kit had news, dropped her cloth, sat on the chair opposite her, and waited.

'He's not permanently paralysed.' Tears of relief prickled at the corners of Kit's eyes.

Amy almost reached out to grab Kit's hand, but thought better of it, and simply said, 'That's brilliant, more than brilliant, it's ...'

'There's a long way to go,' Kit abruptly wiped her eyes on a napkin. 'The muscles in Scott's lower back have been very badly strained and bruised. It is going to take a *very* long time and an awful lot of physiotherapy before he's walking freely again. He might always need a stick.'

'Peggy must be over the moon.'

'She is! She was almost laughing. Nearly her old self, if you ignore the lack of food, sleep, and the terror of living through the past few days.'

'At least she doesn't have to worry about this place.' Amy examined the almost clean café.

'I don't think you can stop her doing that. Not unless you put your career plans even further on hold, and I don't think Peggy would forgive you if you did that.'

'Well, that's rich. When was the last time you wrote something in here?'

Kit shrugged ruefully. 'OK, it's been a while.' After a brief pause, she went on. 'In fact, between you and me, I think I've screwed up the contract I had with the web site I write for.'

Amy was horrified, 'Oh no! Kit, why didn't you say? I could have managed here with Jack.'

'You won't tell Peggy, will you?' Kit hurriedly added, 'I don't want her to feel guilty. Anyway, I think it's for the best. I love writing erotica. And I will definitely go back to it, but there's only so much smut you can write without running out of original ways of describing an erection.'

'Erotica! You're kidding me!' Amy was stunned. 'I assumed you wrote kid's stuff.'

'What? Cuddly lambs gallivanting around a sunny farmyard going baa? Not me!' Kit laughed at Amy's shocked expression, 'I thought you knew! Didn't Jack tell you?'

'Not a word. No wonder Peggy likes your stuff.' Amy was suddenly rather coy. 'Can I read some?'

Now it was Kit's turn to be surprised, 'You?'

'Yeah. I love that stuff, providing it's not cruel. I have some of the Xcite collections knocking about, but recently I've started to read some stuff on a website I subscribe to.'

Kit felt a smile crease her lips. 'You're kidding me! Which one?'

'I like Katrina Island's stuff on *Pearls*, do you know it?'

Kit burst out laughing. 'Know it? That's me! *I'm* Katrina,

180

and I write for *Pearls*!'

'No way!' Amy's mouth dropped open.

'And to think I had you down as a good girl.'

Recovering herself, Amy giggled, 'Come off it! I've been out with Jack too, you know.'

Kit regarded the waitress more seriously for a second. 'I owe you an apology.'

'What for? Secretly boosting my erotic fantasies for the past twelve months?'

'No!' Kit's smile faded as she confessed, 'I was jealous. Not of you, exactly, but of what you had with Jack, and of how well you've handled it all.'

'You have *got* to be joking!' Amy looked at Kit in disbelief. 'Handled it! He dumped me and I ran away. For over a decade! I'm not sure that counts as a true qualification of handling it, do you?'

Kit's mouth dropped open, 'That's why you went to live in Scotland?'

'Yes.'

'I assumed you'd gone up there because of your job. God, that boy has a lot to answer for.' Kit crunched up the damp paper napkin she was holding.

'You are telling me.'

Kit was thoughtful as she continued, 'Shame isn't it.'

'That we both loved him, you mean?'

'Bloody tragic.' They both shook their heads ruefully at each other, before bursting into fits of teenage-style giggles.

By the time Jack had come back from paying in the takings at the local bank, the two girls had made decent headway into a bottle of Peggy's house white.

'Anything I can get you girls? Cushions? A servant to waft you with a fan? A three-course meal while I juggle the other jobs left to do in here tonight?'

'Shut up, Jack, and sit down.' Amy toasted him with her glass as she spoke.

Jack, puzzled at the new-found solidarity before him,

181

shrugged his shoulders, took a glass from the counter, and joined them. 'So, what are we drinking to?'

'Scott.' Kit hurriedly filled Jack in on her telephone call.

'Can he come home soon then?'

'It'll be a little while yet, and there'll be a fairly lengthy gap between coming out of hospital and walking unaided, but at least the ultimate prognosis is good.'

Jack looked from Kit to Amy, 'There's something else.'

'A truce,' Amy gestured towards her fellow female, 'Kit and I have had a chat'

'Which is going to become an extended chat once you have buggered off,' Kit added.

'Exactly,' Amy nodded, failing to suppress a giggle as the wine had an effect on her food-deprived body.

'Oh.' Jack didn't know what else to say, as both girls dissolved into another fit of giggling camaraderie. 'I think I'd better get going then.'

'Night, Jack,' the girls chorused after Jack as he left them to their alcohol and the remaining tidying-up.

After they'd emptied the bottle of wine and cleared the tables, Amy suggested a meal might be a good idea before they both collapsed. Kit sent a text to Phil, getting the all-clear for a girlie night out, and they headed into Richmond.

As they stood in the chilled evening air, which hung thick with the aroma of bonfires and early fireworks, surrounded on all sides by Indian restaurants, Amy suggested, 'Indian food then?'

'Great.' Kit gestured around her, 'The closest one?'

'Definitely.'

Thirty-six

October 26th 2006

They had started to make serious inroads into their complimentary poppadoms before Kit launched into conversation. Emboldened by the wine whizzing about her system, she said, 'You go first. I want the *real* story of your time with Jack. See if it matches up with the version he told me!'

Amy gulped, 'Are you sure?'

'Sure.'

'Only, if you promise to tell me your story straight afterwards.'

'It's a deal, but I should warn you, it's not a pretty tale.'

Amy waved a piece of mango chutney-smeared naan bread around absentmindedly, 'This is Jack; I didn't think it would be.'

Listening to Amy as she told her all about her past, and her renewed, relationship with Jack, warning bells rang loudly in Kit's ears. 'But how can you stand it? If he's been there, just like he used to be, cosy on your sofa, sharing pizza or whatever? I mean, at the end of the day, he'll go off clubbing to find a bloke to screw, and you'll be left on your own.'

Amy felt defensive, but didn't say anything as Kit continued. 'You know what I mean; you're in danger of allowing yourself to live in the past; a fantasy of what life might have been like if he'd treated you better, if you hadn't done a bunk, if he hadn't come out ...'

Amy wiped a finger around the edge of her plate, sucking up the stray sauce. 'I know. But it's worth it.'

'You must really love him.'

'He's my friend.'

'And?'

'And I want him to be happy.' Amy flapped open her napkin as she worked out how to explain it to Kit. 'When I got his tape and read his letter, I genuinely hoped Jack was all right. That he was happy and settled. Part of a couple, I suppose. Content with his life.'

'But?'

'But when I got here and saw him, I couldn't believe how relieved I was that he was single. I wasn't ready to share him I suppose.'

'Perhaps that's understandable, after all those years.' Kit picked up her glass, 'And now you have met him again, how are you going to feel when he finds someone else's sofa to sit on?'

'I'll be sad, but not jealous.'

'Come off it.'

Amy relented, 'OK, maybe a tad jealous, but I won't stand in his way. I might like his future bloke.'

'You can be too nice you know.'

'Don't you start!'

Kit was confused, 'What?'

'It doesn't matter.' Amy re-filled her glass, 'Anyway, I could find someone first.'

Kit sat up; she loved a good bit of matchmaking. 'Really? And where do you go looking?'

'Well, nowhere yet. Maybe someone will come into work.'

Kit regarded Amy as if she was insane. 'Pickwicks isn't going to find you anyone single and under sixty. When was the last time you saw an unaccompanied male in there who wasn't a pensioner?'

'Well, OK, never, but it might happen.'

'Oh, stop it!' Kit clattered down her fork decisively. 'You need to spend less time with Jack, and more time on the pull. Trust me; I know what I'm talking about.'

Amy was emphatic, 'I do *not* go on the pull. Never have.'

'It's time you started.'

'It isn't … is it?' Amy wasn't so sure.

'It is.' Kit didn't sound unsure at all.

They munched happily for a while, talking about nothing and everything, until Amy asked, 'When you were together, did you have any idea? I mean, could you see he was gay?'

Kit studied Amy so closely that she blushed and instantly began to backtrack, 'Sorry, that was a very personal question, forget it.'

'No, no, it's fine; I was wondering how to explain.' Kit scooped up some korma from the central balti bowl, and tapped it off with a satisfying splodge onto her plate, 'I think I sort of knew, in a way. I certainly always assumed he was bisexual, but as he never said anything. I assumed he was happy enough with a woman. Let's face it, you don't really think about your bloke going off with another man while you're in the middle of a relationship with him do you?'

'I guess not. You did think he might be bi though?'

'It was the sex he liked. Very bi-oriented, I'm sure I don't have to paint you a picture.'

Amy blushed a more vivid shade of pink, 'No, I get it.'

Feeling awkward, Kit asked, 'You had no idea then?'

'No. None at all. Naïve I guess, especially in the light of the bedtime preferences you've alluded to. I thought he was more interesting and had more imagination than my past boyfriends, nothing more than that. God, I was such a bloody innocent.'

Kit felt the heaviness of Amy's struggle to understand her own actions, 'You were only young.'

Curiosity keeping her on the theme, yet wanting to move off her own role in the situation, Amy asked, 'What was Jack like, you know, when he first came out?'

Kit put her glass down carefully, 'Much the same really, that's why I found it so tough I guess. Although,' she smiled broadly as she remembered, 'his clothes went temporarily nuts.'

'How d'you mean? Not tight T-shirts surely?'

'Oh yes, tight and white.'

'No way!' Amy clapped her hands with glee.

'With pale jeans and, wait for it … a short-waisted, black leather jacket.'

'Please tell me it didn't have studs!'

'No studs, thank God.' Kit began to laugh at the mental image they were creating.

Amy sighed in mock relief. 'Thank God! Mind you, doesn't sound like he was leaving anyone in any doubt.'

'None whatsoever.' Kit felt strangely satisfied as she shared it all with Amy.

'How long did that fashion crisis phase last then?'

'Six, maybe eight months. It was like he went mad. A new sweet in the sweetie shop, and he made damn sure he advertised so everyone knew where they could get a taste.'

Amy's eyes lowered to the table, and she spoke more quietly, 'He was popular with the lads straight away then?'

'What do you think?'

'Of course, he would be.' The bounce temporarily gone from her voice; Amy contained a sigh.

'And don't forget, it's a different world, it's smaller.' Kit didn't notice Amy's disquiet as she expounded a much-considered theory, 'It sometimes seems to me, at least from the outside, that liaisons in the gay world are much more interchangeable. There's a smaller pool from which to fish, so it's more acceptable for partners to swap and change within a group of friends or associates. Of course, I could be totally wrong about that.'

'If you're right, then that must be very hard sometimes.'

'Bet Jack was hard all the fucking time.'

'Kit!' Amy almost chocked on her mouthful of rice.

'Anyway, enough of Jack.' Kit looked determined, 'Tell me, what would your ideal bloke be like? What was your last boyfriend like?'

Amy wriggled uncomfortably in her seat. 'Jack.'

'Jack?'

'Uh-huh.'

'You've been thinking about Jack for the last thirteen years?'

'Certainly not! I haven't been thinking of anything, really, not until I got down here. I sort of shut down.'

'Bloody hell!' They lapsed into silence for a moment, before Kit peered at Amy's face across the table, making her feel uncomfortable, 'Hang on a second.'

'Have I got curry on my face or something?' Amy lifted her hand to wipe whatever it was away.

'No. I just noticed.' Delight spread across Kit's face. 'You're not wearing any make-up.'

'Well, no, but then, neither are you.'

'Exactly! And here I was beginning to think that I was a freak for not using that stuff when everyone else does, and you don't use it either!'

Amy laughed, aware that Kit was more under the influence of the wine than she'd realised. 'We're probably both freaks, but so what? Why do women all have to look the same anyway?'

'Exactly!' Kit said again, bringing her hand down slightly too hard on the table, causing the waiters to glance their way.

Amy, realising she'd found a comrade, added, 'I hate the way cosmetics make me feel. It's like wearing a mask, like hiding all the time. I do enough hiding as it is.'

'And more to the point,' Kit added, 'where do ...'

Amy joined in, chuckling as they simultaneously said, '... *they find the time to put it on*?!'

Kit topped up her wine glass again, 'I never have a minute to myself when I'm not either working or house-working. When would I find a spare twenty minutes or more to play with slap?'

'No idea! I wouldn't know what to do with most of it anyway. I mean, what the hell does it all do? If my lack of make-up puts people off me, then sod them!'

'I couldn't agree more. Although ...' Kit's voice faltered as she spoke, 'as time goes on I wonder, if perhaps, I should start to use it. Every day I seem to look older.'

'Don't be ridiculous!' Kit was quite taken aback by the uncompromising tone of Amy's voice, 'You're lovely. You have good skin, no wrinkles and beautiful eyes. In fact I think you've probably got all those things because you've never smeared your face in stuff.'

Kit raised her glass, 'You, Amy Crane, are a real find. Thank you.' More content than she had felt in weeks, she put down her fork, 'That was gorgeous.'

'Sure was.'

Knocking back the remains of her wine, Kit said, 'Jack told me we were similar, you and I.'

'Did he?' Amy tucked her hair from around her face to behind her ears.

'I wasn't really in the mood to hear it then, but I am beginning to see that he was right.'

'Well, even Jack has to be right sometimes; law of averages and all that!' Amy laughed into her own glass. 'And what about the music thing? He obviously did that to you as well.'

'It was cute at the start, but to be honest, it's recently begun to get on my nerves.'

Amy nodded. 'I know what you mean. I don't mind it mostly, and sometimes it's nice, especially if he comes up with a flattering lyric, but it can be very annoying.'

'I guess it is part of what makes Jack Jack.'

'I didn't think he'd be so much like he was before.' Amy played with the pilau rice spoon as she talked, 'It's like he hasn't changed at all, and yet so much has happened.'

'Even though that made no sense, I completely agree,' Kit fiddled with the handle of the balti bowl, 'I'm not sure he'll even grow up. He's the Peter Pan of Mortlake.'

Amy sniggered. 'I'm not sure he'd like the Cliff Richard comparison.'

Kit grinned back at her. 'I doubt if Cliff would be too impressed either!'

Dipping her fingers in the water bowl provided as the waiter cleared the last of their plates away, Kit felt happy. 'Thanks, Amy.'

'What for?'

'The company. I can't remember the last time I went out for

a meal with another female. Must have been when I was at college.'

'Don't you ever go out for meals with Peggy?'

'No, she says it's like a busman's holiday.'

'I can understand that. I haven't had a meal out with anyone else for a very long time either. I did go out on work dos in Scotland, but I was always the odd one out in the group. It's nice to have a friend.'

Kit gestured towards the waiter, 'Well, friend Amy; would you like a coffee to top off a good evening?'

'I most certainly would, thanks.'

'Phil, Phil!' Kit rushed into the house and up to the bedroom.

'What is it? Oh God, not Scott?'

'No! Guess what?'

'What?' Phil couldn't help but grin when he saw his wife's wine-flushed face.

'I've got a new friend, Phil. Isn't that fantastic!'

Thirty-seven

October 31st 2006

Had it really been a week? Amy paused in her labours and watched the dance of café life buzz around her. A whole week without Peggy bouncing around the place. A whole week without Scott teasing her with harmlessly suggestive remarks whenever she went into the kitchen for cakes or sandwiches.

Kit was at the counter, polishing the cutlery that had come out of the dishwasher, and Jack had retreated to his bookshop to help Rob with the extra stock they'd ordered in for Christmas. Amy missed his presence, but knew they would manage fine without him now that the barriers between the three of them had finally been broken down.

As Amy topped up the basket of iced pumpkin-shaped gingerbread biscuits that she'd ordered in for Hallowe'en, she reflected on the night before. Jack had taken her to the pub to make up for cancelling a trip to the theatre last week, when another of his friends had needed a shoulder to cry on. Amy was sorry she'd missed the play, but the drink together had been fun, and after all, a friend in need was a friend indeed and all that, so she couldn't really complain.

She was snapped out of her thoughts by the sound of the door opening.

'Peggy!' Amy rushed forward and clasped her employer in a brief hug. 'How fantastic to see you!'

Lifting her head from her work, Kit raised a hand in greeting. Even though she'd only seen her yesterday in Scott's oppressively sterile white room, Peggy looked different out of the hospital environs. Paler, thinner, and certainly more haggard than before the accident, but she was smiling, and that was a sight worth seeing. Kit moved towards her, collecting the percolator jug as she went. 'Coffee, madam? Your usual table?'

Peggy laughed as Kit curtseyed, 'that would be great thanks, but I'll just say hello to everyone first.' Peggy moved around the customers, making sure they were being taken care of, and filling in the regulars on Scott's progress.

'This is where she belongs.' Amy whispered to Kit as they prepared something for Peggy to eat and drink.

'I know. It already feels better in here, and all she's done is walk through the door.'

Peggy ran a critical eye around her domain, 'I wanted to see the old place, and more importantly, thank the three of you properly. Everything is running perfectly. Well done on getting hold of the Hallowe'en biscuits, by the way, the suppliers aren't always reliable.' She glanced around her café again, 'No Jack today?'

'Had to pop over to the bookshop to help Rob. He'll be back to clear up and prepare for tomorrow later.' Kit sat next to Peggy, 'How's Scott? Anything new happening?'

Peggy took a bracing swig of coffee before sharing her news. 'He's doing OK. They've got him on some pretty serious non-steroid anti-inflammatory drugs; otherwise he'd be in a lot of pain.'

She paused to take another mouthful of caffeine. 'But, here's the best bit, they have been able to tell us categorically that not a single vertebra has been damaged. It's incredible. Thank goodness he wasn't driving fast.' Peggy's ponytail swung over her shoulder as she shook her head in joyous disbelief. 'He was such a mess you know. Cut up, swollen, everything, but he has been so lucky. I can't really believe it. To start with I was preparing myself for having no husband, then for the past few days I've been trying to picture living with a wheelchair-bound husband, and now I don't have to. Well, not once his muscles have mended properly.'

'That's so fantastic!'

Peggy's hands started to tremble as she cradled her cup, the magnitude of what might have been engulfing her. 'I thought I'd lost him. I thought I'd lost him, Kit, I thought I'd lost my Scott.'

Kit put her arm around her friend and held her close, while Amy discreetly went to serve a new customer. 'How long will he be in hospital?'

'It all depends on progress. Maybe another four to five weeks, but he's been moved to a normal ward. There'll be heaps of exercises to do to strengthen the muscles, and he's already a bit bored. He has to lie flat on his back without moving too much, so he can't see the television or anything. I'm going to take his MP3 player in later.'

'Hey, why don't you borrow Helena's portable CD player? I've got loads of audio books Scott could borrow.'

'That would be great. You sure she won't mind?'

'She won't even notice it's gone. It lives in a drawer which contains all of those important things she "needs" to keep, but never actually uses.'

Peggy laughed; she could just imagine Helena having such a drawer. 'Thanks that would be great.'

'Oh.' Kit remembered, 'Scott won't worry about it being pink, will he?'

'No,' Peggy laughed, 'he can have proper visitors now, too. He'd love to see you and Phil without the background whining of all that terrifying machinery, not to mention the spectre of Sister hovering in the background to shoo you away.'

'I'll text Phil in a minute, I bet he'll knock off work early and take the CD player and stuff over.'

They paused to nibble some of the apple cake Amy had delivered to them. Peggy surveyed Pickwicks as she spoke, 'This place is surviving wonderfully, thanks hun. So, what else has been happening? You and Amy been getting on well together?'

Kit noticed the mischievous glint in Peggy's eye. 'You knew didn't you? About Jack and her?'

'I guessed.'

'I thought you had.' Kit filled Peggy in on her curry night

with Amy.

'I'm glad you're both OK together. What does Jack think about it?'

'Oh, Jack's too confused to have an opinion! He probably feels a bit ganged-up on I suppose, but that serves him right.'

Peggy grinned, before asking, 'and Phil?'

'Ah. I think I need more caffeine before we have this conversation. I'll make sure Amy doesn't mind coping on her own for a bit longer, and I will confess all.'

'You daft woman! I can't believe you. What were you thinking? Phil is lovely, how could you hurt him like that?' Peggy was horror struck by Kit's confession.

'OK, OK, I know! It was like it came from nowhere, all those things you privately think and feel, which are often wrong, or at least flawed, not to mention horribly disloyal, came rising up and took me over. I know it's an awful thing to admit, but I think that if Scott hadn't had his accident then it would have got worse.'

'Worse how?'

'I'd have kept on speculating about Amy; building it all up in my head. Stupid. I guess what happened to you guys put things in perspective a bit. I was a bitter cow, and I hate that. Am I allowed to have a mid-life crisis at thirty-three?'

Peggy studied her friend's face carefully, 'You and Phil all right now?'

'Yes.'

'Then you're allowed, but don't you ever do anything like that to him again.'

'Trust me. I'll carry that foul taste in my mouth forever.' Kit fished out her mobile. 'I'll text Phil about Scott.'

NOVEMBER

In which Kit meets Toby and more coffee is drunk ...

Thirty-eight

November 15th 2006

'So, are you going to tell me why we are travelling an hour across London for a cup of coffee when Richmond is littered with cafés?' Kit followed Jack into the waiting tube.

'Just fancied a change,' Jack looked shifty.

'Bollocks, Jack. Where are we going?'

'I've come to a decision,' He held Kit's hand as they shot down the District Line, 'from now on I'm going to tell you everything. Involve you in everything.'

Kit couldn't help being touched by what he'd said, but nonetheless felt she had to say, 'I'm not your wife, Jack.'

'No, but I almost lost you once by excluding you from an aspect of my life. I'm not going to make that mistake again.'

Kit put her arm around his waist and squeezed him tight. 'That's lovely, Jack, but you *are* entitled to a private life. Now, where are we really going?'

'I told you, for coffee.'

Jack virtually ran from Leicester Square, dragging Kit after him, right up until he reached the frosted glass door of Ashford's Coffee House. Then he hung back.

'What's the matter?' Kit smirked as realisation dawned. 'You like someone in there, don't you?'

Jack was sheepish. 'How did you know?'

'I may not be your wife, Jack, but I do –'

'Know me very well. You do, don't you. Bitch.'

'Takes one to know one.' Kit grabbed his hand and went to go inside, but Jack drew her back.

197

'I haven't seen him since before Scott's accident; I might be wrong.'

Kit flashed him an evil grin. 'Only one way to find out.' She hauled Jack in after her, taking care to drop his hand the second their feet crossed the threshold.

Walking purposefully to the corner table, Kit rearranged the two chairs so that they could both see all around the café, and not just each other. Jack said nothing, but his eyes shone his 'thank you' anyway.

'Can I take your order, sir, madam?'

Jack seemed to have temporarily lost his power of speech as the waiter approached, so Kit asked for two large coffees and two Danishes.

'Will you take both drinks black and both pastries almond? Or is that just your preference, sir?' Toby's eyes twinkled and his mouth curved into such a devastating smile that Kit felt her insides melting; she didn't dare think what effect it was having on Jack.

As she was the only one who seemed able to speak, Kit replied, 'We'll have the same, thanks.'

'No problem.' Toby turned, but as he moved, said, 'Nice to see you looking more human today, sir.'

As soon as Toby was out of ear shot, Kit verbally pounced on Jack. 'OK, so he remembered your order, that's a very good sign. Now, tell me everything or I'll shout out at the top of my voice that we are married and have twelve children.'

'As I said, you are a total bitch.'

'Woof! Now talk.'

Jack had finished explaining about the one-night-stand that had hoisted him into this very café a month or so before, when Toby reappeared holding a laden tray.

'Jack, what was I talking about?' They'd chattered their way through their food, or rather, Kit had. Jack was furtively sliding his eyes in Toby's direction as often as he could, in a manner that he believed was covert, but very amusingly wasn't.

'*Jack!*' Kit could stand it no longer.

'Sorry?'

'What have I been telling you about Helena?'

'Helena?'

'My daughter! Your goddaughter, heaven help her.'

'Well … ummm … sorry, Kit.'

Kit was secretly enjoying Jack's uncharacteristic uncertainty. 'Why the hell don't you just go and talk to him? You aren't exactly known for hanging back like this.'

'He's probably not interested.'

'Jack! For God's sake, he's looked at you so often that one more smouldering glance is going to set the table on fire.'

Jack's eyes lit up hopefully. 'You think so?'

'Yes.'

Not totally convinced, Jack said, 'Maybe it's you he likes.'

'Don't be so damn ridiculous, if he was a stick of rock he would have "gay" written all the way through him.'

'You're right. Of course you're right.'

'I know.'

'But I can't just go up to him. It's different this time.'

'Because you want to get to know him properly, rather than shag him senseless and run out of his front door before dawn?'

'All right, all right, keep your voice down.' Jack looked anxiously around him, relived that in typical big city fashion, everyone was too intent upon themselves to be listening to their conversation.

Kit leant towards him, conspiratorially. 'I have an idea.'

'You do?' Jack was eager as a child who'd just been offered the chance of sweets.

'Yes. I want you to go to the gents'.'

Jack shrugged. 'Why? He's hardly going to follow me in there, he's at work. Anyway, that sort of thing is too seedy, even for me.'

'No, you idiot!' She thumped his arm, 'Listen, I reckon as soon as you're gone he'll be over here to clean up the table, and he'll say something that will start a conversation.'

'You can't possibly know that.'

'True, but I'll bet you the cost of those coffees that he does.'

'You're on.'

Kit made a *you can talk to me* face at Toby as, just as she'd predicted, he came over to clear up their cups almost as soon as Jack had disappeared.

'Can I get you something else, madam?'

'Not for me, thanks. Jack might want something when he gets back though.'

'His name's Jack?' Toby gestured to where Jack had been sat. 'Hmmm. Suits him.'

'It does, doesn't it.' Kit was pleased he'd picked up on her deliberate name-dropping.

'I wondered,' Toby squatted down so that he was almost on a level with Kit's face, 'would he ... um ... do you think he'd be interested in ...'

'If you ask him out, he'll bite your hand off.'

Toby's face changed from cautious to ecstatic. 'You think so?'

'I know so. He's a nice guy. He already likes you, and would like to get to know you properly.'

Toby's next statement addressed many important questions, without verbally stating any of them. 'You two are obviously very close.'

'We are,' she decided that Jack could be the one to fill him in on that particular area of information, 'I'm Kit, by the way.'

She shook Toby's proffered hand, just as Jack reappeared from the cloakroom. 'Now, if you two gentlemen will excuse me, I don't often get over to this part of town. I'm going to take advantage and do some shopping.' Kit turned to the waiter, 'Nice to meet you, Toby,' before she faced Jack and wiggled her fingers at him in a teasing wave. 'Call me later. Have fun!' and with that she left them to get on with it.

Two hours later Kit's phone announced the arrival of a text message.

Thanks Kit. I owe you one. Jxx

DECEMBER

In which Jack gets told off, Phil comes to a decision, and the coffee flows faster ...

Thirty-nine

December 6th 2006

'Is Scott managing back there?' Kit sipped at her third coffee of the morning as Peggy sat down for a minute.

'Yes and no.' Peggy massaged her temples as she spoke, 'Jack and Rob have rigged up a low work surface so he can make his cakes and stuff. The one good thing about all this is that Scott is spending more time with them. I always worried that he was so shut away in the kitchen before that he missed out on friendship and stuff. The camaraderie. Anyway, the oven door's low-ish, and I've made sure anything and everything is accessible. Though God knows what health and safety will say if we have a visit,' Peggy sighed. 'Still. Providing everything he needs is at waist level it's working fine.'

'Getting used to the wheelchair?'

'Sort of. He gets frustrated about not being able to do everything he used to, but if I tell him it's only temporary, he bites my head off, making me feel terrible. Then Scott apologises, and tells me he feels awful for making me sad, and then the whole cycle starts again.'

Kit appreciated her frustration. 'Why don't I come back and do a shift now and again; help out a bit.'

'Thanks, I'd say yes like a shot, but Scott is determined to manage, so we will manage.'

'Male pride rearing its ugly head?'

'Oh yes,' Peggy produced a packet of paracetamol from her apron, popping two headache tablets into her palm. 'I so badly wanted this you know, Scott back in the kitchen where he ought to be, but I'm sure he's returned too soon. He won't listen though.' She swilled down the pills with some of her friend's coffee. 'It's so damn tiring, Kit. I want to stamp and scream "it's not fair" each time he takes his frustrations out on me.'

'Oh, Peg,' Kit hugged her friend, 'if there's anything I can do, just shout.'

'Thanks,' Peggy forced on a professional smile, 'I know it'll pass, and the physiotherapy is going well. He can already stand on crutches for a short while, which is a miracle if you think about it, but for cooking and stuff he's much better off sitting in the chair.'

'I tell you what, if it helps, I'll pour my own coffee.'

'Well, I guess that will cut out about half my workload!' Peggy laughed, changing the subject, 'How about Phil? Still determined to sell the business in the New Year?'

'So he says. As soon as he's found a new project Home Hunters will be put on the market. It'll be strange, but I think it's for the best. Now Phil's made the decision he's like a new person; it's lovely. Suddenly he's full of life again. I knew it was getting him down, but I hadn't understood how much.'

'I think I understand perfectly,' Peggy spoke wistfully, hauling herself back to her feet.

'Oh Peggy,' Kit was horror struck, 'I'm so sorry. I'm damn tactless sometimes.'

Peggy raised her hand in reassurance, 'Don't be daft. I'm pleased for you. Really I am.' She continued with her earlier line of enquiry. 'Is this a good time for him to find a buyer, do you think?'

'I'm not sure. Christmas and the New Year are his quietest times anyway; it makes sense to tie up loose ends now before he moves on. Maybe he'll put it on the market in the spring.'

'Talking of Christmas, I don't suppose you and the kids would like to come and put up the tree and decorations for me this weekend? Scott and I normally enjoy doing it together, but this year I can't face it.'

Kit put her hand over Peggy's and squeezed it gently, 'Of course, no problem. The kids will love it.'

By two o'clock the dinner time custom had lulled enough for

Peggy to retreat into the kitchen, and Kit called Amy to her table. 'Are you doing anything on Saturday night?'

'Not so far. Why?' She pulled out a chair and sat down.

'Peggy needs to remember what it's like to have fun. Fancy plotting to rescue her for a night?'

You're on, but what about Scott?'

'He and Jack have been getting on like a house on fire. We could put Jack in charge of all things Scott.'

'He might be going clubbing or something.'

'Tough!'

'Fair enough.' Amy stood up again, 'I'm seeing Jack tonight. Do you want me to ask him?'

'No. I want you to *tell* him.'

The pub was surprisingly quiet, but then it was only six o'clock when Amy sat down on a cushion-clad pine settle in front of a roaring log fire. Amy felt the ripple of the flames glow on her face as the reflection of the ember heat stung her eyes, while she watched the sparking of a blazing log jumping and cracking in the confines of the fire place.

'Here you go,' Jack placed a wine glass on the rickety table in front of Amy, before pushing up next to her.

'Thanks,' Amy gulped down the cool liquid. 'So, how's tricks work-wise? Christmas trade picking up yet?'

They settled into comfortable chat about the shop, speculated about how much money Phil might get for Home Hunters, what he might do next, how Kit's novel was progressing, and a wide variety of everything and nothing until about half-past nine, when Jack's mobile burst into song, announcing the arrival of a text.

'Oh, shit'

'What is it?'

'I'm sorry, Amy; I'm going to have to shoot off. It's Nick.'

'Nick?' Amy's brow creased, she was positive he'd never mentioned a Nick before.

'A clubbing mate. Looks like his boyfriend's buggered off. Literally. Can't say I'm surprised. He wants me to go round to his place. Wants someone to whinge to, I suppose.' Jack placed a hand on her knee. 'Sorry, Amy. I hate to abandon you here, especially after I had to leave early at the cinema last week.'

'Don't worry, it can't be helped.'

'Thanks Amy. I'm sure he'll be fine, he's a real drama queen, regular crises, you know? But I should go all the same. Do you want me to take you home first?'

She could tell Jack was itching to leave. 'No thanks, I'll finish my drink and get a cab if I can't face the walk, it's not far.'

Jack leant forward and kissed her cheek. 'You're the best.' He swigged down his beer and virtually ran for the door.

It was only after he'd gone that Amy remembered she hadn't asked him about Scott-sitting.

Forty

December 7th 2006

'Good morning Helena, how are you today sweetie?'

'Hey Jack, what are you doing here this early?' Helena crashed down at the table in her Pooh Bear pyjamas, imperiously awaiting her breakfast.

Kit raised her eyes to ceiling, waiting to see how Jack would reply.

'I stayed over with a friend down the road, thought I'd come and see my favourite godchildren before school.'

'Yeah right, Jack!'

'Helena!' Kit spoke sternly to her daughter, 'don't use that sarcastic tone please.'

'Why doesn't he just say he spent the night at his boyfriend's then? You told us we shouldn't lie!'

Kit couldn't suppress her grin, 'Oh, go and clean your teeth, child.'

'But I haven't had breakfast yet!'

'Go and do them anyway. Go on!'

As Helena was hustled from the room, Jack struggled not to laugh, 'Are you *sure* she's only nine?'

'Don't!'

'I still can't get used to it, you know, you being a mum.'

'Neither can I. My mum says she isn't used to being a parent yet, so I guess I still have time to adjust!' Kit moved around the room, performing the morning tasks on autopilot, 'I take it you had to get up early as Toby has to cross London to get to work.'

'You've got it.' Jack's satisfied face spoke volumes about how he'd spent the previous night.

Kit raised her eyes to the ceiling again. 'Now you're here

you can make yourself useful. Go and shake your godson awake for me. Then, if you're a good boy I'll let you have some toast and jam, and you can help me walk them to school.'

'Cor, ta Mum,' Jack dived off his stool, ducking Kit's attempt to swipe him around the head.

Kit grabbed the sandwich bags with one hand and flicked on the radio with the other, speaking to the DJ sternly, 'I need you to play something to get my brain in gear this morning.'

She laughed as the DJ's dulcet tones announced the next record. 'Thanks, that's just what I needed.' Kit sang along as Queen's 'I'm Going Slightly Mad' filled both the nation's airwaves and her kitchen. Kit's voice was crescendo-ing to full pelt when her mobile hummed. It was a message from Amy.

Once the children were delivered to school and Kit's flustered-mother levels had returned to normal, she got round to asking Jack if he fancied spending an evening with Scott. 'It'll do them both good to have a break from each other.'

Jack nodded in agreement. 'Where will you take Peg?'

'Probably the cinema, she doesn't really go for restaurant trips, so a drink and a film would seem the sensible alternative. I don't think any of us are up to clubbing these days.'

'No stamina, you youngsters.'

'True.' Kit swung her bag over her other shoulder as they walked down Richmond's main street, 'but on the other hand none of us are on the pull, and at our age what other reason is there for going?'

'To have a good time, you sad old thing,' Jack poked Kit in the ribs, 'and anyway, Amy could be. Looking for a partner I mean.'

'Not sure she's interested right now.'

'Why not? Has she found someone on the sly and not told me?' Jack found that although he'd been joking, he didn't like that idea very much.

'Don't be daft. Anyone she was remotely interested in she'd drag around for you to vet.'

'Yes, she would wouldn't she.' Jack felt instantly reassured.

'God help her.'

'And what is that supposed to mean?'

Kit ignored him, and abruptly serious asked, 'Have you introduced Toby to Amy yet?'

'Um,' Jack scuffed his feet in the same way that her son did when Kit was telling him off.

'Christ, Jack, you have told her about him, haven't you?'

'Well, not exactly. I've told Toby all about her though, about all of you actually.'

Kit's face was a picture of righteous indignation. 'Don't you ever learn, Jack Brown? You must tell Amy, or you'll be hurting her all over again.'

'I know,' Jack spoke quietly, 'but I don't know how, we've been so close again, like … I don't know, like …'

'A relationship without sex?'

'Well, yes. How did …?'

'Amy has become a friend, Jack, and women talk to each other. I feel like I'm keeping secrets from her, and I don't like it!' She relented a fraction. 'Please, do something before you screw up again, OK?'

'I suppose you're right.'

'I know I'm right.' Kit linked her arm through his. 'Did you and Toby enjoy the club last night?'

Jack's head shot up, his face pale. 'Club?'

'Sure, I saw you both at about half ten last night outside Heaven; I was over that way with Phil.' Kit looked at him suspiciously.

'Oh right, yes, of course. It was good.'

Arriving at their point of separation, Kit turned to Jack.

'Remember what I said about telling Amy.'

'I'll tell her.' Jack sounded definite.

'Good, now in the meantime go to work, Rob must be fed up of carrying that place on his own.'

'Yes, Mum.'

'Hi,' Kit hailed Amy as she walked through Pickwicks towards her table.

'Morning,' Amy came forward, a mug of already to hand, 'scone or pastry?'

'Scone please, got any cheese ones?'

'Yep, Scott's just taken some out of the oven. They'll be lovely and warm.' Amy disappeared into the kitchen, soon returning with a beautifully aromatic steaming scone and a pile of butter portions.

'That's great, thanks!' Kit arranged her notebooks around the plate. 'Good evening last night?'

Amy, reluctant to let on that Jack had abandoned her, even if it had been to go on another errand of mercy, simply said, 'Yeah, it was nice. Quiet, what I needed really.'

'Phil and I went over to some posh restaurant by the Millennium Bridge, one of his business dinner things. All very suited, booted, and serious.'

'I didn't think you went to those things with him?'

'I don't usually, but this was a posh-do-with-partners thing. Very much the three-line whip, especially in light of the possible sale.' Kit laughed. 'I didn't mind though, my neighbour was free to babysit, and it was great food. We had a moonlit ride on the London Eye.'

'Sounds lovely.'

'It was, oh, and I saw Jack.'

Amy's stomach contracted, 'Really?'

'He was queuing with a friend for one of the gay clubs over that way. You guys meet up early then?'

'Yeah, like I say, I was tired. He must have gone on from me to the club.' Questions somersaulted around Amy's head, but she was interrupted in her tacit pondering by the arrival of a customer. She'd have to do her thinking later.

When her late lunch break arrived, Amy took herself outside into the fresh air. It was drizzling and cold, but she needed to get away for a while. She wanted to believe that Nick really existed. She really wanted to believe that Jack had gone to see him, and in an attempt to cheer him up, had taken him clubbing. Amy wanted to believe it very much, but she wasn't sure that she did.

Forty-one

December 7th 2006

'Are you free tonight, Amy?' Jack's voice echoed down the line, 'I want to make up it up to you for leaving you in the pub last night.'

Immediately on her guard, Amy replied, 'Are *you* free tonight then?'

Completely missing the undercurrent, Jack continued, 'Yes of course, that's why I called. Fancy a pizza out? My treat. I could come and pick you up, about eight?'

'I don't think so, Jack.'

Jack was thrown off balance, Amy never said no, not to him anyway. Perhaps she had a date? After a second's silence, he rallied, 'You busy this evening then?'

'No.'

'Why not come then?'

Fiddling with the objects on the kitchen side as she paced the floor, the cordless phone pressed to her ear, Amy delivered the speech she'd been rehearsing in her head all afternoon. 'It was bad enough being continually stood up, or simply forgotten about, when we were a couple, Jack. I'm not putting up with it again. Not anymore. I'm supposed to be a friend, for heaven's sake. I deserve better.'

Jack's voice became wary, 'What do you mean?'

'I mean, how long into the evening before a mate rings to cry on your shoulder? How much time do we have before someone becomes ill, and you need to go mop their brow? Or,' Amy paused for a lungful of air before she powered on, 'how many minutes before you get itchy feet and decide you'd prefer to be out clubbing like a teenager? Or how long before you find

211

the desperate desire to go and find some bloke to shag too overwhelming to stay for pudding, or coffee, or the end of the film?'

The phone line cracked with static silence. Amy knew Jack was still there, possibly he was considering if there was any point in denying what she'd said.

'How did you know?' When he did speak, his voice was quiet, contrite even.

'At first I didn't. I thought – more fool me – what a nice chap you were, going to the aid of your friends. Then, well, it happened too often, and alarm bells began to ring. I ignored them at first, persuaded myself that I was being paranoid, but then Kit saw you last night outside a club with some mates.'

'Kit?'

Jack spoke flatly, a feeling of betrayal rising in his gullet. Sensing this was the case, Amy continued. 'She wasn't grassing you up, so don't get all precious with her. Kit wondered if I was all right. I think she assumed I called our pub trip off because I was ill or something.'

'Oh.'

Amy let the silence last for a little while before she went on. 'Jack, I don't expect to see you all the time. If you're planning on going clubbing or something, then go. Just don't piss me about, all right?'

'Sorry, Amy.'

'Right. So,' Amy was suddenly business-like, 'if we go for a pizza, will you be staying for the completion of the meal?'

'You mean you'll come?' Jack was both relieved and surprised, and sounded it.

'On one condition.'

'Which is?'

'Your mobile is turned off and you stay for pudding. Then, if you go clubbing afterwards, you'll have something in your system to soak up the alcohol.'

'That's two conditions.'

'True, and there may well be more later!'

Jack couldn't disguise his relief. 'I don't deserve you, Amy

Crane.'

'No, you don't. I'll see you outside the pizzeria on the High Street, and we'll make it seven thirty rather than eight. Do *not* be late.'

Amy hung up. She felt light-headed; she'd been gripping her mobile far tighter than she'd realised, and her fingers ached. Yet she'd been the strong one for once. The one in control, and it felt good.

Trapped in thought, Jack cradled mobile in between his fingers. He should have told her about Toby; it had been the ideal opportunity. Maybe he'd tell her tonight. No. Tonight was about Amy. He'd do it soon though, before she found out on her own and went ballistic.

Forty-two

December 11th 2006

'How's it going, then?' Jack collapsed into the chair next to Kit and, pinching up her notebook, started flicking through it.

Kit snatched it straight back and closed the pages, keeping her hands firmly on the cover. 'Slowly, but I'm fairly pleased with what I've done so far.'

'What's it about then?'

'You'll see when it's finished.'

'And the erotica, oh mysterious one?'

'I emailed *Pearls*, explained the reason for the delay, and filled them in about Scott and my brief holiday from reason.'

'They understood?'

'Of course they didn't! They're kind and everything, but they have a website to run. It's sexy stories they want, not sob stories. It is a business after all.'

'Ah.' Jack waved hello to Peggy as she moved across from the counter to serve some customers with tea and cake.

Kit continued, 'After a bit of to-ing and fro-ing, we've come to an agreement. I'm going to do three more short stories and another two bits of flash fiction for them; just to keep them ticking over while they find a new regular contributor, and then I'm quitting. I'm more than ready to have a go at a few novels, some of which I hope will be erotic. In fact,' Kit picked up her coffee cup, 'I've already approached a couple of publishers to see if they'd be interested in compiling all the other stories I wrote for *Pearls* into one big anthology.'

Jack was impressed. 'You're clearly not as stupid as you look.'

Kit doffed an imaginary cap, 'Why thank you, kind sir!'

'You could call it *Confessions of an Over-Imaginative Thirty-Something*'

'Gee, thanks, Jack, but I think I might work on that title a bit.'

Pickwicks' door creaked opened and Amy came in.

'Does she know about Toby yet?' Kit whispered urgently to Jack.

'No,' Jack hissed back, earning himself a black look from Kit as Amy slumped down unceremoniously next to him.

Amy hadn't expected Jack to be there, but after he'd managed to stay put throughout their entire meal the other evening without seeming even remotely fidgety, Amy had given up being cross with him. It was pointless anyway; somehow she'd always forgive him whatever he did, and they both knew it.

'What's the matter with you? You've got a face like the proverbial wet weekend.' Kit moved her collection of editing pens out of the way, so Amy had room on the table in front of her for some much needed caffeine.

Amy yanked off her rain spattered coat. 'I guessed you might be here. I fancied some company.'

'Here? On your day off? Looks like an emergency coffee stop to me. I'll fetch it, save Peggy's legs.'

Quickly returning, laden with three steaming mugs, Kit said, 'So?'

'I can't find a job.'

'Nothing?' Jack was surprised. After what she'd said a few weeks ago about not searching for work until Peggy was sorted, he hadn't realised Amy had started looking; but then he thought, he hadn't asked her about jobs since Scott had left hospital, 'but you've got so much experience.'

'Oh, I can be a waitress or sweet-talk folk in pubs or shops no problem. I can be an unappreciated temp, scooting around various London offices, getting hopelessly lost in between appointments, or I can go back to being a junior version of what I did before, but I don't want to do that. It was so boring, and most of the advice I gave got ignored anyway, and then the idiot businessmen blamed me when they still went bust.' Amy sighed. 'But I know I can't afford to be picky, not if I want to stay around here.'

'Do you want to move?' Jack surprised himself with the realisation that, despite his initial panic at the prospect of having Amy back in his life, now she was, he didn't want her to leave again.

'Not really. Not now I've found somewhere I seem to fit in.' Amy blushed as she waved her arms around in frustration. 'New job, new home, new life, that was the plan, but it's hopeless. I've got the new home; I've got friends, although I've totally given up on the new relationship part of my new life, but I feel clueless about a career.'

'You're happy working here though, aren't you?'

'I love it, Kit, but Peggy can't afford to pay me full-time, and although I'd work for her for nothing, that won't pay the bills, will it.'

'I didn't mean that really,' Kit felt the stirrings of an idea come to her, but she decided to keep it to herself for now, 'I meant you like working with people, don't you?'

'Yes, but it's also nice not to have to all the time. Sometimes it's lovely to be able to hide behind a computer screen and not have to plaster on a happy face, especially when you have chronic PMT, or feel as sick as a dog, and all you want to do is scowl through the day and eat chocolate.'

'That's true,' Kit agreed, 'I don't know how Peggy does the constantly smiling thing, I really don't.'

Jack laid a hand over Amy's. 'Something will turn up, don't worry.'

Amy sighed again, trying to dispel the image of her dwindling bank account. 'Let's change the subject. How's Rob doing?'

Once Jack and Amy had gone off to their respective destinations, Kit re-opened her notebook and read the last couple of paragraphs with satisfaction, before reluctantly closing it again, and taking a different pad out of her bag. Only five more naughty stories, then she could focus solely on her novel. The idea of that spurred her forwards, as she picked up her pen and began to write lines of kink. It used to scare Kit how easily she dreamt up erotic storylines; now, she was simply grateful, as luridly fun descriptions splashed across the page.

Jack had already got several paces away from Pickwicks when he decided to change direction, and catch Amy up. It was time he took Kit's advice and told her about Toby.

He hadn't meant to keep Toby a secret for more than a day or so, but he hadn't expected things to go quite so well, and then when they had, he hadn't wanted to jinx it by talking to his friends about it. Jack hadn't even properly discussed Toby with Kit beyond their first meeting, and had stalled all her attempts at friendly enquiry into how things were going. He hadn't wanted to tempt fate. But the time to confess to Amy had arrived; it couldn't be put off any longer.

'Amy! Wait a minute.' Jack ran after her, 'Have you got a second? I need to talk to you.'

'Sure, I have nothing planned except more ploughing through soul-destroying jobs papers.'

'You'll be all right, babe; you're bright, cheerful, pretty. You'll get snapped up.' Automatically, Jack put his arm around her waist as they walked, but then pulled it away sharply. Toby might not like it.

'Well, I wish someone would do their snapping-up a bit faster!' Amy looked at him quizzically, surprised by the abrupt withdrawal of his arm.

'Coffee?'

'We've only just had some.'

'So?'

'Good point. Let's have it at my place though, I'd better start saving the pennies a bit.'

'I'll get it, silly.'

'No you won't. My place, or not at all.'

'Yes, ma'am,' Jack saluted and followed her back to Princes

Road.

As Amy dumped her coat and bag down in the corner of the dining room, Jack moved ahead of her to put the kettle on. He'd repeatedly run through how to tell Amy about Toby in this mind. She'd known he'd had some dates recently, but Jack had deliberately let her assume they were all with different men. Beyond a perfunctory 'Good date?' Amy had never asked Jack to elaborate. Now, he wished he'd told her more from the start. Jack had a nagging feeling Amy wasn't going to like having been kept in the dark.

'So, what's up?' Amy sank down next to Jack in their now regular spot on the sofa, the radio humming in the back ground; her spotty-socked feet up on the table. She felt strangely rejected when Jack got up and moved away, repositioning himself on the second sofa across the other side of room.

'Jack?' Amy's skin chilled with anxiety.

'I've got something to tell you.' Amy's face blanched, her brain filling with numerous potential crises 'No, don't panic, it's nothing bad.' His face broke into a beam as he spoke. 'In fact, I think it's rather good.' Jack's smile spread to his eyes and his intentions to break it to her gently dissolved, as he became more animated, his personal happiness got the better of him.

Amy didn't hear his next few sentences, she didn't need to. *Oh God, he's in love. He's met someone.* She fixed a positive expression onto her face, and allowed her years of built-in self-protection take over; making sure she nodded and said all the right things in all the right places as Jack gushed out his words, his joy.

Her brain nudged her ears in time to hear Jack say, 'So, will you meet him? I've told Toby so much about you?'

'Of course.' Amy's facial muscles worked entirely of their own accord, as she smiled with mock pleasure. Jack would have had to be looking at her very carefully to see that her expression was pure fake, and of course, he wasn't. Amy's hands felt colder as she stuffed them into her pockets, while the rest of her body flushed hot, as if flu was about to engulf her. Her head ached. How new was this relationship? Why hadn't he told her before? Why not mention Toby over last week's pizza? Forcing herself to concentrate, Amy said, 'I'd love to.' Her brain prodded her. 'He's called Toby?'

'Yes.' Jack exuded pleasure.

'Not Nick?'

'Who's Nick?'

Amy shook her head, 'It doesn't matter.' And suddenly, it didn't.

Amy sat quite still after he'd gone. Did she mind about Toby? No. Jack had every right to have someone special in his life. Did she mind that that person wasn't her? Amy clutched her arms around her legs drawing her knees up under her chin, protecting herself from the world. Yes, she minded that, however ridiculous, however contradictory. She minded that very much.

Forty-three

December 12th 2006

Kit hadn't paid much attention to the state of her shoes recently. They were merely something she put on every day in the unthinking dash to get the twins to school on time. Staring down at them now as she travelled in the stale-aired, sardine-tin of a tube towards Clapham, Kit saw that the toes were scuffed, and had lost their black shine. They were now the sort of mottled grey which indicated a hole was imminent. She groaned inwardly, Kit hated shoe shopping.

Once she'd disembarked into the enclosed mall at Clapham Junction, Kit took a lungful of the marginally fresher air, and headed towards Phil's office. It had been at least a year since she'd last been there.

She'd worked her idea over and over in her mind all the previous evening. Even watching *Notting Hill* with Phil last night, as they snuggled up on the sofa, hadn't been distracting enough to stop her thinking over the possibilities.

Kit suspected that, even though Phil had made what he called his "final employment decision," he was having trouble letting go of something that had been part of his life for so long. She just hoped he would like her plan.

Perhaps I should have called him first? Kit was unusually nervous as she climbed the stairs to Home Hunters' office. Phil could be anywhere this side of the river, showing clients around, or viewing prospective properties for lease. However, Kit was in luck. He was there, semi-buried beneath piles of paper and bulging files.

Phil caught sight of her, 'Kit! Everything all right?' He

221

waved from his corner of the room.

'Yes, thanks love,' She strode over to him, 'I wondered if you'd like to take me out to lunch.'

'I most certainly would.' Without hesitating, Phil grabbed his coat, and with a friendly nod to his workforce, began to steer Kit towards the door, 'Come on, Mrs Lambert. Let's escape and go Italian.'

The music was marginally too loud for such a small restaurant, but the fact that they got the last remaining table at only twelve o'clock so close to Christmas was a promising sign. The solid, chunky furniture sat awkwardly against the cobbled floor, suggesting that the diner should take care not to rock the table, for fear of knocking off the leather-bound menus and the dainty glass vases which sat centre stage.

They'd munched their way through a mountain of fresh bread and olive oil dip before Phil asked Kit what it was she wanted.

'How did you know I didn't just want to see you?'

'You haven't popped in for lunch since you decided I needed buttering up before persuading me to get the bathroom redecorated.'

Knowing this to be true, Kit grinned. 'I had an idea to help you out of the work rut thing.'

'Go on.' Phil leant forward.

Kit began her pitch. 'Part of the problem, if I understand correctly, is that you can't quite bring yourself to sell the business. You built Home Hunters up from nothing, and getting rid of it is proving harder than you thought it would be.'

'So?' Phil sighed. 'We both knew that.'

'How about not selling it, but not running it anymore?'

'Sorry?'

'Chris is good at his job, isn't he; runs the place when we're on holiday and stuff.'

'Yeah, he does a good job, but he wouldn't want all the responsibility. I've talked to him about taking over before.'

'He's probably scared of letting you down.'

'Maybe; he couldn't afford the place anyway.'

Kit threw down a hunk of half-eaten bread, 'Haven't you been listening, Philip? I said, don't *sell* it, but let someone else *run* it instead.'

'Chris wouldn't want ...'

Kit cut across him, 'No, Chris wouldn't want sole responsibility. But what if he didn't have it? What if he had an equal? Jointly run?'

'Why do I have the feeling you already have someone else in mind?'

'No need to tease me. You only have to say if you hate the idea.' Kit flapped open her napkin and placed it on her lap in readiness for the arrival of lunch.

'I don't know the whole idea yet, do I. Keep talking.'

Kit leant back from the table to let the waiter deposit a bowl of aromatic hot bacon salad in front of her, and a lasagne before Phil. 'I thought that if you kept Chris and employed someone else at an equal level, pay them each a lower wage than you get, but a fraction more than Chris gets now, then you could stay on as director. Perhaps you could still get a small wage, plus you could get a share of the profits, as the business would remain yours? That way you'd be earning while you hunt for a new challenge. It might be easier to let go in stages.'

Taking a draught from her cola, Kit sat back, watching Phil carefully as he considered what she'd just said.

'I'm not sure we make enough money to pay two sets of managerial wages as well as something for me, not after the taxman has taken his share.'

'Could we manage on the profits alone while you search for something else?'

'Maybe. It would be easier though if we paid Chris the same as he got now, but made his new job three-quarter time. Then the new person could do the same, but at overlapping times. That way, the company could operate over increased hours, which would make overseas calls easier.' Phil began to consider his wife's idea. 'It'll take a lot of thinking about, love, and it would cut into the profits a fair bit, but I must admit it's the best plan so far. I don't like the notion of losing touch with it altogether.'

'I know you don't. I don't think you should shut yourself off from it completely anyway, it's been your life for so long.'

'To be honest love, beyond thinking about leaving, I've been putting off any actual decision-making, any real plans. I just don't know what to do next.'

Kit looked at her husband in amazement. She'd been convinced he'd been hatching future plans for weeks. Phil, embarrassed by her surprised expression, pushed a forkful of pasta around his bowl and asked, 'So, when do you want me to ask Amy if she'd like the new job I might be creating?'

Kit laughed, 'Am I that transparent? How did you know I had Amy in mind?'

'Makes sense, she has a good business background, she needs a job, and against the odds, you obviously like her.'

'Yes I do, I think she'd work hard too.'

Suspicion shot across Phil's face, 'You haven't said anything to her already have you?'

'Of course not! You might have hated the idea.'

'Or Jack?'

Kit stretched out her hand to stem Phil's paranoia. 'The only person I have talked to about this is you.'

'What about Peggy?'

'Phil, I have just said, I haven't told …'

'No,' Phil held up his hand to stop Kit's protests, 'I mean, what about Peggy work-wise? Without Amy doing extended hours for half-pay, I'm not sure she'd cope at the moment.'

Kit hadn't thought of that, and certainly didn't want Peggy abandoned when her life was tough enough anyway. 'I suppose I could do it, you know, write there until about eleven, help with the lunch period, and then type up in the evenings.'

'I need to think, Kit.'

'I know.'

Phil put his hand over Kit's. 'Thanks, love.'

'That's what I'm here for.'

'It might not be the right answer, and it will take some serious working out, but I think you might be on to something.

Our savings are pretty healthy these days, so we could live off them for a while if we have to.' Phil talked to himself for a moment, before he returned his attention to his wife, 'Please don't mention it to anyone else for now, though, in case it doesn't come off.'

Kit licked her fork clean, 'Do you really have no idea what you'd like to do next?'

'Not really. More contact with people would be nice. Showing people around is the only bit of the job I'll miss.' Kit opened her mouth to speak, but Phil jumped in, 'And before you say it, no I don't want to work at Pickwicks, not even for Peggy and Scott!'

'That's a relief. I didn't really fancy you breathing down my neck all day.'

'Bloody cheek.' Phil toasted his wife with his glass of water.

'Now,' Kit started to shrug on her jacket, 'pay that bill. I have to embark on the torture that is shoe shopping.'

Phil looked lovingly at his wife. 'What are you like? Most women love shoe shopping!'

'And since when have I been "most women", hmmm?'

Forty-four

December 16th 2006

It had been five days since Jack had first told her about Toby's existence, and Amy still wasn't quite sure how she was felt. She certainly wasn't sure how she was supposed to be feeling. Wasn't this exactly what she had wanted?

Since Jack had confided in her, he'd told Amy all about Toby, the guy he'd slept with last night; the guy who, right now, might well be curled up under Jack's duvet, drinking strong coffee and eating biscuits, a treacherous voice at the back of her head pleaded, *'But that's my spot; that's where I should be.'* She quashed it quickly. 'Damn. I thought I'd got on top of this.' Amy hissed at herself angrily as her insecurities washed over her. *Get a grip, woman.*

It didn't help that Amy knew she only had herself to blame. After their first meeting at Kew, Jack had asked her, on more than one occasion, if she was sure she wanted to be included in that side of his social life. 'Of course', she'd assured him without hesitation, 'I'm happy for you. I missed being part of your life, and your friendship is very, very important to me.' It was a well-practised speech. Amy also knew that it was almost completely true. All those years with Jack as a confused memory were gone, and this was how it had to be now. She just hadn't banked on how challenging it would be to accept that Jack could be happy with someone else. *How arrogant you are.* She berated her reflection in the bedroom mirror. *Just get on with it.* It was high time she started to get ready for Kit's arrival.

'What's the matter?' Kit called through Amy's bedroom door

227

half an hour later, 'Jack said you never took any time to get ready to go out. What are you doing in there?'

Amy glanced anxiously at her closed bedroom door, her once-cream, now faded grey, dressing-gown hanging lonely on its hook. Bubbling with nerves, she took another furtive glance at herself in the mirror. How the hell was she supposed to know what to wear to a nightclub? She hadn't been to one for over a decade. The face staring back at Amy seemed old and wrinkled. Her laughter lines said there was nothing to smile about, and in her mind they could have doubled as the V-shaped valleys her old geography teacher had always gone on about. Her hair hung limply, in spite of its recent wash and straighten at the hairdresser's, and the jeans, which had definitely fitted yesterday, pinched into Amy's thighs and waist accusingly, making her legs resemble the sturdy props of a rhino rather than a young woman. *But you're not a young woman, are you.* Her image taunted her. *You're in your mid-thirties, you're unattractive, no one in their right mind is ever going to fancy you, and any minute now you are going to have to tell Kit that you're scared stiff about going to a club.*

Fed up of hanging around outside the bedroom door, Kit called out, 'Amy, I'm coming in.'

Amy couldn't move; her palms were sweating. The mirror girl had her hypnotized.

Kit peered around the door. 'What on earth are you doing?'

Amy's voice was small, 'I can't come. I'm sorry.'

'Why not? You look great. You're not ill, are you?' Kit flopped down onto the edge of the bed.

'No. And I don't look great, I feel like yesterday's T-shirt.'

'I'm sorry?'

Amy pointed to a pile of dirty laundry that was patiently waiting for its turn in the washing machine. A blue T-shirt languished on the top, creased and stained from a day working at the café. 'That's me. All wrinkled and used up. Yesterday's person. Best hidden in the corner.'

'What the hell are you on about?'

'I can't go out.'

'Amy, this isn't like you.' Kit came closer to her friend, squatting down next to her.

'That's just it, you see. It isn't. Going to a club isn't me. I don't do that. How do I do that? I have no idea. I have no suitable clothes to wear, and no bloody clue how to behave once I get there.'

Kit couldn't believe it. Amy sounded as insecure and illogical as she had herself – before Amy's arrival had forced her to face her own demons. 'I don't do that dressing-up stuff either. You already know that! Your clothes are perfect and you're annoyingly attractive. I can't dance and I've given up behaving well, it never gets you anywhere. This is supposed to be fun, not some sort of inverted torture.'

Amy turned towards Kit, her fingers pulling at each other as she tried to explain. 'I'm sorry, it's been so long. I'm nervous.'

'When did you last go clubbing then?'

'1993.'

'Bloody hell!'

'Exactly.'

'Tell you what,' Kit took a firm grip of Amy's hand and heaved her upright, 'we'll go to a nice wine bar I know down by the river. If we feel like going on somewhere, we will, otherwise we'll stay there and chat.'

'You sure you don't mind?' Amy felt relief flood through her, as she looked hopefully into Kit's face.

'Idiot! Come on, I'll call a cab.'

Despite Kit's reassurances, Amy appeared rather drawn as they travelled the short distance from the house, through the centre of Richmond, and on towards the river. Kit had to physically steer her through the wine bar door.

'You can stop worrying now.' Kit sat Amy at a round table next to the far wall. It was a light, glittery, silvery room bedecked with tinsel and fairy lights; noisy but not deafening. The hum of conversation was accompanied, but not drowned out, by the husky voice of Macy Gray singing 'I Try'. Amy did her best to relax, trying hard not to listen to the lyrics that always made her want to cry.

A waitress arrived swiftly, and without asking, Kit took charge by ordering them a bottle of dry white wine.

Each square table had a group of people around it. Some of the customers were suited after a day at the office, some were done up to the nines, awaiting a posh dinner date or Christmas party, while others appeared to be between destinations, amassing some Dutch courage before being joined by friends or family.

Amy fished around for a conversation which avoided the subject of Jack and Toby. 'How do you know this place then?'

'I used to come here when I was still a college student. It hasn't changed much really, a tad less neon, and a touch more expensive, but mostly it's the same.' Kit scanned the room, 'You see that set of high stools over there?'

'Yes,' Amy eyes roamed over to where a load of executive looking men and women were drinking obscure cocktails and laughing the laugh of folk who probably shouldn't drink any more before they'd digested a hearty meal.

'I always met my college friends over there before we went into the city and hit the clubs.'

'You see them much now?'

'Pretty much never,' Kit gulped back some wine, its cold presence gliding silk like down her throat, 'we all graduated and scattered across the country. I was the only one idiot enough to stay in London. I got a job at the college in the admin department, arranged to keep up my local digs, and then I met Jack.'

'And life was never quite the same again!'

'You've got it! Come on, drink up, it'll do you good.'

As the evening wore on, Amy began to relax. Kit eased her along, progressing from general small talk to gentle enquiries about Amy's life. 'Did you never go out in Scotland, then?'

'Not really.' Her lone meals in the various restaurants of Aberdeen's Union Street seemed another life ago now. 'It wasn't because people weren't friendly. I kept myself to myself.

It was me, not them.'

'That's so sad,' Kit hurled back her third glass of wine, 'and all the more reason why you should make up for it now.'

'I suppose so.' Amy's cheeks had developed a pleasing pink glow. She could feel herself slowly letting go, as the unaccustomed level of alcohol in her bloodstream performed its dance of intoxication, muddling her brain, loosening her tongue, and giving her confidence a boost. Amy blinked as she tried to watch all the women in the room at once, 'Where the hell do these women find time to plaster their faces with all that powder and stuff?'

Kit laughed. 'God knows. They can't have kids!'

'Well, I don't have any kids, but I never seem to have time.' Amy paused, 'Have we had this conversation before?'

Kit laughed again, 'Probably.' She spoke more seriously, 'You've really never ever worn it?'

'Nah. No point. I was a regular tomboy when I was a kid, always up a tree or in a muddy puddle. Then at university, my degree was very hands-on, as you'd imagine. I remember some of my colleagues spending precious time, when they could still be in bed or eating breakfast, painting their nails.' Amy's disbelief at such time wasting dripped incomprehension, 'For God's sake. Within half an hour of starting to excavate, all our nails were scratched to pieces – that's if they didn't get completely broken off. Whatever was the point?'

Kit giggled in the face of her friend's passionate outburst. 'I've never seen you so worked up about something!'

Amy's face flushed in embarrassment, 'Sorry. But I've always thought it so daft. Till now.'

'Now?'

'Perhaps I should have made more effort, perhaps I should start to now, I don't …'

Kit put her hand out to her friend. 'Stop right there, Miss Crane! Before you came, before Jack and I had our spat, I had got myself into a real rut worrying about this stuff. I felt I was too wrinkled, too fat, too thin, too … everything. Phil was despairing of me, and I was making myself miserable.'

231

Amy was surprised, 'But why? You're just fine.'

'I know that now, but I'd got sucked into the spiral. Then you came, a sort of kindred anti-fashion comrade, and I managed to escape the loop. Oh, I sometimes wonder, when I look in the mirror and see crow's feet creeping across my face, if I should use foundation or something, and then the kids call out and I forget all about it, until the next time I have two minutes to criticize myself in front of the mirror. Don't get into the habit of doing something that you'll end up resenting having to make time for for the rest of your life.'

'You're right!' Amy took a glug of wine. 'Anyway, it's good to be different!'

'Too damn right it is!'

Amy, emboldened by such solidarity and more than a touch of alcohol, felt she might be brave enough to try a club after all. 'Perhaps I could face a dance or two, just to see.'

'Really?' Kit beamed. 'That would be great, it's been ages since I had a decent bop. Come on, let's strike while the iron's hot and make total prats of ourselves.'

'OK.' Amy swallowed hard. She could do this. After all, she didn't want to be alone forever, especially now that Jack had someone who wasn't her. She might meet a nice bloke. It'd be fine, especially if she had another glass of wine before they went.

Forty-five

December 18th 2006

'So when are you meeting them?'

Kit stood with her back to the Christmas tree, which the twins had helped her to decorate the night before, and was tastefully adorned in red and gold. She was helping Amy to wipe the tables before Pickwicks opened, so Peggy and Scott could attend a physio appointment. Kit's anti-bacterial cloth smelt of school dinner halls, and was making her feel faintly nauseous.

'Two o'clock.' Amy threw her own cloth violently into the bucket of water and took up a drying towel, rubbing the table so vigorously that it rocked against the floor.

Kit glanced up from her cleaning, 'You OK?'

'Not really,' Amy stopped what she was doing and plonked down onto the nearest chair, 'I'm just so angry.'

'With Jack?'

'No.' Conscious that she'd spoken rather more sharply than she intended, Amy started again, 'No. It's me. I'm so cross with myself.' She sighed, voicing what had been circling her head for some time. 'You'd have thought I'd have learnt after all this time wouldn't you? It took me thirteen years to get on with my life. Then Jack returns my tape and I think, great, a chance for a new beginning. And I come here, and it's great. A bit daunting, scary, not everything I hoped for on the career front perhaps, but I'm happier than I've been for years. I've even been to a club for heaven's sake, where I actually danced rather than doing my famous wallflower impression. And I even enjoyed it!'

Kit chuckled as she remembered Amy's mad, jumpy, immensely uncoordinated, wine-fuelled uncaring dancing. 'How is the head today?'

'Let's just say that I was glad yesterday was my day off and I could suffer in peace.'

'Ah.' Kit, seeing the serious glaze to Amy's eyes, returned to the point, 'So, you were saying?'

'When I met Jack again, apart from the physical stuff, it felt the same.'

Kit, silently remembering how Jack had said the same thing about Amy, spoke gently. 'Except it isn't the same, is it? Not now.'

Amy groaned, 'I'm a fool. He was here; a friend to watch a film with, share a pizza, have a laugh, but for him that was it. But for me? I honestly didn't even realise I was doing it, falling for him all over again. Relying on him and being let down, all over again.'

'Oh Amy! What are we like?' Kit spoke without an ounce of malice, 'that bloody man.' She put down her cloth, wiped her hands on the back of her jeans and hugged Amy. 'You'll go to see them though, won't you?'

'Of course. Call me contrary, but I am glad for him. I'm just not so happy for me.'

Amy picked the towel back up. 'Come on, we have to open in a minute, I'll have to wallow in self-pity later, I haven't …'

Both women jumped as the kitchen door banged shut.

'We're the only ones in the building … aren't we?' Kit breathed out the words, her heart pounding as they tiptoed towards the till.

'Scott!' Kit and Amy shouted in surprise and relief as, unaided, Scott took a few slow tentative steps from the kitchen door to the counter. Peggy stood behind him, her face a picture of love and pride.

'You did it!'

Scott rested against the counter bar and held his arms out for Peggy, who flew over to him, hiding her tears of delight in the safety of his once snug jumper, which now sagged baggily after all the weight he'd lost in hospital.

'So,' Kit sniffed back her own burst of emotion, 'you back with us properly then?'

Scott flashed his brilliantly white teeth in her direction, 'I sure am. I have to go slowly, and only do a couple of steps every now and then to start with, but according to my physiotherapist, the corner has been turned.'

'I'm so glad.'

'Me too.' Amy picked a cup up in each hand, 'Come on, let's celebrate before those customer types start coming in. Hobble over there, you three. I'm taking charge and bringing over coffee and cake. Let's put some meat back on those bones of yours, Scott.'

Producing his wheelchair, Peggy guided Scott sedately across to Kit's corner table, and allowed their friends to fuss over them.

Once their drinks had been poured, Scott raised his cup. 'I want to propose a toast, and in the absence of champagne, Peggy's finest coffee seems most appropriate.' His wife nodded encouragingly. 'To Amy and Kit, thank you. Without you, we might have gone under, or at best, had to win our clients back from the rival cesspit of coffee commercialism.'

Amy and Kit blushed as they accepted his kind words.

'Jack should be here too really,' Amy said fairly, 'he helped too.'

'Indeed he did,' Scott adjusted his position on the chair to get more comfortable, 'but it's to you and Kit; you in particular, Amy, that we owe the most.' He turned to his waitress. 'You've put up with the full weight of my bad-tempered frustration.'

'So has Peggy!' Kit and Amy spoke in unison.

'Ah, yes,' Peggy agreed, 'but on the other hand, I love him.'

Forty-six

December 18th 2006

Kit glanced at the kitchen clock. Amy was late. She'd promised to come straight to Kit's house once her introduction to Toby was over, and had given four o'clock as a rough arrival time. It was now gone five. Kit was torn between worrying that Amy had thrown herself under a bus in the face of the boys' mutual happiness, or relief at the idea that it might be going really well, and Amy had simply lost track of time.

The sound of the twins moving around overhead echoed through the ceiling. Why did they have to bang so much? Kit couldn't be bothered to shout up the stairs to tell them off. There was never any point. After ten minutes of creeping around like mice, they always turned into mini-elephants again.

Perhaps she should text Amy? But if it was going well she didn't want to interrupt. She'd give it another hour.

Amy needed solitude, and space to think. She should be calling Kit, telling her she was fine, but tiredness had invaded every bone, and she didn't feel up to an action replay of the last few hours.

There was very little to say anyway. They'd done all the usual stuff, had coffee and eaten pastries, talked about waiting jobs, the bookshop, their families, and life in general. It was just now there were three of them, not two. It was a question of sharing him. Put like that, Amy thought, as she sat in the closing quiet of Kew Gardens watching a pair of squirrels bury its nuts, it sounds so simple.

A song shot into her head. Jack's influence? Or her own

237

imagination? Amy wasn't sure who to blame as KT Tunstall's 'Other Side of the World' ran through her head, each line of the lyrics increasingly more relevant. When it came to the feelings she couldn't quite put into words, it felt like Jack and her really were on opposite sides of the world.

Amy shook herself, trying to knock the music from her head, before doing up the buttons around the neck of her coat. She wasn't sure what time the grounds closed. It was five o'clock already, perhaps she should move, but the image of Jack's happily flushed face as he fluttered his eyelashes across the table at Toby filled every recess of her soul, and she couldn't force her body to move.

And Toby was lovely. He was funny, kind and obviously adored Jack. In fact, the more they'd talked, the more Amy recognised that she and Toby had a great deal in common, and could quite easily become friends in their own right. She had no problem understanding why Jack liked him.

Her hands were frozen. Amy rubbed them together, but even with her thermal gloves firmly in place, she failed to spark any warmth. Plunging her palms into her overcoat pockets, Amy couldn't remember feeling this cold since she'd lived in that damp orange tent in Wales for a while, all those years ago.

It didn't seem real now. Had that really been her life? Chatty, outgoing, meeting new student archaeologists on an almost daily basis as fresh diggers came and went, on the constantly expanding excavation. Slowly she had revealed hidden Roman treasures with Paul and Rob. Together they'd been quite a team, quite a different group of three altogether.

A rush of shame consumed Amy. Apart from the occasional trip to the cinema, she'd hardly seen Rob since her arrival in London. She'd sidelined him for Jack, in a repeat of the crime of neglect she'd committed over a decade ago. Ignoring the uncomfortable feeling for a moment, Amy turned her attention to her other past cohort, and tried to fix on an image of Paul, as he might be now.

He'd been much taller than the rest of them, chunkier too, a fact that had frequently meant he'd got all the heavy jobs. Paul had always joked that he did so much site clearance he should buy his own pickaxe. So, when he'd moved from student archaeologist to proper archaeologist, she and Rob had presented him with one, complete with a blue ribbon tied around the handle.

Paul had never had much hair, more due to his habit of shaving it off to virtual stubble than premature baldness. Perhaps he was bald for real now. A twinge of regret touched with envy rippled through Amy as she thought about him still living the life she used to have. Still meeting new people all the time and seeing the world. Still twinkling his deep blue eyes at the sophisticated petite blondes that had always been his preference.

Amy caught sight of a green-clad gardener heading her way. It must be closing time. Inclining her head in his direction to indicate she understood the intention to evict her, Amy got up and walked stiffly towards the exit.

Rob had said that Paul would come over. All she had to do was let him know when she was ready. But what with Jack, Scott's accident, more Jack, work, her own paranoia, and then Jack again, time seemed to have dissolved since she'd come south.

Not just time. Her financial status was getting shakier, and she knew that her days at Pickwicks were sadly numbered. It was no good feeling guilty about abandoning Peggy anymore; she needed to earn a wage that covered all of the rent and not just a fraction of it. She was fairly sure that Kit would always help Peggy out if she was desperate.

Kit! Amy fished out her mobile. It was getting late, she'd be worried.

Sorry. Needed time to think. Toby nice. Jack happy. So that's good. See u tomo. Sorry. Ax

Kit's reply came back almost instantly.
Glad you OK. Was bit worried. Tell me all tomo. Kx

As Amy walked up the road from the gardens, she came upon

Reading Nature. Something within her seemed to click into place. She had to act. Without pausing to think, she knocked on the locked shop door, and shouted out, 'Rob! Rob, are you in there?'

'Amy? Whatever is it?' Rob was startled at the sight of her. She had the pallor of a ghost, and her teeth were chattering. 'Come in, come on.' He ushered her straight through the shop and into the kitchen, pushing her down onto the single pine chair. 'What are you doing here? I was about to leave. Where have you been?'

'Kew Gardens.'

'I thought it was shut.'

'It is. I think I was the last one out.'

Rob fussed around, putting the kettle on, turning up the small wall heater. 'I'll give Debbie a call, tell her I'll be late, and then we're going to have a chat. Yes?'

He was so nice to her. Somehow that made Amy feel guiltier than ever. She could hear Rob on the phone apologising to Debbie about possibly missing the girls' bath time and explaining why. It sounded as if Debbie was being nice about it too. It was almost too much. Debbie was another neglected person. They'd got on so well over Sunday dinner, it was a friendship ripe for development, and Amy had ignored it. Too hung up on the shadows of her past to forge out the future she had promised herself.

'So?' Rob poured out the hot water, mixing Amy an espresso, and pushing it into her hands.

'I'm sorry.' Her voice came out as a strangled mumble.

'Pardon?'

'I'm sorry.'

'Yes, but what for?' Rob was perplexed, 'What have you done?' He tilted his head to one side, 'You haven't killed Jack, have you?'

'Jack?' Amy had been concentrating so intently on thinking about Rob, that for a second, the mention of Jack threw her.

Now Rob really was worried. How on earth could Amy have forgotten about Jack, even for a split-second? He made a snap decision. 'Stay right there. I need to make another call.'

Amy couldn't hear who he was talking to this time, but he was soon back, easing the untouched cup out of her hands, pulling her to her feet, and guiding her out of the shop. Amy felt detached from her surroundings, as if everything was happening through a cotton wool of fog.

Rob bundled her into a taxi, and before she knew what was happening Amy was sitting on a comfy sofa, with a real fire warming her, a beautifully bedecked Christmas tree in front of her, and Debbie asking if she'd like a drink before dinner.

It was the last straw. Amy dissolved into floods of tears. It didn't matter that three pyjama-clad little girls were goggling at her, stunned at seeing an adult cry. It didn't matter that Debbie and Rob saw her in that state. And it was just as well she didn't care, because there was nothing she could do about it. The tears kept coming and coming, as if thirteen years' worth of grief, loss, and self-imposed loneliness was being purged out of her.

Amy was vaguely aware of Debbie placing a box of tissues next to her, and of Rob herding the girls out of the room and up the stairs, but still she couldn't stop. Her body heaved, racked with each new sob. She blew her nose over and over again, until it was red and raw, and a pile of soggy white paper had amassed on the thick beige carpet.

Conscious of a muttered conversation a little while later, Amy looked up to see Rob's head peering around the door. At some point she must have stopped crying, she wasn't sure when. Her face felt taut and dry, the lines of her tears were etched upon her cheeks.

Amy ached with release, and felt as if she could sleep the sleep of the dead. Rob came in, put his arm around her, and reading her needs perfectly, said, 'You're staying here tonight.' He put up his hand as Amy opened her mouth to protest. 'Debbie has already made up the spare bed, and the girls are very excited at the prospect of you taking them to school tomorrow.'

'Cunning. There's no way I could disappoint them.' Amy

sniffed into another tissue.

'Exactly. That's why I told them you'd be here in the morning.'

Amy turned to face him. 'I'm so sorry. I've behaved very badly. Especially to you and Debbie.'

Rob shook his head, 'Not for the first time, Amy, I have no idea what you're talking about.'

'I ...'

'No.' Again Rob stopped her before she hit full flow. 'You're too tired. Come on.' He manoeuvred Amy to her feet and showed her to the bedroom. To the side of a large double bed was a table laid out with a tray holding thick hot tomato soup and toast. It was all Amy could do not to burst into tears again.

'One of Debbie's nightshirts is on the bed. There's some moisturiser to smooth over the tear stains, and a spare toothbrush is on the side in the bathroom. Eat up. Go to sleep. That's an order.'

Amy opened her mouth to argue, but thought better of it. Rob had already disappeared through the bedroom door.

Crunching through the toast, Amy remembered how Jack had cooked the same meal the first day that they had kept Pickwicks going for Peggy and Scott. Out of the blue it hit Amy, as she looked around the room, that she'd never seen Jack's bedroom, never even been invited to his home in Mortlake. Trying to reject the notion that he might be ashamed of her, Amy suddenly remembered she hadn't told Rob why she'd gone to see him at the shop in the first place, and that she hadn't mentioned arranging to see Paul at all.

It was the girls that woke her. Amy could hear them laughing and calling to each other as they ran between their cramped shared bedroom and the bathroom in the race to get ready for school. Groaning, Amy yanked the duvet over her head as the evening before flashed in front of her eyes. Filled with embarrassment, she wondered what on earth Rob and Debbie must think of her. All she wanted to do was run away and hide.

Could she sneak out?

Amy sat bolt upright, the duvet dropping from her chest. *Run away and hide*. The thought shot through her. She'd done that before, and where had that got her. Not this time. Not again. So what if she was embarrassed? What was pride anyway? She winced as an image of Jack on one of their last solo coffee breaks before she'd met Toby flashed into her head. He had quoted Duran Duran's 'Ordinary World' at her, something about getting over your pride? She couldn't remember why now. Oh yes. It was something about when he came out to his friends. Well, now it was time she came out; out of her protective shell. The time for personal pride had long gone, especially where Jack Brown was concerned. She'd stood up for herself over being let down in favour of clubbing with his mates; she could do it again.

Hurriedly dressing, Amy was determined not to let Rob's children down. They had been promised her company on the way to school, and that is exactly what they were going to get.

'Hello.' In spite of her private determination, Amy felt awkward as she entered the chaos of the kitchen.

'Amy!' Flora ran over and hugged her around the waist. 'Have you come to play Lego now? You said you would? Mummy says Father Christmas will bring me some more if I'm good.'

A promise made months ago to a child, and she had forgotten. Guilt stabbed at Amy all over again. 'Not now, love. It's school today. Maybe Mummy will let me come soon?'

Amy looked up at Debbie. She nodded in reply. 'Tonight? You could come to supper. A proper supper this time.'

Amy straightened up. 'Are you sure?'

'Of course.'

'You're so kind. You're all so kind.' Amy turned back to Flora, marvelling at how, despite being only two years younger, how different she was from Kit's frighteningly mature children. 'Tonight for Lego then, OK?'

'Yes!' Flora punched her fist in the air and ran off to her

243

breakfast.

Debbie looked proudly at her eldest child before holding out two packets of cereal towards Amy. 'Cornflakes or Malties? I'm afraid breakfast is a rather child-orientated affair in this house.'

'Cornflakes would be perfect, thank you.' Amy sat down meekly next to Flora and smiled as Rose and Lily trailed in shyly, hand in hand, peering up at her cautiously from under puffballs of uncombed hair.

As they waved to the three bouncing girls disappearing through the doors of their primary school, Amy turned to Rob and Debbie, 'I want to thank you.'

'What are friends for?' Rob shrugged.

'That's exactly what I wanted to say. To tell you. It's why I came to the shop last night in the first place.' Amy looked from Rob to Debbie, 'I've been a crap friend for years. I had so many good intentions when I came here from Aberdeen, but then Jack took over. I let him take over, just like I did before. I wanted to say sorry. I was pathetic. I shouldn't have let that happen again.'

Rob looked at his wife for reassurance, before saying, 'Sweetheart, he's a good man, Jack, for the most part at least, but he's a crap boyfriend. You know it, I know it. Even if he was as straight as a Roman road he'd be a crap boyfriend for you.'

'I know.'

'But', Rob continued as he put an arm around Amy's shoulders, 'he *is* a good friend, and it was important for you to see that for yourself. It was bound to take time.'

'I know; and it was time I needed.' Amy replied.

'You've had that now though, I think.'

'Yes,' Amy exhaled a rush of air from her throat, as though a heavy burden had been lifted away, 'yes, I have. Tonight I'll bring a takeaway. No way are you cooking for me. Chinese?'

'Now that,' said Debbie, 'is the kind of friend I like.'

JANUARY

In which a New Year has dawned, Jack and Phil have plans, Amy has to make a decision, and we meet Paul ...

Forty-seven

January 4th 2007

Kit frowned with a sense of foreboding – and *déjà vu*. Jack had sounded so serious when he'd called her to see if she was up for their usual coffee stop. What was it he wanted to discuss so urgently? She remembered all too clearly what had happened last time Jack had told her he really needed to see her.

Kit felt curiously put out when she reached the department store and found that Jack was not alone. He and Toby were sat as close together as the hard chairs would allow. They weren't seated in her and Jack's usual place either; but then, that was only big enough for two. Now there were three of them ...

'Hi boys,' Kit treated Toby to her best smile. 'How's tricks, Toby?'

'Just great, thanks to this guy here.'

Oh my God! They're in love! Amy had told her they were, but Kit had dismissed the idea as too un-Jack. It hadn't occurred to her that it might be true. *But why not?* Jack had been different about Toby from the start. There was no reason why she should be shocked. Kit twinkled wickedly at Toby, 'You obviously don't know him very well yet.'

'Don't you tease me, Kit Lambert, or I shall spill all your innermost secrets.' Jack smirked back at her across his steaming cup.

'You mean you haven't already?!' Kit sat down with her drink, 'So, what's happening? You sounded very serious when you called.'

The two men glanced at each other. Toby gave Jack a 'go for

it' look.

'Well, the thing is. I've decided to do some travelling for a while.'

'Oh?'

'I've got a business, I've got a house, but even though I've got the money I've never done anything else, never been anywhere. Dad and Jane are always sending me postcards from amazing places. I'd quite like to see some of them. Find out what all the fuss is about.'

'And?' Kit began to digest the fact that she was going to lose her coffee partner again after she'd only just got him back.

'How did you know there was an "and"?'

'Because I ...'

'Know me very well. Yes, well ...' Jack fiddled with his spoon, 'it's time for someone else to get to know me really well.' Kit felt stung by his words, her cheeks infused with heat as she listened. 'I've asked Toby to come with me,' he grasped Toby's hand beneath the table, 'I want to take him to meet Dad and Jane. It's time I came clean about my life.'

The gravity of it hit Kit like a sledgehammer. She struggled for proper words, rather than the gurgling noise that was coming out of her mouth. This wasn't simply love, this was borderline serious commitment. Now Kit felt fully justified in being shocked.

Dropping Toby's hand for a moment, Jack asked, 'Kit? You all right?'

She rallied, 'Yes of course,' Kit turned from one boy to the other. They looked young, pink, eager and earnest. 'I'm surprised I guess. It's fab news, Jack, come here.' Kit engulfed him in a massive hug, and whispered into his ear, 'I'm so pleased for you honey, I really am.'

He pushed her back a few steps and held her hands tightly, searching her face, 'You mean it?'

'I only ever wanted you to be happy.'

'I know you did, and I am. Really I am.' The sheer luck and thrill of his new situation clearly hadn't sunk in yet, as he turned to Toby, who reached a hand back to his lover, and covered it proprietarily.

'When do you leave?' Kit sat back down; gratified to find that her pleasure for Jack was genuine, and no longer simply a mask.

'Next month, I hope. There's a lot to arrange yet.'

'And where will you be going?'

'We haven't decided totally, but Spain will be the first port of call. Dad and Jane have rented villa in Tarragona.'

Kit enquired, 'How does Rob feel about it?'

'He's fine.' Jack referred to his partner so that he could take a bite of cake.

'No. He was great.' Toby sounded concerned though, 'you are sure he'll manage though aren't you Jack?'

Jack spoke through his mouthful, 'Sure. He can take on a student or something if things get too much.'

Kit picked up her coffee thoughtfully. Jack certainly didn't have to worry about the financial implications if the shop went belly up. Rob on the other hand, couldn't afford to be so relaxed about his livelihood. Her mind briefly flicked to Phil's plans for Home Hunters, but Kit kept her thoughts to herself; instead opting for the safer ground of listening to the guys plans for their forthcoming adventures, and satisfying her desire for a lot more caffeine.

She had been listening for the front door ever since she'd got in from collecting the twins from school. As soon as Phil walked through it, Kit pounced.

'You'll never guess what?'

Amy sat up in bed. Her bedside clock said it was only six in the morning, but she was already fully dressed. Clutching her duvet up over her legs and under her chin for warmth and comfort, Amy re-read her bank statement for the third time. She was sure she could literally feel her money slipping through her fingers.

She tried to reassure herself by tracing a finger over the amount in her savings account left from the money she'd earned while working in Scotland. It was a fair bit really. Anywhere in the Midlands, say, or back in Scotland, and it would have been enough to secure a deposit on a small house, but not London, especially not with her rent biting a large chunk out every month. Christmas presents hadn't helped, nor had the train fare to her parents for the holiday season. It was time to live a more frugal life. Though it wasn't as if, Amy mused sadly as she sank against her pillows, she was particularly extravagant in the first place.

Forty-eight

January 5th 2007

Rob was kneeling on the floor, the entire contents of the 'Local Flora' bookshelf at his feet, when the shop bell rang. He turned and, only marginally disappointed that the new arrival wasn't a customer, smiled. 'Hello, I wasn't expecting you today. Everything all right?'

'I've had an idea. You got time to talk?'

Glad of the excuse to stop cleaning, Rob stood up and dropped his duster. 'Sure, I'll put the kettle on.' He busied himself in the small kitchen, calling back through to the shop. 'Christmas good then?'

'Great, thanks,' Phil sat on a stool behind the counter, as if trying it for size and comfort. 'The twins had a great time, way too many toys of course. Not to mention not having enough space to find homes for them all. You?'

'The same.' Rob carried two mugs of tea through to the shop. 'So, an idea?'

'You know about Jack going away for a while, I assume.'

'Yes,' Rob ruffled a hand through his recently acquired spiky haircut, 'bit of a surprise, but as he's all happied-up for once, who am I to stand in his way? Anyway, it's more his shop than mine, he can do what the hell he likes.'

Phil stood back up and leant against the counter, 'Will you manage here alone?'

'For now. Jack's rarely in these days anyway. It'll depend how long he's gone for.' Rob started to unwrap a box of books a courier had left on the counter. 'Come March, the tourists will start arriving, that's when I'll need some help.'

Phil put his mug down and quietly surveyed the shop. 'I could help.'

Rob nearly choked on his tea. 'You?'

'Not so mad, is it?' Phil asked.

'No, but ... well, you're a captain of industry, this is just a bookshop.'

'Not *just* a bookshop surely,' Phil lifted up the top book from the pile in front of Rob, and weighed it in his hands. 'You and Jack have a niche market here; I wonder if you exploit that enough.'

'Are you saying,' Rob battled to speak calmly, despite rapidly becoming excited by Phil's suggestion, 'that you could help us in that direction?'

Phil drained his tea, 'How about I nip out and get a couple of sandwiches. You stick all those flower books back on the shelf, and we'll talk?'

'You're on! Tuna and mayo for me please. On white.'

It had been so busy in Pickwicks that Kit hadn't managed to talk to Amy that morning. She watched her friend move around the café, performing her job with her usual neat efficiency. That was the key word though, "performing". Whenever she thought no one was looking, the mask came down. Kit was worried by how fragile Amy seemed, how drawn around the eyes she was. Then, like an actress returning to her role on stage, Amy would plaster on her smile and deliver coffee, cake and sandwiches as if it gave her the most joy in the world.

'She's learnt that trick from you.' Kit called to Peggy as she paused on a return journey from clearing a table.

Popping the tray laden with dirty cups onto Kit's table, Peggy asked, 'What's that?'

'Amy, she's got your "customer first" face down pat. But have you seen her when she lets her guard down?'

'I thought she seemed a bit tired.' Peggy picked her tray back up, 'she said she didn't sleep too well. Money worries, I guess.'

Peggy disappeared into the kitchen, not looking too great

herself. Kit toyed with the idea of helping out, but Peggy had already told her, in a voice that would brook no argument, that she'd ask if she wanted help.

Money worries. That may well be part of Amy's problem. Kit wished that Phil would hurry up and decide what he was going to do about work. She was sure however, that Jack was as big a factor in Amy's ashen face as her finances were. She'd heard all about Amy's pre-Christmas stay at Rob's, and her new determination to get on with her life, but Kit had a sneaky feeling she might not be finding it as easy as all that.

Kit studied the pages of her notebook. She needed to develop a way of linking the next part of her novel with the chapters she'd already drafted, without it appearing disjointed. Today her brain didn't seem up to the challenge. Putting her pen down, Kit picked up her mug. The dregs of coffee that languished at the bottom smelled cold and stale. Her throat recoiled from the idea of drinking them, and Kit picked up her mobile instead

Hey Jack. Words not flowing. Coffee? Kx

Two minutes later she got a reply.

Sounds good, but over at Ashford's. Can you come here? Jx

What a surprise, Kit thought ironically. Toby must be at work. A concept that Jack worried about less and less these days. Kit weighed it up. Did she really fancy crossing London for a cup of coffee? Chances were she'd get no sense out of Jack if he was watching Toby in flirty waiter mode. Not the best time or place to share her concerns about Amy.

Sorry. Need to get kids soon. Maybe tomo? Kx

Tomo good. Old haunt 1pm? Jx

Kit smiled. Maybe it would actually just be the two of them. It suddenly felt like an extremely long time since they'd had time alone together.

Great. Tomo then Kx

Amy's mobile vibrated in her apron pocket. Gathering up some dirty plates she headed through to the kitchen. Dumping the tray down, she fished out her phone. Colour flushed through her cheeks and a broad grin settled onto her face.

'Good news?' Scott glanced over to her from his seat by the cooker, relieved to see a genuinely happy expression on her face for the first time in ages.

Amy re-read the text from Rob.

Paul will call ASAP with visiting date. In Nepal at moment. Come and share takeaway tonight? R x

'Yes thanks. Very good.' Amy started to hum happily to herself as she stacked the crockery haphazardly into the dishwasher, before sending a very positive reply.

Forty-nine

January 6th 2007

'So have you got a rough plan together yet?' Kit took a giant bite of cake, wiping icing from her lips as she did so.

'The trip you mean?'

Kit nodded. Her mouth was too full to risk an audible response.

'Sort of. We've spent hours surfing the Internet for deals and ideas.'

Feeling she could now safely speak without spraying the area with crumbs, Kit prompted, 'And?'

'We've booked a flight into Barcelona on the 1st February, and a coach across to Tarragona.'

'Have you told your Dad that you're coming?'

'Coming out or coming over?' Kit winced at the terrible joke as Jack topped up his cup from the cafetière they were sharing. 'No. That's the tricky bit. If I tell Dad I'm bringing someone, he'll assume it's a girl, making it even harder when I turn up with Toby.'

'And I guess you don't want to tell them you're gay over the phone.'

'No way! That has to be done in person. It may be awful, doing the confession bit, but I owe Dad that.'

'I agree,' Kit's expression showed her approval; she'd been worried that Jack would just drop his father an email or something. 'Any other way would be cruel.'

'So, we've decided to book a hotel room nearby, then I'll go and surprise them at the villa, and *if* all goes well, I'll introduce Dad and Jane to Toby. If not, we'll head off on our travels earlier than hoped.'

Kit gathered her hair away from her face, stuffing it into a stubby pony tail, with the elastic tie she always wore around her wrist. 'How does Toby feel about this?'

'How do you mean?'

'Will he mind having a day, maybe two, alone?'

Jack was confused. 'Why would he be on his own? We're going together.'

'Oh come on Jack, don't be dense.' Kit couldn't believe his short sightedness, 'You can't turn up unannounced after not seeing your Dad for over a year and dive straight in. They'll want to chat, catch up, and eat meals and things. You know; normal family stuff.'

'I hadn't thought of that.'

'Obviously.' Kit despaired of him sometimes.

Suddenly preoccupied, Jack began to tap rhythmically at the rim of his cup, 'Kit, can I ask you something?'

'Sure?'

'Do you think I'm selfish?'

His question caught Kit off guard. 'Why do you ask that?'

Jack ran his hands over his face, 'Ah. So you mean the answer is yes.'

'No!' Kit regarded him carefully, and decided on the truth. 'You can be very self-absorbed sometimes. That's not the same as selfish.'

Jack looked winded. He'd assumed Kit would say "of course not" without even thinking. 'What's the difference then?'

'Selfish is pure thoughtlessness. Self-absorbed isn't ill intentioned. With you I think it's become a form of self-defence.'

Jack laughed, no longer surprised by her insight, 'Thanks. I think.'

'Why did you ask me?'

Jack put his cup down and sat up straight, a guarded expression on his face. 'Something Toby said. We had a bit of a row about stuff and well, it made me start thinking about Amy.'

'That's why I wanted to see you.'

'I know.'

'You did?' Now Kit was surprised, Jack didn't normally notice how other people felt. Not so self-absorbed these days then.

'I'm worried about her. She nods and smiles when Toby's talking, says all the right things. Amy always engages Toby in conversation, asks polite and interested questions. She even joins in with Toby, laughing and joking at my expense.'

Jack waved his hands around as he told Kit how he'd sat back for a few moments the other day and watched Amy and Toby interact. 'They have stuff in common, they like the same things. They could have been friends for weeks, months even. And yet I'm not convinced.'

'Amy's like that, though.' Kit licked some stray sugar from her fingers. 'It's the same at Pickwicks. She talks to customers she's never met before like she's known them for all her life.'

Jack shrugged, 'How am I supposed to know if she's really pleased for me? If she does like Toby, or if she's just being, well, Amy?'

'Of course she likes him, he's lovely.'

'But how can you be sure? You know how well she does the interested stranger bit.'

Kit considered for a moment. 'I can't explain it Jack, but I'm sure that Amy would have let you know if she didn't like him.'

'I guess so.' Jack still appeared troubled.

Kit pre-empted his next statement, 'But?'

'That doesn't mean she's pleased for me, does it, even if she does like him?'

Kit felt on stony ground here, what could she say? How could she explain what she suspected Amy was feeling? It wasn't that long ago that she had felt pushed aside by Amy herself. Now Toby was unwittingly doing the same to Amy. 'I know Amy likes Toby. She told me she did, but I suspect that she is a bit low, that's all.'

'Low?'

Kit moved closer to Jack, using the voice she adopted with the twins when they had a difficult maths problem to sort out, 'Think about it. It must have taken a hell of a lot of guts to

257

come to London after all those years cut off from her friends in self-imposed exile. No sooner is she back and freshly re-instated with you as her main confidant, when her status with you, albeit on a different footing than before, is jeopardised all over again.'

Jack trailed a finger around the rim of his cup, 'I suppose that makes sense. What can I do though? This thing with Toby, well it feels ...' he hesitated, not daring to say the words. 'It may not work out, but I can't not try. I can't not ...'

'Of course not! You have to go for it. Amy would kill you if you didn't, and she'd feel guilty as hell if she knew she'd got in the way of having the chance of, well ...' Kit searched for a phrase that wouldn't make Jack panic, '... a period of happiness.'

'But I thought she wanted me single, so she could keep having me to herself.' Jack sounded confused.

'Don't be daft! Amy is a bit low, that's all. She isn't stupid. You're gay, for heaven's sake, and she doesn't have a problem with that.' Indignant on Amy's behalf, Kit said, 'Amy would love you to be happy and settled. I think it's the timing that's a bit crap from her point of view, that's all.'

Jack sat up; he looked hopeful, 'Is that what she said then?'

Feeling like the piggy-in-the-middle, Kit saw how Rob must have felt when he was at university dealing with the Jack-and-Amy fallout, 'Not exactly, but I know that she's happy you're happy. I also know she genuinely likes Toby. She just feels a bit out of it.'

'But I've included her; she's met Toby a few times now!'

Kit spoke patiently, as if she was again explaining some difficult homework to the twins. 'How many times have you seen her *on your own* since you told her about Toby?'

'Well ... I haven't actually had much time lately, I ...' Jack finally understood. 'She feels left out.'

'Yes.'

'I'll call her; see if she wants to come out with me and Toby tonight.'

'No!' Kit groaned. 'Just when I think you've got it! She

needs to see *you*. You. Her friend. Not on your own every time, but sometimes. She needs to be reminded she's still needed. God knows Amy isn't overly endowed in the confidence area.'

Seeing she had Jack's full attention, Kit seized her opportunity, 'I feel a bit the same if you're interested. The difference is I know it won't always be like this, but Amy doesn't. '

'Why won't it be always like this?' He looked confused again.

'As relationships go on it's nice to spend time apart, as much as it's nice to be together. Amy has never been in a lasting relationship. She doesn't know that yet. I don't suppose you did either!'

Jack shuddered, 'I daren't think long-term like that.'

'Of course you don't, but, as we've said, you can't *not* think like that either.'

Jack drained the last of the cooling coffee into their cups. 'The thing is,' he eyed Kit warily, deciding whether or not to continue, but realising it was probably too late to backtrack anyway said, 'I'm worried that Amy's holding it all in. I'm afraid she'll explode, like you did. I don't want her to spend years suppressing it all. I know that sounds arrogant but, well …'

'Ah.' There was nothing else Kit could say.

Fifty

January 15th 2007

Kit fiddled with her napkin as she let her eyes stray to the window for what seemed like the hundredth time. Phil was late. She wasn't sure if that was a good sign or not.

The waiter came over for a second visit. 'A top-up of wine while you wait, madam?'

Kit was sorely tempted, but declined, wanting to keep a clear head for the conversation that lay ahead.

The little Italian restaurant was quieter today, but then it was already almost two o'clock, and most of the lunchtime diners had already returned to work or hit the shops, enjoying the tail end of the New Year sales.

Phil began to jog. The meeting with Chris had taken much longer than he'd anticipated, and he hadn't wanted to delay things further by stopping to phone Kit. She'd understand in the circumstances. He felt lightheaded as he weaved through the afternoon shoppers, and finally made it to the door of the restaurant. It didn't seem a minute since the lunchtime when Kit had shared her plan with him. On the other hand, it seemed a lifetime ago.

Standing up in relief as she saw Phil push his way through the door, Kit hadn't realised how nervous she was until he was moving towards her. Were they celebrating, or was this meal a re-grouping exercise, a chance to discuss alternative plans and options?

The waiter appeared before they could speak. Kit quickly

ordered the same meals as they'd enjoyed on their previous visit. 'So?'

Phil took hold of both Kit's hands. 'I've done it.'

'Done it?' She hardly dared breathe.

'Yes. Chris loved the idea.'

'He did!' Kit got up and flung herself at her husband, 'Oh Phil, that's fantastic. Tell me everything.'

As they munched their way through lunch, Phil became more and more animated as he described to Kit how excited Chris had been by their plans. He was thrilled to think he'd have more interest and influence in the company's direction, without the pressure of sole responsibility. He also knew his wife would be impressed with the idea of his having an extra day home a week, even if it meant marginally longer hours the rest of the time.

'That's why I'm so late; Chris had a heap of questions. Not least about how we'd manage with me taking a small director's salary, and who his new partner would be.'

Kit sat up straighter, 'But I thought …?'

'Yes, Amy, I know.' Phil looked uncomfortable, 'Chris is worried that they might not get on. He doesn't want me to offer her the job without him having the chance to meet Amy first. Chris wants to run an interview.'

'An interview!' Kit raised her voice, disappointment coursing through her. She's been so sure the job was Amy's for the taking.

'Don't worry! I'm sure they'll get on fine. I'm going to arrange an interview for her as soon as I can.'

'Oh hell, what if Chris doesn't like her?'

Determined to stem the rising tide of his wife's bluster, Phil said, 'Have you stopped to think that Amy might not want to work for Home Hunters?'

Kit stared at him. Phil was right; it hadn't even occurred to her that Amy might not be keen. She'd been so sure it would solve every ones problems.

'You have to admit it would be totally unfair on Chris to dump him with a partner he hasn't even met.'

'I suppose,' Kit pushed her salad around her plate, 'I'm convinced she'd be great though. You should see her with the customers at Pickwicks, she treats them like friends. Even the ones she can't stand or hasn't met before.'

Phil spoke with a placating tone, 'I'm sure you're right. Don't worry. I've really talked her up. Chris is dead keen to meet her.'

Kit looked worried, 'I didn't want to have to tell Amy about the job unless it was a certainty. What if we build her up and then it doesn't happen. I'm not sure she could cope with further rejection right now.'

Phil took a draft of water. 'How's she coping with the news of Jack's imminent departure?'

'Difficult to tell,' Kit dabbed some stray salad dressing from her cheek with a serviette, 'I've hardly spoken to her since the news broke. Pickwicks has been packed with New Year shoppers, I've been submerged in my writing, and each time I mention Jack she changes the subject.'

Phil plunged a fork into his crisp lasagne, 'You know, perhaps we could get round the interview idea.'

'How do you mean?'

'What if I treat Chris to a celebratory lunch at Pickwicks?'

A broad smile settled across Kit's face. 'That's perfect! Amy always treats the customers well, even if she feels dreadful herself.'

'So you keep saying. I could get her talking. Then afterwards I'll see what Chris thinks.'

'Should we tell Amy, or not?' Kit frowned uncertainly.

'No.' Phil was firm. 'That way, if Chris doesn't like her, it'll go no further, and she'll be none the wiser. It probably won't be enough to secure Amy the job, but it seems a good place to start.'

Kit nodded, 'I think I'll tell Peggy if you don't mind, that way she'll understand if Amy seems to be spending a long time at your table. Anyway, we owe her an explanation if we're going to try and poach her only member of staff.'

'Agreed.' Phil continued to scrape his bowl clean. 'Can you

reserve me a table for Wednesday lunchtime?'

'Wednesday? Why not tomorrow?'

'Because,' Phil held his hands up at his wife's impatience, 'tomorrow I have a meeting with our biggest client. I need to explain the shape of things to come. It seems politic to do it in person as he provides most of the company's regular income.'

'Oh God! This is all too grown-up for me!'

'Tell me about it.' Phil laid down his cutlery, 'Now, I think we've deserved a proper drink, and then perhaps I can tell you about another idea that's jumping around my head?'

'That would be great love, there's just one tiny snag.' Kit gathered up her coat, as if to go.

'What's that?'

'The twins finish school in twenty minutes, and I'm half an hour away.'

'Shit!'

Phil gathered up his jacket and frantically gestured for the bill.

Fifty-one

January 16th 2007

'So Jack and Toby babysat for you last night?' Peggy was extracting cinnamon pastries from a huge Tupperware and balancing them on top of each other inside the cake counter.

Kit nodded, 'Yes. It was at rather short notice, but as they'll be disappearing into the wide blue yonder soon, and as Jack definitely owes me one, if not several, I was sure they wouldn't refuse.'

Peggy moved onto arranging the cream cakes, 'What did Helena and Tom make of Toby?'

'Tom's grunt was possibly one of approval, it's tough to tell. Helena on the other hand said he was cool and funny.'

'Praise indeed.'

'Quite.'

Kit had turned up at Pickwicks earlier than usual to see Peggy before Amy arrived. She had already explained Phil's plan, and after the obligatory teasing about stealing her waitress, Peggy had agreed to reserve a table for Phil the following day.

'Why the rushed night out then? Talking over company plans?' Peggy pushed a broom into Kit's hands. 'Be a love and sweep up behind the counter, I didn't get time to do it last night.'

Kit took the brush and set to work while Peggy arranged clean cups and saucers onto the shelves by the coffee machines. 'Phil has had an idea about what he'd like to do next. I had a feeling he was cooking something up.'

'And?' Peggy turned and started to wipe some trays.

'He's come up with a business plan for a shop.'

'A shop? *Phil?*'

'That was my reaction at first, but it's not so mad really. He always said the best bit about Home Hunters was interacting with the public.'

'What sort of shop does he fancy setting up then? Not a café I hope.'

'He doesn't want to set one up, more run one for a time, and then possibly take it over.'

Peggy paused in mid-wipe, 'Kit? Are you saying what I think you're saying?'

'I think so. If you're thinking about Reading Nature?'

'But Jack and Phil don't even get on that well.'

Kit propped up the broom and started collecting the accumulated crumbs with a dustpan and brush. 'They get on much better these days. The point is, though, that Phil gets on really well with Rob.'

'How exactly is all this going to work?'

'God knows, but Phil seems quite excited about it, and apparently Rob is too. They think they can expand the range a bit. Increase internet sales; advertise in US travel brochures that feature Kew Gardens, that sort of thing.'

'And what does Jack think about it?'

'He has no idea yet. Phil is meeting him this afternoon.'

Peggy's eyebrows shot up, 'Should Rob have been told before Jack?'

'Probably not, but Jack isn't at the shop much these days, and when he is, Rob says he's pretty much a waste of space.'

'What if Jack hates the plan?'

'Then it'll be back to the drawing board, I suppose. I hope Jack does go for it though, even if it's just a short term thing while he's abroad. Phil's dead keen.'

'I didn't know Phil was into wildlife and stuff.'

'He's not, but he is into …'

The door opened and Amy walked in. With her came the first handful of early tea drinkers. 'Remember, not a word.' Kit whispered, noticing the dark shadows under the newly arrived waitress's eyes before ducking into the kitchen to see Scott.

A message arrived on Amy's phone as she emptied out the clean glasses from the dishwasher.

Paul called. Will visit soon. Nepal dig almost closed. Rx

She hummed softly to herself, day dreaming about spending time with her two oldest friends, as she started to prepare a loaf of bread ready to make the day's sandwiches.

Half an hour later, Kit was pleased to see Amy's happy expression as she strode over to a newly occupied table to take an order. For the second time this week, Kit noticed how much slimmer Amy was these days, not that she'd needed to lose weight in the first place. If she hadn't been so drawn and heavy around the eyes, Kit would have been extremely jealous.

The hopeless lost look had gone. Bess couldn't hide her relief as she saw her friend move confidently around the room. No longer stiff-limbed, her false smile gone, she warmly greeted her colleagues as she headed to her desk ...

Kit stopped writing as Amy headed in her direction with a drink re-fill. 'Peggy thought it was time you had a top-up.'

'That's great, thanks.' Kit glanced about her, 'Where is Peggy, anyway?'

'Scott's managed some of the morning on his feet, but Peggy doesn't want him overdoing it before his hospital visit this afternoon, so she's trying to coax him back into the wheelchair for a bit.'

'Tricky.'

'Indeed. I'm keeping out of it.'

'Probably best,' Kit gestured to the seat in front of her, 'take a seat while you can.'

'Thanks, I will. Just for a minute though.' Amy subsided onto the wooden chair, 'my feet are killing me already.'

'You're looking good,' Kit plunged straight in, knowing they could be interrupted by a customer at any time. 'I've been worried about you.'

Amy hung her head. She knew she'd neglected Kit a bit recently. 'I've had things on my mind. I haven't offended you, have I?'

'Don't be daft; I was just worried.'

Amy accepted her concern and tried to explain, 'This business with Jack and Toby, I honestly believed that everything was fine and that I'd sorted it all out in my head. Now they're going away, and it feels as if I've broken up with Jack all over again.'

'You should have said; we could have had coffee or something.'

Amy toyed with a stray teaspoon, 'Bless you, but this is old ground now. I've been stupid, and needed time to adjust, that's all. Jack never gave me any impression that he was after more than a friendship. He only ever referred to men when he discussed future relationships. But he was so comfortable to be around. I've been such a fool. I was too ashamed to talk about it, really.'

'Oh, honey.' Kit reached an arm out to her.

Amy acknowledged the offer, but said, 'I finally realised that I've been so wrapped up in Jack, I've been neglecting Rob, just like I did when I left university. I'm going to spend some time with him. Catch up on the good bits of my past, not the painful bits.'

Kit sipped her drink, 'Is that why you're so bouncy today, happy memories?'

'You could say that, you see I've had this text from another old friend passed on to me …' Amy's explanation was cut short by the arrival of a customer.

As Kit watched Amy head towards the new arrival, she contemplated who the text might be from; she privately hoped that the upturned lips on Amy's face would stay in place until after she'd served lunch to Phil and Chris tomorrow.

Fifty-two

January 17th 2007

Excitement rushed through Kit as she read the email for a second time, just in case she'd misunderstood. She hadn't. Kit clutched the news to herself like a precious secret, a positive omen. It had to be a good sign.

Printing out the message, she folded it up, and slid it into her jeans pocket. Kit turned off the laptop. Gathering up her things, she squeezed the piece of paper between her fingers. If all else failed today, at least there was something to look forward to.

Sat in her corner at Pickwicks, Kit ripped a blank page from the back of her notebook, and began to jot down ideas for the new task that demanded her attention. She hardly noticed the customers come and go, her coffee being re-filled, or her empty cake plate being removed. It was almost twelve o'clock when Peggy broke through her concentration.

'You wanted to leave by twelve today, didn't you?'

Kit looked blank; momentarily confused.

Peggy prompted her further as she picked up Kit's drained cup, 'Phil will be here with Chris in ten minutes. You said you didn't want to be here when they talked to Amy.'

'Hell, where's this morning gone?' Kit knocked together the crumpled pieces of notebook that littered the table.

'What on earth have you been doing?' Peggy surveyed the unusually messy nature of her friends work.

'Nothing much,' Kit grabbed her coat, 'must dash.' She turned to Peggy as she waved goodbye, 'Can you text me when they've gone?'

Too restless to go home, Kit headed towards Kew. At least one of the boys would be in the shop this afternoon, and she wanted to thank them.

Phil had been so full of ideas when he'd got home from his meeting with Jack that he'd barely touched his dinner. A pad of paper at his side, he'd jotted down thoughts and numbers, in much the same haphazard fashion as she had in Pickwicks that morning.

Kit was surprised to see that it was Jack sitting behind the counter as she pushed the door of Reading Nature open. 'Hello, I didn't think you'd be here.'

'Of course I'm here. What a cheek to imply I'd neglect my business!' Jack lifted his head from the pile of documents scattered across the counter and grinned impishly at Kit. 'Nice to see you. Coffee?'

'Naturally,' She gestured to the paperwork, 'I'll get it, shall I? You're obviously busy.'

'Thanks,' Jack carried on attacking his inbox. 'This is all due to your husband.'

'Really?' Kit called back over her shoulder as she heaped teaspoons of instant granules into their mugs.

'I'm sorting out all the shop's financial reports, tax accounts and stuff. Best he runs the place with full knowledge of all our quirks and secrets.'

Waiting for the kettle to boil, Kit loitered at the kitchen door. 'It's ever so good of you Jack. Phil is so excited about this.'

'It's good of him, not me.' Jack neatened the documents into groups. 'It means I don't have to feel guilty about running off and leaving Rob. I know it's his business too, but as I own the lion's share, it's down to me if we hit the rocks.'

'I'm sure he'd have coped.' Kit retreated to fetch their drinks, shouting back, 'Rob's very resourceful.'

'I know he is. Thanks,' Jack took his mug, 'but he shouldn't have to cope alone. Anyway, Phil already has more plans for this place than I've had in years.'

Kit grinned at her friend affectionately, 'Where is Rob anyway?'

'Having a well-earned day off. I think Debbie will kill me if I don't start appreciating my partner a bit more!'

'Can't say I blame her.' Kit's eyes twinkled at him as she sat down behind the counter. She looked about her, 'I can't picture Phil doing this though, selling books in a shop. '

'Why not? It's not beneath him!'

'Don't go all indignant,' Kit put down her mug, 'I meant it'll feel strange. I always picture him behind a desk Monday to Friday, not in a shop, Monday to Saturday.'

'Not every Saturday I hope. I'm pushing to employ a Saturday helper, that way Rob and Phil can take it in turns to have a weekend off.'

'Good idea. I'll admit to being apprehensive about entertaining the twins on my own every Saturday.'

'Are you maligning my lovely godchildren?' Jack winked playfully as he took three different-coloured folders from the drawer next to him, and began to put the papers he'd arranged inside. 'I'd considered asking Amy to work the odd weekend, might help her finances a bit. What do you think?'

Kit started to toy with the edge of the mouse mat, 'I'm not sure she'd want to actually.'

'Want to, or need to?' Jack regarded Kit suspiciously. 'You always fiddle when you're not telling me something.'

'What makes you so sure of that?'

Jack laughed, ''Cos, I know you …'

'Very well!' They spoke together.

'Touché!' Kit laughed. 'I can't tell you the details, I'm sworn to secrecy.'

'Not even a clue?'

'Not even if you gaze coquettishly at me through those fluttering eyelashes!'

'Swine.'

'Anyway,' Kit knew she should tread carefully, 'I don't think Amy would want to work for you, Jack.'

'Why not?'

'Oh honestly, Jack, for an intelligent man, you can be so stupid.' Kit felt exasperation rise, 'I'll say it one last time. Amy

271

is happy for you and Toby, but I'm not sure that she needs the fact of your relationship jammed down her throat at the moment.'

'But I wouldn't even be here!'

'Exactly, you'd be away. With Toby.'

Jack creased his brow. 'But ...?'

Kit twinkled her yes at him mischievously, 'Did you know you always look confused when you try and work out why women think like they think? You get a little crease right in the middle of your forehead.'

Jack drank down his coffee. 'Well, it's hardly surprising is it? You're all a bloody mystery to me!'

Checking her mobile again in case she'd failed to hear the arrival of the text she'd been waiting for, Kit sighed. There was nothing. It was almost three o'clock. She stood at the school gates, watching for her children's faces to appear amongst the crowd of rowdy freshly freed pupils. *Why hasn't Peggy texted? Why hasn't Phil? Surely the lunchtime chat couldn't still be going on?*

By a quarter to four, just as Kit thought she was going to go mad with waiting, a text came through. It was from Peggy.

Sorry, been very busy. Amy still sat with them. Xx

Still there! The table had been booked for a quarter past twelve. What the hell were they discussing? It must be a good sign if Amy had been with them over three hours? Or maybe she hadn't been with them the whole time. Perhaps lunchtime had been too busy for her to leave Peggy during the early stages of the meeting? Kit cursed herself for leaving Pickwicks. If she'd stayed then she could have helped Peggy out, and Amy would have been free earlier.

Aware she was becoming paranoid, Kit poured herself a glass of wine. A bit early in the day perhaps, but she felt like she needed it. *Anyway* Kit smiled to herself; *I'm supposed to be celebrating*.

The folded piece of paper in her jeans pocket had been a

quiet source of support all day. Pulling it out, Kit read it yet again. She felt the same excited glow she'd experienced when she'd first seen the message that morning. If Phil would only text, she could share the news. *Funny*, Kit thought as she savoured her wine, *it didn't occur to me to tell Jack when I saw him*. She was dragged out of her thoughts by the ring of the phone.

'Kit Lambert speaking … Oh, hello, it's kind of you to call …'

Fifty-three

January 17th 2007

Ignoring the steaming cup of coffee that Scott had brewed for her, Amy excused herself from Pickwicks as quickly as she could. She could see that Peggy had been looking at her expectantly, waiting for her to say something, but Amy wasn't in the mood to talk. She stalked towards the railway station and the soon to close Kew Gardens.

That morning she'd woken up with the increasingly common feeling of financial insecurity swimming around her head. And now, out of nowhere, she'd been given a way out. A chance of a job. No. The chance of a career. A future in a thriving company. Not a lowly position from which she could work up, but a managerial appointment. That sort of thing just never happens in real life.

Phil had cast his personal knowledge of Amy aside, and had been very professional throughout the impromptu meeting. He'd told her what he was wanted for Home Hunters, why he wanted it, and that if Amy was interested and was confident she could fulfil that role, he would need to see a full CV and references.

Chris, the other manager, had been openly cautious. Explaining, quite frankly, that he required a partner whom he could trust and relate to. Amy had found herself thrown into a position of justifying herself, her past work, her current employment and her future with absolutely no prior warning at all.

She knew she should be thrilled. She'd been more or less promised the post after successfully impressing Chris, and earning a private thumbs-up from Phil. Instead Amy felt angry. Manipulated. She cringed as she imagined Kit and Phil hatching up the plot, arranging to save her, without even thinking to mention it to her first.

Slamming the door of the Princess of Wales Conservatory shut behind her, Amy sat onto the first bench she came to and tried to arrange her thoughts. She didn't doubt that they'd acted in good faith, but surely Kit of all people would have realised how important it was for her to sort her own life out. After years of hiding, of keeping everything safe, of not being brave enough to make herself a future, she had to be the one to do it. To break the mould; to make her own way.

Her mobile vibrated in her pocket. It had gone off several times since she'd walked out of the café, but Amy left the texts unread. They would be from Kit or Peggy, delighted on her behalf. Expecting her to be celebrating, not seething.

Feeling as prickly as the cacti that surrounded her, Amy attempted to calm down. *Logically. I must think logically.*

The first fact she thought, as she watched the last tourists of the day pass her by, was that for the first time since leaving university she had friends that cared for her enough to try and help her. *But how dare ... No, be calm. Think logically.*

The second fact was that she badly needed a well-paid job – and this was a really good one. Amy knew that it was a post she would have applied for anyway if she'd seen it advertised. She'd be able to use all the skills she'd built up in her previous job, as well as the customer relations stuff so recently honed to perfection with Peggy. Work would only take up four days of the week, albeit long days, and in time there would be a salary large enough to secure her rent and living expenses.

Thirdly, she'd meet new people. Phil had said that the office staff were all lovely. 'And let's face it,' Amy muttered quietly to herself, 'I'll never meet the bloke of my dreams at Pickwicks.'

Getting up, Amy began to walk towards the exit, and on through the gloomy, flickering street light darkness of early evening. The initial shock and outrage began to wear off as she considered how nice it would be to have a living wage coming in again. How lovely it would be not to eat Marmite on toast every night for fear of spending too much on food. Kit and Peggy would have been horrified to learn that the only proper meals she'd eaten lately were the pizzas she'd had with Jack, Christmas dinner with her parents, and the free food Scott gave her for lunch, most of which was consumed on the hoof between serving customers.

Amy strode past Reading Nature without a second glance. Rob might well have heard about her job offer by now. Maybe he'd known about it before she did. She was damn sure that Jack would know. Kit talked to him about everything. That meant Toby would know too. She clenched her hands until her fingernails cut into her palms skin.

The first of February. That was when they were leaving. Amy couldn't decide if she wanted the time to go faster, or if she wanted it to drag, so that she could get used to the idea. *Idiot*. There was nothing to get used too. It was nothing to do with her.

Exhaling noisily as her phone buzzed again, Amy gave in and retrieved her mobile from her inside pocket. Four unanswered messages flashed at her.

The first was from Peggy.

You ok? Great news on job. Don't worry about café. Go for it! Peg x

The second and third, spaced about thirty minutes apart, were from Kit.

Heard from Phil. Said offered you job. Fantastic. Are you pleased? K x

Amy? You ok? Peggy says you left work in a hurry. Call me. K xx

It was the next text that stopped her in her tracks however. It had come from Rob.

Got great news. Paul coming next Tuesday. Dig finished early. Ideas for day out??? R x

Amy felt her frown smooth away. Rob hadn't known about the job. Perhaps Jack didn't either then? Surely she'd have received a text from him if he had. Maybe she hadn't been quite as set up as she'd first believed?

After tapping out a message to Kit to say she was fine and thinking things over, Amy read Rob's text again. Paul really was coming to visit. It would be so lovely to see him. *Maybe we could go to Covent Garden, work our way around some coffee stops. Perhaps the National Gallery and then lunch in St. Martin-in-the-Fields vault? Perhaps ...*

Amy's head filled with possibilities as she approached the bustling train station. By the time she'd got home, her indignation over the unexpected interview had evaporated. Kicking off her shoes, Amy picked up the phone and lay back on the sofa. First she rang Peggy and, side-stepping questions about the job by claiming she was thinking things through, made sure she could swap her next day off from Monday to Tuesday. That done, she called Rob, 'Hi honey, can I have Paul's mobile number? I want to arrange something for our day together. You got any ideas about what we should do?'

Amy was quite surprised when she looked at the clock as she put down the phone. Could they really have been talking for an hour and a half? It was a mobile too. Amy panicked as she remembered about her phone bill. Then she remembered that she wouldn't have to worry in that way anymore, not if she took the job.

Sitting back, Amy felt unexpectedly content. Somehow Paul had put it all in perspective. He was right. She was lucky. Her friends needed a vacant position filling; she needed a job, was qualified, had heaps of business experience, and so naturally they'd asked her first. Amy had argued her point to Paul, explaining how wrong-footed she'd felt, and why she needed to break the mould herself.

'But you did break the mould, silly.'

Amy could hear the smile in his voice, but persisted in her belligerence, 'No I didn't. I had no idea about it.'

Paul's soft tone was patient, 'But don't you see, Amy? You broke the mould by coming south in the first place. That took guts. Perhaps this is your reward.'

Amy's stomach grumbled, reminding her she hadn't eaten anything since nibbling a small portion of jacket potato at about 11.30 that morning. As she opened the kitchen cupboards in the hunt for food, she smiled. A reward for all she'd put herself through. She liked the sound of that.

Fifty-four

January 17th 2007

Phil wasn't at all sure how it had gone. Amy had certainly impressed Chris. She'd impressed him too. In a totally ad hoc way they had plunged in with a whole string of interview-type questions. He hadn't intended it that way, and was worried he'd been a bit heavy handed, but Amy's knowledge of marketing, accounts, and all the various facets of business, had been far wider than he'd anticipated. But then, as Amy had explained, in the past she had needed to understand all the ins and outs of a company before she could start setting it right or suggesting improvements to its productivity.

Amy had still appeared rather shocked, though, and Phil had an uneasy feeling that, by having it sprung on her like that, she'd been more offended than thrilled.

He turned the television channel over in an attempt to find something less depressing than the news. There were people arguing. He turned over again. Two people were humiliating a third person, and the audience were evidently finding it hilarious. Despairing of modern programming, Phil switched the set off.

Kit was singing to herself as she came downstairs after saying goodnight to the twins, two empty milk mugs in her hand. 'Cup of tea?'

'Thanks, love,' Phil stood up and followed her into the kitchen. 'Sorry, I should have made it.'

'Don't worry.' Kit went through the motions of hot drink preparation, before regarding her husband carefully, 'I'm sure she'll accept it, don't worry so much.'

281

'You didn't see her face. I'm sure I've upset her in some way.'

'Come on love, it was a huge thing for Amy to take in. It'll be fine. Anyway,' she handed Phil his drink, 'do you think we could change the subject? I've got something to tell you.'

Phil's tea remained undrunk. He'd listened to his wife's news with growing admiration. When Kit passed him the copy of the email she'd received that morning, Phil thought he might burst with pride.

Words hadn't seemed adequate. The erotica Kit sold via the Internet was one thing, and he was proud of her for making a name for herself in such a competitive market. This was something else. Much more. A publisher had expressed an interest in printing and marketing an anthology of Kit's short stories. More than an interest, as the contract Kit had showed him indicated. A book which was all hers. Phil pulled his wife closer and kissed her passionately.

It wasn't until after they'd made love that Kit managed to say, 'I'm glad you're pleased for me.'

'Pleased! It's fantastic. At last you're being recognised in your own right.'

'Not to mention that I'll get the royalties rather than one-off payments.'

'Well, that'll certainly help more than a bit. Especially now I've gone and messed our financial security up.'

Kit kissed him again, cuddling close to his naked body. 'You've done the right thing. It's not as if you've cut us adrift in an open boat! And anyway, you'll continue to make some money from Home Hunters, and if it doesn't work out, you can sell it for a fortune. Face it Phil, we aren't exactly poor, and in the meantime the book will help a little bit.'

Phil looked doubtful. 'I don't want to throw a spanner in the works, love, and the royalties will certainly be extremely useful, but I don't suppose it'll sell that many copies, not with the Internet putting similar stuff out there for free.'

Kit was smug, 'The publishers don't seem to agree.'

'Really?'

'They called me this afternoon. If I agree to their terms, they plan to do an initial run of two thousand. Apparently they sold over four thousand copies of the last erotic anthology they marketed.'

'Bloody hell!' Phil pushed Kit gently down onto the bed, and moved on top of her. 'Come here, you!'

No one said anything else until it was time for breakfast.

'I don't think I'll tell anyone else about this yet.' Kit munched her way through a bowl full of cornflakes as Phil moved around the kitchen, packing himself some lunch.

'Why not? I thought you'd be out there shouting it from the rooftops today. You've worked so hard for this.'

Kit put down her spoon. 'So much has happened lately. I want to savour this between ourselves for a while.'

Phil came over to Kit and kissed the top of her head. 'If that's what you want, love, then you tell everyone when you're ready.'

'Thanks, Phil. Maybe I'll announce it later in the week, when I've got over the shock myself!'

Fifty-five

January 18th 2007

Standing with her back propped against a wall, Amy gazed at the building opposite which had been her place of work since October. In only a few months Pickwicks had become as friendly and comfortable a place to spend her days as she could have wished for. Precisely the fresh start she'd needed.

As she admired the red-brickwork that rose above the café windows, Amy saw for the first time why Peggy and Scott had decided on the name 'Pickwicks'. If you ignored the occasional outbreak of graffiti and modern signage in the street, the architecture had a very Dickensian feel. Perhaps 'The Old Curiosity Shop' would have been more fitting, she thought – but it was too much of a mouthful, and anyway, it wasn't a shop.

She'd have to go inside in a moment. Peggy was expecting her. There was a great deal to do. Extra sandwiches needed to be prepared in advance so that Peggy and Scott could disappear early for another physio session.

Amy hadn't slept much last night. Torn between that nice kind of not sleeping, full of happy hopes, and the guilty kind of sleeplessness, brought on by the knowledge that she was about to leave Peggy hunting for a new waitress. The fact that Peggy was already in the know didn't ease Amy's conscience one bit. In the past Peggy would have managed without any waiting staff for a while, but now Scott was more restricted in both his hours and his movements, good help was essential.

The flowers that filled various pots and vases in the café window were beginning to droop. Seeing them so desperate for water, Amy snapped out of her introspection and headed towards the door. She'd help Peggy out until a replacement was found. If Phil really wanted her to work for him, then he'd surely agree to that.

Even as she thought about it, though, Amy had doubts, a familiar lack of confidence filling her. Maybe she shouldn't be that pushy, or Phil might change his mind. Yet, it felt like the right thing to do, so she'd do it. If she lost out then she'd simply have to go back to scanning the job sheets.

'Are you *mad*?' Peggy looked at Amy as if she'd been teleported in from another planet. 'Don't you dare jeopardise your future for this place!'

Amy was rather taken aback by Peggy's forceful outburst, which went on. 'Scott, come in here and talk some sense into this girl will you.'

Scott wheeled himself into the main café. 'What's the matter?'

'This waitress here,' Peggy pointed at Amy, 'has, as you know, been offered a promising career doing something she loves, but is planning to tell Phil she won't take it until we've found a replacement for her.'

Scott's eyes sparkled as he spoke. 'Oh, stop giving her a hard time, Peg.' He turned to Amy. 'You've been a star. Without you … well. I'm not sure how we would have coped. But you don't owe us anything.'

'I …' Amy stuttered.

'On the other hand,' Scott adjusted his position on the chair, 'you owe *yourself* plenty. So, if the job appeals, take it. We'll be fine.'

Amy stared at her hands and felt tears prick at the back of her eyes. A trembly 'thank you' was all she could manage for a moment.

Scott inclined his head and wheeled himself back into his kitchen. Peggy was smiling at her affectionately. 'He's right; the job is yours for the taking, so take it.'

'I owe you both so much, Peggy.' Amy hugged her boss and, so as not to burst into tears, hurried into the kitchen to wash her hands, before filling a large jug with water and heading off to save the dehydrated flowers.

Squeezing a jet of creamy white mayonnaise into the shards of carrot and cabbage she'd just massacred felt extremely satisfying. Amy shivered as she plunged her hands into the icy-cold mixture, moving the contents of the bowl around until it was evenly mixed. She was on her final stir when her mobile began to ring.

'Scott, can you get that for me? I'm rather sticky.' Amy lifted her coleslaw encased fingers as if to prove her point.

'Sure,' Scott picked up her phone from the kitchen side and flipped it open. 'Hello? Scott here, Amy's on her way, who's speaking please?' Amy giggled at the affected secretarial voice he'd put for the call. 'Oh, hi, Phil, Amy's washing coleslaw off her hands. You OK?'

Amy started to move faster as she listened to Scott chat with Phil. He'd want to know if she was going to take the job.

'Hello Phil. Sorry about that, I was up to my elbows in mayonnaise.'

Scott watched her quietly from his corner. He whistled softly to himself as he weighed out some flour for pastry while Amy told Phil that she would, if he was pleased with her references, be more than happy to take the job.

Fifty-six

January 23rd 2007

Disappointment welled up inside Amy. 'What do you mean, you can't come?'

Rob felt a twinge of guilt as he put on the best fake stuffed-up-nose voice he could muster, 'I'm sorry Amy, but I can't make it. This cold has really got hold, and I'd hate to give it to you guys.' As an excuse, Rob knew it sounded a bit lame. 'Paul's going to be around London for a while. There'll be other times for the three of us together.'

Amy was nervous, more nervous than when she'd caught up with Rob on her arrival in London.

Paul was late. She examined the inside of the intricate medieval stone work opposite her. The doorway to St Martins-in-the-Fields wasn't easy to spot, Amy had walked past it by mistake before she'd come in, and she'd been here before. Maybe the British Museum would have been a better place to meet, or the Victoria and Albert? Amy glanced at the entrance for the tenth time in as many minutes. Paul might not even recognise her; after all, it had been a long time since they'd seen each other.

Her drink was already half gone. Amy checked her phone again. No messages. Giving up, she dug into her bag, bringing out the ever present novel.

Paul had spotted Amy as soon as he'd manoeuvred his six-foot-two frame through the low stone doorway. He'd been confident she would be in the café's furthest corner, and sure enough, there she was. Amy had always adopted a position where she could hide. As he watched her, Paul wondered if it was even something she was conscious of.

There was a coffee cup by Amy already, and the book her nose was stuck into was a paperback of the more ponderous variety of classic. Most of the girls he met these days wouldn't even have considered picking it up.

She was definitely a bit slimmer than he remembered, and her hair was sleeker, tethered back into two shoulder-length bunches that made her look younger than she was. Amy hadn't managed to get them level, and one bunch was noticeably higher than the other. Paul found he was dying to straighten them out for her.

Her clothes were the same as in the old days, though; knowing Amy, Paul thought with a grin, they might well be *exactly* the same. Jeans and a stripy blue jumper, probably with a T-shirt beneath, very probably a black one. The only really noticeable difference between now and then was that she was wearing knee-length boots with a wedge heel rather than trainers.

Rob was right. Essentially, Amy Crane hadn't changed a bit.

Suddenly aware that she was being observed, Amy looked up from her book.

'Hello!'

Her face broke into a welcoming beam. 'I thought you might have got lost.' She stood up and found herself smothered in a massive bear hug. Paul smelt nice; all warm and clean without the overpowering scent of the male perfumes Amy so despised.

'Tube delays. I couldn't get a signal down there to let you know.' Paul felt awkward, not quite sure what to say next, having held her slightly longer than perhaps was normal for a couple of friends. He'd engineered this opportunity to get her alone, and now he was here, he was tongue-tied.

Amy unwittingly came to his rescue. 'You getting a coffee then?'

'Yes, sure. You want a top-up? Black I assume?'

'Yes please.'

'Any cake?'

'No thanks.'

Amy watched Paul flirt with the Polish girl behind the counter as he placed his request. He seemed taller than she remembered. His black hair was still cropped very short, but it wasn't as severe as the shaved style he'd favoured as a student. His jeans were blue rather than black, and his shirt, although crumpled, was smarter than the off-white T-shirts she'd always associated with him. Smarter. He was definitely smarter. A huge brown overcoat, which probably weighed a ton, covered the back view of him almost completely, with the heels of his Doc Martens only just visible below the hem.

How come she hadn't noticed how attractive he was back then? Amy felt taken aback at the alien notion, and abruptly pushed the idea away. Yet that hug ...

Amy reined in and dismissed her wild flight of fancy as Paul returned with their refreshments. After they'd covered a wide range of comfortable reminiscences and laughed heartily at their past selves, Amy brought the conversation back up to date.

'So, is anyone special waiting for you back on site?'

Paul pushed his cup aside. 'No. No one's twiddling their trowel and pining for my return.'

'That's not like you.'

Paul regarded Amy as if she was nuts. 'I'm not stuck in a timewarp, Amy. I'm thirty-four. That pretty much makes me the father figure. I'm the oldest guy on site by at least five years. It's the twenty-somethings that have the trowel-twiddlers waiting for them these days.'

'But surely ...' Amy was genuinely shocked. She was so sure that things would have been just as she'd left them. 'You must meet heaps of nice people.'

'Sure I do. I have many friends, both male and female, right across the world.'

Amy wasn't quite sure why she pushed further, 'But no one special?'

'Not since uni.' Paul sighed, not sure if he was ready to go where this conversation might take them.

'Uni?' Amy couldn't believe it. This was Paul. The guy

every girl had wanted to date back then. Well, every girl bar her. Yet none of the string of young women he'd dated had ever lasted more than a fortnight, and for the life of her, Amy couldn't remember if Paul had especially liked any of them. 'Who was that then? You never said at the time.'

Paul hesitated, before taking the easy way out, 'You never met her. Let's go and explore. Gallery, museum, or a walk in the park?'

Amy was disappointed by his answer, but accepted it for now. She looked at her watch; it had already gone one. 'How about we nip into the National Portrait Gallery, have a quick mooch around and then grab a bit of lunch.'

'Good idea, is there a good café in there?'

'Two; but the Portrait Restaurant is fantastic, you get views right across London. I went in with my friend Kit before Christmas.' Amy paused. 'It's a bit expensive though. We could go into the Lounge, that's better price-wise, although maybe we shouldn't ...' Uncertainty took hold, as Amy's words trailed off.

Paul intercepted her rambling, 'Amy, this is my treat.'

'But archaeologists earn crap money.' Amy blushed as she blurted out the sentence.

'Oh, thanks!' Paul laughed at her, 'Although I can't argue. However, I have news on that front. Come on, I have heaps to tell you yet. Show me these amazing views of yours, and tell me about your new friends.'

They were in luck. After a companionable hour soaking in the diverse art work, they found a two-seater table available at the very edge of the lounge bar. After purchasing a glass of white wine each, they sat in silence for a moment, staring at the world through the window. It was all there. London. Everything the tourist could hope to see in one complete eyeful. St Paul's, the Eye, Big Ben. Everything.

'It quite takes the breath away Amy. All that history.'

Without turning from the view, Amy ran through their personal history as she replied. 'I knew you'd appreciate it.'

The waiter came over and took their order for two bowls of

wild mushroom soup and homemade bread, before leaving them to soak up the panorama. Amy was the first to break the silence, 'You were going to tell me something?'

'Ah, right,' he put down his own glass and sat back in his seat, 'I will, but first I want to know if you saw sense and took the management post you were offered?'

'I did,' Amy took a draft of alcohol, 'thanks to you.'

'Me?'

'You helped me clarify a few things. I was so sure I had been set up, I felt feeling manipulated, but you made me see it wasn't really like that.'

'Of course it wasn't.'

'My friends were just trying to do their best for me.'

Paul was pleased, 'Good. I'm glad. Now I can press ahead with my plans.'

Amy was intrigued, and more than a little impatient, 'Tell me, then!'

'As I said, I'm no spring chicken on the excavation circuit. If I'm not actually running the dig, then I'm at least responsible for a good part of it.'

'That's great. Your CV must be excellent. You always were the only one who could tell an ordinary stone from a Neolithic axe-head.'

Paul smiled in acknowledgement, 'I've seen the world Amy. I've found and seen all sorts of marvellous things. Written thousands of reports, drawn a million diagrams, been cited in heaps of books, but I've had enough.'

Amy was startled. 'But Paul, it's your life!'

'Yes, it is. But I'm fast heading towards my forties, Amy. I have, as I've said, friends everywhere, but no one waits for me when I do get home. Only my parents miss me if a dig is extended at the last minute. It's just not enough anymore.'

Like me, Amy thought. *There's no one at home, not for me anyway.* 'So, what will you do?'

Paul returned his gaze to the view; the people below looked tiny as they scuttled about, oblivious to the fact that they were being observed. 'Is it nice living in London?'

'Bit expensive I guess, and a touch overwhelming sometimes, but I like it.' Amy began to nibble at the soft granary bread which a waiter had placed in the centre of their table.

'Rob loves it, and I guess Jack does. I suppose the night life suits him.' Paul verbally pounced as Amy reddened at the mention of Jack's name, 'What is it? What's he done to you now?'

'Nothing.' Amy put up a hand, 'Really, nothing. I'll tell you all about it later. Go on with what you were telling me about London. Are you coming here to work? Are you?' Amy felt as if she was on tenterhooks as she waited for his answer.

She seemed so eager; Paul felt more hopeful than he had dared allow himself to before. 'I have the chance to. I wanted to know what you thought.'

'And what Rob thinks, of course,' Amy added.

'Oh yes, and Rob.'

Fifty-seven

January 23rd 2007

The air was crisp as they walked through St James's Park. Striding side-by-side with Paul in the fading light of a winter afternoon, Amy took advantage of the comfortable silence and replayed almost every word of the day's conversation through her head. Suppressing the nagging voice at the back of her head, that was desperately trying to tell her she was missing something important, she reflected on Paul's career plans.

After a series of interviews, about which he'd told no one for fear of jinxing himself, Paul had been offered the position of assistant curator behind the scenes at the British Museum, in charge of finding and acquiring new exhibits for the medieval department. Paul had said that, if both she and Rob were staying in the area, then he'd be very tempted to take the job.

Amy had just about been able to stop the internal whoops of joy escaping from her mouth by keeping her face as impassive as possible. Having felt herself manipulated (all be it with good intentions), into taking a job, she didn't want her happiness at having Paul around more often to be a factor in his decision about whether he took the job or not. By the time Paul had finished explaining about it, Amy's facial muscles were aching from lack of expression, as she simply said it sounded great, and that it would be fantastic to see him more than once a decade.

Paul risked a glance at her as they passed Duck Island. After her initial enthusiasm, Amy hadn't even blinked when he told her about the job. She'd said she was pleased for him, and that had appeared genuine enough. *What did you expect?* He had no reason to think she'd gush. They had only ever been friends. Jack had always been the one. *Jack*?

He broke into Amy's companionable silence, 'You were going to tell me something about Jack?'

'So I was. He's found someone at last. A nice guy called Toby. They're going to go travelling together for a while.' Amy, not daring to look at Paul, groaned inwardly at the sing-song tone of her voice.

Paul listened carefully as she brought him up to date, wondering why Amy had flinched when he'd mentioned Jack's name. 'I'm surprised. I assumed he'd play the field forever.'

'I think he did too. Toby was as much a surprise to Jack as everyone else.' Amy was studying the ground as she spoke.

'You OK about it?'

'Yes,' Amy sighed. 'To tell you the truth, I wasn't, but I am now. I was foolish.'

Paul spoke softly, 'Tell me.'

So she told him everything from the very beginning, repeating information he knew, and filling him in on what he didn't. The letter and the tape. How she'd put off meeting Jack at first, but when they'd got together, the old spark had been there, just as before. How on the surface nothing had changed, and yet how everything had – and how something in her had foolishly refused to see it.

'Amy,' Paul sank down onto the nearest bench, pulling her down next to him, 'Jack is a nice person, most of the time at least. But he is a totally, completely, utterly *crap* boyfriend.'

'That's exactly what Rob and Debbie said!'

'I'm not surprised.' Paul was irate, his arms animating his words as he spoke faster and faster. 'He treated you like shit. One minute on, one minute off. God! It was agony watching you so unhappy. He had you hook, line and sinker.'

Amy was so surprised at his explosion that she sat down next to him, open-mouthed. She tried to say she knew that, and that she should never have let it last so long, but her words stuck in her throat in the face of his unexpected rant.

Paul registered her newly pallid face, and stopped talking. 'God, I'm sorry Amy.'

'It's OK,' she felt unsettled as her mind raced. *Why was Paul so upset about it now, all these years later?*

'It was horrible watching you with Jack. You were worth ten of him. Jack was my friend, still is I hope, but for a while I hated him. And now he's gone and hurt you *again.*'

'Paul!' Amy had to shout to get him to stop. 'Please! Listen; in the past, yes, it was mostly him, not all him, but mostly. This time it was me.'

Paul's brow furrowed as he listened, 'What do you mean?'

'It was comfortable being with him. I was in a new place with new people, and he was familiar, easy to relax with after a day's work. I let my imagination run away with me. My fault. My problem.'

'But ...'

'*And,*' she spoke forcefully. 'I'm past all that now.' Amy continued more calmly. 'I've got a new job, friends, and a future. That's why I came here, why I left Scotland. Jack was simply the catalyst, I see that now. He will always be important to me; a special friend, but that's all.'

Accepting what she said, Paul filed the information away to be dealt with later. He stood back up. 'Come on, it's getting dark, let's walk.'

'Have you heard from Amy today? I've been trying to call her. I think her mobile must be off.' Jack was on his hands and knees sorting out a batch of children's books for the Spring window display, before he closed the shop for the day.

Rob, busy at the computer, replied without looking up. 'She's out with Paul today; they're probably in a museum or something.'

'Paul's here? That's great, you should have said.' Jack paused, mildly put out that he hadn't been told one of his oldest friends was in the area. 'I would have covered if you'd wanted to go out with them.'

Rob, his face hidden by the monitor, grinned to himself,

'Thanks Jack, but Paul asked if I'd cry off.'

Jack straightened up, a pile of the stuffed toy chicks and lambs Phil had asked them to order, balanced in his arms, 'Paul did? Why?'

Rob winked at him, 'Why do you think?'

'Paul! No way! Really?' Jack was stunned.

'Oh yes.' Rob felt a childish thrill at shocking Jack where Amy was concerned.

Jack found he had to speak slowly so that his voice didn't waver. 'So, when did he start liking my Amy then?'

'Always, mate. Always. And,' Rob spoke with deliberate clarity, 'she hasn't been *your* Amy for a very long time.'

Jack felt himself go hot as he watched Rob, his head bent as he studied the latest email order. 'Paul liked her? Even back then?' Jack asked quietly.

This time Rob didn't raise his head from his work. 'Even back then, mate, even back then.'

Kit felt bizarrely satisfied as she examined the text from Rob. She'd been thinking about Amy, on and off, as she sat writing in Pickwicks, wondering if Paul had declared himself yet. Rob shouldn't have told her really, and Kit desperately hoped that Amy wasn't going to be the last one to know how much Paul cared for her.

She read the text again.

Told Jack. You should have seen his face! Rx

The damp air had become infused with a light mist as Amy and Paul turned towards the park's Storey's Gate . A distant, unseen church clock began to strike. One, two, three, four, five.

'It can't be five o'clock! We've been together since ten!'

'You don't have to sound so alarmed about it,' Paul's eyes were teasing.

'I'm not; actually I'm sad it's nearly over. Today's gone so fast.' Amy spoke lightly to try and make her statement sound less serious.

'Sign of enjoyment, if the day goes fast.' Paul held her eyes intently, 'So, have you enjoyed yourself?'

'Oh yes.' Amy's eyes flickered over the remaining festive lights that hung across the dusky street.

'We don't have to finish it here. Come out to dinner with me tonight.'

'Dinner?' Amy's heart began to beat out a samba.

'I have a bit of work I need to do first, but I could pick you up about eight?'

'Well,' Amy felt awkward. Today had been supposed to be the three of them, even if it hadn't turned out that way. Dinner though, that was more of a date thing, even if it was only Paul.

'Come on, live dangerously,' Paul winked at her, 'if you come, I promise to spill the beans about the girl from university.'

'That's bribery!'

'I know.'

Fifty-eight

January 23rd 2007

The hands of the kitchen clock seemed to have been turning insanely fast since Amy had returned to Princes Road. It was already seven o'clock, and she still needed to have a bath and, more importantly, she needed to calm down.

Amy had been on the last stage of the tube journey home when the penny had dropped. At first she had dismissed the idea out of hand. It was absurd. Paul was a caring friend who was delighted to see her after so long, but the thought had persisted to gnaw at her. *Am I the girl from university?* All the signs were there.

Her head crammed with questions. *What if I'm wrong? Do I want to be wrong? If I'm right, how long has Paul felt like that? How did this happen? Oh hell, what the hell should I wear?*

Amy felt momentarily shocked at herself. She never worried about what to wear. But then she hadn't been on a date since 1993. *Was* this a date? For God's sake, this was Paul! This was her friend, who, if her suspicions were correct, suddenly felt more like a stranger. Which, she supposed, he was in a way. Despite their day together, Amy realised she didn't know much about his life over the last decade.

Staring blankly into her wardrobe, Amy sighed. There really wasn't anything much to look at. A couple of old work suits, a pair of jeans, a shirt, a pair of aged shiny-kneed black trousers, a grey baggy cardigan she wore in PMT-induced comfort moments, and a semi-smart navy jacket she'd grabbed from a charity shop before Christmas.

Maybe Sarah and James would be home soon and she could

throw herself on their mercy. No. Kit. She needed Kit. She'd lend her some clothes. Help her out, and stop her yo-yoing imagination from making her panic.

Amy's hand hovered over the phone, but then she snapped it back. She could be wrong about all this. In any case, this was Paul. A small voice of reason made an attempt to claim her. If he did like her, then smart jeans and the jacket over a T-shirt would be fine. It would surely be what he'd expect from her. If he was just a friend after all, then it wouldn't matter anyway.

Once Amy had made her, admittedly limited, clothing decision, she tried to think about nothing beyond getting clean, dressing, and brushing out her tangled hair.

Now she was ready, the hands on the kitchen clock seemed to have changed tempo, and were moving extremely slowly, making every minute agonizingly long. Just when Amy had she'd worked the whole thing out, and decided that the idea of Paul finding her attractive was ridiculous, her mind would return to the start of the problem. She waited, a mass of indecision, for Paul to arrive.

It was exactly eight o'clock when the doorbell rang. Even though she'd been expecting it, Amy jumped as the sound echoed through the hallway. Maybe she should pretend to be out; say an emergency had come up, anything to avoid any potential embarrassment. No. She had to know. One way or another.

Muttering her 'new life' mantra to herself as she walked towards the door. Now she'd considered the idea, Amy realised that the concept of Paul as a boyfriend was not totally repellent to her. Would she be disappointed if her suspicions were unfounded? She didn't know. She wasn't sure of anything anymore. Closing her hand around the brass door handle, she took a calming breath, and flung the door open.

They talked of their hopes for their new jobs as they travelled in the taxi. Amy had explained again about how uneasy she'd been about accepting the position with Home Hunters. Accepting her paranoia with patience, Paul put it all into perspective for her once more as they were driven to the

Covent Garden Grill.

'Why, when you say it, does everything seem all right?' Amy felt reassured as she got out of the car.

Paul hugged her to his side as they walked into the packed, oak-panelled restaurant. 'Because everything is all right, silly. Everything is almost perfect.' He bent down and kissed the very end of her nose. It was so innocent, chaste even. Amy was torn between feeling bewilderingly short-changed and tenderly touched.

The meal had been lovely, and even though there had been a couple of rather stilted moments when they first faced each other across the dinner table, Amy had soon relaxed enough to enjoy the food and company. But now they were on the coffee, and Paul hadn't said anything about liking her. He hadn't made any move at all, yet she couldn't bring herself to ask about his mystery girl. Amy found she felt disappointed. *At least that helps me to see how I feel about him.* Somehow that didn't feel much of consolation.

Regardless of the lateness of the hour, the restaurant remained busy. Amy was looking around at the other couples tucking into their steaks, when Paul unexpectedly asked, 'Does Jack still do the song lyric thing?'

Surprised by the question, Amy replied, 'Sometimes. Why?'

Paul hesitated. Should he tell her of the song that he always associated with her? He remembered Rob telephoning him for moral support just before seven, and encouraging him to go for it. So, taking a gulp of air, Paul plunged into his pitch for Amy. 'I always associated you with that *Another Cup of Coffee* song. You know the one? Mike and the Mechanics I think it was.'

'Really?' Amy spoke quietly, turning her attention to her empty square-shaped plate. 'That's quite a sad song. About being alone; about looking back being hard. Regrets and stuff.'

'I knew you'd get that bit.' Feeling uncomfortable, Paul began to fiddle with the corner of the tablecloth, much in the way Amy did when she felt uncertain about something.

'Is that how you see me now, or just as I was back then,

when we were students?' Amy asked, avoiding a gaze that wasn't looking at her anyway.

Paul shifted on his seat, 'Obviously, I *always* associated you with coffee.'

'Obviously.' Amy raised her half empty cup, and flashed him a brief smile in acknowledgment, before re-lowering her eyes to the tablecloth.

'But back then ... I saw you being left, and then left again, that's all. So much of that song seemed relevant, you know, it just summed it all up. You and Jack. Like the whole thing about her wanting to make everything OK, and him making her feel awful all the time. And I didn't seem to be able to do anything about it. It was maddening.'

'Oh?' Amy looked straight at Paul, wavering between being personally hurt, furious on Jack's behalf, and excited that he might finally be getting to the point.

Paul seemed to be waiting for her to elaborate, but Amy sat quietly, cradling her cup. She could feel her frustration rising, but bit her tongue and waited.

After a few minute's peace, which seemed to last hours, Paul banged a frustrated fist onto the table, making Amy jump as he expounded years of suppressed feelings. 'You shut yourself away. Didn't answer calls. Didn't pass on your address. You disappeared.'

'I know. I'm sorry. I explained it all to Rob, and I ...'

Paul interrupted her, 'It's OK. I know, and I sort of understand.' He put down his napkin, transferring his attention to twiddling a silver teaspoon between his fingers. 'But now perhaps ... if you are ready, um ... having started again, like ... to, well, um ...' Paul dropped the spoon down on the table and stood up abruptly. 'I'm going to pay the bill, I'll be right back.'

Amy watched his back with growing exasperation. He'd been so nearly there. She was now convinced of what he wanted to say. Was he worried about ruining their refreshed friendship?

Paul was taking ages at the till, or perhaps it only felt like that. When he did return, a very determined look was etched across his face. Despite the vast supply on the table, he was carrying a folded paper-napkin in his hand. He didn't sit down, but loomed hesitantly over Amy in her seat.

'The thing is, I've tried, but I keep getting jumbled, and well … anyway, would you read this please? Afterwards, I'll either order *you* a cab, or *us* a cab.' Paul thrust the cream napkin into Amy's hands and moved away, turning to stare blankly out of the nearest window.

After a few speechless seconds, Amy unfolded the paper triangle. She found a hastily scribbled note across its centre.

I love you. Sorry!

Fifty-nine

January 23rd 2007

Kit had been expecting the call. Had she got time for a drink? Could she get away?

Jack hadn't sounded desperate as such, but his voice certainly had an urgent edge, which he hadn't quite managed to disguise. Kit had a quick discussion with Phil (who'd rolled his eyes), and agreed to meet Jack at the pub.

Jack's turn at the bar had come and gone once already, and he hadn't even noticed. Observing Jack's distracted air, Kit studied his more-than-usually crumpled appearance carefully, as he eventually purchased two pints of beer, and escaped from the semi-crush of evening drinkers.

'So?' Kit looked at Jack expectantly.

'What?'

Kit positioned her glass on top of the nearest beer mat. 'You have snapped your fingers and summoned me like the genie of the lamp, because …?'

Jack managed not to appear taken aback, even though he felt it, 'I fancied seeing you, that's all.'

'Really? Without Toby?' Kit raised a sceptical eyebrow. 'And the fact that Amy is out with Paul tonight is a total coincidence?'

'Oh, you know.' Jack had the decency to look at least a little bashful as he sat next to her.

'Naturally,' Kit took a mouthful of Worthington's, 'so, as I say. How can I help?'

'Your voice couldn't be less sympathetic if you tried!' Jack, suddenly all charm, smiled with his eyes as he spoke, reminding Kit of the man he had been when she first met him.

'Why on earth should I feel sorry for you?'

'Well, because Amy is out with Paul. I mean, Paul! He's supposed to be my friend, and now I find that all this time … for all these years … and not just now, but then too …'

Jack's words tumbled out at speed, as he pleaded with Kit to understand his feeling of betrayal. It wasn't until he took in Kit's face, her eyes wide, her expression so set in disapproval that his sentence trailed off. He exhaled noisily into his pint. 'You're about to lecture me on double standards aren't you?'

'At least you can see that you've got double standards! Damn it, Jack!' Kit struggled to keep her temper, 'How dare you!'

'What do you mean?' He sounded confused.

'For fuck's sake!' Now Kit did shout, only lowering her voice when she realised she was attracting a small audience from the surrounding tables. 'You're jetting off with Toby in a few days' time. About to declare your relationship to your father, for God's sake.'

Jack placed his glass on the stool-like table next to him, and sat back. The music in the background began to filter into his consciousness. 'Kit, do you remember our chat at Pickwicks, you know when I …'

Not wanting to revisit that particular scene in detail, Kit cut in, 'I remember, go on.'

'I said life for you was like Keane's "Everybody's Changing".'

It was Kit's turn to sigh, 'So you did.'

'It's playing now. Listen.'

They sat together, silently listening, as Tom Chaplin's gentle voice jostled with the chatter, laughter and debate all around them. As the lyrics filled her head, Kit took hold of Jack's hand and placed it lightly over her own. 'Change is scary, isn't it?'

'You're telling me!'

'It'll be all right though. You and Toby will fly off and have some fun. Your dad, who's probably known that you're gay all along, will be cool. I'll write a blockbuster, Rob and Phil will make a huge success of running the shop, and Amy and Paul will live happily ever after and breed you a new generation of godchildren.'

Jack looked at her hopefully, 'You believe all that?'

'Sometimes, you have to live in hope.' Kit spoke lightly and attempted to distract Jack from his unjustified gloom, said, 'Talking of change. Something quite good has happened on the writing front.'

'Yeah?'

'I've got a deal on an erotica anthology. You remember we talked about it a while back?'

Jack put down his pint and threw his arms around Kit, 'No way! That's fantastic. Why didn't you say before?'

'I've only known a while.' Kit extracted herself from his hug, 'I wanted to let it sink in. If I announced it to everyone straight away, it might have evaporated.'

'Well, I'm so proud of you. Tell me all about it.'

It was only after Kit had told Jack all the details of her new contract, they'd had a second drink, and closing time beckoned, that Jack said, 'It's like Del Amitri's "Always the Last To Know"; Paul liking Amy. I mean, I had no idea, Kit.'

Kit groaned loudly as she grabbed her jacket, 'No one knew, Jack. Let's face it, honey, we don't even know if Amy knows yet, do we?'

Sixty

January 23rd 2007

Oh my God!

Amy's brain struggled to register the reality of the situation as her fingers traced over the words *I love you.* She hadn't been prepared for that. An invitation for another meal. A confession of wanting to go out with her. A hidden lust even; but love? He hadn't seen her for years. It was a shock. It had been a whole day of shocks.

Paul was pretending to study London's nightlife through the window. As Amy watched him, false light from the multitude of restaurants, pubs, and clubs gave the sky a luminous effect, highlighting the outline of his broad back. He was barely moving. His jeans were creased around the thighs from where he'd been sitting for so long. The close-cut hair at the nape of his neck showed the first speckles of grey.

Could she do this?

She decided not to think. There'd been too much thinking. Too many years wasted hashing over her past, never bothering to consider a future. It was time to be brave. Time to act instinctively. If this man was in love with her after a gap of so many years, then he must be serious, and if he was mistaken she'd soon find out. Amy stood up rather shakily. Carefully she folded the napkin, and placed it reverently into her jacket pocket, before joining Paul at the window.

Slipping a hand into Paul's cool firm grasp, Amy said, 'It's all a bit frightening, isn't it?'

'It certainly is!' Paul looked down at her, glowing with both relief and joy as he increased the pressure around Amy's soft skin. 'A cab for two, then?'

A sensation of contented happiness flooded through Amy as she felt his hand close around hers.

'Come on,' she said, 'take me home.'

January 24th 2007

When Amy turned her mobile back on the following morning, the crescendo of beeps alerted her to the arrival of a barrage of text messages.

'Good grief!' Sarah exclaimed as she stuffed a piece of wholemeal bread into the toaster, 'You're popular this morning.'

'More last night, I think,' Amy said as she scanned down the eight messages, 'Oh, and yesterday afternoon as well.'

'You got a secret admirer?' Sarah teased as she put on her jacket, ready to dash out of the front door as soon as her toast was buttered.

'Well, yes actually! Although it's not a secret anymore.' Amy's eyes sparkled as she spoke, making Sarah very sorry that she was already late for work and couldn't stay to fish for juicy details. 'I'll tell you about it later.'

The first three messages had been sent yesterday, and were all from Jack. Initially asking if she was free for coffee, and then wondering where she was, and lastly, whether she was OK?

The next was from Kit, asking if she'd had a nice evening, and ditto from that lying bastard Rob, who in the light of things, Amy had decided to forgive for pretending to be ill.

The remaining three were from Paul, and had all been fired off, one after another, between seven and eight o'clock that morning.

Hope you slept well, little one. xxx

You working today? Might come in to say hi? xxxx

Do you like chilli? Thought I'd make one tonight, fancy sharing it? xxxxx

Amy smiled at the increasing number of kisses with each

text. He can't have slept much at all. But then, neither had she. Strange that she didn't feel tired, just kind of high. She replied.

What's sleep?! Am working, but u better not come, u'll distract me!! Love chilli – looking forward to it, v much xxxxxx

Amy and Paul had arrived back at Princes Road a little after midnight. Carrying on their suddenly endless supply of chatter, they'd sat opposite each other at Amy's dining table, arms stretched across its white painted surface, holding hands as they filled in some of the blanks in each other's lives, until it was almost three o'clock in the morning. After many 'I should really be goings,' Paul had finally made a convincing effort to make a move towards home, when Amy asked the question she desperately needed an answer to.

She'd played what she wanted to ask around her head as they'd talked, contemplating putting what needed saying off until tomorrow, but found she couldn't. 'Before you go, there's something I have to know.'

'Yes?' Noting the uncertain edge to her voice, Paul perched back on the edge of his seat and listened.

Amy wasn't quite brave enough to look at Paul as she spoke, 'Love. It's a big word. Are you sure?'

'I'm positive.' He spoke with such firmness that Amy wasn't sure whether to press the subject or not, but this was important.

'But when? When did you first start feeling like this?'

Paul sat down properly and took a deep breath, 'It started that day when Rob and I took you out of the excavation in Wales for a coffee stop in Caldicot. Do you remember?'

'Oh yes,' her brother's tape flashed through Amy's mind, 'my birthday. That has got to be the best coffee stop I've had. Ever.'

Paul grinned as he recalled that day, 'The expression on your face when the café owner stuck candles into those cupcakes. I remember thinking how amazing it could be to have the look of love you gave Rob and I all to myself.'

'But you didn't say anything.' Amy watched him intently.

'I wasn't ready. There was too much fun to be had, and too many temptations. I didn't recognise my feelings for what they were until later. Sorry.'

'No need to be,' Amy lay a hand lightly on his arm, 'we were so young.'

'The idea of you sort of nagged away at the back of my head after that, but then you met Jack and I dismissed it. You were my friend, and that was enough. Until he started hurting you. Then, watching you cry, seeing you withdraw into yourself. I knew how I felt then, and I've never felt so fucking helpless in my life.'

'But you said nothing.' Speaking steadily, Amy squeezed Paul's hand in her soft grip. 'You should have said.'

'You were a mess, Amy.' He spoke gently. 'You wouldn't have heard me if I had told you. You wouldn't have noticed if I'd written it in neon pen across my forehead. Don't you remember how you were?'

Amy cringed at the image of her pathetic former self. Ashamed of her inability to cope, her lack of pride.

'I held you so many times as you cried into my shoulder.'

'Your jumper always smelt of lanolin and cheap conditioner.' Amy felt like sobbing into his shoulder all over again.

'Did it?' Paul was surprised, he'd never noticed.

'Yes. The blue one. It was all chunky, and stretched out of shape.'

Touched that she'd remembered such a tiny detail about him, Paul continued. 'It wouldn't have worked back then, however much I would have loved it to.'

'It wouldn't?'

'I didn't want you on the rebound, Amy. I wanted you to be with me because you wanted to be, not as some sort of consolation prize.'

Amy recoiled at the idea that he should think her capable of that, but in her heart she knew he was right. 'But things are different now.'

'They certainly are. If you'd told me back then that Jack

would turn out to be gay, I'd never have believed you.' Not wanting to go down that particular road yet again, Paul returned to the matter in hand, 'It's OK, Amy. I know you don't love me. But do you think, perhaps, you might learn to?'

'I don't see why not.' Amy leaned forward and kissed him. A kiss which spoke of future kisses to come, and not once did Amy compare the moment to another kiss many years ago.

At that point Paul had declared that his self-control had reached a low ebb. He'd better return to the student flat he was renting, or he'd have to make love to Amy right there, and he didn't think she was ready for that yet.

She hadn't been, but Amy thought, as she threw her toast crusts away, that if he'd made a move she wouldn't have stopped him. She felt an unfamiliar glow spread throughout her body. It was nice to have something to look forward to.

Kit was already installed at her usual table by the time Amy reached Pickwicks front door. Seeing the expression on Kit's face, Amy realised that she had already been told about her date with Paul, and was waiting for details. Amy was surprised to find that she didn't mind. Somehow it wasn't the same as being the last to know about the job.

Peggy also looked knowing as Amy hung up her coat, 'Good evening last night, then?'

Amy turned from one friend to another, 'OK, let's get this over with.' She tried to be stern, but somehow seemed unable to prevent her mouth turning up at the corners. 'Come on Peggy, let's sit with Kit while it's quiet, then I'll only have to go through it once!'

Talking quietly, Amy filled her friends in on the events of the day before.

'So, Paul gave you the napkin, which is a dead sweet thing to do by the way, then what? I mean, has he told you how this all happened?' Kit had a shine in her eyes which betrayed her hunt for good story fodder. 'Why didn't he say anything years ago?'

Peggy, who knew the signs of Kit being desperate to pick up

315

a pen to capture the moment, stepped in, 'Kit, I hope you're not going to exploit my waitress' new-found happiness for writing gain!'

Kit's eyes flashed playfully. 'As if I would!'

'Actually, if you wrote it all down,' Amy laughed with them, 'it might help me make sense of it all!'

Amy had reached the part of her account were she reported the arrival of the morning's texts when work intervened, in the shape of a group of hats, shopping trolleys, and their assorted elderly owners, coming in for morning tea.

Kit watched Amy as she attended to the customers, laughing and joking with them as she took their orders. Pickwicks was going to be a very different place without her. Phil had asked her to suggest the fifth of February to Amy as a good start date at Home Hunters. She felt a bit uneasy about the circumstances with Paul though. Could someone really be in love with a woman they hadn't seen for years? How could Amy go from having no idea that someone liked her – or, indeed, loved her – to embracing the idea so wholeheartedly, so fast?

It might have been eons since Amy and Jack had split, but Kit feared she might find the word rebound flashing beneath Amy's new bubbly persona if she looked hard enough. But then, Kit considered, as a new train of thought wove itself from the current situation into the fabric of her novel, wasn't that how it had been for her and Phil? Hadn't he rescued her from Jack-induced delusions? It had worked for her, was still working. Why not for Amy and Paul? Might he not be the perfect person for her? After all, Paul knew the score with Jack. There were no hidden feelings, no secret skeletons to burst out of the cupboard in twenty years' time.

'What's he like these days?' Kit managed to collar Amy in a lull an hour later.

Amy habitually straightened the serviette holder on Kit's table as she spoke, 'When did you last see him?'

'Not since I was with Jack. He's always here so briefly between digs.'

'Well,' Amy sank down on a free seat, considering where to

start. 'He's kind, quiet, tall, has sapphire-blue eyes, short dark hair, broad shoulders, oh and he's got a job at the British Museum, isn't that fantastic!'

'Amy,' Kit's voice oozed caution, 'this is all a bit quick isn't it? I mean, you can't love him already, can you?'

Amy dragged a chair closer and spoke reassuringly. 'Of course not! But I do like him loads. He's my friend; we have a comfortable history together. I just know he'll never hurt me. He'll never let me down. If that's not a good start for a relationship, I don't know what is!'

Kit said nothing, but looked so suspicious that Amy couldn't help but laugh, 'I know. I know. It's what every woman says about some man at some point, and most are completely wrong. I'm thirty-four years old! He loves me, and I'm sure I'll grow to love him. It isn't like it's a chore! You wait till you see him again, he's gorgeous!'

'Well, I hope you're right. You certainly deserve someone nice after all that crap with Jack.'

'Jack!' Amy clapped a hand to her mouth, 'I'd forgotten all about him. He is not going to like this at all.'

Kit groaned, 'Oh Amy, you're priceless. Only you could worry about what your ex thinks.'

'He's far more important than that, he's my friend. He'll be worried about me. I haven't even replied to the texts he sent me yesterday yet.'

'Which is a good sign.'

'It is?'

'Sure. When you're with Paul, you're clearly not thinking about Jack. Any bloke that can push him from your addled brain has got to stand a fighting chance.'

Amy's face blushed bright pink, 'All the same, I need to tell him.'

Kit laid down the pen she'd been writing with, 'He knows.'

'How?' Amy felt guilt rise in her gullet.

'We went for a drink last night. Rob had told him.'

'And?' Amy, who found she'd been holding her breath, expelled it as Kit replied.

317

'He was fine about it. I'll tell you all later, you've got a new customer.' As Amy reluctantly retreated towards the latest client, Kit called after her, 'Oh, and Phil asked me to talk to you about the new job later, and I've got some news too.'

Amy stood next to the kitchen calendar. She had called Phil as soon as she'd got home from work. Now Amy was staring at the black circle drawn around the fifth of February. It was only twelve days away. The familiar uncertainty of change consumed her. What if she couldn't do it? What if she let everybody down? Would Peggy and Scott take her back if she hated it? Would Kit ever speak to her again if she screwed up?

Through Amy's rising wave of self-doubt, her phone announced the arrival of a text.

Chilli bubbling! Student kitchen bit naff though! See u in 1hr. Can't wait. xxxx

Paul. Amy felt the tension which had been gathering inside her relax a little. In the half an hour she had to spare, Amy stood under the shower, wondering if Paul's self-control would snap tonight. Maybe hers would. Amy wasn't sure if she was ready to sleep with him. She knew it was unusual in this day and age, not to jump straight into bed with your bloke.

'But then,' she told the showerhead with a certain amount of pride, as it pounded wet heat against her shoulders, 'I am unusual.'

Sixty-one

January 25th 2007

Rob had already served three customers that morning, and it was only ten o'clock. Each had been a mother returning home from the school run, lured into the shop by the chance to purchase a fluffy toy from the window display to keep their younger offspring quiet for ten minutes or so. Two of them had also bought a children's natural history book each.

Feeling satisfied with the small upturn in early morning custom, Rob was silently thanking Phil for his foresight, when Paul came in.

'I wondered if you'd come by today.'

'And here I am.' Paul beamed from ear to ear as he lounged against the counter.

'You look like the Cheshire Cat,' Rob wriggled his eyebrows playfully, 'and I would say, judging by that expression, that yesterday's chilli was a success.'

'I think that would be an accurate assumption.' Somewhat self-satisfied, Paul sat down. 'I've come to say thanks for crying off the other day. I also thought I'd better see Jack; make sure he's cool with all this. It's bloody mad really, I mean it's been years since he was with Amy, but I feel I have to clear it with him, as he's a friend, y'know?'

'He'll be in shortly, or so he says.' Rob inclined his head in understanding and began to sort through the morning's letters, 'he has been known not to turn up.'

'An ironic edge to your voice there, Robert?' Paul glanced at his friend knowingly.

'I can't think why!'

Jack had woken up feeling guilty. He was surprised by how shaken he was by the knowledge that Amy was going out with Paul.

He mulled over what Kit had said, about how the way he was feeling right now was precisely how Amy had felt when he'd abruptly introduced Toby into their lives. It didn't make accepting it any easier though. Kit had thought that it was probably a good thing that it was Paul seeing Amy, who already understood his history and tenacious, but lasting, connection with Amy. Jack wasn't so sure that that was such a good thing.

Maybe, Jack thought as he stood waiting for the train, *I should speak to Paul. See if he is serious about Amy or just sampling previously forbidden fruit.* Jack felt a surge of anger. If Paul pissed Amy about, he'd kill him.

By the time he reached Kew station, Jack had convinced himself that Paul simply saw Amy as an easy lay, a target for a bit of post-dig comfort. His forehead thumped with tension, and he was spoiling for a fight. He had to call Paul, sort this out. No way was he going to let anyone hurt Amy. No way.

'The very man.' Paul came forward and enveloped Jack in a hug as soon as he stepped through the shop door.

Feeling the wind blown from his sails, Jack allowed himself to be briefly engulfed by the bigger man, before stepping deliberately back. 'I was about to call you. Rob said you were in town.' Jack's voice wasn't as friendly as usual. Rob eyed him suspiciously.

'I almost emailed you,' Paul also recognised the hectoring tone to Jack's voice, but ignored it, 'then I thought, it's been so long, it would be better to come straight here instead. That's OK, isn't it?'

Disappearing for a moment, Rob reappeared with a mug of extra strong, fully caffeinated coffee and pushed it into Jack's hands. 'Here you go, mate. Come on, I think it's time we all caught up. So much has happened since Paul last dropped by, don't you think?'

Rob brought the extra chair out of the kitchen, and they all sat together, grouped behind the counter. The air between Paul and Jack was tense, but Rob no longer had the feeling that he was about to witness a showdown at the OK Corral.

'So?' Jack dispensed with small talk. 'Amy?'

'Yes.' Paul's reply was a statement, not a question.

'What do you mean, yes?' Jack could feel his hackles rising again, 'What is she to you? Another notch on the famous Paul Donahue bedpost?'

Rob winced, waiting for Paul to explode. Instead the archaeologist put down his mug and said calmly, but with an underlying finality, 'Amy is the woman I love. The woman I have loved since I was twenty. What is she to you, Jack?'

Jack opened his mouth to reply, but Paul jumped in, answering his own question. 'I'll tell you shall I? She's your friend. A loyal girl who, despite being treated like shit by you on more than one occasion, loves you anyway. That's a fact. Nothing will change that. It also has nothing to do with how I feel about her, and how I hope she will grow to feel about me. End of story. Now, tell me mate, what's Toby like?'

Jack's face had flushed dangerously red, but he'd held his tongue and listened while Paul had spoken. Now it was so quiet that only the background ticking of the shop's clock filled the silence as they each digested what Paul had said.

Rob, who desperately wished he'd turned the radio on that morning so it wouldn't seem so quiet, ran his eyes from one friend to the other. He felt rather awkward being there to witness this conversation, but didn't see how he could gracefully exit without highlighting that fact.

Eventually Jack spoke; needing reassurance on one point, 'She's not another conquest then?'

'No. She isn't. Is Toby?'

'No!'

Paul looked expectantly at Jack, his voice returning to its normal pitch, 'Well, tell me about him then. I want to know about the man who's making one of my oldest friends happy. The one Amy describes as having made you see sense and tell your father about your lifestyle. Good on you for that, by the way, can't be easy planning what to say.'

321

'Thanks.' Instantly capitulating under the compliment, Jack spoke eagerly about his boyfriend. 'Toby's great, you should meet him before we go.'

'I'd like that. Perhaps,' Paul glanced at Rob for support, 'we could all go out for a drink or something before you fly out. Spain, isn't it?'

'Amy did tell you a lot.' Jack looked Paul straight in the eye, as if still assessing him.

'I asked her about you. And, like I said, she's your friend.'

Rob, unable to face them going round in yet more conversational circles, stood up and said, 'How about we all get a pint tonight then?'

'Oh, I'm sorry, I'm seeing Amy tonight.' Paul smiled in happy expectation.

'And I'm seeing Toby.' Determined not to be outdone, Jack fished out his mobile so he could set up a date with his boyfriend as soon as Paul had gone.

Rob nodded, 'And I'm probably on bedtime story duty! Oh, what it is to be the only grown-up amongst so much teenage angst. Tomorrow night then?'

'Sure!' they both replied at once, 'no problem.'

'Great.' Rob grinned at his friends. 'Now, Paul, bugger off will you? We've got loads to do before Jack disappears to Europe.'

Kit re-read the dozen paragraphs she'd written that morning. The novel's plot was getting a bit complicated and confusing. She scanned it again, considering how she could make it less intricate.

Bess sighed. How could this be happening? Just when she'd finally accepted that Lee would never, could never, love her, she'd found someone of her own and was feeling genuinely happy for the first time in years, and he'd done a total about-face.

Her best friend, whose advice was always well-meaning, but frequently flawed, had muttered catchphrases and clichés about

Lee wanting to 'have his cake and eat it' and 'only wanting her when someone else did.' Maybe this time she was right. Perhaps Lee had enjoyed the silent power he'd over her, and now it was gone he was desperately trying to claw it back ...

Leafing through the pages she'd written that week, Kit scrutinised her words. The story was certainly moving forward, but it was somehow contradictory. She looked up and saw Amy's happy demeanour as she served a regular customer with a tuna salad and chips, and felt reassured. Life *was* complicated and contradictory, not to mention utterly confusing.

Sixty-two

January 26th 2007

'There's no doubt, we are going to miss her.' Scott rested his weight on his crutches, talking to Kit and Peggy as he watched them refilling the salt and pepper shakers. 'Amy's a star worker, not to mention a big hit with the customers.'

'Have you advertised for a replacement yet?' Kit asked, before failing to hold in a sneeze caused by a cloud of spilt pepper, 'Oh, rats, sorry.'

'Not to worry,' Peggy deftly swept the whole mess into the bin, removed the now unhygienic pepper pot and continued to attend to the salt. 'We haven't, but I think we'll have to soon. It's good of you to help out now and again, Kit, but by Easter, when the first real wave of tourists arrives, we'll need permanent help.'

'You always managed before.'

'Yes, but business has improved so much lately. You must have noticed how busy we are these days.'

Kit supposed she had noticed, but her own work, fine-tuning the anthology, writing it a synopsis, streamlining her ideas for the novel, and outlining future chapters, meant that lately she was largely unaware of what was going on beyond her own coffee cup.

Scott agreed with his wife, 'Part of that success is due to Amy. Word of mouth from our regulars. The pensioners love her. I hope we can find someone as reliable and helpful, not to mention socially acceptable, next time.'

'Socially acceptable? I never thought I'd hear such talk from you, Scott!' Kit was teasing, but nonetheless she wondered at

325

his choice of words.

'I know, I know, but a lack of body piercing and pink spiked hair is a help. Not that such things prevent good table-waiting skills, of course, but those attributes do tend to scare off the over-sixties, and we rely on their custom. This place fills the void left by the fast-turnover coffee houses that the younger generation seem to favour for some reason.'

'Oh thanks Scott! How old do I feel now?!' Kit pretended to be insulted, but she could see the logic of what he was saying. Amy was about as unthreatening and inoffensive as you could get. Should any of the retired regulars find out that Amy had once dated a man who was now gay, they would probably have had apoplexy. 'I'm afraid I don't know anyone after a job at the moment, but I'll keep my ears open outside the school gates.'

'Thanks,' Peggy wiped a cloth over the counter to catch any stray condiment granules, 'a mum who wants a school hours job would be a good start, then we could get a student once the summer holidays start.'

'I'll do my best!' Kit funnelled the last grains of pepper into a waiting pot, and went to wash her hands. 'Now, however, I'd better go and be a customer myself. I have heaps to get done before the publishers can print my book.'

Amy came and sat with Kit for the duration of her ten minute break. 'How's it going?' She gestured to the large pile of notes separating Kit from her cup of coffee.

'Not bad, thanks. My editors sent me some tasks to do this morning. Just lose ends to tie up really, and then I can concentrate on the novel. I have to decide on a jacket cover.' Kit pulled out an envelope. 'While there's no one on this side of the café, it's probably safe for you to have a peek.'

The first proof was of a black silhouette of a woman holding a whip. The second was far more garish, adorned with a scantily clad couple leaving no mystery whatsoever. The last jacket proof was much simpler. Amy let her fingers run over the embossed cream surface, which simply proclaimed the title, *The Anthology of Forbidden Secrets*, in neat copperplate writing, next to Kit's pen name, Katrina Island.

'I like this one.' Amy returned the cover to Kit, who surreptitiously pushed them back into the envelope as if she was hiding a controlled substance in a public place. 'It's simple, and leaves everything to the imagination. Always the best way with erotica, don't you think? Also, it's sort of classy.'

'I totally agree.' Kit nodded, 'I was torn between that one and the black cover. No way was I going with the bizarre couple on the other one. I've no idea what possessed them to even consider it. But if you like it too, then I think I'll go with the cream one. After all, the customer is always right!'

Amy giggled. 'And I'm a customer all right! I'm so pleased all this is happening for you. I can't believe I've been reading your stuff for ages without realising you were a serial coffee-drinker and mother of two. I wonder if …' She stopped and found herself blushing crimson.

Kit finished the sentence for her. 'You're wondering if Paul likes pornography, and if he'll mind the fact that you read erotic fiction?'

Amy's face flushed somewhere between scarlet and maroon, 'Well … yes.'

'He's a man, honey. Show me one who doesn't! It will probably turn him on even more than he is already when he finds out you like it too.'

'Really?' Amy felt a bit alarmed at this. Although nothing had happened between them in that area, Paul had made his intentions pretty clear on their last meeting, and the thought of inflaming him further seemed daunting to say the least.

As if reading Amy's thoughts, Kit laughed, 'Keep that information to yourself until you need to share it. You'll know when the time's right. Trust me; I'm a literary kink queen.' She laughed again as Amy's face reached lobster level. 'I take it nothing of that nature has occurred between you two yet?'

'Kit!' Amy giggled again, embarrassed at being asked such a personal question so directly.

'That's a no then.'

Making a split second decision to confide her concerns,

Amy sat down as close to Kit as she could, 'Nothing at all. I was pleased at first, not being pushed into anything and all that. The whole idea of seeing Paul as more than a friend was enough to get used to. And, well, it's been a hell of a long time since I had any comfort beyond your stories and a bright blue dildo, but well, now …'

'Now you wish he'd hurry up and make a move, 'cos you've realised you fancy the pants off him.'

'That about sums it up, although I am beginning to worry that I won't remember what to do myself!' Chickening out of hearing Kit's response to her confession, Amy made an excuse and retreated to the kitchen, leaving Kit privately chuckling to herself as her friend disappeared out of sight.

An hour later, as she was about to leave, Kit pulled Amy to the privacy of the counter and whispered, 'You'll have to make the first move then won't you. And don't worry, you read my stuff, so you'll know exactly what to do when the time comes. It's like …'

'Riding a bike?'

'Well, riding something anyway.' Kit smirked at the horrified waitress's expression.

Sixty-three

January 28th 2007

'Only seven days to go until you start your new job, then.'

Amy countered Jack's statement with one of her own. 'Only four days till you leave with Toby, then.'

The frosty air smelt fresh and alive with the promise of spring as, sitting opposite each other under the Pavilion's veranda at Kew Gardens, Jack and Amy watched a group of Sunday morning walkers pass by.

'It's going to be very strange without you here, Jack. In fact,' Amy gripped her coat closer about her shoulders as a gust of wind blasted against her back, 'a lot of things are going to feel strange.'

'Are you nervous about the job?' Jack drank from a white china cup, more suited to tea than his shockingly strong espresso.

'You know me, I get nervous about everything. Although I'm not as bad as I used to be I don't think. I'm more concerned about fitting into an established team, being the new girl, than the actual job itself. You nervous about seeing your Dad and Jane?'

'A bit, but not as much as I thought I might be. At least my sister won't be there, I imagine she'll be the one who'll be awkward about all this. Having Toby helps. Perhaps we're growing up at last.'

'Cheek! I don't know about you, but I have no intention of growing up. *Ever*.' Amy threw a screwed-up serviette at him as if to prove her point, 'But you're right in a way. Having someone helps. Just knowing that Paul's there for me helps.'

Jack's eyes flashed for a second, but his voice remained unchanged. 'I'm glad you have someone too, Amy.'

'And yet,' she had seen and understood the disquiet in his eyes, 'you aren't quite comfortable with the idea of me being with someone other than you, even though you expect me to be fine with you and Toby.'

'Are you happy?' Not wanting to admit she was right, Jack looked away as he spoke so Amy couldn't read his eyes.

'Yes I am.'

'Then that's all right, isn't it.'

Amy returned his question, 'And are you happy with Toby?'

'Oh yes, he's great.'

Amy peered up through her fringe at him, 'Then we're both all right aren't we.'

His chair creaked as Jack rocked back, 'I don't know Amy; it's just that sometimes I wish ...'

'No Jack, there'll be no "if onlys," not now.' Amy was a bit taken aback by the sound of her own forcefulness, but it had to be said, and time was running out.

She had spent ages thinking about this. Ever since Jack had retuned her tape to Aberdeen. Ever since she'd upped sticks, moved south, and turned her life upside down, Amy had tried to put her emotions into some sort of order, and attempted to make sense of how Jack fitted into her life, and how she fitted into his. Rob, Debbie, Kit and Paul had all played their part in helping her work through her maze of feelings, and at last she felt as if the puzzle pieces were in place.

'You and I have a friendship that is so close it really isn't a friendship at all.' Jack opened his mouth to protest, 'No, please, Jack, this conversation is well overdue. Listen.' Amy pushed her empty cup away and clenched her hands together. 'We aren't really friends; we're not even like brother and sister. We have something that hangs between friendship and a relationship. A sort of link, something strong, but without definition. Perhaps, in a parallel universe, we are living happily ever after, with 2.4 children and probably a pet Labrador.' Amy paused, stretching out a hand for him to take. 'But we aren't in a parallel universe, Jack. We're here. This is now, and we both have the chance to do something with our lives; separately *and* together. Who else is that lucky, Jack? Don't you think what we have is incredible?'

Jack said nothing, but he stared into her eyes intently, seeing for the first time how far Amy had travelled emotionally since she'd arrived back into his life, and the expression on his face agreed with her. He seemed to be waiting for her to say more before he was ready to comment, so Amy continued, 'We can walk around a garden and admire the same plants. I know five minutes before you do that you want a coffee, and you can always tell if I'm in need of a cake-induced sugar rush. We can talk about anything and everything, and then, at the end of the day, we go back to our partners and have fun with them too. I think they call it "having the best of both worlds" and I think that makes us two of the luckiest people in the world. Don't you think so? Jack?'

Jack continued to watch Amy closely; her greyish-blue eyes were brimming with sentiment. He grabbed the offered hand and held it tightly. 'Not only are you incredible, you're right as well. I love you, Amy Crane.'

'And I love you, Jack Brown. Now let's walk, it's absolutely bloody freezing sat here.'

'So tell me,' Amy asked once they had strolled enough to get their circulation flowing again, 'are you and Toby ready for your European adventure?'

'Sort of, we're all packed up. Just need to order a cab to Heathrow, make sure our hand baggage meets with the new security regulations, stuff like that.'

'It's all happened so fast hasn't it?' Amy knelt to one of the first clumps of snowdrops that had made it through the frosted winter ground.

'You're telling me. I've only been with Toby since the start of December, and yet at the same time I feel I've always known him. Is that silly?'

'Not at all. I, on the other hand, have known Paul for

absolutely years, and it's like I've meet someone new, someone fresh, but with the added comfort of all that's gone before.'

'Paul's looking good. Seeing you obviously agrees with him.'

'Thanks.' Amy started to blush. She wanted to keep how little Paul had seen of her private for now. 'Although I don't expect I'll see too much of him over the next couple of weeks.'

'Why not?'

'I'm starting at Home Hunters, and then Paul starts at the British Museum a week after that.'

Jack was thoughtful, 'Do you think you'll live together?'

'It's only been a few days, Jack.'

'He's the one, though, isn't he?'

Amy noticed there was a new acceptance to his voice, and she inwardly sighed with relief. 'Is Toby?'

'I asked first!' Jack playfully poked Amy in the ribs as they strolled, a favour she pointedly returned, 'Oh, all right, I think he probably is, or will be, in time. You?'

'Possibly. Probably.' They laughed at their mutual reluctance to say what they truly felt. Putting his arm around Amy's shoulders Jack steered her back towards the café. 'Come on, we haven't had any caffeine for at least half an hour. Let's go inside this time and warm up a bit.'

FEBRUARY

In which Jack is missed, and things change faster still for Amy ...

Sixty-four

February 10th 2007

Amy was exhausted. The gravitational pull of the mattress had her firmly in its padded grasp, and her body didn't want to leave the soft cocoon of her duvet. Her first week as a Trainee Property Manager at Home Hunters had been exhausting, hectic, and complicated. Her brain physically ached, packed as it was with new information about procedures, company policies and the role each staff member performed.

Amy had shadowed Phil around the office, been introduced to major clients, and taken to view a number of potential properties. Next week she'd be on her own with Chris. Something she wasn't allowing herself to think about yet.

Mustering all her willpower, Amy poked her toes out into the chill of the room, slowly followed by the rest of her pyjama-clad body. The hands on her alarm clock told her it was already a quarter to ten. It was only the promise of lunch with Paul that spurred Amy towards the bathroom and a hot shower.

Meeting Amy outside the local supermarket, Paul embraced her before they headed to Pickwicks. 'We could go to a pub down by the river or something instead, if you don't want to go back to a work-type place today.'

'Oh, no, I've missed it! I know it's only been a week but, well, I loved working there. Plus I want you to meet Peggy and Scott.'

Paul tugged playfully at the plait that hung down the centre of Amy's back, noticing affectionately that she hadn't quite got all her hair through its tie. Wisps of blonde hair stuck out at odd angles around the red circle of elastic. 'Still prefer coffee stops to pubs then?'

'Definitely!' Amy was emphatic as she expounded on the subject, 'You can go to a café alone or in a group, and neither status is questioned. In a café you can eat something more satisfying than a packet of crisps, and yet less cloying than a gigantic plate of sausage and mash and, should you have to sit near the toilets, the smell of stale urine is unlikely to knock you out!'

Paul laughed, 'All good points.'

Amy paused as her hand rested on the handle of Pickwicks door, 'You ready to go in and be questioned relentlessly about your intentions?'

'Yep.' Paul took her hand firmly in his. 'Come on; introduce me to your friends. I was beginning to think you were ashamed of me.'

Poking him in the ribs, Amy rolled her eyes. 'Idiot! Come on.'

Amy was only mildly surprised to see Kit sitting at her corner table on a Saturday. She had mentioned to Phil she'd be bringing Paul to Pickwicks today. He must have told his wife, and there was no way Kit's curiosity would have let her miss out on that.

Introductions were made to her past employers in between customers, and renewed with Kit, who Paul hadn't seen for years. They both sat with the writer, who hastily piled her notes together, out of the way of prying eyes.

Paul dived into conversation as Scott absented himself, apologising as he wheeled himself back to the kitchen to see to some pies, just as Peggy delivered a tray of steaming hot drinks and a mountain of pastries. 'Any word from Jack and Toby, Kit?'

Kit answered between mouthfuls of scolding coffee. 'Only that they arrived safely, and that his dad has neither killed Jack nor disinherited him.'

'That's great, but I'm not surprised;' Amy paused to pick a

huge Belgian bun off the tray, 'Jack's dad is cool, I bet he had a pretty good idea anyway.'

'Jack's not mentioned anything about taking Toby to meet his folks yet then?' Selecting his own pastry, Paul settled back against his chair, mutely observing the women around the table relax.

'Not as far as I know, but he's not been in touch much, and I haven't wanted to interfere.'

'I guess we'll hear soon enough,' Peggy chipped in as she took a rare opportunity to sit down, 'God, I'm exhausted. We don't half miss you, Amy!'

Habitual guilt shot through Amy, who was about to apologise for abandoning them yet again, when Paul stopped her. 'Peggy was paying you a compliment, silly. Not working here anymore isn't something you should feel bad about.'

'Quite right!' Peggy looked at Paul approvingly, 'You listen to him. I'd soon be complaining if business was slack!'

Kit, whose mind had been elsewhere during this exchange asked, 'Haven't you heard from Jack then, Amy?'

'No,' Amy, who'd been trying not to feel abandoned by Jack's lack of contact, regardless of a couple of "good luck" texts she'd sent, shook her head, 'no, I've heard nothing.'

It was unseasonably mild. Hand-in-hand, Paul and Amy left Pickwicks, and trudged down the now-familiar pavement towards Princes Road. Paul hadn't asked Amy about her contact with Jack, but he'd sensed her disappointment when she'd found Kit had heard from him, and she hadn't. 'You OK?'

'Yes, of course,' Amy looked at him brightly, 'why?'

'I thought you might be missing him.'

There was no need to say who the "him" in question was. 'A bit, but he has new things in his life now', she gripped Paul's palm as she spoke, 'and so do I.'

Paul said nothing as the usual frisson of sexual tension swept over him. He badly wanted to make love to Amy, but the longer they waited the harder it seemed to be to bring the subject up. Never in his life had he felt so awkward about making a move.

Hung up on getting it exactly right, he found himself tongue-tied and frustrated. He simply had to do something before he exploded with an overload of testosterone.

'Amy?' Paul began as they walked through the narrow doorway into the dining area, 'Amy, are the others out at the moment?'

Amy's pulse quickened, her eyes began to twinkle, and a hopeful flirty smile played over her inviting lips. 'No, they're at James' mother's place. All weekend.' *Is he about to take me to bed at last?* His inaction had been driving her neglected body insane; after all, erotic literature was one thing, but a real flesh-and-blood man – now that was something else entirely.

Paul hesitated, uncertain if she wanted him to act, when suddenly Amy heard the echo of Kit's advice at the back of her head, and knew it was time for her to take charge. 'So,' she said, tilting her head to one side as she unbuttoned his massive coat for him, 'are you ever going to take me to bed, or what?'

Wrapped in Paul's arms in her warm bed an hour later, Amy, in a pleasant state of bodily shock, mewed as Paul's fingers began to circle her right nipple. Her relief at being able to remember what to do had been equalled by sheer pleasure at Paul's palpable joy as he revelled in the sight and texture of her naked form, enhancing their mutual and total satisfaction.

'Tell me,' he asked as Amy wriggled closer to his touch and placed a hand flat against his fast-recovering dick, 'if I opened your bedside drawer, would I find anything more interesting than neatly balled socks?'

Amy hid her smirk in the crook of Paul's neck, 'Maybe, why don't you take a peek?'

Twisting away from her, but not so far as to dislodge her hand, Paul slid open the drawer, 'Well, well, Amy Crane. Right up until now, I always believed you were a good girl, and then I got to thinking, seeing as you are such a good friend of Kit's …' He held up a handful of tellingly crumpled erotic short stories she'd printed off the web, and her dildo.

Amy hung her head in mock humility, 'Have I disappointed

you?'

'Christ, no! Come here ...' Dropping the papers, and grabbing the dildo firmly in one hand and her left hip in the other, Paul disappeared under the bedclothes, not emerging until Amy was in the throes of an erotic bliss Kit could never have confined to the world of literature.

Kit re-read her anthologies blurb. She had written it and re-written it more times than she cared to remember. She'd probably worked more on that one short piece of prose than on anything she'd ever written in her life.

'Well,' Kit sat staring at the computer screen in her study, her hand hovering over the mouse, 'here goes nothing.' Clicking *Send*, Kit sent the blurb into the technological ether, heading magically into her new editor's email inbox. She felt strange. Bereft even. The anthology had been sorted into a suitable order for publication, the various last minute pieces of paperwork were in place and the book's jacket had been chosen. Unless the publisher hated what she'd sent, that was it. Now Kit could return to her novel properly, rather than merely pick at it when the time allowed.

Switching off the laptop, she grabbed her coat and bag, and called to the twins, who were playing Doctor Who noisily in their bedroom. On an impulse Kit decided to take them to see how their dad was coping on his first Saturday afternoon at the bookshop, before heading into Kew Gardens to run off some of their ever-excessive energy.

MAY

In which Jack chooses his songs with unusual care and things are resolved ... well, almost ...

Sixty-five

May 25th 2007

As Amy logged off from her computer, she leaned back into the comfort of her soft black leather chair, and inhaled a lingering lungful of air before exhaling it slowly. It had been one hell of a working week. She and Chris had each acquired a new property for the company's books and, more importantly, that very day she had secured her first new corporate client. There had been other individual client gains over the past six weeks at Home Hunters, but this was the big one, and somehow Amy believed her right to work there had been tied up with her ability to win the commission. Now, after nearly four months of calling herself a Property Manager, Amy felt she had as much right as Chris to the title.

Chris was delighted; his enthusiasm was infectious as he congratulated her success. Normally Amy would have agreed to go out with him for the celebratory drink he suggested, but tonight she was busy. Chris had gone home an hour ago, leaving Amy to tie up several loose ends and enjoy a precious moment of peace and quiet before facing the insanity of Clapham Junction at half-past six on a Friday night.

It wasn't the prospect of a crowded and uncomfortable journey home that kept Amy where she was, however. The evening ahead of her loomed very large.

She was looking forward to it, but at the same time the tense knot in her stomach reminded her how apprehensive she was about going. Silly really. The whole point was to be a group celebration, and now she could add to their collective achievements (having already sworn Chris to secrecy), and tell

Phil and Kit about her new American contract. Yet Amy stayed sat where she was.

Paul would be waiting for her at home. He had probably already changed after a day in his dusty old office, hidden at the back of the museum.

Number 8 Princes Road had officially become their home, rather than just her home, almost a month ago. A situation that crept up on them unannounced, rather than being a conscious decision. Paul had spent nearly all his time in Richmond with Amy anyway, so when James and Sarah, who had finally got it together themselves, had decided to get engaged and find a flat they could afford to rent nearer the city centre, it had seemed natural for Paul to move in properly.

In less than a year Amy had gone from being a shy, lonely girl in Scotland, obsessed with an old relationship and avoiding new ones, to a successful London businesswoman with a new group of friends, a live-in partner, and the unexpected luxury of a spare bedroom. Sometimes the ride seemed so fast and intense that Amy wanted to slow it all down for a minute, not to get off, just to stop and admire the view.

If she didn't hurry up then she'd never make it home in time to change for eight o'clock. Amy stood up decisively, thinking about Paul as she made her way out of the office and into the busy street.

He had told her he loved her. He frequently told her, and she always replied that she loved him too. *But do I? Or do I only love the fact that it isn't just me against the world anymore?* The thought frequently nagged at Amy, and did so again as she negotiated her way towards the station. *Maybe I'll know after tonight. Perhaps I need to get this over with to find out how I really feel.*

Having left the children with a babysitter, Kit took Phil's hand as they left the house and headed down the High Street towards Pickwicks.

Uncomfortable in high heels she wasn't used to, Kit walked carefully, leaning against Phil for support, frightened that any minute she could tread awkwardly and twist an ankle.

Phil smiled down at her, 'You don't have to be so nervous.'

'I know, but I don't feel right. I'm not used to these posh clothes, and my shoes are killing me.'

Phil shook his head in mock despair at his wife in her shimmering dress and matching footwear. 'You look magnificent! Just not like you.'

'Thanks a lot!'

'No, really love, you should dress up more often. You're gorgeous.'

Kit remained unconvinced in her black, sequinned evening dress. 'Do you think everyone will come?'

Rob hugged his daughter Lily to his side and, having settled her with her sisters to listen to a story from Granny, went to join Debbie in the kitchen. 'Ready?'

'As I'll ever be.' She was examining herself in the mirror, critically checking the edges of her mouth for stray lipstick.

'Come on then.' Rob pulled his suit jacket on, and ushered his wife towards the waiting taxi.

Toby brushed the last fleck of dust off Jack's jacket. 'Well?' Jack twirled in his new suit, fresh from an Italian tailor.

'Gorgeous.' Toby grinned suggestively.

'We haven't got time for anything like that, young man.' Jack spoke with mock severity. 'Now, are you ready?'

'Yep,' Toby slipped on his shoes and jangled the door keys impatiently, 'come on then, or we'll both be late.'

Peggy and Scott kicked off their shoes. They had barely ten minutes before everyone arrived, and they were determined to take advantage of that time to rest. For days Scott had cooked and prepared food, while Peggy had made sure that the glasses, plates and crockery shone.

Aprons discarded, they sat, Peggy voluptuous in a magnificent low-cut maroon dress, and Scott striking in a black tuxedo. His crutches were propped against the wall in case he needed them. Tonight, however, he was determined not to.

The outfit hung in its plastic wrapper against her wardrobe door. There were literally ten minutes until she was expected at Pickwicks, but Amy felt she couldn't move any faster.

Paul had welcomed her home with a hug, a kiss and a coffee. Recognising that she was having a silent battle with her nerves he'd said nothing, but steered her towards their bedroom, leaving her alone to get ready.

Amy had neither heard from, nor seen, Jack since February. Kit had told her he'd been back for a week, but she hadn't attempted to call him because he hadn't attempted to call her. *Childish. Why is everything with him so fucking childish?* She had genuinely believed they'd reached some sort of understanding before he'd gone away. Paul always said that Jack was a game-player, and Amy had reluctantly come to agree with him, but still ...

The pale lilac outfit glared at her. They had cost a small fortune. Paul had said she looked great in them, and if she was honest with herself, she knew she felt great in them too. Fighting against the fatigue of the week, and the tension which bubbled within her, Amy stripped off her business suit and headed for the shower.

Twenty minutes later, washed, dried, hair brushed, with her outfit and stockings in place, Amy presented herself to Paul. 'Well?'

'Bloody hell!'

'That bad?'

'Are you kidding? Here, put the shoes on.' Paul passed her the delicate silver kitten heels that completed the outfit. 'Wow! I don't know about the meal, but I can't wait for afters.'

Amy coloured with pleasure at his response, and risked a look in the hall mirror. Her boned, sleeveless top tucked her in at the waist, enhancing her small cleavage, while the flowing skirt completed the slimming affect, making it appear as if she was wearing a dress and not a two piece. She felt good, sexy even. Maybe she should have bought some mascara or something? No. She felt strange enough as it was.

346

Butterflies continued to jangle and flit around Amy's stomach, but as Paul took her hand and escorted her towards Pickwicks a new strength began to build within her. 'I feel like I'm in disguise. Like I'm different somehow.'

Paul held her proprietarily to his side, 'Is confidence included in the disguise?'

Clinging to the memory of the contract she'd fought for and won, Amy replied, 'I think it might be.'

'Good girl. Come on, I want to show off the most beautiful woman in the world.'

Amy knew how she felt about him then. She was certain.

Sixty-six

May 25th 2007

Pickwicks was transformed. The majority of the tables and chairs had been pushed to one side of the room, and were shrouded with cream tablecloths. The straw blinds were down at the windows to provide some privacy from the outside world, and rows of little oil lamps and tea lights lit up the room.

Six rectangular tables, covered in burgundy cloth and bedecked with flowers and candles, had been arranged in an approximate square in the centre of the café. Wine sat in coolers and the table was laid with several rounds of cutlery for the meal ahead. Megan, Pickwicks' new waitress, poked her head out of the kitchen door. Peggy had asked if she'd stay to serve the first course, and then she could scoot off.

Peggy turned the music up a fraction. She'd toyed with the idea of playing some of her favourite musical compilations, hits from the eighties and nineties mostly, but in view of Jack's vast repertoire of lyrical associations, she had taken the safer option, and decided upon classical.

She looked at her watch; they'd all arrive any minute now.

The 'wow, you look fantastic!' and the 'I don't think I've ever seen you in a skirt!' comments had been given and received. Peggy and Scott had been thanked and praised for sharing the beautiful setting, and now the male partners were gathering drinks while Kit, Amy, Debbie, and Peggy sat chatting around the table.

'Just Jack and Toby to come then.' Amy glanced towards the door, hoping they'd hurry up and get the initial meeting over

349

with.

'He's always late when it's important,' Kit smoothed down her dress, unaccustomed to sitting on so much excess fabric, 'he'll make the grand entrance soon enough.'

'Have you heard much about his travels?' Amy had been dying to ask Kit about Jack, but hadn't liked to admit she'd heard nothing from him herself. Now she seized the offered opening.

Kit, who knew Amy hadn't received any contact from Jack, shook her head dismissively, deciding to play down her own frequent contact with him, 'Bits and pieces. He went from Spain to France to Italy, and I know he's relieved his Dad is cool about his lifestyle, but beyond that it's all been very quiet.'

Armed with alcohol, the men joined them. 'Here's to us,' Scott announced as he sat down, his dazzling grin as wide as ever, 'and to our future success, health and happiness.'

They raised their glasses, echoing his sentiment, before Peggy diplomatically said, 'Perhaps we should wait for Jack and Toby to arrive, love?'

'We've waited long enough.' Scott was decisive. 'Anyway, I'm starving, and I bet Megan is dying to go home after almost ten hours on her feet.'

'Won't they mind?' Amy wasn't sure, 'I mean, this is partly their welcome home dinner.'

'Tough! Anyway this isn't only for them; they should have been here on time. I said eight, and it's nearly nine o'clock already.' Scott stood up and waved to Megan, who started to dish up the food as quickly as she could.

Their plates were piled high with Scott's delicious cooking, and the chatter was flowing like the fast-disappearing Merlot, when the door opened and Jack walked in. 'Sorry everyone.' He sat straight down at the table and helped himself to some wine. 'I lost track of time. Food smells incredible, any for me?'

Scott raised an eyebrow and Rob looked at him questioningly. Jack was alone.

'I'll fetch your plate from the oven.' Peggy spoke tartly as she headed to the kitchen.

'Do we need to ask where Toby is?' Paul passed the wine bottle back towards Amy for a top up.

'He's out with his mates, of course. Just like I'm out with mine.'

Amy's palms instantly began to prickle with perspiration. *Is this a dressing-up game to him? Would he rather be out with Toby and his other mates? Are we an inconvenience?* 'Peggy and Scott,' she glanced at their hosts, whose smiles had faded, 'have provided food for ten people. We were all under the impression that Toby was coming with you.'

Jack took in the eight sets of enquiring eyes, and had the decency to seem abashed. 'Come on, guys. He hasn't seen his friends for months!'

'True,' Amy's voice remained calm even as she continued as unelected spokesperson, 'and it is totally understandable that he wants to see them. All you had to do was call Peggy, or any of us, and say he wasn't coming. Not a big thing, just courtesy. That's all.'

After a brief lapse into stunned silence Jack said, as he respectfully regarded Amy in full Property Manager mode, 'I didn't think any of you would mind.'

'You didn't think at all,' Amy stared defiantly into his eyes, daring him to turn away from her.

Jack turned to Scott. 'I'm sorry. Amy's right. I should have called you. Sorry.'

A few seconds passed before Scott broke the tension. 'Well, you've said sorry now.' He looked wryly at his guest. 'Now, come on everyone, we're here to enjoy ourselves. Eat up!'

He raised his glass, and the moment's discomfort was broken. 'To us.'

'To us,' they chorused, before tucking back into the feast.

As the last of the plates were cleared away and the glasses were refilled, Scott stood before the assembled friends.

'I haven't got a long speech prepared, so don't worry! But we arranged all this, not just to welcome Jack and Toby home, not so we had an excuse to dress in posh clothes for a change, but because I believe we all have something to celebrate. And Peggy and I,' he took his wife's hand, 'wanted to say thank you properly.' Scott put up a hand to stop the general murmurings of "there's no need."

'You'll notice,' he continued, 'that I'm standing to say all this. You will also notice that my crutches are well out of reach. So first, to you Amy, for working stupid hours on so little pay with no complaints. To you Kit, for helping Amy, totally unpaid, and to Jack for the same. Not to forget you, Rob, for running the bookshop alone so that Jack could help out, and you, Debbie, for not strangling Jack for taking advantage of your husband. Finally, to you all, for your visits to the hospital, your messages of support, and your love. We couldn't be more grateful. Thank you.'

Scott sat down to choruses of 'No problem!' and 'Don't mention it!' before Phil pushed his chair back and rose to his feet. 'If this is the time for speeches, then I feel I should also raise a glass. I would like to propose a toast, to Kit.'

Kit blustered as she looked up at her husband, 'Phil, honestly, you don't need to.'

'Oh, but I do. You've achieved something incredible.' Phil turned back to their friends, 'Kit, as you know, has recently started a novel. I believe she is about halfway through?' He turned back to Kit, who almost imperceptibly inclined her head. 'And, even more than that, her book, *The Anthology of Forbidden Secrets*, is to hit the streets in four months' time. I trust, despite our varying sexual dispositions and tastes, that you will all be buying a copy! So, would you raise your glasses to Kit, and toast the success of her short stories and her future blockbuster!'

'Here, here!' Taking the floor, Jack echoed Phil's sentiments. 'And a toast to Phil himself.' Phil looked puzzled, as Jack took his turn. 'For saving my business.'

'Too right,' Rob chipped in, 'You've turned that place around. We're doing far better than ever before.'

'Which is why,' Jack picked up the lead, 'Rob and I

wondered if you'd like in properly?'

'Really?' Phil's face lit up.

'Yep,' Jack looked hopefully at Phil, as he continued, 'I'm thinking of selling up. What do you think? Fancy buying me out?'

Phil glanced at Kit, the satisfied expression on her face telling him she loved the idea. 'I think I'll need to think about it. But don't you dare offer it to anyone else!'

Jack laughed. 'As if I would!'

Phil stood up again, 'Well, if we're going down that line, then I think a glass should be raised to Amy. Without her, so Chris tells me, Home Hunters wouldn't be doing so well.'

Amy's cheeks went a pleasing ruby colour that was only partly due to the wine she'd drunk. 'Thanks. Um, actually I have a bit of an announcement about that.'

'What is it?' Kit leant forward.

Amy spoke quietly, unused to being in the limelight, even before friends. 'I've secured a contract today. A big one, with a company in Texas. I feel I've maybe earned my place at Home Hunters properly at last.'

Paul looked on with pride and admiration as, once she was thoroughly flushed from everyone's congratulations, Amy said, 'As this appears to be the time, I would like to propose another vote of thanks, if that's all right.'

The general babble died down, and all eyes focussed on Amy, who took Paul's hand for support. 'Firstly, I would like to thank Jack for ...'

Jack interrupted, 'You have *got* to be joking! I've only ever caused you hassle, I –'

Amy cut back in, her eye shining, her voice warm, ' ... for sending back my tape. If you hadn't, well, I wouldn't be here now, amongst friends. Perhaps you wouldn't have met Toby. I certainly wouldn't have re-met Paul, and right now that thought is unbearable.' She held his hand tighter, and Paul realised, as she turned towards him, that she loved him for real, not just because he desperately wanted her to. His face shone with happiness.

'It's the little things that make the big things happen. My Grandpa used to say that, and he was right.' Amy turned to Peggy, sounding for all the world as if she was gracefully accepting an Oscar, 'I'd also like to thank Peggy and Scott for giving me a job in this, the best of coffee shops, Kit for her unexpected friendship, and Phil, for giving me the chance to try a career that I love already. Finally, to Rob and Debbie, for their constant friendship and support. They don't know it, but without them I would have fled back to Scotland months ago.'

Amy picked up her glass. 'Now, is there any pudding, or are we all going to sit here and drown in a pool of sentiment?'

Their desserts devoured and the coffee brewed, the nine friends relaxed back against their seats. Bellies full, their bodies and inhibitions freed by too much alcohol, a comfortable hush fell around the table as Peggy pushed down the plunger of the huge coffee pot, which was then manoeuvred from place to place.

When all the cups were full, and Phil had scooted out to the kitchen to fetch his lone cup of tea, Jack stood up.

'Come on Jack, we've done all the soppy speech stuff,' Kit beckoned for him to sit down again, but he shook his head.

'I've something to share with you all. If that's all right?' He glanced around the table, looking at the faces before him. They all shrugged, each trying to guess what bombshell Jack was going to drop on them now.

'Although Toby and I have been back for a week, I've not been in touch with you. You may have wondered why.' Jack turned to Amy, but as her face gave nothing away. 'There is a reason. I hope you will think it's a good one.'

He rummaged in his coat pocket, pulled out an unmarked CD, and placed it on the table mat before him. Amy and Kit's eyes flickered to it instantly, both feeling their own private horror rising.

'As Amy said earlier, this all started with a tape. A blank tape her brother gave to her before she set off to university for the first time, over sixteen years ago.'

Amy's mouth had gone dry.

'And Amy did record a couple of songs,' but then I ruined it. I messed up everything, including her tape.' Jack spoke fast, not wanting to dwell on any specific event, 'I took it away, not returning it for years and years. Of course, you know all of this ...'

'Jack, really ...' Amy found her voice, but he interrupted.

'With Toby's and my dad's help, I got a lot of things straight in my head while I was away. I did a lot of thinking. Not just about Amy's tape, but about another tape that I never recorded, even though I promised I would. And about all of you, my friends, who I know I frequently take for granted.' Kit clenched her hands in her lap, not daring to look at Phil as Jack went on.

'You all know I'm crap at expressing myself, and I've always relied on song lyrics to help me out. Well, I've done it again.' He picked up the CD case and passed it to Scott. 'The first tune is for Amy, the second for Kit, the third for Paul, Rob and Debbie, the fourth for Peggy and Scott. The fifth and final track is for you all. I chose very, *very* carefully. I listened to and assessed every single word. It has taken me all week. Every song says what I'd like to be able to say, but without screwing it up, which, let's face it, I would. Scott, will you put it on? Will you play it for me?'

Glancing again at the assembled faces, Scott waited for their unanimous approval before he moved towards the stereo. No one spoke. Amy instinctively put her hand out to Paul, who took it, the gesture helping to calm her feelings of trepidation.

As the first track came on, Amy felt relief sweep through her.

Jack turned to Paul, 'If it's all right with you, I'd like to ask Amy to dance.'

Paul agreed with only slight reluctance. Understanding and accepting that this was Jack's way of finally giving her up, as he passed Amy's hand over to his.

As Robbie Williams sang 'Angels', Jack whispered the lyrics with him into Amy's ear. 'If ever a girl was an angel, Amy, it's you', he murmured softly.

Amy and Jack danced slowly. They knew that this was when

it ended; this was when they let go of each other properly. Amy wasn't sure if she felt sad, happy, or immensely relieved as she let silent tears fall freely down her smiling face.

By the time Kit and Jack were to dancing to the perfect melodies of 'God Only Knows' by the Beach Boys, the whole room was on its feet, swaying around the café, each person eager to hear the tune that Jack had chosen for them.

EPILOGUE

In which we say goodbye ...

October – Three Years Later

In spite of the optimistic forecast, it was drizzling, and the sky was grey. To Amy, though, it was a beautiful day. Her dress hung expectantly from the wardrobe door. Cream, simply cut, and stunning.

Rob had already popped in to see her, a visit to wish her luck and lots of love, and to deliver a single red rose from Paul, before he dashed off to perform his best man's duties.

Kit and Debbie were downstairs with Amy's parents, fussing over their five children in their bridesmaid and pageboy outfits, checking there were enough buttonhole flowers, and generally worrying about anything and everything.

Amy, content to escape the chaos, walked over to her bedroom window. The view looked pretty much the same as it had the first time she'd stared down at Richmond's back streets almost four years ago. Damp, dull, but somehow full of hope. Full of future.

Peggy and Scott would be busily preparing last minute items for the buffet, which was to be held at Pickwicks when the simple ceremony was over.

Phil had left Reading Nature in the care of the newly appointed Saturday girl, and was currently helping Chris to clean their cars, which were to be used to ferry the bride and bridesmaids to Richmond's registry office.

She thought of Jack. Alone again. Toby and Jack's initial happiness had begun to wane for reasons that Jack was, beyond quoting a couple of obscure song lyrics at Amy, keeping to himself. He'd taken Toby's defection a month or so ago, to a charismatic assistant bank manager, surprisingly well. Amy hadn't liked to point out to him that Toby seemed inexplicably drawn to men with money. It wouldn't have helped.

Jack wasn't coming today. He'd said, honestly and openly, that he couldn't watch her get married, not even to a friend. He just couldn't, and hoped Amy wouldn't mind and could understand. She minded very much, and hadn't understood at all. It wasn't even as if he wanted her for himself. Still, Amy told Jack, he should do what was best for him. So he'd gone to stay with his dad and Jane for a while, and thought that maybe he'd come home and do something with the horticultural qualification he'd worked for at college over the past two years. Or perhaps he'd travel some more, try America or Australia? He wasn't sure really. He'd come back, though; he'd always come back.

Amy glanced at the clock. She had two hours of being Miss Amy Crane left. After that she would be Mrs Amy Donahue. It felt strange as she played her future title around her tongue.

Excitement gripped Amy as she headed towards the kitchen.

Her 'new job, new home, new life' plan was complete. It was time to get ready for the first day of the rest of her new life.

'But first,' she told her wedding dress, 'I'm going to grab one more cup of coffee …'